IAN HAMILTON MYSTERIES

EDINBURGH DUSK

ALSO BY CAROLE LAWRENCE

Ian Hamilton Mysteries

Edinburgh Twilight

IAN HAMILTON MYSTERIES

EDINBURGH DUSK

· CAROLE LAWRENCE ·

THOMAS & MERCER

This is a work of fiction. Names, characters, organizations, places, events, and incidents are either products of the author's imagination or are used fictitiously. Any resemblance to actual persons, living or dead, or actual events is purely coincidental.

Text copyright © 2018 by Carole Lawrence
All rights reserved.

No part of this book may be reproduced, or stored in a retrieval system, or transmitted in any form or by any means, electronic, mechanical, photocopying, recording, or otherwise, without express written permission of the publisher.

Published by Thomas & Mercer, Seattle

www.apub.com

Amazon, the Amazon logo, and Thomas & Mercer are trademarks of Amazon.com, Inc., or its affiliates.

ISBN-13: 9781503903906
ISBN-10: 1503903907

Cover design by Ed Bettison

Printed in the United States of America

For Liza Dawson, the best friend anyone could wish for.

Revenge, the sweetest morsel to the mouth, that ever cooked in hell!

—Sir Walter Scott, *The Heart of Midlothian*

PROLOGUE

Edinburgh, 1880

She stood over his bed, savoring the moment. This was the pinnacle, the flowering of all her plans and aspirations. As the sun dipped beneath surly gray clouds, she watched him begin to sweat, beads of perspiration glistening on his forehead like translucent pearls. His breathing deepened as his face turned pink, then scarlet, and he began to moan faintly. This was the moment she had been imagining, awaiting patiently during many days and weeks of planning. The anticipation was sweet, and she had drawn it out as long as possible, but nothing equaled the fierce joy of watching a life in the balance between this world and the next. Her body swelled with pleasure far greater than mere sexual longing. It was as if her blood had turned to silk, caressing her veins with every pulse of her heart.

It was time.

She lifted the covers and crept between the sheets to lie next to him. Her own breathing quickened in response to his labored breaths, her limbs hollow with desire. She lost awareness of the room around them, watching the reflection in the window as the sun slid across the

Edinburgh sky in its journey westward. She could just make out the Nelson Monument, perched upon the summit of Calton Hill, thrusting bravely into the wintry sky. The clock on the wall continued its relentless ticking, the hands moving inexorably forward as the man's fingers twitched and clenched the blankets spasmodically, as his moaning crescendoed.

"Shh," she whispered, cradling his head between her hands. "It will all be over soon."

But not too soon, she thought as her hand snaked its way down his body. Gently she unbuttoned his pajamas and caressed his limp manhood, fondling its downy softness, until it began to stiffen in her hand. It was always a marvel to her—how, even on the brink of death, bodies responded to the pull of life. Soon, he'd shuffle off this mortal coil, but first, she would savor the sliver of life yet left in his body.

As she stroked him, she pushed a damp lock of hair from his forehead with her other hand, kissing his neck and whispering in his ear.

"You see," she said, "I told you I'd never leave you."

At that moment, in a slaughterhouse deep within the bowels of the city, a pig squealed as a sharpened blade pierced its throat.

CHAPTER ONE

On a cold Monday in November, Detective Inspector Ian Carmichael Hamilton entered the High Street police station with a feeling of foreboding. His superior officer, Detective Chief Inspector Crawford, had not been himself lately, and no one seemed to know what the matter was. Not a particularly cheerful man under the best of circumstances, DCI Crawford had been even moodier of late, muttering under his breath, looking peeved and distracted. Worse, he had become absentminded, forgetting orders he had given and countermanding others. Morale was shaky, the men under him jumpy. Officers were coming in late, if they showed up at all, and a sense of chaos pervaded the squad room.

After hanging his cloak on the rack, Ian sat at his desk in the corner, turning his attention to the growing mound of paperwork. But he found it difficult to concentrate, sensing expectant looks from the other officers around him. Conversation had ceased when he entered, and there were low murmurs he couldn't make out, the words lost in the room's lofty ceilings. It was clear something had to be done.

DCI Crawford was not the sort of man to take anyone into his confidence, but DI Hamilton was the closest thing he had to a friend on the force. Though it was more of a father-son relationship—and a fraught one at that—Ian knew if anyone could break through the chief's intimidating personality, he could.

He didn't relish the idea of confronting Crawford—his commanding officer's tirades were legendary and, over the years, had reduced more than a few recruits to tears. Ian looked up to see Constable Bowers hovering nervously nearby. His blond eyebrows were knit with concern, terror in his deep-set blue eyes.

"What is it, Constable?"

"Well, sir, he won't talk to anybody—just sits there in a black mood, starin' out the window, y'see." Like Ian, Bowers came from Invernesshire, but DCI Crawford had the ability to intimidate even the Highlanders on the force.

"And you're waiting for me to do something about it, I suppose?" said Ian.

Constable Bowers fiddled with his truncheon and bit his lip. "Well, are you going to, sir?"

Several other policemen stared at him from their desks. The tension in the room was as thick as the evening fogs that rolled in from the Firth of Forth.

"All right," Ian declared, standing up and squaring his shoulders. "I'm going in."

He felt all eyes on him as he strode toward Crawford's office, projecting a confidence he did not feel. The chief inspector's office was at the front of the building, separated from the main room by a wood-and-glass partition, the door facing the larger central chamber. Ian knocked on it crisply and waited. No reply. He looked back at Bowers, whose face had gone a shade paler.

"He's in there, sir," the constable said.

Ian knocked again more sharply—still no response. He took a deep breath and opened the door. He braced himself for reprimand, but the figure slumped behind the desk barely moved to acknowledge his presence. The seat was turned toward the window, so all he saw was the back of the chief inspector's bald head over the top of the chair.

"Sir?" he said.

"Do you know what I hate, Hamilton?" Crawford said without turning around.

"What's that, sir?"

"I hate this whole blasted existence. We eat, we sleep, we trudge off to work, return home again only to eat and sleep some more. What's the bloody use? That's what I'd like to know."

"We also catch criminals, sir. We make the city a safer place to live."

"Do we, Hamilton? Is it really safer?"

"I should venture to say so, sir."

"How can you tell? Because it feels like a cesspool to me right now."

"Then imagine what it would be without us."

Ian's remark was met with a thin sigh. "I can't really imagine anything at the moment—that's the trouble."

"Would you care to talk about it, sir?"

Another sigh, then what sounded like a muffled sob, and DCI Crawford slowly swiveled around toward Hamilton.

Ian was shocked by the sight of his superior officer's face. It had a pasty greenish cast, as though all the blood had drained from it. His cheeks sagged, his eyes were dull and lifeless—even his bushy red muttonchops seemed to droop. Normally a robust, portly man, he looked shrunken and pale.

Ian took the liberty of sitting in the chair in front of Crawford's desk. Usually a stickler for rules, the chief inspector didn't take any notice of this violation of protocol. Crawford gazed at Ian listlessly, twisting a piece of string restlessly between his fingers.

"Sir," Ian began, "the men have noticed something is wrong, and—"

Crawford interrupted him with a laugh—a short, bitter burst of air. "Oh, they have? Bully for them! Perhaps we should promote them all to the rank of detective, eh?" He gave another laugh, but it caught in his throat, becoming a deep, shuddering sob. His body shook as he let his head fall forward to rest on his folded arms.

Ian watched Crawford give in to his grief, his large, ungainly body racked with weeping. Ian felt for the man, but he knew the policemen on the other side of the glass partition could hear them, and when DCI Crawford returned to his senses he would be horrified at the public nature of his breakdown.

But for now there was nothing to be done except sit and wait. Crawford's sobs were punctuated by sounds from outside—the clop of horses' hooves, shouts of street vendors, and the cries of gulls. The birds were a constant reminder of how close Edinburgh was to the sea, the Port of Leith on the Firth of Forth lying only a couple of miles from the center of Old Town.

Finally, Crawford's grief wore itself out. Wiping his face with a blue kerchief, he blew his nose loudly and cleared his throat.

"Well," he said, "that was damned embarrassing."

"'Everyone can master a grief but he that has it,'" Ian said gently.

Crawford's eyes narrowed. "Another one of your Shakespeare quotes?"

"Much Ado About Nothing."

Crawford grunted. "Well, at least this one's appropriate."

Ian was relieved to hear the inspector sounding more like himself, some of the old vinegar creeping into his voice.

The chief stood and stretched his bulky form. Well over six feet tall, Detective Chief Inspector Crawford was an imposing presence. Curly red whiskers grew in reckless abundance upon his chin, as if to make up for the hair that had long since abandoned his head. A pair of magnificent bushy eyebrows, black as a chimney sweep's broom, presided over his face. Everything about him was writ large—his long, oval face; bulbous nose; and thick lips, all set atop a big-boned, fleshy body.

"Are you quite all right, sir?" Ian asked.

"We'll speak no more of this, Hamilton," he said, straightening his cuffs and brushing lint from the sleeves of his uniform. "Now then, what did you want to see me about?"

Ian hesitated. "Well, sir—"

Crawford's small eyes narrowed. "Did I give you permission to sit?"

"No, sir, I—"

"Just thought you'd take advantage of my inattention, eh?" Crawford said, giving his nose another mighty blow into the kerchief.

"No, sir, it was just—"

He was interrupted by a knock on the door.

"Who is it?" Crawford barked, settling back in his chair.

"Sergeant Dickerson, sir," came the voice from the other side.

"Come in, Sergeant."

The door opened to admit a short, unprepossessing young man with ginger hair and pink skin. Hamilton gazed at him gratefully—not only because he had interrupted an uncomfortable moment, but also because Dickerson was Ian's most trustworthy and loyal colleague. In spite of his unimpressive appearance, he had proven to be resourceful and brave, if a bit plodding at times.

"What is it, Sergeant?" said Crawford.

Dickerson cleared his throat and glanced apprehensively at Ian.

"Out with it, man!" Crawford barked. "We haven't got all day."

"I was wonderin' if I could work an extra shift today, sir, in exchange for next Friday off."

"Why did you not take this up with the shift sergeant?"

"I did, sir, and he said I was t'see you."

"Well?"

"I have a—er, commitment."

Crawford frowned. "What sort of 'commitment' could possibly take precedence over your work as a police officer?"

Ian noted with some relief that the sergeant's presence seemed to have invigorated DCI Crawford. Perhaps scolding his subordinates was just the thing to conquer his melancholy. Poor Dickerson was squirming uncomfortably, sweat gathering on his ruddy face.

"Well, sir, y'see . . . I'm in a play."

"A *play*?" Crawford bellowed. "You're in a *play*?"

"Not just any play, sir—*Hamlet*. I've been given the role of the Second Gravedigger."

"Well done, Sergeant," Ian remarked, but Crawford glared at him.

"And who has made the colossal error of casting you in this—*play*?" he inquired.

"It's a charity event, sir—the Greyfriars Dramatic Society. All the proceeds go to feed the needy."

"And were you required to demonstrate your fitness for the role of—what is it?"

"Second Gravedigger. Yes, sir—I had t'audition for the part."

"'Alas, poor Yorick,'" the chief inspector remarked with a smug smile at Hamilton.

"That's Hamlet's line, sir," Ian corrected him.

"What difference does it make whose bloody line it is?"

"The Second Gravedigger gets to ask, 'Who builds stronger than a mason, a shipwright, or a carpenter?'" said Dickerson.

The chief inspector thought for a moment. "I give up—what's the answer?"

The sergeant blushed. "Er, I dunno, sir."

Crawford scowled. "Why not?"

"'Cause that's when Hamlet enters, and Shakespeare never answers the riddle."

"That's bloody rude of him," Crawford muttered. "All right, go ahead—and tell the shift sergeant next time not to bother me with such bosh and bunkum."

"Yes, sir—thank you, sir," Dickerson said, backing out of the office. As he did, he bumped into Constable Bowers.

"What is it, Bowers?" asked Crawford.

"There's a lady here, sir. Says she won't leave until you see her."

"What sort of lady?"

A strident voice behind Bowers led Ian to think that perhaps the term "lady" had been misapplied. "It's murder, I tell you, plain and simple!" The accent was English, a bit plummy—probably central London, Ian guessed.

"Good heavens," Crawford said, his thick eyebrows rising halfway up his shiny forehead like climbing caterpillars.

The personage herself barged past Constable Bowers, shouldering both him and Sergeant Dickerson out of the way. She strode across the small office to stand in front of Crawford's desk, hands on her broad hips, breathing heavily. Clad in a plain black bodice over an ample gray skirt, she was nearly as tall as Ian, her dark hair parted in the middle and pulled back into a severe bun at the back of a muscular neck. Her eyes were dark and rather deep-set, over a small, determined mouth and firm chin. Though she was no beauty, Ian observed that her brusque manner and style of dress conspired to make her less attractive than she otherwise might have been.

She crossed her arms over her impressive bosom. "I demand an investigation!"

"Into what, madame, if I may be so bold?" Crawford inquired.

"The death of Mr. Thomas Caruthers."

"And how did he die?"

"He was poisoned."

"And you know this because—?"

"I recognize the signs of arsenic poisoning."

"Who are you, if I may ask?"

"Dr. Sophia Jex-Blake."

9

Crawford's mouth fell open. Jex-Blake was one of the most famous—and notorious—women in Edinburgh. She and six other women had attempted to upset centuries of tradition by petitioning the university to let them study medicine. Known as the Edinburgh Seven, they were derided and savagely attacked; there was even rioting in the streets. Crawford shot a look at Dickerson and Bowers, who had been watching from just outside the office.

"Close the door, Constable, and go about your duties. I'm sure you must have plenty to do."

"Yes, sir," Bowers gulped, swinging the door shut reluctantly, leaving Ian and the chief inspector alone with their visitor.

"Assuming you are who you claim to be," Crawford began, "why—"

"Why on earth would anyone pretend to be me?" she interrupted impatiently.

Knowing her reputation, Ian was convinced she was exactly who she claimed to be.

Evidently the chief inspector agreed. "Very well," he said. "Pray be seated."

"That's more like it," she said, settling her sturdy form into the nearest chair.

"Now then," said Crawford, "exactly why do you believe a murder has been committed?"

Jex-Blake returned his gaze. "Are you familiar with the symptoms of arsenic poisoning?"

"Some of them, yes."

"Then you are perhaps aware that it can easily be attributed to other causes, such as stomach viruses, dropsy, or even cholera."

"What in particular leads you to believe Mr. Caruthers is the victim of arsenic poisoning?"

"His fingernails display pronounced horizontal striation."

Crawford's broad face puckered. "Horizontal stri—?"

"White lines along the width of the nails," she explained, as though addressing an exceptionally slow child. "It is a telltale sign of arsenic poisoning."

"I see," Crawford replied, stroking his ginger whiskers.

"What relationship have you to the victim?" Ian inquired.

Dr. Jex-Blake squinted at him as though he were an unusual laboratory specimen.

"Why is that of any consequence?"

"In any investigation, it is crucial to identify the persons surrounding the victim," he replied, uncomfortable under her scrutiny. "You are the one to report this crime—if indeed such it is—so I am starting with you."

"Mr. Caruthers' wife has been under my care since her pregnancy."

"Under your care?" said Crawford.

"You are evidently unaware that I run a clinic for women on Grove Street," she said drily, as though their ignorance was an offense against her honor.

"Ah, yes—quite commendable," Crawford said with a little cough. "So Mrs. Caruthers informed you of her husband's death?"

"Actually, no. I was the one who found Mr. Caruthers after his demise."

"How did that come about?" Ian inquired, exchanging a look with Crawford. It was a given in crime investigation that the person who "discovers" the body must be considered as a potential suspect.

"I did not poison Mr. Caruthers, if that's what you're thinking," Dr. Jex-Blake snapped. "I happened to be checking in on Mrs. Caruthers, and not finding her at home, I thought to wait for her."

"How did that lead to the discovery of the body?" said Ian.

"Mrs. Caruthers had given me a key to her home. When I let myself in, I felt something was not quite right, so I went into the bedroom, where I found Mr. Caruthers."

"I see," said Crawford. "Upon which you diagnosed arsenic poisoning."

"Precisely."

"And where is Mr. Caruthers at this moment?"

"His poor wife was quite beside herself with grief, so we had him taken to the city morgue."

Listening to Dr. Jex-Blake, Ian Hamilton thought this seemed a very interesting case. He had no way of knowing it would prove to be far more than that.

CHAPTER TWO

It was nearly ten o'clock, and Sergeant William Dickerson had just poured his second cup of tea, when Detective Inspector Ian Hamilton burst forth from DCI Crawford's office.

"Come along, Sergeant," he called, throwing his long black cloak over his shoulders. Some on the force felt the old-fashioned garment was an affectation, but Dickerson thought the detective looked rather dashing in it.

"Where to, sir?" he asked, scrambling to fetch his own coat from the rack.

"The morgue," Hamilton replied, and the sergeant's heart sank.

The place made Dickerson extremely uncomfortable, though he would never admit it to anyone. He knew their trip was something to do with the lady who had barged in demanding to speak with DCI Crawford. He'd never seen such cheek in a woman before. He admired her, but women like her scared him—another fear he was unlikely to admit.

He donned his long uniform coat and barely had time to button it as he hurried after Hamilton. They emerged into a bright, windy day, skirting the edge of Old Town on their journey to the morgue. Dickerson dodged a group of schoolboys playing hoops and sticks, nearly tripping over one of them as he scrambled to keep up with Hamilton's long strides.

"That lady—ye seemed t'recognize her," he said. "Who is she?"

"A very brave woman, Sergeant. She managed to get permission to study medicine at the University of Edinburgh—caused a lot of trouble, too. You've heard of the Surgeons' Hall Riot?"

"When were that, sir?"

"About 1870, I believe. My family had just moved here around that time."

"So she's a doctor?"

"Yes, but she got no joy from the University of Edinburgh. She and six other women attended lectures but were never given degrees. It would seem progress in Scotland crawls rather than marches on."

"A right pity, sir—I'd think a lady like that would make a good doctor."

"Well, she eventually got her medical degree—from a German university, I believe."

"I'm glad, sir. There's somethin' about her inspires confidence, if y'know what I mean."

"I do," Hamilton said. "I only hope for her sake that her accusation does not land suspicion upon her."

"Beg pardon, sir?"

"It is not uncommon for criminals to pretend to 'discover' a victim they have in fact murdered. They do this hoping to divert attention from themselves, but some killers also derive a perverse thrill from remaining close to the investigation. This allows them to relive their crime all over again, as well as keep an eye on the progress of the police."

"That's disturbin', sir."

"The criminal mind is a dark place, Sergeant."

The city morgue was an imposing stone building located on Cowgate, so named after the herds farmers brought from the west of Edinburgh to sell at the Grassmarket. It was as dismal as Dickerson remembered. The hollow clang of a bell announced their arrival, and the attendant appeared shortly afterward, swinging open the heavy wooden door to admit them to the underground chambers. The sergeant remembered him from their last visit—a stringy-haired Welshman by the name of Jack Cerridwen. Dickerson was wary around the Welsh, who could be surly and secretive. Most of all, they tended to be ill-disposed toward the English, and being from Lancashire, Dickerson had met his share of unfriendly Welshmen.

But Jack Cerridwen didn't seem to care about anyone's origins so long as they supplied him with alcohol, and he greeted Detective Hamilton with a broad smile. "Come right in, gentlemen—I've been expectin' ye, as it were."

He was not disappointed—Hamilton produced a bottle from beneath his cloak, which the Welshman stashed in a drawer of a wooden filing cabinet before leading them through dusky corridors to the back of the building. Dickerson winced as the smell of mildew and formaldehyde assaulted his nostrils. He heard a slow, steady dripping sound as they entered the main chamber. Three bodies were laid out on marble slabs, their chalky white feet protruding from the none-too-clean sheets covering them. Jack Cerridwen pointed to the body nearest them.

"There he is, gentlemen, fresh as a daisy. Hasn't been here but a few hours."

"Why were you expecting us?" said Ian as he gazed at the sheet draped over the dead man.

"Well, the lady who came earlier said ye'd be along soon."

"Did she now?"

"Wasn't the type ye'd argue with, either—a right ol' battle-ax, I'd say."

Dickerson looked at Hamilton, who was smiling faintly.

"But she was right enough—here y'are," Cerridwen remarked. "An' now if you'll excuse me, I'll leave you gentlemen to it," he added, rubbing his hands eagerly.

Dickerson noted that the gift of whisky had the dual advantage of procuring Cerridwen's cooperation as well as his absence. Hamilton no doubt appreciated this as well; he nodded gratefully as the Welshman left them.

Dickerson swallowed hard, praying his stomach would behave as Hamilton pulled back the sheet to reveal the body on the slab. He felt it lurch at the sight of the waxen, blue-tinged skin, but willed his breakfast to remain where it was. Even drained of life, Thomas Caruthers clearly had been an exceptionally handsome man. His high cheekbones, thick, wavy hair, and noble forehead looked as if they belonged to a romantic poet rather than a laborer. Hamilton bent to examine the victim's fingernails, holding the man's cold hand close to his face. Dickerson shuddered but stood his ground—he knew such squeamishness was unbecoming to a policeman and was determined to reveal nothing to the detective.

Hamilton turned and beckoned to him. "What do you make of this, Sergeant?"

Dickerson took a step closer.

"Come along. He won't bite you."

The sergeant complied, and Hamilton lifted the dead man's fingers so the pale light from the windows fell on them. Intrigued in spite of himself, Dickerson bent closer and saw that each one bore clearly visible horizontal white stripes.

"Is this what the doctor lady meant, sir—those marks on 'is nails?"

"This is indeed a strong indication of the presence of arsenic—over a period of time, I should think. Whoever poisoned this man took their time about it, probably did it slowly, over weeks, maybe even months."

"That's cold, sir, if you don' mind my sayin' so."

Ian looked down at the body on the slab. "'It is not, nor it cannot come to good.'"

"I recognize that one, sir. It's—let's see . . ."

"Act One, Scene Two, if I'm not mistaken."

"Right you are, sir, as usual," Dickerson said, then suddenly shivered violently.

Hamilton stared at him. "Are you quite all right?"

"Yes, sir. I were jus' thinking how Hamlet begins with a murder as well."

"Quite right, though it takes place before the play starts."

"'All that lives must die,'" Dickerson added with a sigh. "I believe that's from the same scene, sir."

"Well done, Sergeant," Hamilton said, continuing his examination of the body.

"Thank you, sir," he replied. "Do you believe in ghosts, sir?"

"Not really—why?"

"I were jus' thinking how it's a ghost what comes t'tell young Hamlet his father were murdered. Otherwise, his uncle—Claudius—mighta got away wi' it."

"I fear many a murder goes undiscovered and unpunished, Sergeant—likely more than we'll ever know."

"An' if it weren't fer Miss—er, Dr. Jex-Blake, we might never a' known 'bout this one, sir."

"True enough," Hamilton said with a smile, "though Dr. Jex-Blake is hardly a ghost."

"No, sir, that she isn't," he replied, thinking what a comfortingly solid presence Dr. Jex-Blake was. Her sturdy corporeal existence seemed to banish the entire notion of otherworldly creatures. Dickerson took a deep breath to steady himself. He could hardly wait to get out of that wretched place of death and decay and into the light of day.

CHAPTER THREE

Half an hour later, Ian Hamilton stood in DCI Crawford's office, waiting for him to return.

"How long ago did the chief inspector go out?" he asked the desk sergeant who entered to deliver a pile of paperwork.

"I'd say an hour, sir—he seemed very agitated."

"And he didn't say when he'd be back?"

"No, sir," the sergeant replied. He closed the door quietly, leaving Hamilton alone in the room.

Ian sighed and gazed out the window overlooking the High Street. Beyond the crooked streets and crumbling tenements of Old Town stood the clean neoclassical buildings and straight, wide avenues of New Town. Edinburgh was not one city, but two. The privileged lives of the lawyers and bankers of Princes Street were made possible by the chimney sweeps, cobblers, and dockworkers who lived in dilapidated and dangerous buildings. As a policeman, Ian straddled the two worlds, not always comfortably. The job often presented more philosophical quandaries than he could handle.

Ian heard the click of the doorknob and turned to see DCI Crawford, looking worn and worried.

"Well, was it murder?" he said, slinging his coat over the back of his chair.

"Dr. Jex-Blake is correct, sir."

Crawford sat heavily behind his desk. "And you know this because—?"

"The striations she described were present upon the victim's fingernails."

"And that's conclusive, is it?"

"An autopsy would leave no doubt."

Crawford rubbed his forehead. "Littlejohn is a busy man, but I'll see if he can fit it in."

Dr. Henry Littlejohn was Edinburgh's police surgeon as well as the city's first medical officer of health.

"Shall I open an investigation?"

"I suppose so—at least it will keep that blasted woman off our back," Crawford said, fishing around in his desk drawer. Pulling out a worn bit of string, he twisted it around his fingers, staring vacantly out the window.

"Sir?" said Ian.

"What is it, Hamilton?"

"Is something wrong?"

Crawford scowled, and Ian braced himself, but the chief inspector's shoulders fell and he sighed deeply. "It's my wife."

"I thought she was doing better, sir."

"She had a setback."

"I'm sorry to hear that. Is there anything I can do?"

"As a matter of fact, that brother of yours—"

"Donald?"

"Is he still around?"

"He's staying with me whilst studying medicine at the university."

What Ian didn't say was that his older brother was not the easiest of houseguests. Prickly by nature, he was even more irritable than usual since his recent decision to abstain from drink.

Crawford looked down at the string between his fingers. "You, uh, mentioned something about him helping me find a specialist."

"What are her symptoms?"

Crawford gave a little cough and gazed out the window. "It's to do with her digestion. If your brother could pop 'round in the next few days, I'll explain it to him."

"I'll see what I can do, sir," Ian said. He left the office, returning to his desk to catch up on paperwork. Darkness fell long before the end of the working day in Edinburgh in November. With the autumn equinox well behind them, the citizens were gearing up for the onslaught of a cold, dark Scottish winter.

Shortly after five, Ian stepped into the street and turned west toward his flat on Victoria Terrace. He had not gone ten steps when he heard a familiar voice behind him.

"Hello, Guv'nur!"

He turned to see the grimy face of Derek McNair—street urchin, thief, pickpocket, and one of Ian's most valuable assets.

"Hello, Derek. How are pickings these days—hit any good marks lately?"

Derek's face fell into a mock frown as he pushed a lock of unkempt brown hair from his forehead. "I tol' you, I gave all that up." His accent sported the laconic consonants and rolling vowels of England's West Country.

"And I really believe you," Ian replied without slowing his pace.

Derek trotted to keep up. He was slight and delicate of build and looked younger than his ten years, except for his skin, tanned and rough from life in the streets. "It's true, I swear it!"

"I'm glad to hear it."

"You know what yer problem is, Guv'nur?"

"I have always longed for someone to enlighten me on that subject."

Derek studied Ian's face, then burst out laughing. "Yer a sly one, so help me."

21

"Is that your diagnosis?" Ian said as they rounded the corner onto George IV Bridge.

"I was about ta say yer problem is that you're suspicious of everythin'."

"I should think a healthy dose of skepticism is a virtue in a police officer."

"You've an *unhealthy* dose, is what I'm sayin'."

"Whereas you're just a sweet, trusting fellow, I suppose?"

"What kinda sense would that make fer an orphan like m'self? I'm forced to live by me wits, day by day, on Edinburgh's hard an' bitter streets."

"While your eloquence is admirable, I cannot say the same for your honesty."

Derek stood, arms crossed, barring his way. "Jes what do y'mean by that?"

"On Thursday last you were spotted pilfering meat pies from the butcher shop on Candlemaker Row—"

"Who says they saw me stealin' pies?"

"—and on Saturday I saw you working the crowd at the Grassmarket."

"I were jes havin' a look at the ladies."

"And if you don't keep your hands to yourself, you may lose one of them someday."

Derek frowned. "They don' do that sort a thing anymore."

"You mean chop off people's hands for stealing?"

"Yeah," he said. "They don', do they?" Though still just a child, Derek liked to glide his hands over women's bottoms. And in a thick crowd, he usually got away with it.

"This town is full of thugs and toughs. If you should chance to prey upon the wrong girl, she's likely to have several sturdy brothers who would enjoy nothing more than pummeling some sense into you."

"Don' worry 'bout me, Guv'nur," Derek insisted, but he looked uneasy.

Ian hoped the boy would take his advice. He would rather have Derek frightened than lying battered in back of a dark alley.

"Heard you were at' morgue today," the boy said, trotting after Ian as he resumed his brisk pace homeward.

"How do you know that?"

"I've eyes an' ears in t'street, don' I? Someone get murdered?"

"We don't know yet."

"Well, let me know if I kin help. You know where t'find me."

Ian smiled—it would be more accurate to say that Derek knew where to find him.

"Right," he said.

"I mean it, Guv," the boy said, peeling off as they reached Victoria Terrace. "Remember how I helped ye last time!"

"Wait—don't you want some money?" Ian called.

"You kin pay me when I do some work," Derek shouted back, disappearing around the corner as a gust of wind lifted a pile of leaves to scatter them into the night.

Ian couldn't imagine how the boy could help, but he had no idea how the case would develop. It was, as his aunt Lillian would say, "early days yet." He lowered his head and pulled the collar of his coat higher, pushing forward into the relentless Scottish wind.

CHAPTER FOUR

Aunt Lillian arrived at precisely half past six. Ian was a frequent guest at her house—their Sunday-night dinner had become a ritual—but the previous night she had been out late visiting a sick friend, so on this night he insisted on cooking for her instead. Ian had bought the best lamb chops he could find, serving them with neeps and tatties. Donald had evening classes on Mondays, but Ian cooked a couple of chops for him to have later.

"My, this is good," Lillian declared, accepting a second helping and lifting her wineglass for a refill. "I see you're working a murder case."

"How on earth—"

"You are unusually preoccupied. A case of petty thievery seldom produces such a distracted state of mind that you attempt to pour the wine before it has been uncorked. And twice you paused to listen as though you were expecting someone."

"I thought Donald might come back early."

"Now you're just blethering," she said with a smile. Lillian enjoyed sprinkling her conversation with Scottish slang. "If you'd rather not talk about it, just say so."

"I'd rather not talk about it."

"Fine," she said crisply, pinning a wisp of hair back into the loose chignon at the nape of her neck. Aunt Lillian had the same lanky build and clear blue eyes as Ian's mother, her only sister. Though she was nearly seventy, her spine was as straight as it had been in her youth, and her hands, though increasingly gnarled from arthritis, were steady as ever. They sat in silence for a few moments.

Finally, Ian said, "It's a case of poisoning."

Her eyes lit up, and her whole body snapped to attention, like a pointer on the trail of a grouse. Lillian Grey was in many ways a typical Scottish matron of her era, but she had the same fire and thirst for adventure that burned in Ian's breast. He described the singular encounter with Sophia Jex-Blake and his subsequent visit to the morgue.

"Well!" she declared. "It sounds to me as though you have a real mystery on your hands. What do you know about this Thomas Caruthers?"

"He worked as a lineman for Caledonian Railway, though I've yet to find out much else."

"You'll have the help of that appealing little sergeant—"

"Dickerson's a good man. But DCI Crawford won't be much help; he's much preoccupied with his wife's health."

"What's the matter with her?"

"She's been unwell, and he's very concerned. I'm going to ask Donald for help."

"I'm glad your brother has finally gotten hold of himself."

"The death of our parents took a greater toll upon him than me."

Lillian placed her napkin next to her plate and leaned back to gaze into the yellow flames of the fire. "Life takes things from all of us, Ian. Perhaps not evenly, or fairly, but loss is universal. You can wrap yourself in your own grief, or you can move forward. There is no middle ground."

"But if we don't stop to acknowledge loss and grief, how can we possibly go on?"

"The problem arises when we become lost in our grief, and it becomes more attractive than moving forward. We become frozen."

"What are you trying to say, Auntie?"

She looked out the window, where a blustery wind shook the tree branches as if they were naughty children.

"Ian," she said, "do you think it's natural for a young man to have no one special in his life?"

Ian sighed; he knew where this was headed. "I know you and Uncle Alfred were blissfully married, but—"

"Can I tell you something about love?"

"Can I stop you?"

"You are young and handsome now, and no doubt attracted to pretty girls."

"Auntie—"

"But that is not what love is. Love is like this bench," she said, indicating the crude but sturdy wooden bench he kept near the fireplace, lopsided and riddled with ancient termite holes; it had been one of the few things to survive the fire.

"Your great-grandfather made it from an old oak tree on his land. The tree had provided shade and shelter to him and his flock of sheep all his life, and when it was felled by lightning, he saved the trunk and fashioned this bench. He was no carpenter, as you can see. And the years hav'nae been kind tae it," she said, slipping into her native Glaswegian. "Eaten by termites, discolored by smoke and pipe ash, full of holes and nicks. But the more it ages, the more you love it, true?"

"Yes, I suppose that's right."

"My love for Alfred was the same—I loved him not in spite of his nicks and scars but because of them."

"I know you loved Uncle Alfie, but—"

"This is not about my marriage to Alfred, nor is it about your parents, God rest their souls. It is about you."

"Forgive me, but surely I may choose how best to live my own life?"

"You are mistaken in the notion that your life is separate from all others. That is a fiction. Your choices have an effect upon the people around you," she said, pouring them both another glass of wine.

"Fair enough, but—"

"Especially those who care for you the most."

"Are you suggesting I live my life to please others?"

"What I'm saying is sometimes you should *listen* to what other people have to say, and not be so bloody-minded. Your father was like that, God rest his soul—went his own way even when everyone around him was screaming at him to go the other way." She paused, as if she'd said too much.

Ian leaned forward. "Aunt Lillian, was my father a good man?"

"Don't ask me that. I am not the one to judge."

"What do you mean?"

"Good heavens, look at the time," she said, indicating the grandfather clock in the corner. "I must be off. I'm working the clothing booth at the charity jumble sale tomorrow."

She fairly leapt from her chair—as much as her stiff joints allowed. Ian rose from the sofa and dutifully fetched her coat from the rack.

"I do appreciate your concern, Auntie, but—"

She took his hand in hers. Her fingers were thin as chicken bones, the skin around them loose and dry. But he could feel the strength pulsing through her veins—age had not diminished the force of her personality, nor dimmed her vitality.

"You know I regard you as if you were my own son."

"Aunt Lillian—"

She put a finger to his lips. "Let me speak. I love my daughter, but as you know, Harriet and I . . . she was her father's child, and when he went—well, we have never been close."

"I am truly sorry."

Harriet Grey lived in Dumfries somewhere—last Ian had heard, she was working as a schoolteacher, still unwed.

Lillian buttoned her coat and drew on a pair of yellow kid gloves. "I long ago gave up any hope she would marry, and resigned myself to a life without grandchildren. But you—there is hope for you yet, Ian. Don't disappoint me."

"I can't—"

"I would regard any child of yours as my very own grandchild," she said, pulling her hat down over her abundant gray hair. "Surely you know that."

"I do," he said, his throat thickening. "And I want more than anything not to disappoint you."

"Then don't."

"Let me call you a cab."

"Don't be ridiculous—it's not far, and the walk will do me good."

"But it's late."

"Thank you for an excellent meal. Good night," she said, and slipped out the door.

Ian watched her lean, straight figure negotiate the cracks and potholes in the sidewalk as she threaded her way down Victoria Terrace, disappearing around the bend as it curved toward the center of Old Town.

CHAPTER FIVE

She sat in the warm nook of her kitchen, planning her next move. There was nothing so delicious as the anticipation and preparation, the sweet fantasy of conquest. She gazed out the window as her cat, Blackie, rubbed against her shins, his arched back and half-closed eyes a perfect manifestation of contentment. Cats were so wonderfully expressive and supple in their unselfconscious enjoyment of sensual pleasure. Their movements were so controlled, so graceful, the ultimate in economy and efficiency. If only she could be more like Blackie, she thought as he leapt to the table in one smooth move.

"What do you think, my darling?" she asked, stroking his silky head. "Shall we do another?"

He smiled at her in the way cats do, narrowing his eyes to emerald slits.

"Who's a lovely boy?" she said, rubbing the white, diamond-shaped patch of fur between his ears. "Who's Mummy's little charmer?"

Blackie purred and rubbed against her hand.

"I have a treat for you," she said, spooning a bit of chopped liver onto his dish. "Come along, now, have your dinner."

Blackie sidled up to the bowl and took a few delicate bites.

"Why can't people be more like cats?" she murmured as she poured a fine white powder from a small green tin into a slim glass vial. Dosage was so important, and she was still adjusting to find just the right amount.

She gazed out the window onto the small patch of earth where she grew herbs and roses. She would bury him there, beneath her favorite rosebush. And in the spring, when it produced fragrant pink blossoms, she would think of Blackie.

CHAPTER SIX

After dinner with Lillian, Ian was in the study reading when he heard the front door open and close, followed by his brother's heavy footsteps and the sound of low cursing.

"Bloody hell . . . organic chemistry."

As usual, Donald was muttering to himself. When he was alone—or thought he was—he was given to endless, rambling monologues about a wide variety of topics. Ian had enjoyed spying on his brother when they were young, and would occasionally remind him of something he had said the day before, much to Donald's irritation. The enjoyment Ian got from this more than made up for the epithets his brother invariably hurled at him.

"Goddamn ridiculous," Donald muttered from the front hall. "Why even bother with it?"

There was the sound of a boot dropping to the floor, then another, followed by a louder crash. Ian sprang to his feet and dashed to the foyer, where he found his brother standing over the fallen coatrack. Donald blinked when he saw Ian.

"What are you doing up?"

"Reading," Ian replied, stooping to lift the coatrack.

"It's all right, old man—I've got it," Donald said, bending over his substantial belly to retrieve the fallen rack.

As portly as Ian was lean, Donald Hamilton was a whale of a man. Well over six feet tall, he towered above the average Scot, a fact he'd used to avoid bar brawls back in his drinking days. Aware of Ian's eyes on him, he brushed street dust from his coat before hanging it up. "Don't worry—I've not been drinking. The hallway was dark and I tripped."

"I didn't say anything."

"I wouldn't blame you if you were suspicious—I would be in your place."

The concession was unusual for Donald, and out of character, but Ian accepted it gratefully.

"The thought never crossed my mind."

"Now you're the liar," Donald replied. "Of course it crossed your mind."

"The point is, you haven't been drinking—let's just leave it at that. What did you trip over—the cat?"

"Don't think so. Where is the blasted creature, anyway?" His brother pretended to loathe Bacchus, Ian's black-and-white cat, but on more than one occasion Ian had found Donald asleep on the sofa, the cat draped happily over him.

"I expect he's on mouse patrol, this time of night."

"I'll join him, then," Donald said, lumbering toward the kitchen. "Except that I'll be on beef patrol. You do have a joint around somewhere, I suppose?"

"There are a couple of leftover lamb chops from dinner," Ian said, following him.

"Even better. How was dinner with Auntie Lillian? Did she give you an earful about your love life, or lack thereof?"

"How did you know?"

Donald laughed. "My dear brother, Lillian has been agonizing for weeks over whether to broach the subject with you."

"You *knew* about that?"

His brother pulled the plate of lamb chops from the icebox. "Are there any tatties to go with this?"

"On the bottom shelf. So she already spoke to you about all this?"

"We didn't scheme together, if that's what you're worried about. She asked me if I thought it was a good idea to say something. I told her absolutely not, so naturally she did it anyway." He scooped a generous serving of mashed potatoes onto the plate with the lamb. "Got any cress?"

"There are turnips."

Donald shuddered. "Thanks, anyway."

"Still don't like them?"

"I strive for consistency. Makes life easier. Be a good lad and fetch me a bottle of ginger beer, will you?" he called over his shoulder as he headed out to the parlor with his plate.

As Ian opened the cupboard next to the sink and reached down to grab a bottle, his hand brushed against something furry. He jerked away with a yelp.

Bacchus poked his head out of the cabinet.

"How the devil did you get in there?" Ian said.

The cat purred and rubbed against his leg.

"What's going on?" Donald called from the other room. "A man could die of thirst around here."

"Coming," Ian yelled back, seizing a bottle and closing the cupboard door decisively. The cat sauntered into the parlor behind him. Donald was bent over the grate, stoking the fire. Silhouetted in the orange flame, his face looked almost childlike, but Ian could see puffiness and lines beneath his eyes.

"I don't see why Lillian goes on about my love life, but doesn't seem troubled about yours," Ian said.

"My case is more . . . complicated."

"You mean because of your weakness for drink?"

Donald rubbed his hands over the fire. "I should think a policeman's salary would allow you to spend a bit more for heating."

"I seem to recall a saying about beggars and choosers," Ian remarked, handing him the ginger beer.

"Steady on," Donald replied, lowering his bulk into one of the armchairs in front of the fire. "You know once I'm a proper doctor, I'll pay you back tenfold." He took a hefty swig from the bottle, then looked at it ruefully. "Not the same as the real thing. I do miss it. Don't worry—I'm not giving in to temptation."

"See that you don't," Ian said, lowering himself into the chair opposite Donald. He winced as a stab of pain shot through his upper back.

"Shoulder bothering you?" Donald asked.

"No," he lied. Admitting it might lead to a discussion of the fire that killed their parents. The burns on his back were a constant enough reminder, and since Donald's return, they had done their best to skate around the subject, a large hole in the ice of their carefully maintained smooth surface.

Bacchus sniffed at Donald's plate and attempted to jump on the armrest of his chair, but Donald pushed him away.

"He likes you more than me," Ian remarked.

"He likes my lamb chops—or would if I'd let him."

The cat circled the chair, rubbing against Donald's shins.

"No bloody chance," he informed Bacchus, who began energetically grooming himself. "This lamb is quite decent. Where'd you get it?"

"Marchand's."

"I don't trust that Frenchie. But then, I don't trust anyone."

"That must be a liability in medical school."

"I don't have to trust my instructors—I just have to learn from them."

Ian smiled. "That reminds me of what I once said to DCI Crawford about Derek McNair."

"That young ragamuffin who's always lolling about?" Donald said, his mouth full of potatoes.

"I said I didn't have to trust him, I just had to make him useful."

"And have you? Made him useful?"

"He seems to think so. He was sniffing around today for more work."

"He and this cat have a lot in common," Donald remarked, licking his fingers, his chin glistening with lamb grease. "Quite the pair of opportunists."

"You should talk," Ian muttered, and instantly regretted it.

Donald put down his lamb chop. "If you want me to leave, why not just say so? May I remind you that it was you who invited me to stay."

"I'm sorry. I shouldn't have said that."

"I know I showed up out of the blue, but you took me in. You shouldn't punish me for accepting your offer."

"Quite right—you would have done the same for me."

"It's not so easy, you know, being in school again after all these years."

"I heard you cursing about organic chemistry when you came in."

"I suppose they know what they're doing, but it seems odd having to study some of these subjects. Hard to see what they have to do with being a doctor."

Donald lit a cigarette, with a quick glance at Ian, who disapproved of smoking. Ian ignored it but saw an opening.

"I wonder if you would do me a favor."

"How could I refuse?"

"Crawford's wife isn't well—"

"What's the matter?"

"It seems to be digestive."

"Her name's Moira, isn't it?"

"How did you know?"

"I met them both years ago, when Father—before the fire."

"Where was I?"

"Probably out mucking around with your delinquent rugby friends, or at a wrestling match—God knows. It was exhausting just to watch you. I used to wonder which one of us was adopted."

"Clearly you were. Father was athletic, like me."

"Fat lot of good it did him."

Once again, Ian could feel them teeter on the brink of the subject, then back away. He breathed a sigh of relief when his brother heaved himself to his feet and set his plate on the mantel. Bacchus followed, purring.

"You can give him the lamb bones," Ian said.

"Keep his teeth sharp for murdering mice, eh?" Donald replied, tossing a bone on the hearth. The cat crouched over it, purring even louder. "He certainly likes his food. Maybe I should take him with me when I leave."

"Please, no more of such talk. Stay as long as you like."

Donald stretched and yawned. "I'd better turn in soon. But first I want some pudding and a strong cup of tea to help digest all that lamb."

"By the way, are you familiar with the signs of arsenic poisoning?"

"Some of them."

"Have you come across fingernail striation?"

"That can be a sign of several disorders, depending on the nature of the marks. Are they horizontal or vertical?"

"White horizontal stripes."

"That would likely indicate the presence of a toxin. Arsenic is a good possibility."

"But not the only one?"

"No, though I couldn't give you a complete list. Why?"

Ian told him about the curious appearance of Sophia Jex-Blake and his subsequent trip to the morgue.

"Extraordinary woman," Donald murmured.

"You've heard of her, then?"

"Certainly—though her reputation around the medical school is not entirely untarnished. Doctors are by nature conservative, and academics even more so. You can imagine their reaction to her attempt to upset that particular apple cart."

"Do you think her accusation credible in this case?"

"It depends upon the toxicology report."

"Assuming it's positive for arsenic—"

"I'd say you have a poisoner on your hands. Now then, how about some pudding? I believe I saw a mince pie in the pantry."

Ian shook his head. "Does nothing disturb your appetite?"

Donald patted his considerable belly. "As Lillian would say, are ye struck blind, man?"

"I suppose a strong stomach is a useful attribute for a doctor."

"To compensate for my less than useful ones."

"Do you still have a photographic memory?"

"Yes, assuming years of overindulgence haven't destroyed it. Now, how about some of that pie?"

CHAPTER SEVEN

The next morning, Ian dragged himself into the station at half past nine. Crawford was not at his desk, but Dickerson was waiting for him, his blue eyes bright as the copper buttons on his uniform.

"Lab results came back, sir."

"Read it to me, Sergeant," Ian replied, pouring a strong cup of tea to soothe his throbbing head.

"'Marsh and Reinsch tests both confirm large amounts of arsenic in victim's system. Cause of Death: Arsenic Poisoning. Manner of Death: Undetermined.'" Dickerson frowned. "How can it be undetermined, sir? Don't poisoning mean he were murdered?"

"Not unless we can prove it."

"That lady what came in yesterday—"

"Dr. Jex-Blake."

"She seems pretty well convinced he were murdered."

"It's possible the fatal dose was taken accidentally."

"Isn't that unlikely, sir?"

Ian sat at his desk and pushed the gathering mound of paperwork to the side. "Do you recall the Bradford sweets poisoning in England? Twenty people died from eating candy accidentally laced with arsenic."

"Yes, but that were before the passage of the Pharmacy Act, weren't it?"

"Good on ye, Sergeant," Ian said. "How did you know that?"

"My dad were a pharmacist, an' he used to grumble 'bout havin' to keep a poison register. Still, he knew it were a good thing in the long run."

"Then you also know arsenic is present in many common household compounds. For example, it is the main ingredient in rat poison."

"But who swallows rat poison on purpose, like?"

"That's what I mean to find out. Come along—we have a call to make."

"Where we goin', sir?" Dickerson asked, fetching his coat and hat.

"To pay a visit to Dr. Henry Littlejohn."

In addition to his post as police surgeon, Henry Duncan Littlejohn taught at the university. According to Donald, he lectured from eleven until one on Tuesdays and Thursdays. Ian pulled his watch from his waistcoat pocket. It was nearly ten.

"We'd best be quick about it," he urged Dickerson as they descended the stairs to the street. "If we don't catch him before he goes into the lecture hall, we shall have a long wait."

The police station was located in the middle of the busy High Street, so it wasn't difficult finding a cab. Within minutes they were rumbling over South Bridge. Dr. Littlejohn's office was snuggled into a turret overlooking Drummond Street.

"Is he expectin' us, sir?" Dickerson asked nervously as they ascended the winding steps to the third floor.

"No, but I hope he will see us nonetheless," Ian replied, though his confidence was growing as narrow as the twisting staircase.

A knock upon the door brought a mumbled reply. Ian pushed the door open slowly. Seated behind a broad, cluttered desk was a powerfully built man of about sixty with pale, sunken eyes and a curved beak of a nose set over a thin, determined mouth. His abundant silver hair was parted in the middle and slicked back, emphasizing his prominent cheekbones.

"Well?" he said without looking up. "What is it, what is it? I have a lecture to prepare for—haven't got all day, you know. Not all day." His voice was surprisingly light for such a substantial physical presence, his accent suggesting Scotland's western coast.

"DI Ian Hamilton, at your service," Ian said, fighting the urge to click his heels.

Dr. Littlejohn looked up, his stern face relaxing into a smile. "Ah, yes—you're one of Robbie Crawford's men."

"Yes, sir."

"Come in, come! Close the door, would you?"

Ian glanced at Dickerson, who obliged, standing stiffly at attention.

"How is old Robbie these days?" Littlejohn asked warmly, suddenly appearing to have all the time in the world.

"Fine, thank you, sir," Ian lied, impatient to get to the matter at hand.

"Give him my regards," the doctor replied. "Now then, now then, what can I do for you?"

"I was wondering if you would be so kind as to give us your opinion as to the likelihood that a victim ingested poison accidentally."

"Ah, yes—the arsenic case," he said, leaning back in his chair.

"You know of it?"

"Dr. Jex-Blake has made certain everyone knows of it," he said, frowning, though Ian thought he detected a note of admiration.

The doctor rose and came around to the front of his desk, leaning upon a pile of blue examination booklets. Not an inch of the desktop was visible beneath the pile of books, folders, and knickknacks littering its surface. Littlejohn crossed his arms thoughtfully.

"It is possible the man in question was accidentally poisoned, though I rather doubt it. The amount present in his system suggests a more sinister event. Rather more sinister, I should think."

"But you cannot say for certain that the manner of death is homicide?" Ian said with a glance at Sergeant Dickerson, who hovered respectfully in the corner, his pale-blue eyes wide.

"I am reluctant to declare it with finality, as it casts suspicion upon the people close to the dead man."

"I appreciate the delicacy of your position, but what do you think is the most likely scenario?"

"If you put it that way," the doctor said, stroking his chin, "I would have to say it likely that a murder has been committed. Extremely likely."

"Given the facts, then, you would advise an investigation?"

"Most certainly, most certainly. There's no telling what you'll find if you begin turning over rocks. You can tell Robbie Crawford I said so."

"Thank you—I will, sir," Ian replied, turning to go.

"And tell Old Muttonchops that I haven't forgotten he owes me five pounds. Five pounds sterling."

"Uh, yes, sir," Ian said, following Dickerson out the door.

"He won't get off so easy!" Littlejohn called after him. "Not so easy."

"Who woulda thought it, sir?" Dickerson said as they walked toward the high gate guarding the entrance to the school. A wind had picked up, tossing dead leaves into the air, rustling them in papery swirls. "DCI Crawford with gamblin' debts."

"You don't know that it's about gambling, Sergeant. Hamilton's Third Rule of Investigation: 'Never leap to conclusions.'"

"How many rules are there, sir?" Dickerson asked as they stepped into the swarm of pedestrians and carriages on South Bridge.

"Currently ten, but they are subject to expansion. The main thing is that police investigation must be treated as a discipline—a science, if you will."

"Should I go 'round to the chemist shops and see if there's been a run on rat poison an' the like, sir?"

"I thought about that, but it's so readily available I fear it would be a waste of valuable time. Anyone can get their hands on it."

"Oiy, watch out!" Dickerson yelped as the rear wheel of a brougham nearly rolled over his foot.

"Steady on, Sergeant," said Ian, turning onto Chambers Street.

"Isn't there quite a lot o' guesswork involved, sir?"

"My aim is to reduce that to a minimum."

"Don't you ever have—*hunches* about things, sir? For example, I have a hunch this poor fella were poisoned by someone he knew."

"That's more of a statistical probability than a hunch."

"Why d'you say that?"

"Consider how difficult it would be to deliver poison to someone you were *not* acquainted with. How would you ensure they ingested it? You'd need access to their food or drink. And how would you do it without being observed? Think how much easier it would be to do away with someone you knew—the more intimate the acquaintance, the higher likelihood of success."

"So we're lookin' for someone close to the victim, sir?"

"I expect so, though we must keep an open mind," Ian replied as a couple of students hurried by, clutching massive textbooks, their long robes fluttering behind them like black sails. "I suggest we begin by interviewing Mrs. Caruthers."

"Horrible thought, that a man's own wife would do such a thing."

"Poisoners are an ugly lot. Can you imagine planning to kill someone in such a painful and terrifying manner, then having the sangfroid—"

Dickerson frowned. "Sang what, sir?"

"It means 'cold blood' in French. Imagine plotting it out, then delivering the fatal dose to your unsuspecting victim."

"Give me an old-fashioned crime a' passion any day. Poor bloke comes home, sees his wife in flagrante delicto, as it were, an' jus' snaps, like. Coupla minutes later, we've a dead wife and the chap is in a daze, hardly realizin' what he's done. But somethin' like this—"

"There are more things in heaven and earth than are dreamt of in your philosophy, Sergeant."

"Right you are, sir," Dickerson agreed as they approached the broad stone walls of the police station, its tall, latticed windows frowning down on them. As he yanked on the heavy wooden door to the entrance, a gust of wind nearly wrenched it from his grasp. Ian steadied his hand, holding the door against the draft while the sergeant grabbed for his hat. "Thank you, sir," he said as both men slipped into the building.

Across the street, a pair of eyes watched them, wondering how much they knew and what to do about it.

CHAPTER EIGHT

"How are you getting on with the Greyfriars Dramatic Society?" Ian asked as they headed into the station.

"'Tween you an' me, sir, it's a bit thick, y'know. Half the time I dunno what they're sayin'."

"You're lucky to have a comic part."

"Some a' those jokes musta been side splitters back in Mr. Shakespeare's time, but I confess I don' quite get all the humor," Dickerson said, following him up the marble steps.

"I envy you, being so close to all that genius, a mouthpiece for immortality."

"For example, 'A knavish speech sleeps in a foolish ear.' What's the meanin' a that, sir?"

"Hamlet has just told his friends Rosencrantz and Guildenstern that the king is just using them, but they don't understand, so he calls them fools for not heeding his warning."

"Sounds t'me like he's insultin' them."

"It's ambiguous. 'Knavish' could mean sly or crafty and clever. I think he's telling them they're fools for not understanding his clever advice. My aunt would accuse me of much the same thing," he added with a smile.

Dickerson shook his head. "It's all a bit deep for me, sir."

"Do you think I might come to a rehearsal sometime?" Ian asked, nodding to the desk sergeant as they entered the broad room with its high ceilings.

"I s'pose so—I'll ask the director."

"Don't worry—I shan't criticize your acting."

"I weren't worried, sir," Dickerson replied, though his tone suggested otherwise. "Per'aps you'd like to join the society, seein' as you like Shakespeare so much."

"I'm not really looking for a hobby," Ian said, hanging his cloak on the bentwood rack in the foyer.

"It's nice havin' something like that when you're feelin' lonely."

"What do you mean by that?"

"Nothin', sir; I just thought—"

"That I was lonely?"

"I were jus' saying—" Dickerson began, sitting at his desk across from Ian's.

"I'm surrounded by people all day. For God's sake, I have a bloody roommate—"

"Your brother, sir?"

"And if you think it's easy living with him, Sergeant, I assure you—"

"I'm sure it's no walk in the park, sir," Dickerson replied, busying himself sharpening a stack of lead pencils.

"You don't know the half of it. He comes in at all hours, fills the house with cigarette smoke, snores like a room full of bears—"

"There's all kinds of lonely, sir."

"Have you been talking to my aunt?"

"Why, no, sir. Excuse me, but it's my turn to make tea."

Ian watched Dickerson trundle over to the tea station, where a couple of constables stood conversing. He was trying to puzzle out what the sergeant meant by his comments when his attention was caught by the late-morning sun glinting off the brass buttons on the men's uniforms, scattering into a thousand shards of light. He gazed at them, mesmerized, before a familiar voice shattered the station's relative calm.

"Good Lord, Hamilton, why on earth were you bothering Henry Littlejohn? He has more important things to do than answer your questions."

Ian looked up to see DCI Crawford bearing down on him. Hatless, looking like an enraged walrus in his gray coat, the chief inspector turned every head in the station with his entrance.

"How did you know we saw him?"

"I went to see him on another matter, and he told me he had spoken with you. Why didn't you ask me first?"

"You weren't here, sir."

"You should have waited."

"Murder waits for no man," Ian murmured, and instantly regretted it. He braced himself, expecting the full fury of Crawford's wrath. To his relief, the chief inspector sighed and drew a hand across his brow.

"I suppose you're right," he muttered. "But for Christ's sake, Hamilton, follow protocol, would you? If it's not asking too much," he added sarcastically, heading for his office.

"I'll do my best, sir," Ian replied, following him.

Crawford closed the door behind them. "So what did he say?"

"He gave you his regards and asked you to pay the five pounds you owe him."

"About the *case*, Hamilton!"

"He believes it is most likely murder."

"Very well, have your investigation. I can spare one man—take your pick."

"I'll take Sergeant Dickerson."

"Thought you might," Crawford said, removing his coat. "Did you notice how Dr. Littlejohn repeats everything twice?"

"Yes. I was wondering what that was about."

"Some kind of compulsion, I suppose. And yet he manages to accomplish more in one day than most men do in a week. He must never sleep."

"And you, sir? How have you been sleeping?"

"Not so well." To Ian's surprise, a smile crept over Crawford's face, and he gave a strange little giggle. "'Macbeth does murder sleep,'" he said proudly.

"Well done, sir—though it's considered bad luck to quote that play backstage."

"Good job we're not backstage, then," Crawford shot back.

"Sorry, sir. Well done, sir."

"Never mind, Hamilton," he muttered, but Ian could tell his feathers were ruffled.

"I wonder, sir," he said, "would you like to go with me to see Sergeant Dickerson in *Hamlet*?"

Crawford frowned. "I should think crime solving would take precedence over a stage play."

"I just thought perhaps—"

"So he's still nattering on about that bloody five pounds?" Crawford said, pulling on his whiskers.

"I had the impression it was more of a joke."

"Ha! Henry Littlejohn has no sense of humor when it comes to money, I can assure you."

"If you don't mind my asking, did you lose it in a card game, sir?"

"Good Lord, Hamilton, I'm surprised you would dare suggest that Henry Littlejohn is in the habit of collecting gambling debts."

They were interrupted by a commotion in the front room. Crawford opened his office door to discover loud shouting and cursing coming from a short, squat fellow with the shoulders of a bull and a neck thick as a butter churn. He wore coarse overalls, thick-soled rubber Wellingtons, and a well-worn, wide-brimmed hat. His clothing and sunburned face left no doubt as to his profession: he was a farmer.

"Yer a bag a shite!" he roared in a voice ragged as a cheese grater. "Yer bum's oot a windae!"

The last time Ian had heard that particular epithet was from Aunt Lillian, when she was displaying her Glaswegian roots.

The target of the fellow's anger was Constable Turnbull, whose pockmarked face had turned bright crimson. Turnbull was a sneaky, narrow-shouldered young man who sought to hide his premature baldness with a musty toupee that looked like a dead cat someone had dug up.

"What's going on here?" Crawford demanded.

"I observed Mr. McAllister riding furiously and recklessly in front of St. Giles'," Turnbull replied acidly.

Mr. McAllister clearly disagreed. "Ye call that riding recklessly? I'll wham yeh, yeh fuckin' wee basturt!" he bellowed at Turnbull, who continued to fill out a warrant. Though making a show of calm, the constable flinched at McAllister's words.

"Threatening a policeman with bodily harm is hardly likely to advance your case," Crawford remarked.

"Git tae fuck, all a ye! Yer a load a basturts, so y'are!" McAllister declared.

Crawford turned to Turnbull. "Constable, why don't you write this gentleman a summons so he can pay his fine and get out of my station house?"

"Just a moment," Ian said. "Do you have a first name, Mr. McAllister?"

"Course I do! Ye think I wa' raised by wolves or sommit?"

"What is it, then?"

"Angus."

"You're Glaswegian, aren't you?"

"Wha's it tae yeh?"

"My aunt is from Glasgow."

"Bully fer her," he replied, suspicion warring with curiosity in his red-rimmed eyes.

Ian turned to Constable Turnbull. "What kind of conveyance was Mr. McAllister driving?"

The constable glanced at the farmer contemptuously. "A turnip cart."

"Is this your first offense?" Ian inquired.

"I ne'er been dragged in by the coppers afore, if tha's wha' ye mean."

"I'm sure there was a reason you were in such a hurry," Ian suggested to McAllister, who scowled and twisted his cap between his filthy fingers.

"An' wha' if I did? Ye still gonnae fine me?"

"I should like to hear your excuse."

Crawford frowned. "Now see here, Hamilton, we can't ask every miscreant why he broke the law."

"I am only asking Mr. McAllister, sir," Ian answered politely. "Perhaps there are mitigating circumstances."

The chief inspector threw his hands up in the air and retreated to his office.

"Now then, Mr. McAllister," Ian continued. "What do you have to say?"

"I'll admit I wa' drivin' a wee bit fast, but I'm shorthanded on the farm a'cause me youngest boy took ill. I wanted tae make delivery afore market opened. No chance a' that now," he added bitterly.

"I'll tell you what," Ian suggested. "If you promise never to do it again, perhaps Constable Turnbull will see his way to letting you off with a warning. What do you say, Constable?"

Constable Turnbull's mouth tightened and his eyes narrowed. "There's schoolchildren roaming those streets, you know!" He shot a furious glance at Sergeant Dickerson, who shrugged. "Very well," the constable replied tersely. "So long as he gives his word."

The farmer nodded blankly, then a wide smile parted his lips to reveal several missing teeth. "God bless ye," he said to Ian. "I won' fergit yer kindness."

"I have no doubt of that," Ian replied. "Now, I'm sure you'd like to be on your way. Sergeant, would you see Mr. McAllister out?"

Dickerson complied, leading the farmer past the row of desks and through the swinging door.

Ian turned to Constable Turnbull. "I apologize if you think I trod on your toes."

Turnbull's pitted face was flinty as steel, his jaw working, but as he opened his mouth to respond, they were interrupted by a sharp summons from Crawford.

"Hamilton!" he yelled from his office. "Get in here, now!"

A couple of other policemen snickered nervously.

"Uh-oh," one of them said. "You're in for it, Hamilton."

"Sergeant, would you please find out where Mr. Caruthers lived?" Ian asked Dickerson calmly as he came back into the room.

"I'll get started on that right away, sir," the sergeant replied, glancing nervously at the chief's door.

"I'll be right back," Ian said, squaring his shoulders and marching into Crawford's office.

CHAPTER NINE

"Close the door behind you," Crawford said when Ian stepped inside. He complied, and the chief inspector peered at him from behind his desk as though Ian was a piece of three-day-old fish. "Let me ask you something."

"Yes, sir?" Ian said, maintaining a placid expression that did not betray the hollow feeling in his stomach.

The chief inspector's voice was unusually calm—a bad sign. "Do you think your fellow officers are stupid, Hamilton?"

"Quite the contrary, sir."

"And Constable Turnbull—do you think he's an idiot?"

"Not at all."

"And how would you feel if one of your colleagues interfered with your investigation?"

"I expect I shouldn't like it much, sir."

"Then why the *hell* would you intervene when the poor fellow is making an arrest? Answer me that!" The chief inspector's voice had lost its pretense of serenity, gradually climbing in pitch and volume. His face had a decidedly purplish cast, and droplets of sweat beaded on his forehead.

"I wished to put Mr. McAllister in my debt."

"Why on earth would you do that?"

"In order to make him useful."

"I don't follow."

"It seems to me there are a number of ways to proceed as a policeman," Ian said, choosing his words carefully.

The chief inspector frowned and tugged at his muttonchops. Ian could read Crawford's mood in how he treated his whiskers. Tugging was not a good sign. "Such as?" he said, peering at Ian, his small eyes nearly obscured by the opulence of his shaggy black eyebrows.

"We can keep the peace by arresting criminals, and try to prevent crime by locking them up."

"Or—?"

"We can gather allies—forge relationships with people who might be of help to us in the future."

"I don't see what that has to do with letting a fellow get away with breaking the law."

"Did his name not ring a bell?"

"McAllister? It's a common enough Scottish name."

"And his appearance was unfamiliar to you?"

"He looked like a farmer."

"Do you recall James McAllister of Gullan's Close, jeweler and notorious resetter?"

"Resetters," who received and resold stolen property, were an important link in the chain of Edinburgh's criminal underground. Without them, thieves had little hope of profiting from their escapades.

"Of course I know him," Crawford replied. "But I don't see . . . hang on a moment! Come to think of it, the two of them look so alike they could be—"

"Brothers."

"I was about to say twins."

"Perhaps. But I certainly would put money on them being brothers."

"Just so long as you don't bet with Henry Littlejohn." Crawford chuckled.

"I thought you said he didn't gamble."

"Certainly not!" Crawford snapped. "I was joking," he added lamely, but they both knew better.

"With Angus McAllister in our debt, it may be possible to get a step ahead of some of our more prolific burglars—or at least be not three steps behind."

"You really believe Angus will rat out his brother?"

"I was thinking more along the lines of his brother owing us a favor."

"But will they see it that way?"

"Isn't forgoing a minor fine a small price to pay to find out?"

"I suppose so," Crawford murmured, stroking his chin thought-fully, which indicated his mood had improved.

Ian decided to get out while he was ahead. "Will that be all, sir?"

"Yes, yes—dismissed. Fancy that," Ian heard him mutter as he left the office, "bloody twins."

The other constables' faces sagged with disappointment when Ian emerged from Crawford's office. There are few things as delicious as witnessing a colleague receive a tongue-lashing, and deprived of the expected fireworks, the men looked decidedly grumpy. Ian was not tremendously popular. Regarded as standoffish, he was respected for his dedication and success as a detective but resented by less diligent policemen. He knew this, and was determined not to let it bother him.

There was no sign of Constable Turnbull, who had probably returned to his beat around St. Giles'. It was a busy area, but not a ter-ribly crime-ridden one, being rather close to the police station and far enough from the worst slums of Old Town.

"I were 'fraid Crawford would let you have it, sir," Dickerson remarked as Ian returned to his desk. "But I didn' hear much shoutin' in there." Ian couldn't help noticing even the loyal sergeant looked disappointed.

"I managed to smooth his feathers," Ian said, taking a seat behind the desk. "Did you locate Tom Caruthers' address?"

"Yes, sir," Dickerson replied, running his finger down the second column of the city registry. Though the original document was at city hall, the police kept a copy for reference. "His address is—or was—Nineteen Reid's Close."

"Come along," said Ian. "If we hurry, we can make time for a late luncheon."

"Right you are, sir," Dickerson said, grabbing his coat. "I'd watch yer back if I were you, sir," the sergeant added, hurrying down the marble staircase after Hamilton. "Constable Turnbull were pretty angry at what y'did."

"Thank you for the warning, but I expect I can withstand his indignation."

"He's a nasty piece of work, sir," Dickerson said as they swung through the front door of the station house. "Be careful, is all I'm sayin'."

A wintry chill crept over the city as the two men turned east on the High Street. Behind them, Edinburgh Castle stood silhouetted in the gathering gloom, still and watchful atop its rocky perch, as the reluctant sun slunk toward its looming parapets.

CHAPTER TEN

She gazed out the window at the dried vines crawling up the side of the building, and at the dead leaves scattered across the ground. The sky overhead was slate gray, the color of river stones. She took a sip of strong tea and smiled. The gradual dying of Nature in autumn always flooded her with a fierce joy. Bitterness blossomed in her heart like a black flower; the withering of living things filled her with satisfaction. It was a reminder she was not alone in her misery—all life came to this, in the end. She had dedicated herself to serving her darkest fantasies, and it was fitting she should embark upon this quest at a time when Nature herself was loosening her hold on life. The once-supple green earth no longer pulsed with growth but lay still and dormant all around her.

She looked at the white powder in the tin cup on the table. So soft and white, innocent as a baby's caress, yet so deadly. She basked in the delicious irony as she planned her next conquest. The last one had gone smoothly—so much so that she needed to be wary of complacency. She could not relax her guard, become sloppy, or it would be her undoing. No, she would be careful this time as well, and leave no trace.

Gazing at the steam curling up from her cup, she was transported to another kitchen table, over a hundred miles away, many years ago. It was the dead of winter; fresh snow covered the landscape in a thick blanket of white, muffling sounds, softening the edges of objects, lending a dreamlike atmosphere to the frigid air. Lights blazed in the big house on the fen day and night; the gas was always lit, burning brightly late into long winter nights.

Footsteps echoed up and down the narrow staircase at all hours, the creaking boards complaining of their burden, groaning beneath the weight of an endless parade of women. But the women were attending to their own burden, who lay weak and barely moving in the bedroom at the end of the hall, swathed in blankets, his shrinking body dwarfed by the carved mahogany headboard looming above him like a great dark sail.

She would hover at the kitchen table and listen for the footsteps to die away as the patient drifted off and his caretakers sank exhausted into fitful sleep. Then, when all was quiet, she would pad up the steep staircase in her stocking feet, and down the long, narrow hall, until she came to his room. Pausing with her hand upon the doorknob, she listened for the sound of his labored breathing before pushing it open slowly, creeping softly into the room to avoid waking him.

The man in the bed lay still, the only movement the rising and falling of his chest, the only sound the faint, sickly rattle in his throat. She tiptoed to stand beside him, studying the familiar planes of his face in the faint glimmer of moonlight filtering through the curtains. Perhaps it was the pale-blue light, but he looked younger than before the illness. The worry lines on his forehead had all but disappeared, his skin glistening with a feverish sheen that mimicked the dew of youth.

She bent over him, inhaling his aroma. He smelled as he always had, in spite of the illness. It was a manly scent—cinnamon and allspice and freshly chopped wood. Lifting the covers, she crawled in beside him and wrapped her arms around his body, pressing her heart against his. After sighing deeply, she wished fervently she could preserve this moment for all time—there, in the feeble light of the moon, she hugged his body to hers.

By day he was surrounded by women, but tonight he would be hers alone. She sighed and drew her father closer to her.

CHAPTER ELEVEN

Vickie Caruthers was a slight, sallow woman with sad eyes and a wan, worn-out face. Her loose-fitting bodice, shawl, and hand-knit skirt made no attempt to conceal her advanced pregnancy. There was something disturbing about the sight of a protruding belly on such a diminutive person; looking at her, Ian had the disquieting thought that she was about to give birth to a demon or other monster. He attributed this unpleasant association to his recent reading of *Frankenstein; or, The Modern Prometheus*, by Mary Shelley. The book was much in vogue in Edinburgh, and Aunt Lillian had recently given him a copy.

Mrs. Caruthers led the men into a dingy but tidy room that appeared to serve as combination parlor and dining room. Beckoning them each to a chair, she attempted to perch upon a milking stool, but Ian would have none of it.

"Please, madame," he implored, indicating a tattered blue armchair. "In your condition, you should take the weight off your feet."

She did not argue, and sank wearily into the chair. In her cloth cap and shawl, she looked anything but a murderess and sat demurely with her hands folded, waiting patiently for Ian to speak.

"I am so very sorry about your husband's tragic and untimely death," he began.

She gave a shallow sigh, her thin shoulders barely moving, as if that was all the energy her small body could muster.

"He was a good man, my Tom," she said in a low voice. "Don' know what we'll do weaout 'im."

"'We'?" said Ian.

"Me an' the baby," she said, patting her distended abdomen.

"Do you have anyone to look after you?"

She shook her head and stared into the distance. "Lost me mum an' da in the cholera. Tom's folks live in Aberdeen—s'pose I could go live with them, if they'll have me. Unless they think I did 'im in. You don' think I killed my Tom, do you?" she said, a flush creeping into her pale cheeks.

"Of course not," Ian blurted out, startled by her directness. Sergeant Dickerson caught his eye and frowned, but Ian pretended not to notice. The truth was, he didn't think she was guilty. Her innocence and lack of guile, stooped shoulders and quiet grief—surely these were not the traits of a cold-blooded poisoner. Of course, she could be putting on a show, but if so, she was an actress of preternatural talent. Ian's instinct told him she was as much a victim as her unfortunate husband. "We'd like to question you," he said, "to help us find the person who did this."

"Oh, aye," she said earnestly. "I'll do whatever I can t'ketch poor Tom's killer."

"Can you think of anyone who would want to hurt him?"

"I've thought of naught else, but nae one comes to mind."

"Did he have any friends we can talk to?"

"Ye might talk to 'is mates at the rail yards."

There was a light, quick knock at the door, and she struggled to rise from her chair.

"Please, allow me," said Ian.

He opened the front door to see a bright-eyed young woman with an abundant crown of blond hair holding a basket in the crook of her arm. She frowned upon seeing Ian but, spying Vickie, waved cheerfully.

"I just popped 'round to see how you're getting on. I've brought you a wee parcel of food."

"You're an angel, Abby," said Vickie. "Come in fer jus' a moment."

"I can't stay long—I'm on my way to the clinic," she said, laying the basket on the dining table. "Why, Billy Dickerson!" she exclaimed, seeing him. "What a surprise, seeing you here—and how dashing you look in that uniform!"

"Hello, Abby," he said, blushing.

"It's very naughty of you not to mention you were a policeman," she said, wagging a finger at him. Turning to Ian, she pulled off her gloves, and he caught a whiff of jasmine as she extended her hand. "Abigail McNaughton," she said, giving him a frank look and a firm handshake. "I'm one of the nurses at the clinic where Mrs. Caruthers is a patient."

"Detective Inspector Hamilton," Ian said. "I see you already know Sergeant Dickerson."

"Yes, we're in a play together."

"Ah, so you're in *Hamlet* as well?"

"I have a very small role, but Billy is really quite good. You should come see him!"

"Perhaps I will," Ian said with a glance at Dickerson, who fidgeted with the brass buttons on his uniform.

"I didn't realize you were a nurse, Miss McNaughton," he mumbled.

"The good Lord knows this city needs more of them," she replied. "You're here about the terrible tragedy, I suppose?"

"The poisoning, yes," Ian replied.

"It was poison, then? How very dreadful." Her gaze fell upon Mrs. Caruthers sitting meekly in her chair, and she turned pale. "Surely you don't think—Vickie would *never*; I mean, it's unthinkable!"

"We are not in the habit of jumping to conclusions of any sort, Miss—"

"McNaughton."

"It is standard procedure to interview anyone who knew the deceased."

"Of course. Forgive me; I feel protective where my patients are concerned."

"You work with Miss Sophia Jex-Blake, I believe?" asked Ian.

"Yes, I'm one of her colleagues—employees, really. She writes the checks, so that makes me an employee."

"And how do you get on with her?"

"I don't think it would be overstating it to say I am in awe of Dr. Jex-Blake. But then, I'm hardly alone—most of us worship the ground she walks on."

"You enjoy working for her, then?"

"Well, she can be difficult—geniuses often are, you know. But few people have done what she has for the poor, not to mention her devotion to women's rights. Anyone who works so tirelessly for the downtrodden deserves respect, don't you agree?"

Her earnest brown eyes searched Ian's face for a response, and he felt his cheeks burn.

"Yes, indeed."

Sergeant Dickerson stepped forward. "How well did y'know Mr. Caruthers?"

"Not well. I saw him when he accompanied Vickie to the clinic."

"Can y'think of anyone who might wan' t'harm him?" he asked, writing something in the notebook he always carried.

"Not a soul, but we only had a nodding acquaintance. Now, if you'll excuse me, I must get back to the clinic."

"Thank you, Miss McNaughton," said Ian.

"My pleasure," she replied, giving Vickie Caruthers a warm hug. "Don't you worry, love—we'll look after you."

Vickie nodded passively, a dazed expression on her face. The rest of their interview yielded little helpful information—yes, there was rat poison in the house, but none seemed to be missing or tampered with.

"Lovely young woman, don' you think?" Dickerson remarked as they waited for a cartload of cabbages to clear the intersection. The dapple gray pulling it was half asleep, his heavy head nodding, his hooves scraping the paving stones. The driver didn't seem to mind—perched atop his cart, the reins slack in his hands, he whistled a Highland melody Ian recognized but couldn't place. Seeing Dickerson's uniform, the driver tipped his hat cheerfully before disappearing around the corner, the sound of his whistling absorbed by the cacophony of an Edinburgh street.

"Which young lady are you referring to?" Ian asked, though he knew perfectly well.

"Miss McNaughton, a' course," the sergeant replied as they crossed to the other side of Canongate. "I near didn' recognize her in that nurse's getup. Wonder if she has a fella."

"Are you no longer seeing Miss Tierney?"

Sergeant Dickerson's love life was the envy of the entire constabulary. Short and ginger-haired, with a soft, chubby body, he had managed to attract the interest of the lovely Caroline Tierney, of raven hair, pink cheeks, and inviting red lips. His colleagues were forever moaning and wondering at his good fortune, a puzzlement Ian shared, though he would never say so.

"Miss Tierney don' enter into it," the sergeant answered. "It were you I was thinkin' of, not me."

"I'm too busy to cultivate an interest in what Aunt Lillian calls the 'flowers of Edinburgh.'"

Dickerson chuckled. "That sounds like your aunt, sure enough."

"'A madness most discreet,' Sergeant."

"Y'mean t'say your aunt's mad, sir?"

"I was speaking of love—or rather, Shakespeare was."

"I don't recognize that one, sir."

"*Romeo and Juliet*, the balcony scene. And how is your Juliet, anyway? Does the course of true love still run smooth?"

"I am still seein' Miss Tierney, though I wish the fellas at' station would leave off askin' what she sees in me."

"If your colleagues cannot perceive what Miss Tierney sees in you, it speaks to their lack of imagination—and no doubt their envy as well."

"I appreciate that, sir."

"And, in turn, I would appreciate you not pressing me on the subject of my private life."

Dickerson's face fell; he looked like a chastised puppy. "Not another word, I promise."

"Very well—we'll consider the matter closed."

"Where to next, sir?"

"I believe we have arrived at our destination," Ian replied, stopping in front of the White Hart. "My brother swears this is the best steak and kidney pie in Edinburgh. Shall we test his theory?"

Dickerson's face broke into a toothy grin. "I s'pose I'm up to the task."

"Good," said Ian. "This one is on me."

"Ta very much, sir," the sergeant replied, following him inside, his pudgy body sighing with contentment. Across the street, a lone figure darted into an alleyway, hidden in the shadows between the buildings.

CHAPTER TWELVE

After lunch, Ian and Dickerson trudged down to the rail yards to interview Thomas Caruthers' coworkers. Situated beneath Waverley Station, the yards were dirty, noisy, and dank. Smoke from the constant stream of locomotives hung in the air, turning the atmosphere a grainy, pervasive gray. The clank of tools and shouts of workers filled the intervals between trains as they clattered by, steel wheels screeching and rattling on the iron rails. The tracks occupied the steep valley separating the slums of Old Town from the shining neoclassical buildings of New Town. From a distance, the sloping tenements and winding streets of the medieval Old Town looked picturesque, but Ian had walked those streets long enough to know otherwise.

Picking his way carefully across the muddy ground, Sergeant Dickerson behind him, Ian headed toward a group of laborers gathered around a switch lever. Their heads swung in his direction, cap brims shadowing their eyes. There were three of them—the tallest and stockiest was evidently the leader, judging by how the others looked to him for his reaction. His rolled-up sleeves revealed brawny arms festooned with tattoos.

"Good morning," Ian said briskly. The gap between him and these men was as wide and deep as the valley separating New Town's elegant streets from the festering warrens of Old Town. He would not be surprised if one or all of the men had criminal records. The workers made no reply, and Ian did a quick mental calculation. He and Dickerson were outnumbered three to two, and the roar of the trains would drown out any sounds of a fight, so he could expect no one to come to their aid. Careful to show neither fear nor hesitation, he strode forward confidently. "I'm Detective Inspector Hamilton, and this is Sergeant Dickerson of the Edinburgh City Police."

The shortest of the three men spit on the tracks and gazed at Ian calmly without wiping his mouth.

The big one who was the leader crossed his massive forearms and cocked his head to one side. His eyes were a bloodshot blue, and he had the shoulders of a mastiff. "What d'ye need from us, then?"

"It concerns your coworker, Thomas Caruthers," Ian replied.

"Tom? He didn' report in today."

"That's because he's dead," Sergeant Dickerson blurted out, evidently going for shock value, but unfortunately his voice shook, spoiling the effect.

"Yer pullin' my leg," the big one said with a laugh.

"I'm afraid not," said Ian. "The fact is, he was murdered."

The leader's face hardened. "There's nobody'd kill poor Tom. He's meek as they come."

"I assure you, he is deceased."

"Well, I'll be shot tae fu'," the man said, scratching his day-old bristle. "Wha' happened?"

"It were one a' those woman he kept on't side," the spitter mused, revealing a Geordie accent. He was thin and ill-nourished-looking, with a yellowish complexion and dark greasy hair.

The third man nodded in agreement. He was a rather handsome lad, with dirty-blond hair in need of a trim and a frank, open face. "Bill's right—bet you twenty to one, it was over a woman."

"What woman is that?" Ian asked.

"Oh, Tom always had a bit on the side," said the big fellow with a smirk. "This latest one was outta his class—leastways, that's what he said."

"Do you know her name?"

"I dunno 'er name, but she were trouble, I kin tell ya that," the little Geordie replied, suddenly anxious to be helpful.

"He was always talking about her," the young blond agreed. "How he was hiding it from his wife but didn't know how long he could keep it up."

"And he never mentioned a name?" said Ian.

The three men shook their heads. "Not far as I kin remember," the leader said.

"Did he say anything else about her?"

"Liked her better than th'last one," said the Geordie.

"That's true enough," agreed the leader.

"Why is that?" asked Dickerson.

The three men exchanged a glance, and the big one snickered. "Last one kep' sayin' she wanted t'join a convent."

"Did she?" said Ian.

The leader shrugged. "Don' know. But Tom was sick o' hearin' 'bout it."

"How did he die?" asked the good-looking young one.

"He was poisoned," Dickerson said ominously.

The Geordie smiled grimly. "Aye, that'll be woman's work fer sure."

"Was he a good worker?" asked Ian.

"Good as they come," the big one replied with a shrug.

"Did he have any trouble with his coworkers?"

"Nah, apart from bein' randy, he were a pussycat. Sometimes the fellas took the mick out o' him on account of his looks, but he didna' seem t'mind."

"So there was no one who had it in for him?"

69

"His wife, I 'spect," the leader replied with a grim smile. "Maybe the husband of one o' his mistresses."

"I don' think this one were married," the Geordie said. "Leastways, that's th'impression he gave."

"He lied to them, you know," said the young blond.

"About being married himself?" said Ian.

"That an' 'bout what he did fer a livin'," said the Geordie. "Used to brag how he convinced them he were a law clerk or a sommit."

"He could put on quite the posh accent, too," said the blond.

The leader nodded. "Aye—had quite the talent fer it. Used to keep us in stitches imitatin' folks."

"Like who?" asked Dickerson.

The big man shrugged. "Everyone. Our fellow workers, the fops on Princes Street—'e did a braw take on our boss."

"Oh, yeah," the Geordie said. "Pure dead brilliant."

"It sounds like he was pretty charming," said Ian.

"Oh, he were right charmin' enough," said the Geordie. "That an' 'is good looks were like sugar to t'ladies."

The leader nodded. "I'm gonnae miss 'im, poor Tom."

"Do you know of any other friends we might speak with?" Ian asked him.

"Naw, I think we were 'is best mates."

The Geordie nodded. "Between 'is marriage an' all the lady friends, Tom didn' have much spare time."

Ian gleaned no more useful information from the men, though once they began talking, they seemed reluctant to stop and go back to work, trading jokes and gossip about their colleagues and bosses.

"You've been most helpful," Ian said. "Sergeant Dickerson will collect your names and addresses, and feel free to contact me if you remember anything else, no matter how seemingly insignificant."

"So you don' think one a them done it, sir?" Dickerson asked as they made their way back over the muddy earth, stepping over the tracks crisscrossing the rail yard.

"Did you observe their reactions when you told them he was dead, or were you too busy trying to gain the upper hand?"

"Well, I—"

"I was watching them carefully, and to a man, their faces betrayed shock. I wouldn't rule any of them out, but I think it's unlikely."

"So we're back t'square one?"

"On the contrary," Ian said as they climbed the steep set of stairs up from the embankment. "Thomas Caruthers was having an affair, and if that's not motive for murder, I don't know what is."

CHAPTER THIRTEEN

The sun retired early in Edinburgh in November, and by the time Ian and Sergeant Dickerson left the rail yards, a thin twilight threaded its way through the tumble of city streets. After bidding the sergeant good night, Ian watched him climb the hill to South Bridge before turning his own steps westward. Feeling restless, Ian did not go straight home, but wandered down to the Water of Leith, following the river past the botanic garden until he reached the Warriston Cemetery. He roamed the grounds aimlessly, feeling oddly at home among the overgrown headstones as he contemplated the thin line between life and death. A patch of fresh earth here and there signaled more recent arrivals, and his thoughts turned to his parents, interred in the cold, hard ground. Finally fatigue drove his footsteps homeward, and he trudged back along the river as a silvery crescent moon rose in the night sky.

Donald was already in bed when Ian arrived, and sound asleep, judging by the snores emanating from his room. Ian closed and latched the front door, slipping quietly into the front parlor, where a single lamp was lit. Upon the table next to it was a note scribbled in his brother's hand.

FED CAT. GONE TO BED—DO NOT DISTURB!! CHEMISTRY EXAM TOMORROW.

Peeking into his brother's bedroom, he saw a familiar black-and-white lump sprawled over Donald's stomach. He felt a little jealous the cat had transferred his loyalty to his brother, but also relieved. Bacchus was not an accommodating bedfellow, and disliked being dislodged from whatever inconvenient position he was occupying. He usually protested with his claws, and Ian bore many scratches as reminders. Now the cat had managed to curl up on top of Donald's generous abdomen and was also sound asleep. Ian tiptoed to his own room and crawled into bed.

He lay staring at the moon for some time. He watched it rise higher as it shrank in size, becoming more distant in the night sky, until he could see the stars all around it, the faint flicker of far-off flames. As a result of a recent trip to Scotland and professed passion for the Scottish people, French writer Jules Verne had become immensely popular in Edinburgh of late. His novel *Around the Moon* had everyone talking about the possibility of life on the moon or remote, undiscovered planets. Gazing at the stars, Ian wondered if, somewhere in those distant worlds, a detective much like himself was chasing down miscreants in a city that resembled Edinburgh.

He closed his eyes to sleep, but the waxen face of Thomas Caruthers appeared before him. Despite having never known the man in life, Ian felt a sacred duty to represent him in death. He was reminded of the solemnity of death every time he gazed upon a corpse, but there was something about poisoning victims that eroded his very notion of humanity. To take a life was a terrible thing, but to plan and execute such a torturous demise was monstrous.

What he hadn't told Dickerson was that he hoped the killer was not a woman. Ian knew his attitude was old-fashioned and sentimental, putting women on a pedestal whether or not it was deserved. He didn't dare admit any of this to Aunt Lillian, who was already too invested in his private life. She would no doubt find it ridiculous, perhaps even contemptible. Still, when he thought of his mother, he couldn't find a single fault in her—in his memory, she was as pure and loving a spirit as ever lived.

He turned over in bed and fluffed the pillow, hoping to lure recalcitrant sleep to his bed. Just as a welcome drowsiness was overtaking his limbs, he heard the creak of a door hinge and shot upright in bed as a familiar silhouette sauntered into the room.

"Good Lord, Bacchus," he muttered. "Timing isn't your strong point."

The cat responded by bounding upon the bed, settling his solid body on Ian's knees, and energetically licking himself. Ian turned over, pulled the blanket up to his neck, and put a pillow over his head to drown out the rhythmic whirr of the cat's purring. Tomorrow, he thought, he would buy a dead bolt for his bedroom door.

Sleep, when it came, was not an amiable companion—monstrous creatures roamed the landscape of his dreams. He found himself in a dank alley, unfamiliar and strange, filled with vague, shadowy forms. Ascending a narrow flight of stairs, he entered the parlor of Vickie Caruthers' tenement and was disturbed to hear screams coming from the bedroom. He rushed to her side; she was about to give birth, attended by Abigail. He had never seen a woman in labor and was appalled at the sight of her contorted face, purple and slippery with sweat. Abigail barked instructions at him as the slimy, bawling creature slid out of Vickie's tortured body.

Abigail held the child up to the light, and Ian saw with horror that it was a deformed child, a miniature Frankenstein's monster, with terrible, vacant eyes and a deathly gray complexion. She held it out to him, and he shrank back as a scream formed in his throat.

"Ian, wake up, for God's sake!"

He opened his eyes to see Donald standing over him, shaking him by the shoulders. The cat was nowhere in sight.

"W-what are you doing here?" he stuttered, dazed.

"Your screams were enough to wake up the entire neighborhood," Donald replied irritably, lighting the gas lamp next to the bed.

"Sorry. I was dreaming."

"Remarkably, I managed to reach that conclusion on my own. Are you in the habit of vocalizing while asleep?"

"Not that I'm aware."

His brother yawned and rubbed the back of his neck. "Lillian's right—you need a woman."

"What makes you say that?"

Donald threw his hands up in mock despair. "Must I spell it out?"

"I don't know why you think that would help."

"Then you're even more naïve than I suspected."

"Anyway, I'm not interested in *that* sort of woman."

"My dear brother, *everyone* is interested in *that* sort of woman—unless they're interested in something else altogether."

"Why are we having this conversation?"

"Good question. Oh, I remember—it's because you woke me *at three o'clock in the morning.*"

"I said I was sorry."

"The question remains: What on earth were you dreaming?"

Ian recounted the hideous apparition of his nightmare, and when he had finished, Donald shook his head and picked up the book lying on the nightstand.

"Why are you reading this?" he inquired, holding up Mary Shelley's opus.

"Aunt Lillian gave it to me."

Donald sighed. "Not only does she plant notions of monsters in your head, she also frightens you by insisting you pursue women in spite of your aversion to them. No wonder you're having bad dreams."

"You can't blame this on Aunt Lillian. The relationship to the poisoning case is clear. And why do you say I am averse to women?"

"I should think it would be obvious," Donald replied with a yawn. "Forgive me for not wanting to stay up all night discussing your nonexistent love life, but I have a chemistry exam tomorrow."

"I'm sorry I woke you."

"I shall do my best to return the favor sometime. Until then, good night."

"Good night," Ian replied as his brother shuffled out of the room. "That's my robe you're wearing."

"And it still looks better on me," Donald called over his shoulder before closing the door.

Ian lay awake gazing at the moon, still and bright and surrounded by its mantle of stars, until dozing off shortly before dawn. He was awakened by the cat's cold little breath on his face. Dragging himself out of bed, he trudged to the kitchen, where another note from his brother greeted him.

DON'T ALLOW BACCHUS TO BULLY YOU INTO SECOND BREAKFAST. I ALREADY FED HIM. FRESH EGGS, ETC. IN ICEBOX.

Ian opened the icebox to find there were indeed eggs. He ignored the cat's attempt to gain his attention by winding around his legs and was just finishing breakfast when there was a knock at the door. Still in his pajamas, he padded to the foyer and threw open the door to see Sergeant Dickerson standing there, sweat lining his pink face. He was dressed in street clothes—Ian could see a white shirt and tweed jacket beneath his greatcoat.

"Beg pardon for disturbin' you, sir, but there's been a—development," he said, panting.

"Catch your breath, Sergeant."

"Yes, sir—sorry, sir."

"Now then, what's happened?"

"There's been another death, sir. Suspicious circumstances, you might say."

"Poisoning?"

"That's what I'm thinkin', or I wouldn't a bothered you."

"Damn," Ian muttered. "Damn it to hell."

"It's bad luck t'swear before breakfast," came a voice from behind the sergeant.

Ian frowned—the voice belonged to Derek McNair, who tipped his cap to the detective.

"Kin we come in?" the boy said. "It's cold as a witch's tit out here."

Ian opened the door to admit the two of them into the foyer.

Derek grinned at him. "Told ye I'd be of use in this case," he said cheerfully, tracing a finger over the antique mirror on the wall.

"That has yet to be determined," Ian replied, firmly removing the boy's hand from the mirror.

Dickerson gave a nervous little cough. "Well, y'see, sir—"

"Spit it out, Sergeant."

"It were the lad what found the body. I were jus' returning from seein' my sister off to school when he turns up on my doorstep, hoppin' up an' down like he's fit ta be tied, swearin' he's found another victim."

"I see," Ian said, looking down at McNair, who wore a beatific expression on his grimy face. Ian wasn't taken in—a profligate pickpocket and thief, the boy was too clever by half. "And where exactly did you come upon this body?"

"Holy Land," McNair said with a sly smile.

"Hardly surprising," said Ian.

Holy Land was a notorious tenement off the Canongate, and together with its neighbor, Happy Land, housed a fair percentage of Edinburgh's underclass. It was a bastion of thieves, prostitutes, and criminals of all kinds, as well as poor unfortunates who had nowhere else to go.

"I won't bother to ask what you were doing there," said Ian.

"I were visitin' a friend," the boy replied.

"No doubt."

"Not that kinda friend. Though I wouldn' mind—"

"That's disgusting," said Ian. "You're ten years old."

Derek grinned. "I'm old fer my age."

"Where was the deceased when you last saw him?"

"I tol' Kate—"

"Are you referring to Fair Kate?"

"Yeah. You know 'er?"

"What did you tell her?"

"That if she didn' move the body, I'd give 'er half a crown."

"And where did you propose to procure those funds?"

"From you, a' course. Listen, Guv," Derek said, trying to peer around him, "I've not had breakfast yet, an'—"

Ian turned to Dickerson. "Sergeant, would you see that he gets something to eat while I get dressed? Keep an eye on the silver—and anything else that isn't nailed down."

"I'm affronit by that, after all we been through together," Derek said gloomily. "Th'unkindest cut of all."

"Sergeant?" said Ian.

"Yes, indeed, sir—will do," Dickerson responded, casting a wary glance at McNair.

Ian left the two of them to get dressed, and when he reappeared, the boy was happily devouring a plate of eggs and rashers.

"Where did you get the bacon?" Ian asked the sergeant, who was sipping a cup of tea while petting the cat. Bacchus pranced back and forth, back arched, purring loudly.

"Found it in t'icebox, sir, tucked away behind a bit o' mince pie."

Ian smiled to himself—his brother had been secreting food away as long as Ian could remember. As a child, Donald had kept a stash of sweets and cakes under his bed, and sometimes Ian could hear him munching on it late at night. He always seemed to enjoy food more if there was a secretive element involved, as if furtiveness itself was an appetite stimulant.

"Very well," he said, tying his cravat for the third time—a task he invariably performed poorly when in a hurry. "If you are quite finished with your breakfast, shall we be off?"

"Jes about done," McNair muttered, cramming a biscuit into his mouth.

"You're done now," Ian said, throwing on his cloak.

Derek slid from his chair and left the table, but not before grabbing a couple slices of bread and jamming them into his coat pocket.

"Aren't the Sisters of Mercy feeding you?" asked Ian, opening the front door.

"I'm a growin' boy. Anyway, yer food is better."

"I'll bear that in mind next time I invite you to dine," Ian said, exchanging a look with Sergeant Dickerson as he closed the door behind them, leaving Bacchus alone in the silent flat.

CHAPTER FOURTEEN

It was too bad about the pregnant wife, she thought as she gazed out her window onto a bare patch of ground. A black squirrel dug industriously into the dull earth, no doubt looking for nuts stored earlier in the fall. The wretched woman would be better off without him, though—men like him did not deserve to live. And she would think of something to help his widow—she didn't know what yet, but she felt a responsibility toward the poor little thing. After all, they belonged to the same sisterhood.

She remembered the first time it happened. The intervening years had done nothing to dull the memory. Instead, they had burnished it, like the binding of a well-worn book, just as vivid as the day it occurred. It was a windy day in October; her mother and brother had gone to town to do some shopping. She would have joined them but was recovering from a cold, so she stayed behind at her mother's insistence. She lay on her bed with her doll, Lucinda, listening to the intimate sounds of the big house—the furtive scurrying of small creatures in the attic, the ancient shutters creaking under the onslaught of the wind, blowing in from the North Sea.

As she combed Lucinda's wheat-yellow hair, she became aware of a new sound—footsteps upon the stairs. Quiet, steady, and firm, it was the tread of someone who was determined but in no hurry. Alarmed, she put the doll down and rose from her bed, hesitating as she reached for the doorknob. But the door swung open by itself, and she nearly fainted with terror. Relief flooded her limbs like cool water when she saw the figure filling her doorway was her father. He smiled at her broadly, a lock of light-brown hair falling over one eye. Her father was a handsome man, and until that day, the sight of his face made her feel protected and loved.

"Did I frighten you?" he said. "I'm sorry. I had few customers, so I closed the shop early. I figured anyone in need could go to Blackmore's."

Her father was one of two chemists in their town, the other being Henry Blackmore, whose pharmacy was at the other end of the High Street.

"May I come in?"

She opened the door wider.

"Hello, Lucinda," he said, seeing the doll upon the bed. "You're looking pretty today."

"I just combed her hair."

"Well, it looks very nice," he replied, sitting on the bed. "How are you feeling?"

She frowned and pulled at her earlobe, a nervous habit. "Fine, but I wasn't allowed to go shopping."

"Your mum knows what's best for you. Come sit beside me," he said, patting the bedspread, which was pale pink with little purple flowers.

She complied, sitting cross-legged, her frock spread out around her like the feathers of a brooding hen.

"Shall I teach you a game?"

"All right," she said, curious, since her father rarely had time to play with her.

"Close your eyes and put out your hand."

She did as he said. She heard the rustle of wool, and then he took her hand and laid it on something that felt like a soft, skinny wrist.

"Can I open my eyes yet?" she asked.

"Not yet," he said. His voice sounded muffled, and she was aware of his breathing, which seemed louder.

He closed her fingers around the strange appendage and began moving her hand back and forth over it, faster and faster, as his breathing quickened. Though she did not understand what was happening, she knew it was not good. He made little moaning sounds, punctuated by strange little squeaks she recognized, having heard them coming from her parents' room late one night when she couldn't sleep.

His fingers closed tighter around hers so she couldn't pull away, and then his other hand snaked across her lap and beneath the folds of her frock. Her body stiffened as she felt his fingers digging into her undergarments.

"Oh," he moaned. "Oh, oh, oh, my darling!"

This confused her even more. She had heard him refer to her mother as "darling," but he never called her that. She winced as his fingers made contact with her bare flesh, and squeezed her eyes shut more fiercely, not wanting to see, wishing she could make them both vanish.

"Oh, ooooh, aaaahhh," he groaned. "Aaaah! Oh, I die—oh, oh, *I die!*"

She felt something wet and sticky on her fingers. As his body went limp and silent, hot tears slid down her cheeks.

"Thank you, dearest girl," he said, hugging her, his breath smelling of whisky and cigars. "We won't tell anyone about this, eh?"

She shook her head numbly, afraid to make a sound. When finally she heard the click of the door latch, she opened her eyes to see Lucinda lying on the floor, her yellow hair tangled and wild, an accusatory look in her unblinking glass eyes. Snatching the doll up, she threw it across the room. She felt soiled, wretched, and unutterably, unbearably sad. Her deep sense of abandonment would only grow with time.

She was seven years old.

CHAPTER FIFTEEN

The landscape of Scotland, ripped apart by volcanoes, torn and scraped by centuries of glaciers, pockmarked by lakes and crags, was like its inhabitants—besieged by internal warfare, blown and scattered by invading armies, and dotted with remnants of tribes hardy enough to eke out a living from its rocky soil and rugged climate. The descendants of those tribes loved the land with a fierceness born of centuries of deprivation and hardship. Scotland's harsh beauty inspired dogged devotion from a people given to excess, in love with the romance and nobility of suffering.

Nowhere in Edinburgh was this suffering more apparent than in Holy Land, the ironically named swamp in the neighborhood known as the Canongate. Just as the Irish ghetto on the west end of town lay in the shadow of Edinburgh Castle, the Canongate's tenements slumped directly below the posh residences of Royal Terrace and Holyrood Palace. Stark poverty was bracketed on every side by extreme affluence—no doubt contributing to the city's violent and bloody past.

These cruel disparities were not lost on Sergeant Dickerson as he alighted from the hansom cab carrying himself, DI Hamilton, and Derek McNair at the entrance to Holy Land. A couple of grubby children peered through soot-covered windows at the unfamiliar sight of a hackney carriage invading their dim and dusky corridors.

Detective Hamilton's knock upon the front door was met with silence—Dickerson glanced up to see the children's mother pull them away from their window perch. Hamilton tried knocking again, but to no avail.

"Why don' they answer?" the sergeant asked.

"Folks 'round here don' much like coppers," Derek observed.

"How do they know we're policemen?" Dickerson said.

"They can smell us," replied Ian.

"C'mon," said Derek, darting around the side of the building. "Follow me."

He led them to the back, then up some rickety stairs that hugged the stone walls, a rusted handrail the only thing between them and the cobblestones below. Hamilton pounded loudly on the second-floor landing door; what was left of its green paint peeled off in flakes beneath the blows of his fist.

"I know you're in there," he called. "Open the door or we'll break it down!"

The door swung open abruptly to reveal a large, fleshy woman of indeterminate years, dressed in a low-cut yellow frock. Her skin had the pale hue of one who rarely saw the sun; her hair, an unlikely shade of copper, was tightly curled around her flushed, round face.

"Why would ye want to do that, now, lovey?" she asked Ian. "You know Kate's always glad to see your handsome face. Who's this fresh young thing?" she asked, giving Dickerson a look that made his cheeks burn.

"This is Sergeant Dickerson," said Ian, "and this is—"

"Oh, no need to introduce young Master McNair," she responded with a laugh that was meant to be lewd and worldly, but the sound of it filled the sergeant's heart with sadness. She turned to Dickerson. "Pleased t'meet you. 'Round here they call me Fair Kate."

Unsure of the proper response, Dickerson nodded and tipped his hat. She grinned, revealing crooked front teeth, and crossed her plump white arms over her bulging bosom. She was the picture of degraded femininity, yet he could not ignore his body's response—her presence excited him. Kate smelled of camphor and oil soap and freshly laundered linen; she was motherly and sensual and wholly, utterly different from his lady friend, the proper and exquisite Caroline Tierney. He adored Caroline with all his heart, yet there was something wild and thrilling about Fair Kate that shook Dickerson to his core. Confused and perplexed, he wiped the sweat from his upper lip and shoved his hands into his pockets.

"Well?" said Ian. "Are you going to invite us in?"

"'Will you walk into my parlor, said the spider to the fly,'" she replied, holding the door open for the three of them.

Dickerson was startled to see Derek McNair run his hand over Kate's buxom behind. She swatted it away but seemed neither surprised nor annoyed by his rude familiarity.

"Cheeky little scamp," she muttered.

The boy winked at the sergeant before sauntering into the building.

This confused Dickerson even more. He was utterly flustered by the fallen woman, with her outrageous curls and insinuating smile. Not for the first time, William Chester Dickerson felt himself an outsider, a clumsy interloper in a society whose rules he did not understand. He stumbled after Hamilton, hoping the detective did not notice his discomfort.

The room they entered was evidently a kitchen, judging by the bubbling coming from the far corner where a gas stove sagged beneath the weight of a gigantic cast-iron pot.

"I'd offer ye some," Kate said, observing Dickerson eyeing the pot, from which steam poured with such abandon a thin film of mist covered his entire face. "Trouble is, I don't think ye'd want any." She walked over and dipped a wooden spoon into the boiling cauldron, lifting forth a sopping garment he recognized as a pair of women's bloomers. He felt himself blush helplessly as she threw back her head and guffawed, full-throated and hearty as a sailor. "Round here, there's as likely to be laundry cooking as dinner, lovey," she said, wiping the sweat from her own brow.

Detective Hamilton seemed less than enchanted by her quips. His ascetic face was stern, his gray eyes glimmering with impatience. "Would you be so kind as to take us to the scene of the crime?" he said.

"Don't get yer knickers in a twist—we're on the way," she said, wiping her hands on a dirty dish towel.

Dickerson couldn't help marveling at how at ease she was in the company of two policemen and a lewd street urchin. The presence of the police put most people on edge, but Kate was as relaxed as if she was entertaining old friends. They followed her through a beaded curtain and down a narrow hallway with peeling flowered wallpaper. She stopped in front of a door at the end of the corridor.

"This is the room where he—well, we left him just as we found him, like the lad told us," she added with a glance at Derek.

Ian turned his gaze on the boy. "Just exactly what *were* you doing at an establishment like this?"

"Told ye, I were visitin' a friend. Anyway, wha' diff'rence do it make? I found ye another victim, innit?"

"That remains to be seen," Ian remarked. "We may find the poor blighter died of natural causes."

"Well, have a wee look-see fer yourself," said their hostess, swinging the door open to reveal a midsized bedroom.

The interior was dim; the only source of illumination was the feeble sunlight struggling to penetrate the layers of soot and grime covering the windows. The room was sparsely furnished, with a simple pine dresser between the two windows and a brass bed against the wall at the other end. The atmosphere was musty and damp, the stale air suggesting the windows had not been opened for some time. There was another odor Dickerson recognized immediately.

It was the smell of death.

CHAPTER SIXTEEN

The dead man on the bed was fully clothed, for which Dickerson gave silent thanks. William Dickerson had never enjoyed the sight of another man's body, finding it especially embarrassing to gaze upon a naked dead man. In addition to being personally distasteful, it always struck him as a violation of privacy, a final indignity, so to speak. Luckily, that was not the case with this gentleman, who had apparently been overcome by death before he could divest himself of his garments.

The dead man appeared to be in early middle age, with a solid physique, well-groomed and prosperous-looking. His beard was neatly trimmed, Van Dyke style, and his dark-blue wool suit was of the finest gabardine. The jacket hung from the bedpost behind his head; the matching waistcoat and trousers he wore appeared quite new and in excellent condition.

But the body itself was shocking. His limbs were twisted grotesquely, splayed at unnatural angles, and oddly stiff, more than the usual effects of rigor mortis, as if he had died in the midst of violent convulsions. His face was contorted into a mockery of a smile, the teeth bared, and the sergeant could make out a faint rim of dried foam around his mouth.

Derek McNair pulled off his cap and clutched it respectfully between his grubby fingers, bowing his head. Hamilton and the sergeant were hatless, but both went silent for a moment, the solemnity of death pervading the room. Even the garrulous Kate was quiet, crossing herself rapidly, her lacquered nails flitting from one side of her swelling bosom to the other. In spite of the influx of Irish laborers following the cholera epidemic, Catholics were still in the minority in Edinburgh. Dickerson wasn't good with dialects and wondered if Kate herself was originally from the Emerald Isle.

"This is how you found him?" Hamilton asked her.

She nodded vigorously. "We left the poor fellow jus' as we found 'im, like the lad said."

The detective glanced at Derek. "And no one else has been in this room?"

"Not a soul, cross my heart an' hope ta die," he said with a smug smile.

"I believe you were promised monetary remuneration for your cooperation," Hamilton told Kate.

She licked her full red lips. "The lad said—"

"He was not authorized to make any such promise, but I will honor it nonetheless."

"Thank ye kindly, sir. I'm glad t'be of service to the police whenever possible."

"I'll be sure to remember that," Hamilton said, fishing some coins from his waistcoat pocket. "I trust this will suffice?"

Her eyes widened with surprise; evidently the detective was more generous than she had expected. "Ta very much," she said, tucking the coins into the voluminous folds of her skirt.

"Now then, what can you tell me about this gentleman?"

"You'd best speak ta Big Margaret. He was her—er, that is, he came here t'see her."

"Where might I find her?"

As if on cue, there was a shuffling step in the hall. Kate went to the door. "Is that you, Margaret?"

"Aye," said a voice so throaty and low Dickerson might have taken it for a man's.

"Can you come in here a moment?"

A singular personage appeared in the doorway. Nearly as tall as Detective Hamilton, she was built like a drover, sturdy of limb and broad shouldered, but her stooping posture gave the impression of submission rather than strength. Her hair was a thick chocolate brown, and her unlined face was youthful—Dickerson estimated her to be not much older than himself. Her visage was long and somber, with high cheekbones and thin lips. The large, deep-set eyes were her most attractive feature, expressing an aura of gentle sadness. She reminded him of a doe he had once seen peering through a thicket in an upland wood. In contrast to Kate's yellow dress and gaily painted nails, she was dressed simply in an ivory muslin frock, the only touch of frippery a tortoiseshell comb holding her hair in place.

"This is Detective Hamilton and Sergeant Dickerson," said Kate.

"How d'you do?" Big Margaret responded, giving a little curtsy.

"An' I'm Derek," the boy piped up with a glance at Ian.

The detective fixed him with a withering gaze. "Don't you have urgent business to attend to?"

"Naw, I—" he began, but sensing the warning in Hamilton's expression, he took a step backward. "Oh, right, I do have ta be somewhere—sorry, ladies," he said with a gallant tip of his hat. "I s'pose I'll see you later," he told Ian.

"No doubt," said the detective.

"Right, then, I'll be off," McNair said reluctantly. He sidled toward the door unenthusiastically, lingering with his hand on the knob.

"Good*bye*, Master McNair," Ian replied firmly.

"Don' worry, Guv—I'm goin'."

He slipped into the hall, closing the door behind him. Ian turned to the newcomer, who gazed at him expectantly, her large-boned hands dangling at her sides. Her expression was apprehensive yet strangely resigned, as if she would not be surprised by anything that happened to her.

"So then, Miss—"

"Folks call me Big Margaret," she said with a barely perceptible shrug.

"I am given to understand that you were acquainted with the deceased?"

"He was one of my regulars." Her accent was not low class—in fact, to Dickerson's ears, she sounded rather educated.

Hamilton looked at her as though he were trying to process the idea of this strange, solemn creature as a fallen woman. Dickerson was having trouble picturing it himself—there was something oddly virginal about her. He did not find Margaret sexually enticing, as he had Kate. In fact, she made him want to weep. He was keenly aware that she was someone's child, and possibly someone's sister as well. Being intensely protective of his own sister, Dickerson felt an urge to whisk her away from this place—but to where? The idiocy of the idea struck him with full force, along with realization of his own foolishness, and he blew his nose loudly to cover his feelings.

"Can you tell me his name?" Hamilton asked Margaret.

She glanced at Kate, who gave an encouraging nod. "It's all right, dolly, you can tell him. Can't hurt now the poor fella's dead."

"I knew him as Geoffrey Pritchett," said Margaret. "But I don't know if that's his actual name, y'see. Many gents don't use their real names."

"Do you know anything about him?" asked Ian.

"He was a banker, I believe. Usually came by on a Wednesday, when the banks were closed for the half day."

Sergeant Dickerson wanted to ask a question but knew better than to interrupt.

"And were you the last to see him alive?" said the detective.

She nodded sadly. "This was our regular meeting. He showed up on time but didn't look well. I asked if he might like to reschedule, but he said he had a busy week ahead, then suddenly began twitching. And then he—" She gave a shuddering sob and pressed a handkerchief to her mouth.

"Take your time," Ian said gently.

"His body started twisting most horribly, his back arching, and this terrible grin came over his face. He wasn't able to speak at all, frothing at the mouth like a rabid dog. I dashed out to get help, but when I returned with Kate, he—well, you can see for yourselves."

"Thank you," said Ian. "I know what a shock all of this must have been for you."

"What do you think happened, Detective?" said Kate.

"There can be no doubt he was poisoned."

The two ladies reacted with a gasp.

"Arsenic?" asked Dickerson.

"No," replied the detective.

"What, then?" said Kate.

Hamilton gazed out the streaked window, as if the answer to her question was lurking in the tumbledown warren of streets and alleys below.

"Mr. Pritchett died of strychnine poisoning."

CHAPTER SEVENTEEN

Ian's pronouncement produced a stunned silence, and no one appeared more surprised than Big Margaret. Her mouth hung open in astonishment, and her lips moved silently, like a fish gasping for breath. Kate was the first to speak.

"How d'you know it's strychnine, then?"

"The signs are unmistakable. Convulsions, including arching of the back and spasms of the limbs, frothing at the mouth, the odd facial expression resembling a smile. All indicative of acute strychnine poisoning."

Margaret trembled and turned pale. "You don' think I—"

"At this stage of the investigation, we must consider everyone who knew the deceased a potential suspect," Ian replied—perhaps a bit too harshly, Dickerson thought. The young woman gasped and clutched the bedpost to steady herself.

"She n'er would harm a fly," Kate declared, wrapping a fleshy arm around her friend. "Why, Margaret's the gentlest soul on earth, so she is! Ask anyone."

It appeared that they might soon have the opportunity to do so. Dickerson heard footsteps and furtive whispering in the hallway. Opening the door, he saw half a dozen young women—and some not so young—gathered outside the room. Kate took charge immediately—striding across the floor, she stood in the doorway, hands on her fleshy hips, and fixed them all with a stern glare.

"Just what d'ye think you're all doin' out here, ear waggin' like a bunch o' cluckin' hens?"

One of the women stepped forward, a comely blonde in a scarlet frock that looked as though it had been hastily donned. "If aught's happened, we've as much right as anyone tae know whae's goin' on."

"And so ye shall," Kate said. "Until then, there's no need t'interfere with a police investigation."

"It's quite all right," Ian said. "I should like to interview each of you, especially anyone who saw or heard anything."

A murmur arose from the assembled company—judging by their expressions, the women had no objection to being questioned by the handsome detective. Several blushed and tittered, which surprised Dickerson, given their manner of employment, but he was familiar with the effect DI Hamilton had on women.

Though the ladies were eager to report anything they could, the interviews turned up nothing of interest. Most of them were asleep during the time in question, having labored late into the previous night, and no one had anything of import to add to Margaret's account. While it was generally agreed Mr. Pritchett was indeed a banker (or claimed to be), no one seemed sure if that was his real name or which bank employed him.

It was late afternoon by the time Hamilton and Dickerson were finished. Before leaving, they asked Kate to leave the body where it lay a while longer. She nodded sadly and led them through a narrow hallway with peeling flowered wallpaper to a dingy foyer.

"Look," she said as she slid back the heavy dead bolt on the door, "I don' want t'appear unfeelin', but is there any way t'keep this outta the papers, love?"

"We have little influence over the press," Ian answered. "We can withhold certain details about a case, but there are often leaks."

"Sometimes press coverage can help apprehend a criminal," Dickerson suggested helpfully.

"I want the killer caught, a' course," Kate said quickly. "It's jus' that—well, you know how people talk, and I'm afeard—"

"It's bad for business?" Ian said.

"I don' want ye thinkin' I'm heartless, Detective. I got half a dozen girls dependin' on me, and—"

"I understand," said Ian. "But I can't promise anything."

Taking their leave of a rather gloomy-looking Kate, the two men stepped outside into the squalid streets of the Old Town slum. The morning's splendid sunshine had been replaced by a thin, spitting rain that stung the sergeant's cheeks as he followed Hamilton toward the Canongate. They had not gone two blocks when they heard a familiar voice coming from a side alley.

"How's yer investigation gettin' on, Guv?"

They turned to see Derek McNair leaning against a lamppost, hands in his pockets, chewing on a bit of beef jerky.

"I thought I told you to make yourself scarce," said Ian.

The boy shrugged. "Yeah. I din' believe ya."

"If you want to make yourself useful, go to the station house and ask DCI Crawford if we might bother Dr. Littlejohn to come and provide his professional opinion on a poisoning."

Derek's eyes widened. "So it *were* murder, then!"

"Do as I say, and there'll be half a crown in it for you."

"Right you *are*, Guv!" the boy said, and took off at a run.

"Tell him I sent you!" Ian called after him.

Then the detective pulled his collar closer and headed off at a half lope down the street. Dickerson puffed along beside the detective for a quarter of a mile or so before speaking.

"Any theories, sir?"

"Theories are only useful when there's evidence to back them up."

"Where are we going?"

"To avenge a foul and most unnatural murder."

He led Dickerson through the wynds and closes of Old Town until they reached Princes Street, the broad thoroughfare separating it from New Town.

"This is as good a place as any to begin," Ian said when they reached the Bank of Scotland. "It's the bank closest to Holy Land, so we may get lucky."

But luck was not with them—their inquiries were met with blank stares. Not a single employee had failed to turn up for work that day, an uncommon occurrence in a city plagued by wretched weather and ailments from cholera to catarrh. No one had heard of a banker by the name of Geoffrey Pritchett, and Ian's description of the victim brought no signs of recognition. Half an hour later they were back outside the neo-Grecian building. Dickerson gazed at the chunky white columns with distaste; he found that style of architecture stodgy and old-fashioned.

"This will never do," said Ian. "We need a picture of the deceased, especially since Geoffrey Pritchett may not be his real name."

"We don't even know if he's really a banker," Dickerson added.

"Indeed. It's time to pay a call on Aunt Lillian."

This time they took a brougham cab, much to Dickerson's relief. He had lost half a stone since working with Hamilton, but his pudgy body was not equipped to keep up with the detective's long strides. Trudging up and down the hills of Edinburgh left him constantly out of breath, and in the evening, he had taken to soaking his aching feet in magnesium salts.

It took some work to persuade Ian's aunt to accompany them to the bawdy house, but in the end, they bundled her into the cab, along with her camera, which took up half the seat. Dickerson squeezed himself uncomfortably next to Lillian, her bony shoulder digging into his arm. She smelled of rose water and lye soap.

"I don't see why you need me so urgently," she complained as they bounced over the ruts in the pitted streets of the Canongate. "Surely a dead man won't suddenly sprout wings and fly away."

"The sooner we identify him, the sooner we can apprehend his killer," said Ian as the cab swerved to avoid a coal cart.

The interior of the cab was stuffy, and Dickerson broke into a sweat. He removed his hat and wiped his damp forehead, gazing out the window at a gaggle of schoolchildren playing rounders in the street. He wondered how Pauline was getting on—he had seen little of his younger sister of late, her being busy with school and him dashing from work to rehearsal. He was beginning to regret his decision to be in the wretched play, even though Pauline had encouraged him to try out for it.

As the vehicle rounded the corner onto the High Street, passing stalls of tobacconists, butcher shops, and bakeries, the aroma of fairy cakes floated into Dickerson's nostrils. His stomach contracted in futile anticipation. He loved fairy cakes, and it had been hours since breakfast, but there was no point in mentioning it. When Hamilton was hot on a chase, he regarded food as an unwelcome distraction. Dickerson sighed and tightened his belt to lessen the hunger pangs.

"And are there no police photographers who can accommodate you?" asked Lillian.

"We are shorthanded at present," Ian replied. "There are only two, one being away in the Highlands attending his sick mother, and the other having come down with an attack of shingles."

"Won't DCI Crawford be annoyed at you bringing me in?"

"You know perfectly well he asked you to consider working for the constabulary earlier this year. I know you remember, so don't pretend otherwise. You told him you would, and frankly, this is a good time to start."

Dickerson thought he saw a satisfied little smile at the corners of Lillian's mouth.

"Well," she said, "so long as it's *urgent*."

"We don't even know if this fellow is a banker, or if his name is Pritchett. A decent photograph will help identify him."

"No form of identification in his wallet?" said Lillian.

"If there was, it's not there now."

"What about printing his picture in the papers, sir?" Dickerson suggested. "That might bring out some folks who knew 'im."

"Capital idea, Sergeant," said Ian. "Why don't you take the photo 'round to the *Scotsman* later?"

When they arrived at Holy Land, this time they were admitted via the front door. Kate seemed to be expecting them, looking more anxious and frazzled than during their previous visit.

"Thank goodness ye came," she said, peering out the door before closing it behind them. "There's a very peculiar gentleman upstairs—a Dr. Little something or other."

"Dr. Littlejohn," said Ian. "Is he examining the body?"

"The lad brought him," Kate said, indicating Derek McNair, who was lurking at the far end of the narrow entrance hall.

"I fetched 'im, jes like y'asked," Derek declared, brushing a sweep of dark hair off his forehead.

"Here's half a crown, as promised," Ian replied, fishing a coin from his pocket.

"Ta very much," the boy said, slipping it into his oversized trousers, fastened around his slim waist with a bit of twine.

"This is my Aunt Lillian," Ian told Kate. "She's come to photograph the body."

"How d'you do?" Kate said, extending her hand. "Folks call me Fair Kate."

Sergeant Dickerson thought Ian's aunt might disdain to shake a bawdy house keeper's hand, but Lillian treated Kate with the respect she would give a duchess.

"Pleased to make your acquaintance," she said. "I am deeply sorry to hear of your misfortune."

"Ta very much," Kate responded. "Though I'm 'fraid the misfortune is poor Mr. Pritchett's more than ours."

"Detective, if I may, may I have a word?"

Ian turned to see Dr. Henry Littlejohn descending the stairs. He looked as dapper as before, his glossy silver hair catching the light that seeped through the heavy damask curtains on the front windows. He wore a pinstriped three-piece suit and carried a black medical bag in one hand and a towel in the other.

"Thank you so much for coming, Doctor," Ian said.

"Of course, of course—a tragic case, this. Tragic. Good afternoon, madame," he said, tipping his hat to Lillian.

"This is my aunt, Mrs. Lillian Grey," said Ian. "May I present Dr. Henry Littlejohn."

"It is an honor to meet you," said Lillian. "Your efforts on behalf of the citizens of Edinburgh are unparalleled."

"You are most kind, most kind," said the doctor, wiping his hands on the towel, which he folded and put in his bag.

"Your improvements to the sanitation system are worthy of praise, and your founding of the Royal Hospital for Sick Children—"

The great man coughed modestly. "My wife will be quite cross if I return home tonight with my head too swollen to fit through the door. Quite cross, indeed."

Derek frowned. "What's 'e talkin' about?" he whispered to Ian. "Why would 'is head swell up, like?"

"It's a figure of speech," said Ian. "It refers to someone having an inflated opinion of himself."

"Oh," Derek said with a sly smile. "Like you."

Dickerson thought Hamilton looked as if he wanted to cuff the boy but perhaps felt it inadvisable after Lillian's remarks about Dr. Littlejohn's noble efforts on behalf of children.

"The victim was poisoned, then?" Dickerson asked the doctor.

"The signs are classic. Convulsions, muscle spasms, risus sardonicus. Classic."

"Risus whatus?" said Derek.

"The positioning of the facial muscles in a grin. Highly characteristic of strychnine."

"Can you rule out suicide?" asked Ian.

"Suicide by strychnine ingestion is uncommon, but not unknown. I'll leave that determination up to you. But as to cause of death, it's a fairly straightforward case. Fairly straightforward."

Ian nodded, though it seemed to Sergeant Dickerson that very little in this case was straightforward.

CHAPTER EIGHTEEN

"I'll be off, then," said Dr. Littlejohn, buttoning his overcoat. Tipping his hat to the ladies, he started for the front door, then turned back. "May I have a word with you, Miss, er—Kate, was it? A quick word, yes?"

"Don' see as why not," she replied, but Ian could see she was nervous.

"In private, I think," the doctor suggested. "In private, eh?"

Kate shot a look at Ian, then led Dr. Littlejohn to the parlor, where Ian heard them conversing in low tones.

"Wonder wha' he wants?" Derek muttered, scuffing his toes on the tattered hall carpet.

"Stop that," said Ian.

"Why?" said the boy.

"It's not your carpet."

"But what's he got ta say to the likes o' her?"

"Probably to warn her to stay away from the likes of you," Lillian suggested.

The boy looked at Ian. "Wha's he been tellin' you about me, then?"

"Nothing but the truth, I'm sure," Lillian remarked as the doctor returned, followed by a chastened-looking Kate. Her eyes were swollen and red.

Dr. Littlejohn put on his hat and turned to Ian. "Tell Toshy Crawford I'll be in touch. I'll be in touch."

"'Toshy'?" Derek smirked.

Ian glared at him. "Thank you again, sir," he said to Littlejohn.

"Think nothing of it, nothing." With another bow to the ladies, the good doctor was gone.

"What'd he say?" Derek asked Kate.

"Well, I'll be a monkey's uncle," she murmured.

"What did he say, dear?" Lillian asked.

"He tol' me that if me an' the girls ever needed medical attention, I should send for 'im. Can ye credit that—a famous doc like 'im, eh? Carin' about a bunch o' bumpots like us."

"I wish you wouldn't speak of yourself that way," Lillian said. "You are merely women down on your luck, surviving as best you can."

Kate looked down and bit her lip. "There's not many would see it that way."

"Well, I am glad to hear there is compassion within the medical establishment," Lillian said. "And now, would someone please conduct me to the whereabouts of this unfortunate gentleman?"

It didn't take Aunt Lillian long to photograph the body. Ian was impressed at how efficient she was, briskly setting up her equipment and taking pictures from several different angles. Mr. Pritchett's grotesque appearance seemed to bother her not at all.

"That should do it," she said when she had finished. "I'll get these developed straightaway in the Photography Society darkroom and should have them for you shortly."

"I kin pick 'em up fer ye," Derek suggested from the doorway, where he had been loitering.

Ian was having doubts about using McNair's services quite so much, but in the end, he agreed to give the boy another half crown to deliver the photographs to him. He decided to send Derek back in a cab with Lillian, warning her to keep an eye on him.

"He'll rob you blind when you're not looking," he told her.

"Just let him try. He'll find I'm sharper than I look."

"Now you're fishing for a compliment."

She drew herself up indignantly. "When have I ever resorted to such measures to induce my favorite nephew to say nice things about me?"

Ian smiled. "Very well, Auntie—you're sharper than most women half your age."

"And don't you forget it," she replied, pinching his elbow. It was the same gesture his mother used to make. He wondered if such things were inherited.

After procuring a cab for his aunt and McNair, Ian went back inside to find Kate. He located her in the kitchen, serving a bowl of cock-a-leekie soup to a famished-looking Sergeant Dickerson. It was only when he smelled the broth that Ian realized it had been many hours since their last meal.

"Sorry, sir," Dickerson said, leaping to his feet.

"It's all right, Sergeant—you must be hungry."

"I am at that, sir."

Kate waved the ladle at Ian. "Would ye like some?"

"Thank you, but I arranged to meet my brother for supper—I fear I'm already late."

"Suit yerself," Kate replied, sounding a bit put out. "You don' know what yer missin'—right, Sergeant?"

"Oh, yes!" he responded, his chin shiny with chicken grease. "It's totally brilliant."

Ian looked around the otherwise unoccupied kitchen. "Where are—the, uh—"

"My girls?" Kate said with a smile. "I tol' 'em to make themselves scarce. I 'spect they've gone out shopping. Why, do ye need to speak with 'em?"

"No, I just wondered where they'd gone."

"I said I didn' want 'em gettin' in the way of the learned doc, but truth be told, I thought they could do wi' a few hours away from this place. It's not so nice sharin' a house with a dead person, y'know."

"I'll send someone from the morgue to pick up the body as soon as possible."

"I can go fetch someone, if y'like, sir," said Dickerson, slurping up the last of his soup.

"Thank you, Sergeant—that would be helpful."

Taking their leave of Fair Kate, the men ventured once more into the dusky streets of the city, joining the army of lamplighters, night watchmen, and pub crawlers out for the evening. A faint pink glow lingered in the western sky, and the air was crisp as an apple, tart with the promise of fall. Ian filled his lungs with the aroma of lamb stews simmering over peat fires. Light-headed with hunger, he envied Dickerson his full stomach. The sergeant was the first to speak as they turned from Leith Wynd onto the Canongate.

"I don' buy the idea it could be suicide. Why kill hisself in a place like that?"

"Indeed—what man wishes to be discovered dead in a house of ill repute?"

"An' to die such a horrible death."

"The question remains whether the killer, knowing where Mr. Pritchett was headed, gave him just enough that he didn't die immediately. Instead he collapses in the presence of Miss Margaret, thereby casting suspicion on her."

"But you don' suspect her?"

"I have rarely met a less likely murderer."

"Still, must keep an open mind, eh, sir?"

Ian looked at him curiously. "Perhaps you noticed something I missed?"

"No, sir—it's just that you're always sayin' we mustn't jump to conclusions, so I—"

"Quite right, Sergeant—thank you for reminding me."

"But if the killer knew exactly how much to give Mr. Pritchett, then doesn't that mean—"

"That he most likely has medical knowledge. Which makes him even more dangerous."

"Beggin' pardon, sir, but do you think poison is a woman's tool?"

"The government certainly thought so."

"How's that?"

"In 1851, there was a failed attempt in the House of Lords to pass a law forbidding women to buy arsenic. But I'm not convinced. That traditional bit of wisdom overlooks the fact that most murders are committed by men. And if she did indeed time it, as we suspect, where would a woman get such precise medical knowledge?"

"You said Miss—I mean, Dr. Jex-Blake—"

"An extraordinary woman but hardly a common poisoner."

"I weren't suggestin' it were her, sir, but per'aps a nurse might have enough knowledge—"

"Interesting notion—not out of the realm of possibility, by any means. And here I must leave you," Ian said, stopping beneath a flickering gaslight. "I promised my brother I would dine with him tonight, if he has not completely given up on me. You are headed in the other direction, I believe?"

"To the morgue, yes, sir."

"Until tomorrow, then."

"Yes, sir—good night, sir."

Ian watched as the sergeant disappeared down the dark and winding lanes, wondering what other secrets the city held within its ancient, twisting streets.

CHAPTER NINETEEN

Ian arrived at the White Hart half an hour late, exhausted and famished. His brother had commandeered a corner table and was studying an anatomy book.

Donald Hamilton swiveled his bulky body around to face his brother. "Hello there."

Ian scrutinized him for signs of intoxication, which did not escape Donald's notice.

"Ginger beer," he said, lifting the glass at his elbow. "Cheers, old boy." Seeing Ian's discomfort, he smiled. "Don't stand there like Lot's wife, man—what are you having?"

Ian hesitated.

Donald rolled his eyes. "I won't dissolve into a puddle of tears if you have a pint, for God's sake!"

"Heavy ale, then."

"That's more like it." Donald heaved himself from his chair. "Guard our table from the riffraff, will you?"

"I see a fair number of medical students," Ian replied, recognizing several of Donald's classmates.

"That's the worst kind of riffraff," Donald shot back, heading toward the bar.

Ian slid onto the chair next to the one his brother had vacated. The table was none too clean, and as he pulled a handkerchief from his pocket, he heard raised voices from across the room. Squinting through the haze of tobacco smoke, he spotted a pair of inebriated youths taunting a tall young woman trying to squeeze past them. Her face was hidden by a mass of copper curls, but her hunched shoulders expressed the embarrassment of her predicament.

"Well, if it isn't Miss P-p-prissy P-pants," the shorter man said, waving a soiled handkerchief at her. He had a crooked nose and small black eyes, and reminded Ian of a small burrowing animal.

"Such a lady wants to dirty her dainty white hands dissecting corpses," said the other, a hulking blond fellow sporting a grimy bowler. "Whatever will her dear old mum think?"

"She'd b-b-better look to her mater, as she's not likely to f-f-find a husband," his companion declared, and the two of them bellowed with laughter.

Ian was across the room in three strides. A smart blow to the solar plexus sent the larger one sprawling to the floor as he seized the other by the back of his collar. Lifting the little fellow half a foot off the floor, Ian pulled his face close enough to smell cheap whisky oozing from his pores.

"P-p-please," the man squeaked, terror in his little eyes.

"I'd rather not skin my knuckles on a shrimp like you," Ian hissed in his ear, "but I'll give you half a minute to collect your friend and clear out of here."

The crooked-nosed fellow nodded, swallowing hard. Ian let him drop to the floor, and he stumbled toward his companion, who was on his feet, brushing the sawdust from his trousers. He tugged at the yellow-haired giant's sleeve, but his friend was having none of it. Rolling up his sleeves, he glared at Ian, squaring off for a fight. The other patrons had cleared to the sides of the room, leaving a wide circle. Caught up in the intoxicating aroma of violence, they shouted taunts and encouragement. If there was one thing that united all Scots, it was their thirst for a good fight.

"Oiy, take 'em, Gordon!"

"Avenge the lady's honor, mister!"

"I'll put a fiver on Gordy!"

"You're on, mate!"

Ian's opponent licked his lips and grinned, the bowler hat still clinging improbably to his head. Ian sized him up as being the heavier by at least two stone. He braced himself as the large man lunged at him, swinging with both fists. Ian managed to duck a left hook, but a hefty roundhouse caught him on the side of his head, sending him reeling backward into the circle of onlookers. A couple of stout fellows caught and steadied him.

"Don't let 'im get the better a ye!" urged one of them.

"Good Lord, Ian, can't I take you anywhere?" said the other. It was Donald.

Splinters of pain shooting through his forehead, Ian staggered back into the circle, where his opponent was waiting for him. Though intoxicated, the man was obviously skilled in the art of fisticuffs. Ian revised his strategy. Doing his best to keep his distance while his head cleared from the blow, he circled his adversary, never taking his eyes off the man as the shouts of encouragement for both combatants continued.

"C'mon, Gordon, make mincemeat o' the skinny fella!"

"Don't let Gordy bully ye, boyo!"

The barkeep's feeble attempts at breaking things up were met with jeers and ridicule.

"If you don't cease and desist, I shall call the police!" he whined.

"Christ, man, he *is* the police!" Donald yelled, but no one paid him any mind.

Ian's training was in wrestling, where getting close to your opponent was essential, but his adversary's size and the speed of his meaty fists made that a dangerous gambit. Another punch to the head might well knock Ian unconscious. He needed to gain an advantage—but how?

"What're ye waiting fer?" the towheaded colossus growled. "Come an' fight like a man!"

He lurched forward, the bowler still perched atop his head, and Ian saw his chance. Reaching up, he flicked the hat deftly off the man's head. Instinctively, Gordon grabbed for the hat as it fell, and Ian took advantage of his momentary distraction. Sweeping in low, he tackled his opponent around the knees, bringing him heavily to the ground. Gordon hit the floorboards with a grunt, Ian on top of him. Gasping for air, his opponent struggled to get to his feet, but Ian held him tightly in a headlock. Twisting the crook of his arm around the man's neck, Ian applied pressure to his windpipe until his face turned scarlet and his body went limp. Quickly releasing his hold, Ian staggered to his feet amid cheers and applause.

"Attaboy—you showed him, by God!"

"Well done, Skinny Malinky!"

"What's the matter, Gordy—havin' a wee snooze?"

Panting heavily, Ian rested his hands on his knees and looked down at the prostrate form of his opponent, who lay very still. Alarmed, Ian knelt beside him and loosened his collar. He didn't appear to be breathing. Panicked, Ian looked around wildly at the crowd, but their attention was already turned to collecting bets and ordering the next round of drinks. The young woman whose honor he had defended had vanished, as had Gordon's comrade. Ian felt a hand on his shoulder and looked up to see the concerned face of his brother.

"What's the matter?" asked Donald.

"I don't think he's breathing."

Donald knelt beside them and felt the man's neck. "His pulse is uneven."

"What does that mean?"

"It's not a good sign. Stand back!" he commanded, removing his coat and placing it under the unconscious man's shoulders. Grasping his arms at the elbows, Donald brought them over Gordon's head, then back down, crossing them over his chest. He repeated this gesture, in a vigorous rhythmic motion, until Ian saw the victim's chest began to rise and fall.

"He's breathing!" Ian cried.

Perspiring from the unaccustomed exertion, Donald wiped his brow and felt for a pulse. Ian realized the room around them had become silent as everyone stopped to watch his brother's ministrations.

"The Silvester Method," a slight, bespectacled young man murmured. "Well done."

"You, there!" Donald called to a couple of burly lads at the bar. "Help me carry this fellow outside, and be quick about it!"

Even with the four of them lifting him, Gordon's inert weight was considerable. Once outside, Donald hailed a hansom cab.

"Royal Infirmary, fast as you can!" he barked at the driver as they slid the unconscious man onto the seat. Donald and Ian squeezed in as best they could, holding their charge upright between them.

"Will he be all right?" said Ian as the cab clattered across the cobblestones.

"His breathing is steady, but I don't like the fact that he's still unconscious." Still puffing a little, Donald made another swipe across his damp forehead with his handkerchief. "Was that vulgar display of fisticuffs really necessary?"

Ian didn't reply as the unconscious man's head lolled to one side and came to rest upon his shoulder. The irony of the scene wasn't lost on him—there he was, crammed into the backseat of a cab in intimate proximity to a man who minutes ago was attempting to pummel the life out of him.

"One of these days your temper will get you into serious trouble— if it hasn't already," Donald remarked.

"I couldn't just stand by without doing anything!"

"The flaw lies rather in the manner of your intervention."

"What was I to do?"

"It seems to me you resort to violence more often than not."

"I merely wanted them to leave the young lady alone—I had no desire to engage in a fight."

"And yet somehow you managed to end up in one."

"Get stuffed," Ian muttered, staring gloomily out the cab window as "Gordy" drooled a thin rope of spittle onto his shoulder.

CHAPTER TWENTY

It wasn't far to the Royal Infirmary, and the cab slid to a halt in front of the front doors. Donald leapt out with surprising agility, immediately commandeering a gurney and a pair of orderlies to help transport the injured man. Within moments they were wheeling him down the scrubbed tile corridors. White-clad nurses pushed patients in wheelchairs as doctors brushed by on their rounds with medical students in tow. Other patients hobbled along on crutches and administrators with clipboards strode briskly past visiting families dressed in their Sunday best. Limping a little, Ian scrambled to keep up as his brother urged the orderlies to "step along smartly."

As they passed a tall doctor surrounded by a gaggle of medical students, a somewhat high, metallic voice rang out.

"Hamilton!"

"Hang on a minute," Donald commanded the orderlies. "Yes, Dr. Bell?"

The doctor peered through wire-rimmed spectacles at the injured man. Even through the lenses, Ian could see his eyes were a deep, piercing blue. A handsome man in the prime of life, he had an aquiline face with a long jaw and high cheekbones suggesting the keen mind inside. "What have you there?" he asked.

"A fight casualty," Donald answered. "The victim's airway was compromised. Breathing was restored using the Silvester Method, but the patient has yet to regain consciousness."

"How long has he been out?"

"Approximately twenty minutes."

Dr. Bell turned to the students hovering around him. Several hugged textbooks to their chests, gazing at him reverently.

"Differential diagnosis?"

"Brain swelling," suggested one.

"Possible hemorrhage, coma," declared another.

"Treatment?" asked Bell.

A voice came from the back of the group. "This man is an alcoholic."

A smile crossed the doctor's lean face. "I was wondering when someone would realize that. Well done, Doyle."

"Thank you, sir." The voice belonged to a muscular young man with serious eyes and an elaborately waxed mustache.

"How did you arrive at your conclusion?"

"The clubbed tips of his fingers and his yellow pallor indicate poor circulation as well as jaundice as a result of persistent, chronic alcohol abuse. There is also a suggestion of rhinophyma."

"Rhino what?" Ian whispered to his brother.

"Drinker's nose," Donald said. "The lower part of the nose becomes swollen."

"Doyle is correct," Bell said. "This man suffers from chronic alcohol abuse. How does that influence treatment?"

"If his coma persists, he may well go into alcohol withdrawal," Donald replied.

"Which could prove fatal," Bell added. "Suggested treatment?"

The students were silent.

"What about introducing small amounts of alcohol into the bloodstream intravenously?" Donald suggested.

The other students stared at him as though he had just proposed decapitating the patient. Bell, however, looked at him thoughtfully. "Intriguing idea, Hamilton."

"In addition to glucose or saline solution, one might inject controlled doses of alcohol to prevent potentially fatal withdrawal symptoms."

"You may have something," said Dr. Bell. "Bring your patient to Operating Theater Three—I'll join you in fifteen minutes, when I finish my rounds." He strode off down the hall, the medical students scampering after him like ducklings.

"Follow me," Donald said to the orderlies who had been standing by patiently. The men complied, wheeling the gurney after him as Donald strode confidently down the polished corridors. "You know, it occurs to me that we might ask Dr. Bell if he'd be willing to have a look at your boss's wife. I hear he's quite the diagnostician."

"If you're willing to approach him, I'm sure DCI Crawford would be most grateful," said Ian. He had completely forgotten about his promise to Crawford, and his head felt fuzzy as he followed his brother through the halls of the infirmary.

Ian had not been in a hospital since his treatment for burns sustained in the fire that killed his parents, and as he trailed after his brother, his left shoulder began to throb and pulse. It all flooded back—the sharp odor of antiseptic, the hollow ring of footsteps in hallways, the murmur of voices as they passed various wards. He felt dizzy and light-headed as they turned the corner toward the surgery ward. He blinked in an attempt to dispel the dark spots darting through his field of vision.

As they neared the entrance to the operating theater Ian's legs felt rubbery and weak. Clutching the air, he stumbled and pitched forward as the black spots swelled and became a thick curtain of darkness. He was vaguely aware of his brother's hand on his shoulder as he plummeted into a long black tunnel.

Voices, when they returned, were thin and faint, as if coming from great distance.

"Wait—he's coming 'round. Ian, can you hear me?"

He knew the voice belonged to his brother, but at first Ian didn't know where he was. He imagined he was lying on the sofa in the sitting room of his own flat. Then he caught the scent of rubbing alcohol and oil soap and remembered. He fought to open his eyes, but it felt as though someone had draped a cloth over his face. His vision was blurred, even as he squinted to bring the room into focus. The light hurt his eyes, yet everything was so dim. He heard footsteps, followed by more voices, farther away this time.

"What happened?" It was a man's voice—authoritative, sharp, commanding.

"He fainted." Ian recognized Donald's voice.

"So now we have two patients instead of one."

Two patients . . . A cold blade of panic sliced Ian's stomach as he remembered what he had done. He struggled to sit up, to will himself into full consciousness, but felt hands upon his shoulders. It was then he realized he was dressed in a hospital gown instead of his own clothes.

"Easy, now." The voice belonged to the other man . . . Dr. Blue . . . Bull? Bell, that was it. "You've had a nasty fall."

"Dr. Bell, I think this man is coming 'round." The voice belonged to a young woman—a nurse, Ian supposed—but it came from the other side of the room.

"Your patient seems to have recovered before we could try your treatment, Hamilton," the doctor said. "Too bad—it would have been interesting."

"His recovery is the most important thing, sir," Donald replied.

"Of course, of course," said Bell. "Still, it's a pity we didn't get to test your theory."

Ian's brain fought to bring back the details of what had transpired. Something about alcohol and a coma . . . but the effort was too much, and he sank back onto the pillow, letting go of the need to figure anything out. He was so tired . . .

He awoke to a view of starlight. The tall windows looked out onto a clear night, and above the flicker of gas lamps, constellations shone bright and cold in the November sky. Feeling wide awake and rested, Ian sat up in bed. A sharp pain in his left shoulder distracted him momentarily—perhaps he had injured it in the fall—but he rested his weight on his other arm and surveyed the room.

His bed was in the middle of a Nightingale ward, a large room containing multiple patients, the beds lining the walls on either side of the chamber, creating a wide corridor in the middle. All the other patients appeared to be asleep; he heard snoring and the occasional murmur coming from the beds around him. Next to his bed, slumped in a chair, his brother, Donald, slept. Ian didn't know whether to wake him or not, so he pulled his covers off and climbed quietly out of bed.

"I say—you probably shouldn't be up."

Ian turned to see the tall, muscular medical student they had encountered in Dr. Bell's entourage.

"It's all right—I'm quite recovered now," he replied.

"You're Donald's brother, I believe?"

"Detective Ian Hamilton, Edinburgh City Police," he answered, not wishing to be known simply as "Donald's brother."

"Yes, he mentioned something about having a brother who was a policeman. Arthur Conan Doyle," he said, extending a hand. "Fourth-year medical student."

His grip was firm, the hand strong, matching his athletic build. Ian was taller, but Doyle was broader, with thick, strong legs and a powerful torso. It was, Ian thought, the body of a sailor rather than a physician. He was a fine-looking fellow, with an oval face and strong chin beneath the elaborately twirled mustache.

"You're one of Dr. Bell's students—the one who diagnosed chronic alcoholism," Ian said. "That was very clever."

"I was merely applying Dr. Bell's methods," Doyle replied. "He has taught us to observe patients closely and deduce from what we see."

"That's exactly what I do in my line of work."

"Indeed? My father always claimed you lot rounded up likely suspects and beat confessions out of them."

"Regrettably, he's not entirely mistaken," Ian said with a wry smile. "But I intend to reform the way police detectives approach their work."

"That's a rather tall order, I should think."

"I'm sorry medicine has already claimed you—we could use more chaps like you on the force."

His companion smiled, causing pouches to appear beneath his heavy-lidded, almond-shaped eyes. There was something exotic about his face—manly and leonine yet with a suggestion of the Orient in his wide-set eyes.

"It doesn't take much of a diagnostician to see you've a nasty contusion and possible concussion," he said, gazing at Ian's face.

Ian put a hand to his temple, swollen and hot to the touch.

"That's why I fainted?"

"I should imagine so. How do you feel now?"

"Not too bad. A little shaky."

"Go easy for a while, if you can."

"Where is the man we brought in?"

"Ah, you mean Gordon Kinsey. He's gone."

"He's been released already?"

"Not exactly. He regained consciousness and staggered out, against medical advice. Muttered something about finding a drink before the pubs closed."

"That sounds entirely in character to me."

"Do you mind if I ask a rather personal question?" said Doyle.

"As long as it relates to medicine or murder."

Doyle smiled. "How did you come by that scar on your shoulder? I noticed it when we removed your shirt."

Ian took a deep breath and considered lying. After all, he had just met Doyle, and owed him no personal information. But something about the man's open, honest demeanor made lying seem small and dirty. "In a fire," he said, hoping the medical student would probe no further. To his relief, Doyle seemed satisfied with his answer.

"Does it bother you much?"

"Sometimes."

Doyle shuddered. "Nasty thing, burns. I once helped treat a woman who was disfigured when a jealous lover threw carbolic acid at her."

"Did they catch him?"

"They did, may he rot in prison forever. You mustn't be too impressed with my diagnosis today," he added with a rueful smile. "I'm afraid I've had rather more experience of the effects of chronic alcoholism than I'd like."

Ian was at a loss for how to respond to this confession.

"My father suffers from the condition," Doyle explained. "Since childhood I have had ample opportunity to observe its devastating effects."

This personal revelation from a man he had just met made Ian uncomfortable. He had an impulse to mention Donald's struggles with alcohol but felt it inappropriate. He had no idea what his brother had revealed to his fellow students and colleagues.

As if aware of Ian's thoughts, Donald stirred in his sleep, then jerked up in his chair and opened his eyes.

"Ah, I see you're out of bed," he said to Ian. "What are you doing here, Doyle?"

"I came to check on your brother."

"Couldn't resist, eh? Came to compare notes?"

"I don't know what you mean," Doyle replied unconvincingly.

"Don't pretend with me, old man. I can see right through you." Donald stood up and stretched his massive frame. Taller than Ian and considerably heavier than Doyle, he loomed over them like a watchful schoolmaster. "Arthur is fascinated by crime," he told Ian. "When I mentioned my brother was a detective, he expressed a desire to meet you." Donald fumbled through his waistcoat pockets. "I say, old boy, do you happen to have a cigarette?"

Doyle sighed and produced a cigarette from his lab-coat pocket. "Your brother has a habit of cadging cigarettes from his friends. I can't help but think it's intentional."

"You've got his number, all right," Ian said, smiling. "He's already commandeered my dressing gown. Lolls around the flat in it night and day."

"This is the fourth one this week, Hamilton," Doyle said, handing him a cigarette.

"If you insist, I shall bring you an entire bundle of cigarettes one of these days," Donald replied huffily, lighting it.

"And you will no doubt continue to pilfer them from me."

Donald sucked deeply on the cigarette and exhaled a plume of air into the room. "I can't imagine why you occupy your brain with such petty things."

"If you think this petty," Doyle responded, "then you are the only medical student in Edinburgh unconcerned with money."

A couple of patients stirred in their beds, and one murmured something in his sleep.

"We should go out into the hall lest we wake someone," Ian suggested.

"Always the considerate one, my brother," Donald remarked drily, but with a hint of affection.

The three of them tiptoed into the hall, with its gleaming marble floors and scrubbed tile walls. Despite the late hour, activity still swirled around them. Orderlies and nurses wheeled carts and gurneys to and fro, and the air was filled with the sound of footsteps and muted voices.

"I could use a drink," Doyle remarked. "What do you say, Hamilton?"

"I'd better see my brother home safely, then hit the books," Donald said. "Otherwise I shall never pass the anatomy exam Friday."

Doyle sighed. "I wish you hadn't reminded me."

So then, Ian thought, Doyle must be unaware of Donald's condition. Or did he suspect it, and was merely pretending not to see? His demeanor was at once serious and good-natured, making him difficult to read.

"I'm sure my brother will give you some tidbits about crime solving next time you meet," Donald said.

"How is he?" called a female voice from the other end of the corridor.

Ian turned to see the young lady he had rescued in the pub, striding down the halls as if she owned them, dressed in a crisp white nurse's uniform.

"Well?" she repeated impatiently. "Did he survive intact?"

Doyle turned to Ian. "Detective Hamilton, allow me to introduce Miss Fiona Stuart."

She frowned. "You were a fool to take on Gordon Kinsey. He should have made mincemeat out of you."

"I shall endeavor to remember that next time," Ian replied.

CHAPTER
TWENTY-ONE

"A policeman," Miss Stuart said, looking him up and down. "That follows. So, did Gordy recover?" she asked Doyle.

"He should be all right, if he doesn't drink himself to death."

"That's a relief. We wouldn't want our gallant detective brought up on murder charges," she said, wrinkling her nose at Ian. She gave off a faint aroma of lemon and lavender.

"How is it you know such a disreputable fellow?" Ian asked.

"Oh, he used to work here as an orderly. Got fired because of his drinking, so he's bitter about it."

"Why does he dislike you so much?"

"I was the first to raise concerns about his behavior. He probably blames me for being fired."

"Nurse Stuart is never one to step away from confrontation," Donald remarked.

"So I observe," said Ian.

Nurse Stuart gave him a sharp look.

"If you'll excuse me, I must check on a patient," Doyle said, making a hasty retreat.

"Coward," Donald muttered under his breath.

"I wasn't exaggerating, you know. He could have killed you," Fiona Stuart told Ian. "He and his unsavory little companion frequent that particular establishment."

"I was only trying to save you—"

"I can handle myself quite well, thank you," she replied tartly. "I'm in no need of a knight-errant to come to my rescue."

Her utter lack of gratitude was galling. Instead of basking in praise, as he had anticipated, here he was defending himself to this slip of a girl! It was downright humiliating.

"I shall take care to remember that next time I see a damsel in distress," Ian responded coldly.

"See that you do," she shot back. Turning smartly on her heel, she strode briskly away.

Donald watched her go. "It appears you two are made for each other."

Ian glowered at him. "Your attempt at humor is not appreciated."

"I am perfectly serious. She is clearly attracted to you."

Ian felt his ears redden. "That's absurd."

"Perhaps you failed to notice the widening of the eyes or the facial flush, not to mention the increase in respiration—classic signs of sexual arousal."

"That's enough!" Ian hissed, looking around to see if anyone was taking in their conversation. Fortunately, the occupants of the infirmary had enough on their minds, barely glancing at him as they passed.

Donald smiled. "You are very good at deciphering the workings of the criminal brain, less so when it comes to the feminine one."

"No man in his right mind understands women. I risk life and limb, and what thanks do I get? She upbraids me for coming to her rescue!"

"Ah, I see the attraction is mutual."

"Don't be ridiculous. I never met a more irritating person in my life!"

His brother laughed. "I rest my case. Now then, let's get you home—you look done in."

As Ian was still weak and Donald was not one for walking much, they hailed a cab. The route the cabbie chose took them past the location of their old house. Ian usually did his best to avoid that particular street, and driving down it now, he felt a familiar swelling in his throat.

Grief was a strange companion. At first it had hit hard and strong, like a blast of frigid wind, a shuddering blow that left no air in his body. Then it subsided for a while, rising up from time to time like an adder, coiled and poised to sink its teeth into the flesh of its victim. Ian had tried outrunning it, then fighting it, but quickly found the best thing was to lie still and let it crash over him like a wave.

In the years since his parents' deaths, his grief had subsided to a quiet trickle, a thin, sad stream running beneath everyday life. He and Donald had never truly discussed it; the air between them was heavy with unspoken words and unexpressed feelings. Now, sitting beside his brother in a hansom cab hurtling through the crisp November air, Ian felt an urge to speak of long-buried events.

"Do you ever . . ." he began, but his tongue felt thick and useless. He was having trouble forming the words, or even remembering which words to use.

"Do I ever what?"

"Never mind," he mumbled, afraid Donald would rush him back to hospital. He had an overwhelming urge to sleep, and longed for his own bed.

"I live with it every day, as do you," said Donald. "For years it drove me into a spiral of despair."

"How did you—"

"I decided I could live with it. It was either that or die. I knew I was killing myself slowly, but for a while drink worked—I could forget for periods of time. Then it stopped working, and I had a choice to make."

"So one day you just decided—"

"It wasn't nearly as dramatic as that. It was more a gradual realization that I didn't really wish to die. I mean, what do we have, really? A few brief moments in the sun, a little joy and pleasure, and, if we're lucky, love. I realized, in spite of all the wasted years, I could choose to live."

His brother's unexpected frankness took Ian so much by surprise he feared any response might sound trite or shallow. He had always taken it as a matter of faith that his brother was the weaker one, but it suddenly occurred to him that perhaps Donald felt more deeply, and suffered more. Ian tried to put his realization into words, but exhaustion overcame his efforts.

"I didn't know—I mean, I couldn't—"

"It's all right," Donald said. "We all think our grief is nobler than everyone else's. It's hard to admit the fact of another's suffering."

Ian stared at his brother as if for the first time. He had never thought of Donald as wise—intelligent, certainly, but not wise. They lapsed into silence for the rest of the trip, but Ian sensed a shift. The air between them was somehow clearer and yet more complex.

Arriving home, Ian had barely climbed into bed before sleep overtook him, whisking him into blessed oblivion.

CHAPTER
TWENTY-TWO

She sat at her kitchen table, the night huddled around her like a co-conspirator, her body suffused with the excitement she felt whenever she took another victim. She imagined the aftermath: the discovery of the body, the shock and horror of onlookers quickly leading to fear and confusion, followed by a frenzied search for the perpetrator. It thrilled her to think she was the cause of all this activity and emotion. Her limbs tingled with contentment as she contemplated the sweetness of ultimate control over existence itself. The more she indulged her dark fantasies and desires, the more the terrified and confused girl of seven receded from her memory—until finally, she hoped to forget her forever.

She pulled the curtains aside to reveal the canopy of stars rising over the chimneys and steeples of the town. Cold, hard, and bright, they burned with a distant fire much like her own.

Gazing at them now, she remembered another night, much like this one, many years ago. He had come to her bed late, creeping in while she was asleep. She awoke to find his hand sliding up her thigh, secretive as a snake, until his fingers found the lips between her legs. Parting them, he slid a finger inside her, all the while cooing and coaxing, as if she were a willing partner.

"There now, doesn't that feel good? You like that, don't you?"

She maintained a stubborn silence through his murmuring and moaning as he unbuttoned his pants with the other hand. She heard the wet flapping sound as he stroked himself, listened as it increased in rhythm and tempo, faster and faster, until she felt the warm spurt on her leg, heard him shudder, felt his body spasm and tremble.

"Oh, oh, my darling girl," he gasped, but she recognized these not as words of love but of control. He had power over her—absolute power, and even now, the memory filled her with shame.

But something else happened that night. Opening her eyes, which, as usual, she had shut tightly, she saw a yellow band of light fall across her bedspread. The door was ajar, and the light came from a lamp in the hall—a lamp someone was holding. She was aware of a flash of flannel, the swoop of an arm, and the throaty, tormented cry of her mother. It was a sound she never heard her mother make before or after—the piercing wail of an animal in agony. She buried her face in the pillow to the sound of blows falling upon her father's shoulders. He was surprisingly quiet, making no protest other than a few low whimpers. Uncovering her face, she saw the full force of her mother's fury, her arms flailing like windmills.

Her mother did not find words until she had exhausted herself, panting and spent.

"Get—out!" she gasped, her breath coming shallow and fast. "Don't—you—*ever*—go near her again!"

She saw her father scuttle from the room without a word and waited for her mother to embrace her, to apologize, to make it all right. But her mother ran a hand wearily over her own eyes and said simply,

"Go to sleep." Without another word, she left the room, closing the door behind her.

And so she sank back on the pillow, alone again with the cold and heartless stars, high and remote in the night sky. She gazed at them until her eyes watered, imagining being up there, far removed from a world she had learned, suddenly and violently, was not to be trusted.

CHAPTER
TWENTY-THREE

When Ian awoke the next morning, Donald had already left. Ian's head throbbed—he felt as if he had been run over by a lorry—but at least sleep had cleared the cobwebs from his brain. Ravenous, he devoured four eggs, two lamb sausages, half a loaf of bread, and several boiled potatoes, washed down with a strong pot of coffee. The cat curled around his ankles while he ate, even though Donald had left a note saying Bacchus had been fed.

"Not a chance," Ian told the creature, who gazed up at him with wide green eyes, which were unusually round and a bit off center. His long nose and lopsided eyes gave him a comical look, which was augmented by his ungainliness. But his lack of grace did not dampen his thirst for gymnastics. Ian often entered a room to see Bacchus tumbling off the back of a wing chair or sliding off a bookshelf, having miscalculated the leap.

But he was an excellent mouser, and kept the rodent population down. His clumsiness seemed to vanish when it came to hunting. He liked to perch atop the kitchen table at night, waiting for the mice to venture forth from their hiding place beneath the stove. Then he would pounce, so swiftly the doomed mouse didn't have time to flee. What happened next was better left to the imagination—Ian didn't want to interrupt Nature's course, but he often wondered what sadistic impulse impelled a cat to torment a mouse before killing it. The behavior reminded him too much of the worst criminals Edinburgh had to offer, which led to the uncomfortable conclusion that cruelty was a fact of life.

"You win," he said, tossing the cat the last bit of sausage before taking his plate to the sink. "Don't tell my brother."

After gobbling up the meat, Bacchus launched into an industrious cleaning of his whiskers.

Ian arrived at the High Street station to a stern summons to appear in DCI Crawford's office. When he entered, Crawford was standing at the window, a shaft of sunlight falling on the semicircle of ginger hair that ran around his mostly bald head. The sight reminded Ian of the bowl-shaped moraines he had seen in Wales.

"Now see here," Crawford said. "You know how I feel about that thieving little street rat of yours."

"I can't say I blame you."

"Then why on earth did you insist on using him as a messenger?"

"Because it was convenient. I had an important message to deliver, and he was there."

"How did you know he would perform the task?"

"He's never failed me before."

The chief inspector ran a hand over his high forehead. "Good Lord, Hamilton, you can't go about using any wretched street urchin—"

"He's not 'any' urchin—he's exceptionally bright and capable."

"He was in that godforsaken brothel, wasn't he?"

"Yes."

"What business does a child have in a house of ill repute, I'd like to know?"

"That makes two of us, sir."

DCI Crawford grunted and sank wearily into his desk chair. Ian would have liked an invitation to sit, but as it was not forthcoming, he continued to stand.

"Well, I don't trust him farther than I can throw him," said Crawford.

"He did deliver the message, though?"

"You know he did." He plucked a sheet of paper from his desk and thrust it at Ian. "Dr. Littlejohn sent me the official report of strychnine poisoning as the cause of death. Honestly, I don't know when the man sleeps."

"It looks as though you could do with a bit of sleep yourself, sir."

Crawford rubbed his forehead wearily. "My wife had a bad night."

"I'm sorry, sir," Ian said. "I wanted to tell you, my brother knows a doctor who has a reputation for being a brilliant diagnostician. He's going to ask if he'll have a look at your wife."

"What's his name?"

"Joseph Bell."

"Is he the one who treated those cuts on your face?"

"Uh, no," Ian said. He had forgotten the signs of his fight were all too evident.

"I heard you were involved in a bar brawl."

"Who told you that?"

"I have my sources."

"Street urchins of your own, sir?"

"So it is true, then?"

"A young lady needed assistance, and I stepped in to offer some."

"I see how that turned out for you."

"I assure you, my opponent—"

"I know—he looks worse." The chief inspector dug a piece of string out of his desk drawer and twisted it between his forefinger and thumb. "See here, Hamilton, we can't have our policemen involved in pub fights. It doesn't look good."

"I don't imagine it does, sir."

"See that it doesn't happen again. Oh, and this came for you this morning," he added, handing Ian an envelope.

In it were the photographs of Mr. Pritchett that Lillian had taken. In black and white, he looked even more horrific.

"That the victim, is it?" Crawford said, looking over his shoulder. "What's his name?"

"Geoffrey Pritchett, though we can't be sure that's his real name."

"These are rather good," Crawford said, admiring the photographs. "Who took them?"

"My aunt."

"Ah, so she *is* working for us, then?"

"I wouldn't want to speak for her, but I think she has a knack for this."

"Tell her we'll pay her as much as we pay our regular chaps."

"That reminds me, sir—Dr. Littlejohn gave me a message for you."

"Oh?" Crawford asked. "What was it?"

"He said to tell 'Toshy' Crawford hello."

Crawford turned away and coughed. "Very well—that will be all, Hamilton."

"'Toshy,' sir? How did you come by that nickname?"

"I said that will be *all*, Detective!"

"May I say one thing, sir?"

"What?"

"You don't look like a Toshy to me."

Crawford's ears reddened, and his eyes narrowed dangerously, but Ian slipped out the door before the inspector could respond.

Sergeant Dickerson was seated at his desk going through a stack of papers. He held up a fistful as Ian approached. "I've got five complaints about Mrs. McGinty's pig in the last week alone. That animal's likely to be the death o' me."

"We have more important matters than porcine miscreants, Sergeant."

"That's jus' wha' I'm on about, sir! Don't seem right t'me that we have ta look after a pig when there's murderers out there."

"Agreed. If you can tear yourself away from the allure of paperwork, I have several inquiries to make."

"Right you are, sir," Dickerson said, grabbing his coat and hat.

The day was brisk and bright; a wicked wind whipped in from the coast. The men held on to their hats as they crossed North Bridge toward Princes Street. Below them, Old Town teemed—unruly, rough, and rude. Ahead, the gleaming crescent of New Town beckoned, seductive as a desert mirage. As they left the bridge, they stepped aside to let a cart full of cabbage pass. The driver wore the wide-brimmed farmer's hat, and Ian was reminded of the favor he had done Angus McAllister.

"I wonder if a poisoner might also be a thief," Ian murmured.

"Why d'you mean, sir?"

"Assuming Pritchett was indeed a banker, could the motive this time be money?"

"I see what you're drivin' at, sir."

"Once we've established Mr. Pritchett's real identity, we need to find any possible connection between the two victims."

"It's two different poisons, right? What if it's not the same person what did 'em both?"

"An excellent question, and the answer may lead us closer to our prey. Shall we start here?" Ian said, stopping in front of the Royal Bank of Scotland on St. Andrew Square.

This time their inquiry met with more luck. As soon as the young bank teller behind window one laid eyes on the photograph, he blanched and waved over a thin, middle-aged man in pinstriped trousers with sharp black eyes behind thick spectacles.

"Efrim Winslow Jr.," he said officiously. "I'm the manager. May I be of assistance?"

"DI Hamilton and Sergeant Dickerson, Edinburgh City Police," said Ian, holding up the picture. "Was this gentleman employed by your institution?"

Efrim Winslow Jr. peered at the picture. "That's Geoffrey Pritchett. He failed to appear at work this morning. What on earth is wrong with his face?"

"I'm afraid Mr. Pritchett won't be coming to work anymore," Ian said bluntly. The bank manager's officious manner irritated Ian, and he had an urge to rankle the man.

"What do you mean?"

"He's dead."

The bank manager dropped the picture as if it had stung him. "Oh, dear me. Dear, dear—how was he—I mean, what happened?"

"He was poisoned."

"You mean—murdered?"

"Very probably."

"What shall I tell the others?" he said, his small eyes flitting around the lobby.

"I'd appreciate it if you would gather the staff and make an announcement with the sergeant and myself present."

"Very well," Winslow said. "What should I say?"

"Tell them Mr. Pritchett was poisoned."

"Where was this picture taken?"

"I am not yet releasing that information."

"As you wish," the bank manager said.

The staff was duly summoned as the remaining customers were escorted out, and the front doors were locked, the shades pulled down to obscure any view from the street. There were about a dozen employees, ten men and two women. Once everyone had gathered around the manager's desk, a very nervous-looking Winslow made the announcement.

"I am sorry to inform you one of our employees has met with an unfortunate turn of events," he said, wiping the sweat from beneath his shirt collar with a linen handkerchief. "It seems he was poisoned."

A collective gasp arose from the assembled company. Ian studied the face of each person carefully. Most looked genuinely shocked, but one young woman—one of the clerks—appeared puzzled, as if she didn't believe what the manager had just said.

The others peppered him with the usual questions—where, how, when, and so on. Ian stepped forward, to the evident relief of poor Winslow, who was wilting like a flower under the pressure. After introducing himself, Ian held up his hands for silence.

"Mr. Pritchett's death is under investigation; therefore, some of the details are not yet being released to the public."

"Why not?" said a tall young man with a long nose and curly brown hair.

"I can only say that it is police procedure to withhold some details of an investigation from the general public."

"Was it murder?" asked a solid-looking older man with a bristly white mustache.

"That is at present undetermined."

That was met with a chorus of murmurs and speculation.

"Who'd want to kill Geoffrey?"

"Wonder if it was one of us?"

Ian held his hands up again for silence. "Sergeant Dickerson here will take down your names and addresses. After we interview each of you, you will be free to go. It is up to Mr. Winslow as to whether to remain open or close the bank for the remainder of the day. If anyone has information they feel might pertain to Mr. Pritchett's death, I urge them to come forward at this time."

His words had an effect upon the young woman who had responded so curiously earlier. She bit her lip and stared at the wall clock over the front entrance, a pensive look on her face. Finally, she seemed to come to a decision. Squaring her shoulders, she marched over to Ian.

"Beg pardon, sir, may I have a word?" she said timidly. Her accent suggested a certain degree of breeding. She wore a forest-green skirt with a short matching jacket, smartly cut, hand embroidered. Though she wore no wedding ring, Ian imagined her delicate figure and light-brown hair and eyes attracted a fair number of suitors. He wondered if any of her colleagues numbered among them.

"Of course, madame," Ian said formally. The more attractive women were, the more reserved his manner.

"Not here," she said, looking around nervously. "Can we go into the back?"

"If you think it prudent, Miss—?"

"Garvey. Eleanor Garvey."

"Please, lead the way, Miss Garvey."

She took him down a narrow hall to a small chamber that appeared to serve as both break room and smoking parlor for the employees. A row of cupboards sat over a small gas stove with a well-worn teakettle. Half a dozen chairs were scattered around a rectangular table; several decks of cards were visible, as well as ashtrays, teacups, and sugar bowls.

"Now then, madame," said Ian. "What did you wish to tell me?"

She fidgeted with the buttons on her jacket. Her hands were soft and pink and well cared for. "I don't know if it's important or not, but Mr. Pritchett was—I don't quite know how to say it."

"Take your time," he said kindly, though curiosity bubbled up inside him. No matter how impatient he was, it was never a good idea to hurry witnesses. It could make them flustered and forgetful, and sometimes they clammed up entirely.

Miss Garvey took a deep breath and squared her shoulders. "Mr. Pritchett was—well, he was free and easy with the ladies. There, I've said it," she concluded, sounding relieved.

"Did he force himself upon you?"

"Kathy and I would catch him staring at us—in an indecent manner, you know? He seemed to fancy himself a bit of a ladies' man, judging by the way he fawned over the female customers. Mr. Winslow spoke to him about it once or twice, but then he just did it when Mr. Winslow wasn't watching. And sometimes he—well, he would touch us."

"How so?"

"At first it was just friendly, like, but gradually it became . . ."

"Inappropriate?"

"Yes. When we told him to stop, he would just laugh it off and say he couldn't resist. It would stop for a while. But then he'd be at it again after a few days."

"And you think this might relate to his death because—?"

"It could be a jealous husband. I don't know what Mr. Pritchett gets up to on his hours off, but isn't revenge a good motive for murder?" Her eyes were shining as she gazed at him expectantly.

"Do you read many penny dreadfuls, Miss Garvey?"

"Only the ones my brother brings home," she replied, blushing a deep scarlet. "I'm not being fanciful, if that's what you're getting at," she added hotly.

"I merely found it curious that a refined young woman such as yourself would be contemplating motives for murder. My apologies if I've offended you in any way."

"You haven't," she said with a toss of her head.

"Is there anything else you wish to tell me?"

"No."

"Since you have been both observant and helpful, may I ask you something?" He hoped she wouldn't see the flattery for the manipulative ploy it was—though, as with all good flattery, there was a good deal of truth in it.

"I suppose so," she said.

"Did you ever see Mr. Pritchett with any ladies outside the bank?"

"No—though no doubt a man such as he had a slew of them."

"Thank you for your assistance," he said, escorting her from the room.

The rest of the employee interviews yielded nothing of particular interest, though Ian made sure Sergeant Dickerson took copious notes nonetheless. No one could think of Pritchett mentioning any friends outside the bank; his only family was apparently a wedded sister in London, but no one knew her married name. When they finally finished, and trudged up the hill toward the High Street station, the sun was in its last lingering throes before disappearing behind the ancient volcanic structure of Castle Rock.

"The victims have at least one thing in common," Ian said, watching the lights of New Town flicker on one by one, as Edinburgh's army of lamplighters set about their work.

"What's that, sir?" asked Dickerson.

"Ill behavior toward women. I'm beginning to think your notion of la belle dame sans merci might be close to the mark after all."

"What's that, sir?"

"It's French for 'beautiful lady without mercy.'"

"Woman or man, there's not much mercy in this killer, is there, sir?"

"Indeed, there is not, Sergeant," Ian answered as the sun dove behind the cover of Edinburgh Castle and the sky deepened into a melancholy midnight blue.

CHAPTER
TWENTY-FOUR

She watched as the two men parted, the shorter one turning north, the taller wending his way eastward. She decided to follow him, as he was the leader, but also because he was good looking, with his curly black hair and leonine face. He looked like a romantic hero straight out of Sir Walter Scott. She devoured books, escaping into fiction as much as possible—she had read *The Heart of Midlothian* five times. It was thrilling to imagine herself a character in one of Scott's romances. The detective reminded her of her father in some ways, which she found both thrilling and sickening—the angular build, the upright, economical gait, supple as a jungle cat.

But she was the predator this time, she reminded herself as she slunk after him, always in the shadows. She was good at trailing people, and this time of day was perfect for remaining unseen. Workers were heading home or to alehouses, just as denizens of the dark—lamplighters, night watchmen, and whores—clogged the narrow streets, turning Edinburgh into a mass of humanity. She lowered her head as a group of dockworkers strode by, feeling their eyes upon her, hating them, wishing them dead. Filthy creatures, with their calloused hands and rough ways, sunburned necks creased with grime and soot. At least her father had smooth hands, with perfectly manicured nails—there was nothing common or crude about him.

She had made a mistake, she knew that. In her zest to experiment with different substances, she had miscalculated. The poison had not worked as quickly as she'd expected—maybe the banker's constitution was sturdier than it had seemed, but in any case, he'd left her before it took effect. She felt unfulfilled, missing the climax she craved, the intoxicating moment when life moved over to let death in. That alone was disappointing, but far worse was that she did not know what he had said or to whom. She suspected he was visiting his dirty whore, but she didn't know for certain. Now, they had managed to locate his place of employment—but how?

She would have to find out, she thought as she ducked behind a pie shop, watching the handsome detective climb the steps leading to Victoria Terrace. So this must be where he lived, unless he had a lady friend. The thought filled her with rage.

Hidden by the shop awning, she watched as he turned the key in the lock and went inside. Pulling her bonnet low over her face, she darted into the crowd, keeping her head down as she retraced her steps toward the heart of Old Town. Now she knew where he lived. The rest would be child's play.

CHAPTER
TWENTY-FIVE

When Ian emerged from his flat Friday morning, Derek McNair was leaning over the railing, idly tossing pebbles at people in the street below.

"Oiy—stop that!" Ian said.

The boy wiped his hands on his trousers. "Yer up late," he said, falling into step next to the detective as he headed east toward the police station.

"What do you want?"

"Thought ye might like ta see this mornin's paper."

Ian took the broadsheet from the boy's grimy hand. The headline assaulted him in boldface.

MURDER IN OLD TOWN!!

PROMINENT BANKER FALLS VICTIM TO MAD POISONER

Police baffled—is anyone safe?

"What d'ye think? Pretty dramatic, ain't it?"

Ian gave Derek a dour look. "How much did they pay you for the information?"

"That cuts me t'the quick! Half a dozen folks could've told them."

"What else did you tell them?"

"C'mon, now, Guv—I'm yer mate, you know that."

"What I know is that you'd do just about anything for money."

"Kin ye blame me?"

"I just wish you had asked me before you went blabbing about details of the crime."

"I din' tell 'em anything they couldn't a found out on their own."

"What were you doing in that brothel?"

"Nothin'."

"You're far too young to be around women like that. Why were you there?"

"Non' o' yer business."

"Do you wish to aid in this investigation or not?"

Derek kicked at a stone, sending it skittering into the gutter. "I was lookin' fer someone."

"Who?"

"Me maither."

"Your mother is—?"

"Last I heard. They said they'd try an' help me find 'er."

Ian fell silent. He had not anticipated this response. He'd never inquired about Derek's past, assuming anything the boy told him was likely as not a lie. He had no doubt it was unsavory, but Edinburgh was full of people with tragic histories. He had a tendency to shut out any facts not relevant to an investigation. He realized this character trait, like most, cut both ways, and could be a virtue or a flaw, depending on the circumstances. At the moment, he felt it made him rather callous.

"When did you last see your mother?" he said, stepping aside to let a wagon heaped high with hay pass. It teetered dangerously as it rounded the corner onto George IV Bridge, the driver invisible behind the teeming mound of straw.

Derek shoved his hands into his pockets. "Three years ago. It were me birthday, and she got stone-cold pissed an' passed out. Had ta drag 'er to bed."

"Was that here, in Edinburgh?"

"Nope. It were in Leith."

The nearby town of Leith was noted for harboring "rough trade"—the dockworkers and longshoremen who unloaded cargo from the ships coming in from the Firth of Forth. Houses of ill repute sprouted in the port's back alleys like mushrooms after a spring rain. The thought of Derek watching his mother service that stinking, carousing clientele made Ian's head throb.

"And your father?"

"Me da's a devil. Yer better off not goin' near him, 'specially when 'e's got the drink in 'im."

"Why do you wish to locate your mother? It sounds as if she wasn't much use to you."

"I dunno—maybe because you's only got one family. Maybe I hope she's diff'rent."

Ian stopped at a fish-and-chip stand and handed the vendor two shillings.

"Will that be two orders, sir?"

"Yes, please," he said, watching as the man plunged two thickly breaded strips of haddock into the bubbling kettle. The oil splattered and hissed as the smell rose to envelop them, and Ian was reminded of his own family's Friday-night dinners of fish and chips. Both his parents were Protestant, but his mother had Catholics on her maternal side and carried with her the ritual of eating fish on Fridays. He looked at Derek, whose eyes were fixed on the boiling oil with the golden-brown chunks of fish bobbing up and down.

"Ta very much," he said when Ian handed him both servings. "What're you havin'?"

"I had breakfast."

"Yer too skinny," the boy said, swallowing half a portion in one gulp.

"DCI Crawford doesn't like you, you know," said Ian as they continued east beneath George IV Bridge.

"I don' much care for him, so that makes us even."

"When he sees this headline, he's not going to be happy."

"I've always thought happiness were overrated, m'self," Derek said, starting on the second portion of fish. "I mean, wha' does it get ye? Happy people never do any damn thing."

"If you want to continue working for me, you'd best stop selling information to the press."

"Speak o' the devil, look who's waitin' fer ya, Guv," Derek said as they approached the police station.

"Damn," Ian muttered.

Loitering in front of the High Street station house was a figure he recognized only too well. Standing barely five foot four and weighing nine stone soaking wet, a worn tweed cap perched jauntily on his head, was the *Scotsman's* chief crime reporter, Jedidiah Corbin. Tireless, resourceful, and dogged, he was known to boast that "if there's a story out there, Jed Corbin will sniff it out." Ian did not consider the boast an idle one. When Corbin saw Ian, a smile broke across his ferret-like face. His dark eyes remained watchful—Ian suspected they missed very little.

"Detective Hamilton—just the man I was hoping to see!" He beamed.

"How fortunate my presence brightens your day so wonderfully."

"And how delightful to see your much-vaunted irony is sharp as ever," said Corbin, winking at Derek. "Hello, Master McNair."

"Mornin'," Derek mumbled through a mouthful of haddock.

"I see my associate here is known to you," Ian remarked.

"I owe half my career to this lad and others like him," Corbin said, chuckling.

"I'm sure you pay them well for their trouble," Ian replied. The reporter's high spirits were getting on his nerves.

"Bollocks," Derek protested. "I ain't never—"

"We'll discuss it later," Ian told him. "Now then, Mr. Corbin, if you'll excuse me, I have work to do."

"Just one or two questions—please?"

"I'm afraid the interests of your newspaper are not entirely the same as those of the Edinburgh City Police."

"A tragedy of my profession, Detective. I would like nothing more than to aid in your investigation—"

"And yet you have already printed information we wished to keep classified."

"How was I to know what was secret and what was not?"

"By paying us a visit before you printed the story."

"Ah, but by then the *Caledonian* would have beaten us to the punch."

"Next time you are in a rush to press, perhaps you will consider our perspective."

"Indeed, I shall—I promise."

"I am glad to hear it," Ian said, his hand on the doorknob.

"Please, just one question?"

Ian considered the advantage of having Corbin on his side rather than against him. "One."

"Do you have any leads?"

"Yes."

"What are they?"

"I agreed to one question. Good day," he said, opening the door.

"Oiy!" Derek said. "Wha' about me?"

"If I were you," Ian replied, "I'd make myself scarce. DCI Crawford likes to eat little boys for breakfast—especially ones who blabber to the press."

Derek gave a derisive snort, but his eyes widened.

"Can I just get a quote from you, Detective?" Corbin called out. "Something to reassure the public, perhaps?"

Ian turned upon the doorsill. "We will apprehend this criminal, and when we do, a hangman's noose will be waiting."

"Capital!" Corbin cried. "That will make excellent copy."

As the door closed behind him with a hollow thud, Ian wondered if his bravado would come back to haunt him.

CHAPTER
TWENTY-SIX

Ian found Sergeant Dickerson at his desk engrossed in a bound manuscript. With his pale eyes and pink skin, he looked like a balding cherub. When he saw the detective approaching, he quickly slipped the book under some other papers.

Ian sat at his own desk across from Dickerson. "What have you got there, Sergeant?"

"Uh, I were jus' havin' a look at me script, sir. *Hamlet*, I mean."

"Studying your lines?"

"It's not so easy—I'm not good at memorizing, like."

"Would you like some help?"

The sergeant's brow furrowed. "Such as what, sir?"

"I can help you rehearse by reading the other parts."

"What—now, sir?"

"When your shift ends."

"You'd do that fer me?"

"'All the world's a stage,' Sergeant," Ian said, looking around the room.

Several constables loitered at the tea station having a chat, while the rest prepared to go on their beats. It was a few minutes past nine, when the day shift replaced the officers returning from the night shift. A couple of very young constables entered the station, yawning, bleary-eyed, and sleepy. The night shifts tended to go to the newer members of the force—those with seniority had their pick of more desirable times. Ian had always enjoyed the night shift when he was a young recruit. He liked the solitude, the empty streets, the sensation of being awake while thousands slept all around him. Edinburgh always seemed more itself in the dead of night.

Dickerson lowered his voice. "You ever been in a—er, play, sir?"

"Once or twice, when I was younger."

"It's not as easy as it seems. So much t'think about, like, y'know?"

"Speaking of which, Sergeant, any thoughts about this case?"

"Funny you should ask, sir. It occurs t'me—"

He was interrupted by the entrance into the room of a familiar personage—the formidable Sophia Jex-Blake. Breezing her way past the desk sergeant before he could object, she strode over to Ian and Dickerson, planting her solid figure before them. She wore a worsted gabardine suit jacket over a matching gray skirt with crimson trim, her dark hair pulled back into a severe bun at the nape of her neck. Ian noticed once again that, in spite of her efforts to disguise it, she was a handsome woman. Her large eyes with their dark brows were her best feature, though the rest of her face was attractive as well, with its determined chin and delicate, Cupid's bow lips. Her deliberate attempt at plainness seemed to insist she be treated as an equal.

"Well?" she demanded, brandishing the same broadsheet Derek had shown him earlier. "Is it true—is this the same killer?"

"That is precisely what we are trying to determine, madame," Ian said, rising politely from his chair.

Sergeant Dickerson followed suit, so hastily that he nearly spilled his mug of tea.

"Why does the *Scotsman* claim it *is* the same person?"

"I make it a practice to believe very little of what I read in the papers."

"Hmm—wise enough, I suppose," she said, frowning.

"Please, have a seat," he said, pulling over a chair.

"Thank you. Forgive me—I'm afraid years of dealing with university administrators has left me with a rather short fuse. I've been told my manner irritates people. Do you find that?" she asked, fixing him with her luminous dark eyes.

"Not at all," Ian said, "though I suppose some people may find you intimidating."

She chuckled and drew her jacket around her broad shoulders. "You would make a good politician, Detective. You lie like a professional."

"Then may we get to the point?"

"By all means. If more people came out and said what they really mean, there would be far less nonsense about."

"What brought you here today?"

"I have some information about Mr. Geoffrey Pritchett."

"Oh?"

"It would be indiscreet to mention this if he were alive, of course, but—"

"Anything that might help us apprehend his killer must outweigh other considerations."

"It may be useful to you to know that Mr. Pritchett came to our clinic to be treated for what is commonly referred to as the French disease."

"Syphilis? Not surprising, I suppose, considering where he died."

"Ah, yes, the article made mention of that."

"But I thought your clinic was exclusively for women?"

"It is not unusual for us to treat the occasional gentleman who desires our discretion to maintain his anonymity. Perhaps someone who wishes to avoid revealing a particular condition to his own physician.

You know how this town is—people of a certain class are terrible gossips." Her implication was clear: neither she nor Ian belonged to the class in question.

"How long had Mr. Pritchett been your patient?"

"Less than a month. According to my appointment book, he came in Thursday last for a follow-up."

"And his treatment?"

"The usual—tincture of iodine. If that does not suffice, we use mercury."

"And was it working?"

"His symptoms had abated somewhat, but that is not uncommon. The disease can lie dormant for periods of time, which does not necessarily indicate a cure."

Sergeant Dickerson shivered. "Makes y'think, don't it?"

She regarded him with a lofty gaze. "Meaning what, exactly?"

"I—uh, jes mean that a man's gotta be careful, is all."

"And women? Do they not deserve consideration as well?"

"Well, a' course they do. I don' mean to suggest—"

"It's quite all right, Sergeant," Ian said, rescuing him. "I'm sure Dr. Jex-Blake wasn't implying that you—"

"My apologies," she said quickly. "I'm sure you meant no offense. That's one of the things people find so irritating about me, you see."

"On the contrary, madame," Ian said. "Your commitment to defending your sex does you credit."

"Really, you do belong in politics!" she said with a laugh.

"Is there anything else about Mr. Pritchett you wish to tell us?"

"He frequented houses of ill repute—not just Kate's, but others as well."

"Would you happen to know which ones?"

"I'll ask my staff, and if there is anything else of interest, I shall come to you at once."

"When might your staff be available for an interview?"

"They are all quite busy—I'd appreciate it if you direct any further questions to me."

"I should like to at least question the nurses responsible for his treatment."

"Very well," she conceded. "I'll arrange for it. And now if you'll excuse me, I have patients waiting."

"Thank you for coming in," Ian said, rising from his chair. "Shall I escort you out?"

"Very gallant of you, Detective, but my legs are quite as sturdy as they look."

Ian thought she winked at him.

When she had gone, Sergeant Dickerson shook his head. "That woman gives me the willies."

"I think she's rather impressive."

"I'm not sayin' otherwise, sir, but she's frightenin'."

"'Angels and ministers of grace defend us.'"

"Sir?"

"Surely you recognize that quote."

"It's, er, Hamlet speaking to 'is father's ghost, ain't it?"

"We'll make a thespian out of you yet, Sergeant."

"I shouldn't wonder, sir."

"Come along," Ian said, springing to his feet.

"Where are we off to, sir?"

"We're going to a funeral."

CHAPTER TWENTY-SEVEN

She sat watching through her kitchen window as the sun slid lower in the November sky, her tea growing cold beside her. She stared at the pattern of leaves at the bottom of the cup and sighed. It was a pity, but it couldn't be helped. She had no choice. If there was even a chance the girl knew too much . . . She had no hate in her heart for the poor strumpet, but that would only make her task easier—no emotions to cloud her judgment.

She knew how men talked to their whores—she could imagine him, as soon as the symptoms came on, blabbering on about having just come from her place and eating the soup she served him. It wouldn't take much to make the connection—even a poor prostitute could figure it out.

She put on her nurse's uniform, piled her hair on top of her head, and smoothed out the folds of her crisp white tunic before grabbing her medical kit.

It was a short walk to Holy Land, and when she knocked, she saw the curtain drawn aside on the front window, the flash of inquisitive eyes, followed by footsteps and the click of a heavy dead bolt. A blowsy redhead with a broad Irish face opened the front door and looked her up and down, hands on her ample hips. She wore a sheer negligee over a black lace bodice; her lips and cheeks were an unnatural shade of scarlet.

"Now what can I do for ye?" she said, a hint of the Emerald Isle in the roll of her vowels.

She pointed to her medical kit. "I've come to check up on your girls."

The woman's expression brightened. "Ah! Did Dr. Littlejohn send you, then?"

"Yes," she replied. Luck seemed to be with her tonight. Everyone in Edinburgh knew who Littlejohn was, though she wondered what he would have to do with such a place. Men couldn't be trusted—no doubt below the surface he was just another degenerate.

"Come in, then," the woman said, opening the door. "'Round here they call me Fair Kate."

"I'm—Suzanne," she said, picking the first name that came to her.

"Can I fetch ye a cuppa?"

"That would be nice, thank you," she replied, taking in the peeling yellow wallpaper and sad, tattered hall carpet.

"I'll just be a minute. Why don't you have a seat in the parlor?" Kate said, indicating a small room separated by a stained red velvet curtain.

"Thank you," she said, peering into the dimly lit chamber.

The upstairs floorboards creaked, a door clicked open, and she heard the patter of bare feet, followed by the squeak of bedsprings and stifled laughter—a man and a woman. Her shoulders tensed at the thought of what was happening in that bedroom.

"There now, doesn't that feel good? You like that, don't you?"

Her face burned with shame when she remembered that sometimes it almost did feel good, or at least not as bad, which was disturbing and confusing. She knew it was wrong, that it wasn't her fault—she dreaded those nighttime visits, and yet found herself craving his attention. As she grew older, the secrecy made her feel special. "It will be our little secret, just the two of us, right?" His voice still reverberated in her ears. "Yes, oh yes. Daddy's Precious Little Girl." That's what she was, Daddy's Precious Little Girl.

The laughter upstairs subsided, replaced by low moans and the rhythmic creaking of bedsprings. She cursed this wretched building with its thin walls, frayed rugs, and peeling plaster. Such places weren't fit for rats, let alone human beings. She wanted to run, to escape into the night, but just then Kate appeared carrying a tea tray.

"There now, we'll just have a nice sit-down, and then you can see the girls."

"Thank you," she said, pulling off her gloves and laying them carefully on top of her medicine bag.

"You'll have to forgive me," Kate said, plopping onto a tattered French settee that didn't look up to the task of supporting her. She poured tea from a blue flowered pot into two chipped, mismatched cups. "Normally I'd offer you some biscuits, but it's been such a crush 'round here since what happened, y'know." She was unable to hide a certain relish in her voice.

"Terrible thing, that—the papers said it was a banker, I believe?"

"Yes, I'm 'fraid so. One of Big Margaret's gents, he was."

"Was it foul play, like the papers said?"

Kate leaned in, her breath smelling of whisky and onions. "It was poison, somethin' called strych, er, strike—"

"Strychnine?"

"That's it."

"Do they know who might have given it to him?"

"Not a clue, love."

"They don't suspect Big, uh—"

"Margaret?" Kate leaned back on the settee, her thighs bulging to escape the sheer fabric of her robe. "Hardly the killing type, poor colleen. Mild as a mouse, she is."

"Did she talk to the police?"

"We all did. Not that it did 'em much good, mind you."

"Why not?"

Kate pulled a wayward lock of hair from her neck and pinned it on top of her head. "Weren't much t'say, really. I'm 'fraid we weren't much help."

"Not even Margaret?"

"You can ask her yourself."

"That's all right," she said, sipping her tea. "It's none of my business."

"She's not occupied at the moment."

She put down her teacup and wiped her mouth delicately. "Yes, that would be fine, thank you."

CHAPTER TWENTY-EIGHT

Sergeant William Dickerson did not like funerals. The dimly lit church was dank and drafty—it felt colder indoors than out. Pulling his overcoat closer, he struggled to fasten the middle buttons, but to his dismay, they wouldn't reach. Too many fairy cakes, that was his problem. He'd always had a sweet tooth, and Edinburgh winters made him hungry all the time. It was so blasted cold and dark, and he craved the comfort of the soft sponge cake with its perfect layer of creamy vanilla icing . . . He sighed and gave up his attempt at buttoning the coat.

Standing next to him, Detective Hamilton surveyed the crowd, his gray eyes watchful. Straight as a rod, Dickerson thought, and skinny as one, too. Some men might envy his superior officer, with his curly black locks and lean, intense face, but William Dickerson was not that sort of man. His feelings toward the detective tended more toward admiration—perhaps too much for his own good. And if there was much to envy about Hamilton, he thought, there was at least as much to feel sorry for. His was not a sunny spirit—he could be brooding, moody, restless. Always had to be on the go, fighting evil wherever he found it. If there was one thing Dickerson had learned in his brief life, it was that there would always be evil in the world. No amount of justice would root it out finally and totally, so to his way of thinking, there was no point driving yourself into the ground over it.

But Detective Hamilton was a man obsessed—anyone could see that—and Dickerson had no desire to live inside that tormented head. He was perfectly content being William Chester Dickerson, born and bred in Lancashire. He was proud of his working-class origins, though determined from a young age not to end up a coal miner like his father and grandfather before him.

He and Hamilton slipped into the last pew as the priest proceeded slowly up the aisle, swinging a silver container filled with incense. Dickerson's childhood near the mines had left him with compromised breathing even in ideal circumstances; in situations like this, he was given to asthma. He choked as the air thickened with incense. He hated the foul stuff—the smell reminded him of attending mass with his parents. He never could understand the comfort his mother seemed to take from religion—the pious declamations of the clergy always left him with more questions than answers.

As the priest and his retinue reached the pulpit, muffled sobs could be heard from the front row. Surrounded by flowers, their scent mingling with the smell of incense, the casket perched precariously on its flimsy-looking stand. He found himself wondering what would happen if it suddenly tumbled to the floor. Would there be gasps, tears, a few nervous titters? He always had inappropriate thoughts in church—he imagined priests loudly passing gas or bursting into uncontrollable laughter. As a child, he'd often imagined himself doing these things, just to see what would happen.

He never did, though—Billy Dickerson was a good boy, dutiful and obedient, traits he carried into adulthood. He respected authority, even religious authority, because he was at heart a traditionalist, craving order and rules of behavior. That as much as anything was at the heart of his decision to join the police force, turning himself into an enforcer of law and order. Having been bullied throughout childhood by local ruffians, he knew all too well the effects of mankind's baser instincts.

"We gather here today to remember our brother Thomas," the cleric intoned in the familiar singsong voice.

Dickerson followed Hamilton's gaze around the somberly dressed congregation, a sea of dark colors, surprised to see the church so full. The notoriety of Caruthers' death no doubt had brought the usual share of gawkers, but sniffling and stifled sobs in the first few rows gave him the impression a fair number of people would truly miss the poor chap. Dickerson wondered who would miss him if he died suddenly—or worse, was murdered. Would that be ironic, he mused, or just plain sad, a copper ending up a murder victim?

His reflections were interrupted by Hamilton's fingers gripping his elbow. He looked at the detective, who nodded in the direction of a rear pew across the aisle.

"There," he whispered. "You see?"

"See what, sir?"

"Observe the young woman at the far end of the pew."

The sergeant did as he was told. A young girl of about twenty was shaking with silent sobs, her face buried in a black lace handkerchief.

"What about her?"

"Does it not strike you as odd that she is sitting all alone, so evidently distraught but doing her best to hide it?"

The sergeant continued to watch her, and noticed that, as her sobs subsided, she glanced around nervously from time to time.

"She seems to be waitin' fer someone, sir," he whispered.

"Or hoping someone does not show up."

"Who, I wonder?"

"And so we send our brother Thomas into the afterlife," the priest intoned pompously, "committing his body to dust as we release his spirit into the arms of the Lord."

The mourners stirred hopefully in their seats, perking up as the service drew to a close.

After the service, they sat watching the mourners leave the church, Hamilton scanning their faces for signs of—what? Dickerson wasn't entirely sure, but he knew better than to disturb his concentration with foolish questions. Caruthers' young widow passed by, leaning heavily on the arms of two young men—her brothers, perhaps—her stomach even more distended beneath her black dress. He wondered how she was going to get by with a child on the way—the timing of her husband's murder seemed too cruel to bear.

"Why, hello, Detective Hamilton."

They turned to see Jed Corbin, a grin on his sharp face. Dickerson wondered why he always seemed to be smiling, and why the sight of that smile filled him with such misgiving.

Hamilton frowned. "What are you doing here?"

"Same as you, I expect. Any developments in the case?"

"None that I care to share with you."

"No luck, then, eh?" the reporter said with a knowing nod.

His arrogance might be a ploy, Dickerson thought, but it was damned irritating. He saw Hamilton's eyes narrow, always a dangerous sign.

"Don't you have better ways of spending your time?" said the detective. "Surely this town is full of stories. Every time the sun creeps behind the clouds, someone has a row with their wife, or a stranger appears at the door, there's a potential story in the making."

Corbin smiled. "You should be grateful I'm writing about your case. There's many who'd appreciate it."

"I'll make a note of that."

"The public has a right to know."

"And to be scared half to death by your sensationalist headlines?"

"They don't need my newspaper for that, Detective—they're already terrified."

Ian's voice became very quiet, but Dickerson could hear the quaver of anger in it. "You know, Mr. Corbin, you might consider spending more time checking your facts and less inventing ways to frighten your readers."

"I'm afraid that wouldn't sell as many papers."

"I should remind you it's a crime to interfere with a police investigation."

"Oh, dear, are you going to arrest me?"

The church was nearly empty now, but a few people turned to look at them.

"Nothing would please me more," Hamilton said in a low voice. "But you haven't broken the law—yet," he added, as he and Dickerson rose to join the queue of people leaving the church.

"Ah, well, it's early days," Corbin replied cheerfully, following them. "There's time enough for that."

And with that, he darted into the crowd, mingling with the sea of somberly dressed mourners. Among them Dickerson recognized the pretty young nurse who had come to Vickie Caruthers' flat when they were there.

"That man is trouble," Ian said, looking after Corbin. "Mark my words—he will be underfoot before this investigation is over."

As they stood in front of the church, the sergeant noticed two men in overalls with spades slung over their shoulders standing in the shadow of the eaves. One was long and stringy as a pole bean, the other short and wide as a pumpkin. They made a comic pair, and the uncomfortable realization dawned on him that they were gravediggers.

"Fine day fer a funeral," the tall one said, chewing on a bit of straw between his stained teeth.

"Aye, if it don' rain," said the other, looking up at the sky, which, though the usual dull gray of an Edinburgh winter, showed no signs of precipitation.

The tall one shook his head. "That's th'trouble with ye—always expectin' the worst of a situation."

"It's a sight better 'an bein' disappointed all th'time."

"Ach, yer jes a dour fella, an' that's all there is t'it."

"I'm a realist. There's a diff'rence," he said, spitting.

"Gae on wi' ye," said the tall one. "Come along, we'd better get tae work afore the worms get too hungry fer their dinner."

"Better a hungry worm than a hungry devil," his companion said, shouldering his spade and following him in the direction of the graveyard.

Dickerson looked at Hamilton to see if he had heard any of this, but the detective was busy scanning the crowd.

"Ah! There she is," he said.

Dickerson followed as Hamilton strode briskly after the sobbing, solitary woman they had seen in the church. Head lowered, she spoke to no one, skirting the crowd and heading toward the heavy iron gate separating the churchyard from the street.

"Excuse me, miss," he called as they caught up with her. "May I have a word?"

She turned, and the sergeant was taken aback by the intensity of grief stamped upon her face. She wasn't exactly pretty, but there was something about her clear white skin with its faint rose blush, her face framed by light-brown hair, that reminded Dickerson of his own dear Caroline. Caroline's hair was darker, but there was some likeness in the facial features.

The young woman pulled her blue-and-green tartan shawl around her narrow shoulders and faced them warily.

"Detective Ian Hamilton, Edinburgh City Police," Ian said. "This is Sergeant Dickerson, Miss—?"

"Eleanor Atkinson. What do you want?"

"I noticed you among the mourners at Mr. Caruthers' wake. Might I inquire as to your relationship to the deceased?"

She focused her clear blue eyes on his. "No, you may not." Her voice was soft but firm, the accent revealing her working-class roots, though her elocution suggested some education.

The sergeant was surprised to see the detective's face redden, though with anger or embarrassment, he could not tell.

"I must advise you, Miss Atkinson, that this is a murder investigation," he said tightly.

"I have nothing to say to you about my 'relationship,' as you call it, to Mr. Caruthers, other than I knew him."

Hamilton's face turned a deeper shade of scarlet. "I shall give you the benefit of the doubt by assuming you are unaware it is a crime to hinder a police investigation."

"Arrest me, then, and have it done with."

The detective gazed at her for a moment, as if memorizing the lines of her face, then said softly, "I see. You wish to protect his wife from shame and scandal."

"I can neither confirm nor deny that."

"By God, spoken like a lawyer!" Dickerson blurted out, regretting it immediately.

"You obviously cared about Thomas Caruthers," said Hamilton, "or you would not have risked your reputation to attend his funeral."

She clenched her jaw but did not respond.

"Do you not wish to bring your friend's killer to justice?"

It was her turn to study his face, as if searching for signs of weakness or hesitation. Dickerson was glad he was not the object of her scrutiny—there was something discomforting in the calmness of her measured gaze.

"I need your assurance that whatever I tell you will be kept in strictest confidence, not only for my sake but for the sake of his wife and her unborn child."

"I give my word that anything you say will go no further than Sergeant Dickerson and myself. No one else need know."

"And it will help you catch whoever killed Thomas?"

"That I cannot guarantee, but if you keep silent, it could help a murderer escape—one who has likely taken other lives already and may yet take more."

She blanched and swallowed hard. "It is true, then? Thomas is not the only victim?"

"We have reason to think so."

She squared her shoulders and tilted her head ever so slightly. Dickerson couldn't help but notice the angle was a flattering one, minimizing her weak chin.

"Very well. As you no doubt have guessed, I was Thomas' mistress."

"Your candor does you credit."

"In my defense, I did not know he was married until quite recently. When I found out, naturally I broke it off with him."

"When was that?"

"About a month ago. He hid the fact from me, but I chanced to see him with his wife at the Grassmarket."

Ian frowned. "You were grievously misled."

"That does not excuse my wanton behavior, especially as I am about to take the vows in less than a month."

"Vows?" said Dickerson. "You mean you—"

She smiled shyly, and in spite of what she called her "wanton behavior," he saw there was something pure and unblemished about her.

"The Sisters of Mercy."

"May I ask why you have made this choice?" Ian said.

"Why do you want to know?"

"I have my reasons."

"I won't pretend I felt called by God, or anything like that, though I do have faith. I just want to live a simpler life, free from the complications of society or desire. Can you understand that, Detective?"

"Yes, I can."

"What will you do?" Dickerson asked.

"I am trained as a nurse and hope to administer to the poor."

"Very noble of you," Ian remarked.

"If one cannot be useful to one's fellow man, then there does not seem to be much point to this life. Do you not agree, Detective?"

Ian smiled at her. "The Sisters of Mercy will be fortunate to count you among them. Can you think of anyone who might have wished to harm Mr. Caruthers?"

"It could very well be a jealous husband. In my experience, men who cheat on their wives do not stop at one transgression. They make a habit of it."

"You seem to understand the ways of the world rather well."

"That is reason enough to enter a cloister."

"To escape?"

"There is no such thing, Detective. I am not so deluded as to believe otherwise."

Once again, Hamilton reddened, though Dickerson saw a faint smile creep onto his face.

"Your powers of observation are impressive for one so young."

"I regret I cannot be of more help."

"You have been most helpful. Thank you for your time," Ian said, tipping his hat.

"Good day, then, Detective," she said. "Sergeant."

"Good day, miss," said Dickerson.

She turned to go, and Hamilton watched her get as far as the gate. As her hand was upon the handle, he called to her.

"One more thing?"

"Yes?" she said, turning.

"Who were you waiting for at the church?"

"What gave you the impression I was waiting for someone?"

"My mistake. I do make them sometimes," he added with a glance at Dickerson.

"Yes," she said, but her hand twitched upon the gate handle, and her voice climbed half an octave. "And now I really must be off."

"Good day, and thank you," said Ian, watching her go. "'Get thee to a nunnery,' eh, Sergeant?" he murmured.

"Yes, sir," Sergeant Dickerson said, wondering why such an intelligent and self-possessed young woman was such a bad liar.

CHAPTER
TWENTY-NINE

As the sun sank behind Castle Rock, Margaret Callahan wandered down Queen Street, peering into shop windows, with their elegant frocks and dainty satin slippers. She lingered in front of a lemon-yellow silk dress, wondering what it would be like to be the kind of person who wore such a dress, a lady of wealth and leisure whose greatest daily challenge was choosing which gown to wear to a ball.

"Big Margaret" had never spoken to such a lady, nor was she ever likely to. The closest she would ever come to high society was entertaining a groomsman or a valet at Kate's establishment. Still, it didn't bother her overmuch. She was old enough to know that even the lives of the fancy people were plagued by disappointment and tragedy. She had learned long ago that wanting what you couldn't have never brought anything but grief.

She knew she had to get back soon for the evening's trade, but her steps took her to the end of Queen Street, where it turned into Albany. Skirting Moray Place, she entered the Dean Gardens, inhaling the aroma of freshly turned soil. Margaret liked to wander the streets of Edinburgh all hours of the day and night. She liked its sounds and sights, and even—God forbid—its smells. Born on a potato farm in Kilkenny, she had always dreamed of city life. She got her wish when the Great Famine (which her parents stubbornly insisted on calling by its Gaelic name, *Gorta Mór*) swept across the land, withering crops and people alike.

Fleeing their homeland, her family had joined the great migration pouring out of Ireland. They went first to Glasgow and on to Edinburgh, where they prospered until her parents were struck down in the cholera epidemic a few years later. Orphaned at the age of fourteen, Margaret worked selling cress and turnips for a greengrocer until one day she found she could sell something else. Always tall for her age, she could pass for older, and though she wasn't exactly pretty, she had thick, straight hair and skin as white as skimmed cream.

It wasn't the worst life. Kate, in keeping with her nickname, had always been fair, and Margaret was careful with her money. Of course she liked her drink—who in this town didn't?—but she never lost control. She was getting on in years now, but still had her regulars, who bought her stockings and trinkets, and protective Kate made it clear that Edinburgh's "rough trade" were not welcome at her house.

Twilight deepened into dusk as Margaret walked the path leading down to the Water of Leith, the river winding through Edinburgh like a thin blue thread woven into a garment. Born in the misty mountains of the Pentland Hills, it snaked through the landscape of Midlothian, finally emptying into the arctic waters of the Firth of Forth. As she neared the banks of the river, she heard footsteps behind her. She turned to see a figure emerge from the shadows cast by the majestic oak trees lining the path.

"Oh, hello," she said. "Fancy seeing you here." Smiling, she walked toward her companion. As she did, the branches of the weeping willow along the stream shuddered as a crow took off from it, its harsh caw cutting through the November air.

CHAPTER THIRTY

Ian liked to wander through the National Gallery in his spare time, a habit he'd acquired from Aunt Lillian, who was considered quite an artist in her youth. The gallery was open late on Friday, and was a short walk from his flat. His lack of success in the case was making him restless, and he needed to take his mind off it. He skirted the western edge of the Princes Street Gardens, the twittering of birds just audible over the rumbling from the underground train tunnel buried beneath its mounds of flowers and greenery.

His footsteps took him, as they did so often lately, to the room containing the work of seventeenth-century Spanish artist Diego Velázquez. He was especially fascinated by the painting *An Old Woman Cooking Eggs*, dazzled by its rich textures and remarkable realism. He was staring at the shine on the ceramic bowl containing the eggs, marveling at the painter's ability to render such stunning details, when he became aware of someone entering the room from the far side.

He saw with displeasure it was Fiona Stuart, the nurse on whose behalf he had intervened at the White Hart, and whose subsequent ingratitude so rankled him. He looked away immediately, but it was too late—she had seen him.

"Oh," she said, "it's you." She made no attempt to hide her disappointment.

Ian longed to blurt out that people should be grateful to strangers interceding on their behalf.

"Nice to see you again," she said.

"If you insist," he muttered.

"Remarkable painting," she said, gazing at the Velázquez.

"Yes, it is," he replied tightly.

They stood uncomfortably studying the painting for a while, then he turned to leave.

"I'm sorry if you thought I was rude, but I didn't ask for your help, you know," she said.

"I beg your pardon?"

"You needn't have troubled yourself on my account. I can look after myself."

"You've made that abundantly clear."

"I understand you meant well, but it's people like you who are responsible for—"

He wheeled around, dizzy with fury. "For what—the rising crime rate in Edinburgh? The orphans and widows who go hungry every night for lack of bread? For desperate young mothers who smother their children because they can't afford to look after them?"

Her face reddened as she looked away, and he realized everyone was staring at them. He was acutely aware of how silent the room had become. He heard the street sounds outside, the clatter of horses' hooves and the rattle of carriage wheels on cobblestones. He was desperate to be out there—or anywhere—rather than in this chamber with all these people gaping at him as though he were one of the paintings.

"I was *about* to say that it's attitudes like yours that keep women as second-class citizens," she said in a low voice.

"You don't have the slightest idea what my 'attitudes' are."

"You thought I was someone who needed rescuing."

The other patrons pretended to be looking at the paintings, but Ian could tell they were still listening.

Very well, he thought peevishly, *I'll give them a show.*

"What I *saw* was you being bullied by a man who outweighed you by at least eight stone. It had nothing to do with you being a woman."

Her nose wrinkled, and a little frown line appeared between her eyebrows. "He wasn't attacking me physically."

"Let me tell you something I know a bit about, Miss—" In his anger, her name suddenly escaped him.

"Stuart."

"Miss Stuart, I spend my days apprehending the worst offenders this town has to offer. I can assure you that fellow I rescued you from has done bodily harm to any number of people."

"Is that any reason to go and get yourself battered about? He could have killed you."

"Yet here I stand—sound of body, if not of mind."

"You acted like a fool because you thought it would impress me."

"Impress *you*?" Ian sputtered. "You give yourself far too much credit, I assure you!"

"Then who were you aiming to impress?"

"I was merely attempting to correct an injustice."

"If you really cared about injustice, you would be petitioning to improve conditions for the widows and orphans you mentioned earlier."

"How do you know I'm not?"

She narrowed her eyes, which were a warm green, the color of dark jade. "You don't strike me as the petitioning sort."

"What I am is a bloody good detective, and I've put away a fair number of criminals who prey upon your widows and orphans."

"Oh, now they're *my* widows and orphans?" she replied, a faint smile playing around her mouth, with its moist, rosy lips.

Ian realized with disgust that he did find her physically attractive, which was unacceptable, maddening creature that she was.

"Yours, mine—what difference does it make? The point is I am working daily to protect them—and everyone else in this blasted city."

"Then presumably you have plenty of opportunities to play the hero in your profession," she observed.

He stared at her. "I assure you that nothing about my work remotely resembles 'play.'"

"That's a pity," she said. "If one cannot find a measure of joy in one's occupation, then life is indeed a dreary drudge."

"Good Lord, what's the use?" he said, confounded by her relentlessly confrontational attitude. "I bid you good day, Miss Stuart." He tipped his hat awkwardly and began to walk away. His brain was tied up in knots, and his head buzzed with frustration.

"Why don't you show me?" she said.

He turned to face her. "I beg your pardon?"

"Show me what you do all day. I should be most interested."

"Why would that possibly interest you?"

"Because I am a student of the world, most especially people."

"Best of luck in your studies," he said icily.

Turning once again, he strode away resolutely. He could feel her eyes upon him as he left the room and could not shake a sense of her presence even as he descended the long, winding staircase to the ground floor.

As he walked home, Ian couldn't stop thinking about Fiona Stuart and her insufferable behavior. A "student of the world"! *How arrogant,* he thought as he strode homeward for an early bedtime. He liked to be at his desk on Saturday morning, when it was quieter than during the week, and he could attend to neglected paperwork and catch up on correspondence.

He awoke early Saturday morning, and as he left the flat, he saw Derek McNair huddled in the doorway of his building. His frown was replaced by a look of concern when he saw the boy's stricken face.

"What is it?" said Ian. "What's wrong?"

"It's—it's Big Margaret."

"What happened?"

"She's dead," he said, and burst into tears.

CHAPTER
THIRTY-ONE

By the time Ian arrived, a crowd of onlookers had already gathered in the Dean Gardens, along the banks of the Water of Leith, craning their necks to catch a glimpse of the gruesome sight. They were held in check by two stocky constables guarding the crime scene. Pushing his way through the crowd, Ian heard the comments and observations of Edinburgh's citizenry, no strangers to murder and mayhem. From the nefarious Deacon Brodie to famed garroters Burke and Hare, Edinburgh seemed to breed criminals as promiscuously as it did poets and philosophers. The onlookers huddled close as the weak November sun struggled to break through a thin cloud cover.

"Who's the victim?"

"Some lass, a'think."

"I haerd it wa' a prostitute."

"Did ya? How'd she die, then?"

"I haerd it were suicide."

"Why all the coppers, then?"

Half a dozen uniformed policemen were combing the banks of the river, backs bent, examining the ground for evidence. Ian spied Sergeant

Dickerson standing a few yards from the corpse, hands in his pockets. Relief swept over Dickerson's ruddy face when he saw his superior officer.

"There you are, sir! How d'you get 'ere so quick, like?"

"Derek McNair fetched me."

Dickerson looked puzzled. "How'd he find out, then?"

"Sometimes I think he's in league with the devil."

"'Cause I dispatched Constable Bowers to get ye ten minutes ago—"

"Yes, yes," Ian said impatiently. "Where is she?"

"I'm 'fraid it's—" he began, but before he could finish, Ian strode over to look at the dead woman.

She lay on her back, fully clothed in a cream-colored frock, her bare flesh fish-belly white. She was just beginning to bloat; she couldn't have been in the river long. Bits of seaweed and lily fronds clung to her hair, as if she were a mermaid merely resting on the shore before diving back into her watery home.

"It's her, all right," he muttered. "Damn it to hell."

"There's no clear-cut evidence of foul play, sir. Could be suicide."

"Oh, it's murder, all right."

"But how kin we prove it?"

"Who found her?"

"Coupla lads playin' by the river saw her, dragged her on t'shore."

"They see anything else?"

"No, sir. Constable Bowers took their statement an' addresses, then sent 'em home."

"Cause of death appears to be drowning?"

The sergeant nodded without turning his head in the direction of the body.

"Strange you chose to be a policeman," Ian remarked, "considering you can't stand dead people."

He regretted his words even before the mortified look crossed the sergeant's earnest face. "I s-s'pose you're right, sir."

"Never mind," he said, laying a hand on Dickerson's shoulder. "Why don't you go see if the constables have turned up any evidence?"

The sergeant scampered away gratefully, and Ian knelt beside Big Margaret. Her hair was disheveled and her clothing was soaked, but there were no obvious signs of a struggle. Her eyes stared up at the overhanging dome of willows, their feathery branches bending over her as though longing to enfold her in their embrace. Ian sighed. No matter how long he did this job, he always felt solemn in the presence of death.

Gently lifting Margaret's hands, he studied the fingernails. They were intact, neither chipped nor broken. Around her wrist was a silver bracelet—the same one he had noticed earlier at the brothel. Peering at it closely, he observed a single long hair threaded through its interlocking rings. He carefully extracted the hair, holding it up to the light. It appeared to be a different shade than Margaret's own brown hair, though whether light brown or auburn, he could not tell. Wrapping it carefully in his handkerchief, he tucked it into his breast pocket. He was struck by the similarity of her death to Ophelia's, and Queen Gertrude's description of the young woman's drowning ran through his head.

> *When down her weedy trophies and herself*
>
> *Fell in the weeping brook. Her clothes spread wide;*
>
> *And, mermaid-like, awhile they bore her up*

Ophelia's death sounded almost peaceful described this way—alas, Big Margaret's demise was no such thing. She was one of the unlucky ones, to live the life she had and then to come to such an end—it was ungodly. As he stared down at her, the scar on his shoulder began to throb. He straightened up and stretched his back, but it failed to relieve the pulsing pain. The doctors had said there was some permanent nerve damage, but at the time, his physical pain had seemed nothing compared with the loss of his parents.

A groan escaped him as a sliver of pain shot down his left arm. He looked up to see Sergeant Dickerson headed his way, and composed his face as best he could, but it was too late.

"You all right, sir?" Dickerson asked.

"Quite all right. Did you have any luck?"

"I'm 'fraid not, sir—there's not much in't way of evidence so far."

"Tell them to keep searching. They may turn up something yet."

"Very good, sir. You sure you're all right, then?"

It took every bit of will Ian had not to snap at him, but he took a deep breath, letting it out slowly. "I'm fine."

"Right you are," said Dickerson unconvincingly.

"You can transport the body now," said Ian through clenched teeth. "The autopsy should give us the cause of death."

He brushed the dirt from his hands, drew his cloak around his shoulders, and started back up the path. The crowd had thinned, though a few stragglers remained, watching eagerly as the constables lifted the body onto a stretcher.

"Where are ye headed, sir?" Dickerson asked.

"To Kate's. I have a few questions to pose."

"Shall I come wi' you?"

"I'd rather you stayed here to oversee matters."

"Yes, sir," he replied, sounding disappointed.

As Ian headed up the bank, he saw a man striding toward him. He sighed when he recognized the wiry form of Jed Corbin.

"Who's the dead girl?" the reporter said, falling into step with him.

"No one you know."

Ian increased his pace, but Corbin matched it.

"It's been a bad week for you. Must be taking its toll. You don't look so good."

Ian started to reply but winced as another stab of pain shot up his shoulder.

"Is your shoulder acting up again?"

Ian stopped walking and fixed his eyes on Corbin. "What did you say?"

The reporter met his gaze. "I asked if your shoulder is acting up again."

"How do you know about that?"

"I'm a reporter. It's my business to know things."

"Do me a favor, Mr. Corbin, and find someone else to harass, will you?"

"But I like you, Detective."

"I assure you, the feeling is not mutual."

Corbin put his hand to his heart. "That wounds me deeply."

Ian didn't reply as he turned onto Albyn Place.

"It pains me to leave you," Corbin said, "but I'd better get to the crime scene before my rivals beat me to it." He started off toward the river. "Be seeing you," he called back.

"Not if I can help it," Ian muttered as a gaggle of schoolboys dashed past him, chattering excitedly.

"Is it still there, ye think?"

"Dunno—think we'll get close enough t'see?"

"Aw, it's prob'bly swarmin' wi' coppers."

They ran off, heels clattering on the pavement, their clear, high voices vanishing in the mist rapidly descending over the city. Their curiosity about death didn't offend Ian—he understood the callousness of youth. Right now, however, his own childhood seemed very far away.

Of course, they didn't know Margaret, and he found himself wishing he didn't, either. He knew when he closed his eyes to sleep that night he would see her blank ones staring up at the gently waving willows.

When Ian arrived at Kate's, she met him at the door, wringing her hands. "Thank goodness ye've come." She wore a pink flowered apron over her usual attire, which might have been comic on a less solemn occasion.

"Where is everyone?" he said, noticing the house was unusually quiet for a Saturday.

"I sent them all out."

"Why?" he said, trying to contain his irritation.

"I figured they needed some time away from this place. Besides," she said, removing her apron, "no one likes to do their business in a house w'one dead person, let alone two."

"I'm going to need to question them."

"Can't you leave 'em be for just a few hours, love?"

"Who told you about Margaret?"

"I did."

Ian turned to see Derek McNair lurking in the corner of the hall.

"I suppose you told the papers as well," Ian said.

"If they found out, it weren't from me, mate."

"Why don't you go get something to eat, lovey?" said Kate. "I left some colcannon on the stovetop for ye."

"Ta very much," said Derek, patting her generous behind.

Ian glared at him, but he scampered off to the kitchen.

"Why do you put up with that?" he asked Kate.

"He's just a wee lad—he don' mean nothin' by it. Harmless as a lamb, he is."

"He may be small, but he's more fox than lamb."

"Don' worry—I'd never leave me cashbox around 'im. You know, I feel bad about what I said about murder being bad for business," she said mournfully. "And now this. Almost as though I were bein' punished, y'know?" Tears gathered at the corners of her eyes.

"Tell me everything you remember while it is still fresh in your mind."

"She went out fer a walk, as she often does before entertainin' gents on Fridays."

"Did she say or do anything out of the ordinary?"

"Not that I noticed."

"Did she seem frightened or preoccupied?"

"If anythin', she was more cheerful than usual. Maybe it was on account o' seein' the nurse Dr. Littlejohn sent over."

"Oh? Who did he send?"

"Her name was Suzanne somethin' or other—nice young woman."

"Did you catch her last name?"

"No, love, sorry."

"And she came to check up on you all?"

"That's right. But Margaret was th'only girl available jus' then. The others were entertainin' customers."

"Had Margaret been suffering from ill health?"

"She was always healthy as a horse, bless her. Lately she'd been havin' some stomach upset, but nothin' serious."

"May I look at her room?"

"Upstairs, last on the right."

Ian climbed the rickety staircase, which creaked beneath his weight, followed by Kate. Derek trailed after them, chewing on a hunk of bread. When they got to the landing, Ian turned to the boy.

"Isn't it high time you—"

"Went home? Is tha' what y'were gonna say?"

"I don't see why you should hang about."

"Look, mate," Derek said, hands on his narrow hips, "I'm th'one what brought ye the news, ain't I?"

"Very well," Ian said. "But don't get underfoot."

Kate led him to a closed door at the end of the musty, narrow hall.

"This is—was—her room."

"She didn't share it with anyone?"

Kate shook her head, red curls bouncing. "She's been here the longest, and came to live here permanent like 'bout two years ago. I let her have her own room."

"This isn't the same room where Mr. Pritchett died."

"No, he likes the center room with the bigger bed, so she entertained him there."

"I need to have a look around—alone," he added, with a meaningful look at Derek.

"Come downstairs an' have some more stew, dearie," she said, taking the boy by the shoulder.

"Aw, bugger all," he said, with a backward glance at Ian.

When they were gone, Ian opened the door to Margaret's room, which was shabby but homey. A frayed hooked rug covered the floor, and a tattered lavender bedspread with tiny yellow flowers was tucked neatly into the corners of a four-poster bed. On the bed was a hand-crocheted pillow with the words "Bless Our Home." The notion of anyone thinking of a dilapidated brothel in Holy Land as home struck him as more than a little sad. Still, the little touches gave the room the personality of its owner. The thick layer of dust clinging to the cheery yellow curtains and the coating of grime on the windowpanes only made her attempts at comfort more touching.

Ian never enjoyed intruding on another person's private space, especially when they were dead. Even though Margaret was gone, her scent lingered in the room—peppermint and Castile oil soap. He almost had the feeling that she was watching him—even more strangely, that she approved of what he was doing. The closet contained a few frocks and high-laced boots, as well as a pair of red satin slippers. He looked through the drawers of the plain pine dresser in the far corner and, finding nothing of interest, was turning to leave when he noticed something poking out from beneath the bed. Pulling it out, he saw that it was a small metal trunk filled with hand-knitted baby clothes.

He straightened up, a tiny blue cap still in his hand, stunned by the revelation. Could it be that Big Margaret was pregnant? And if so, might that help locate her killer?

He made his way downstairs to the kitchen, where Kate was seated at the table darning a pair of black stockings. There was no sign of Derek McNair.

"Where's the boy?" Ian asked.

"Said he had t'go meet a friend," she answered without looking up. "You needn't be so hard on him, y'know. He's just a wee lad."

"He's a thief and a pickpocket."

"And you wouldn't be if you were livin' on the streets?" she said, deftly looping the needle through a stitch and tying it off.

"Is it true you're helping him find his mother?"

"Could be. Tryin' don't mean succeeding."

"I have an important question to ask you."

"Ask away," she said, biting off the thread.

"Was Margaret expecting?"

She stared at him. "Why d'ye ask, then?"

"I found baby clothes in her room."

"Sweet Mary, Mother of God," she said, letting the stockings drop to her lap. "That would explain the stomach troubles. She said it were somethin' she ate."

"Why would she hide her condition from you?"

"Isn't it obvious, then? Wha' man wants t'bed a pregnant whore?"

Her bluntness was disconcerting, and Ian felt his face redden.

"Thank you for your time," he said.

"Anythin' ye need to catch the monster that'd kill a poor defenseless girl like her."

"Monster" might have seemed like a strong word a few days ago, but now Ian thought it an appropriate description.

CHAPTER
THIRTY-TWO

It was past six when Ian trudged wearily homeward, to find his brother waiting with a joint of beef and a glass of claret for him on the sideboard.

"Good on ye, as Lillian would say," Ian said, dropping gratefully into an armchair by the fire.

"Good on me indeed," Donald replied as he carved off a thick slice onto a plate piled high with potatoes and peas. "Goes nicely with tatties and peas, eh?" he said, setting it in front of his brother.

"Nothing better," Ian mumbled through a mouthful of food.

"Oh, by the way, Dr. Bell is keen to do the autopsy," Donald said, lowering his bulk into the wing chair opposite Ian.

"What autopsy?"

"The dead girl—what's her name?"

"Margaret. How on earth did he know about—"

"My dear brother, word travels fast in this town. He's made arrangements for the body to be transported to the infirmary—he intends to use it as a teaching tool."

"I'm not sure how I feel about that."

"You can observe."

"When is it?"

"Tomorrow, first thing."

"On a Sunday?"

"Justice never rests, dear brother."

"Very well, I'll be there."

"Have you ever attended an autopsy before?"

"Not really. And you?"

"I've helped dissect cadavers. Can't say I enjoy it much."

"Presumably they'll be able to tell if she was expecting?"

Donald's eyes widened. "Do you have reason to believe she was?"

"I do."

"The autopsy would certainly reveal that, yes."

Ian fell silent thinking of Margaret, with her friendly, horsey face, lopsided smile, and warm eyes. He took a long swallow of claret and looked up to see his brother staring at him, licking his lips.

"Sorry if it makes you uncomfortable, old man," said Donald, "but I do miss it."

"The taste or the effect?" Ian ventured cautiously, not sure this was an area he wanted to explore.

"Everything," Donald said. "The earthy aroma of a pint of bitters, the sharp sting of gin, the hint of oak barrel and peat in a glass of single malt. The warm glow that envelops a room after the first glass of Bordeaux. The way it makes other people so much less irritating. The problem is, I never stop there. Or after the second, or third, or fourth. If I could, I'd still be drinking." He held up his hands. "Remember how they used to tremble? Steady as a rock."

"What do you say when your medical colleagues ask why you don't drink?"

"I make up some malarkey about an adverse physical reaction to the stuff."

"And they believe you?"

"One of the fellows was so intrigued he wanted to study me!"

"How did you respond?"

"I told him I was too busy turning other people into laboratory specimens to become one myself. He was sufficiently amused and dropped the subject."

Ian nodded—but he preferred sharp, caustic Donald, wry, ironic Donald, or dry, remote Donald to vulnerable, confessional Donald. He knew his brother's prickly personality was a façade, but he relied upon it to shield them both from dangerous intimacy. Now that ice seemed to be melting, and he feared being pulled into the vortex of his brother's need. Since their parents' death, Ian had carefully constructed a world to keep other people at arm's length. Relationships were safe and predictable: colleague, boss, ally, victim, suspect. At the end of the day he could go home, close the door behind him, and retreat into solitude.

But now something messy and chaotic had presented itself. Donald's presence in his flat and in his life was confusing, and he found himself longing for things to be as they were. But as the weeks stretched into months, he began to realize those solitary days were over, perhaps forever. The thought needled him as he watched his brother stare into the dancing flames of the fire while sipping his ginger beer. He could not understand Donald's weakness for drink—intellectually, perhaps, but not in a deep and personal way. He could not, as it were, walk in his brother's shoes, which filled him with guilt and anger. Guilt because, through some inexplicable whim of fate, he had been spared the same affliction, and anger because he felt somehow culpable for his brother's unhappiness.

"Well," Donald said, draining the last of his ginger beer, "it's high time we turned in, don't you think?"

As he bent over to turn off the gas, Ian felt the handkerchief in his pocket with the hair he had taken from Margaret's body. Sliding it carefully out, he turned to his brother. "Donald?"

"Yes, O Brother Mine?"

"Do you have access to a microscope?"

"I do indeed, at the medical school."

"Do you think I might use it to examine something?"

"What?"

"A hair I found on Margaret's body."

"Ah! A clue, perhaps?"

"Possibly."

"Why don't you come 'round and observe the autopsy, and I'll see what I can do."

"Thanks very much."

Donald stood up and stretched, like a bear waking from hibernation. "'To sleep, perchance to dream.'"

"Hamlet's talking about death there, you know, thinking about what it would be like to take his own life. You're not—I mean, you don't—"

"Everyone's rehearsing for death all the time, don't you think? Life is one big death rehearsal. Oh, that's quite good—'death rehearsal.' Get it?"

"Unfortunately, yes."

"Where's your sense of humor? You used to be so jolly."

"Really?"

"No, come to think of it, you were always a glum bastard."

"At least I'm consistent," said Ian.

"Cheer up—if there were no murderers out there, you'd be out of a job."

"And if no one ever got sick, you would be, too."

"Odd we both chose professions that profit from other's people's misery," said Donald.

"At least we're attempting to alleviate that misery."

"There's suffering enough to go around in this world, I suppose."

"True enough. Good night."

"Sweet dreams," Donald said, cocking his head and raising an eyebrow.

It was a gesture Ian had seen all his life, but now it occurred to him how personal it was, one of the countless details that made up a person. If he could accept that little quirk as part of Donald, why could he not accept his weakness for drink? Were they really so different?

He pondered these questions as he laid his head upon the pillow before drifting into a deep and dreamless sleep.

CHAPTER
THIRTY-THREE

The next morning broke bright and sunny, not a cloud in the bluebell-colored sky. Donald prepared a hearty breakfast of coddled eggs, sausage, and potatoes—he was doing much of the cooking now, an arrangement Ian found highly satisfactory.

As the day was fine, they walked to the surgical hospital on Drummond Street, zigzagging through the wynds and closes on either side of the Cowgate. The brothers shared a fondness for taking circuitous routes to their destinations, wandering the streets of the city as they had roamed the hills of the Highlands when they were young.

"Do you believe Margaret's death is somehow related to her condition?" Donald asked as they turned south on Infirmary Street.

"If not, it strikes me as an unfortunate coincidence."

"Dr. Bell claims that, in medicine, there are no coincidences."

"One might very well say the same of police work."

"Another way in which our professions are not so dissimilar," Donald remarked as they approached the heavy, ivy-covered buildings of the surgical hospital. They were met at the door by Dr. Bell's assistant, Arthur Conan Doyle. Ian was surprised by how glad he was to see the young medical student. He did not form friendships easily, but Doyle's open, earnest face instantly put him at ease.

"Right this way," Doyle said, leading the brothers down a spotless corridor. The floor was so shiny the sunlight reflecting off it from the tall, narrow windows hurt Ian's eyes. "Dr. Bell is waiting in the east wing surgical ward," Doyle added. They followed him past offices, patient wards, and nurses' stations, finally passing through a set of double doors into a large operating theater.

"I must assist Dr. Bell now," Doyle said. "Perhaps I'll see you later." He slipped back through the swinging double doors, leaving Ian and Donald alone in the rear of the room.

Ian was taken aback by the number of people packed into the steeply raked seats—medical students as well as older men he supposed were physicians and professors. Below them, at the center of the operating "stage," stood a lone gurney. Upon it lay a body covered by a white sheet; next to it was a tray of gleaming surgical instruments. The air was electric with anticipation, the low voices of the spectators buzzing with excitement. He had never been in such a place before, and seeing so many people crammed into the room made him light-headed. He had never reacted well to crowds or enclosed spaces, a condition the fire had only worsened. As he followed his brother up the stairs, Ian was seized by a wave of dizziness. He grasped the wooden rail on either side of the steps to steady himself, closed his eyes, and took a deep breath.

"Are you all right?" Donald said.

"Give me a moment."

He opened his eyes just as the rear stage door opened, and through it strode Dr. Joseph Bell. Clad in a long white laboratory coat, wavy gray hair swept back from his high forehead, the deep-set eyes thoughtful and piercing, he looked the embodiment of the scientist as intellectual.

"Gentlemen," he said, "today's lecture involves the forensic autopsy of an unfortunate woman who may have been the victim of foul play.

Most of you are familiar with me already, but for those of you who aren't—"

The rear door opened again, and Conan Doyle appeared. His deference to the older man was evident. He seemed bent on taking up less space than his powerful build would allow; his head inclined and his shoulders stooped forward as he gazed at Dr. Bell with reverence.

Bell's momentary expression of impatience was replaced by a wry smile. "Your timing is impeccable as always, Doyle."

This brought an appreciative chuckle from the audience, which Bell clearly relished. No less showman than doctor, it seemed, he displayed a theatrical flourish.

"My apologies, sir," Doyle said softly, but the hall's acoustics were such that Ian heard every word.

Bell gave him a magnanimous smile, which Ian thought was meant for the onlookers.

"As I was saying, I am Dr. Joseph Bell, and this is my assistant, young Conan Doyle. We are here to perform a forensic autopsy upon a young woman who appears to be a drowning victim. The literal translation of 'autopsy' is 'self-seeing,' or to 'see with one's own eyes.' I suggest that is a good model for any physician to hold in mind. And not merely to see but to *observe*."

An appreciative murmur arose from the spectators. Dr. Bell permitted himself another slight smile.

"What are some of the things one would expect to find in a drowning victim?"

A flurry of hands shot up. Bell nodded at a thin, dark-haired young man in the third row wearing thick spectacles. "Yes, Jenkins?"

"Water in the lungs, sir."

"What else?"

Another round of hands, but fewer than the first time.

"McNee?" Bell said, indicating a pudgy student in the front.

"Fluid in the paranasal sinuses."

"Excellent. Anything else?"

Donald raised his hand.

Bell squinted up at him. "Yes, Hamilton?"

"Thickening of the lungs and swelling of the stomach, due to water aspiration and swallowing."

"Very good. Now, before beginning the autopsy, we may ascertain a few facts about the victim."

A hush fell over the assembly as each man leaned eagerly forward, attention focused on the tall physician in the white lab coat. According to Donald, Bell was renowned for dispensing pearls of knowledge based upon observation. Ian himself was curious to see him at work, and his own throat was a little dry with anticipation.

Bell pulled off the sheet with a flourish, and a respectful silence fell over the crowd. Ian felt a little sickened at the sight of poor Margaret lying naked in a room full of men, but comforted himself with the thought that the autopsy could help bring her justice.

"The subject is a woman of early middle years, well preserved and carefully groomed." He lifted her hands and studied them carefully. "She does little or no menial labor but is not a member of the upper classes. She is not married, though her appearance is important to her, possibly due to her line of work. She is relatively organized and disciplined, a bit set in her ways, accustomed to routine. She is of a calm, phlegmatic disposition, though lately something has happened to upset her."

The pudgy student in the front raised his hand. "Beg pardon, sir, but how do you know all that?"

"Her hands are neither calloused nor worn—in fact, they show unusual signs of care, the nails recently trimmed and filed. Her feet also show signs of regular grooming. This would suggest a person of some discipline and routine—and furthermore, that her appearance is important to her. Since she is not married, it may relate to her profession."

"How do you know she's not married?" asked the thin young man with thick glasses.

"Her hands show evidence of sun exposure, there being no difference in the color on her left ring finger. If she wore a wedding ring, one would expect the skin of that area would be several shades lighter."

"And her calm disposition?"

"Though she is no longer young, her forehead is remarkably free of worry lines. Yet the index finger on her right hand shows signs that she has recently begun chewing on her cuticles, a habit she had rarely indulged in prior to this."

"What about her social standing?"

"Though well groomed, I surmise she is not a member of the upper classes due to one key thing."

"What is that?"

"The fact that she is unmarried. An upper class, well-groomed woman of her age would most certainly have a husband—the fact that she does not leads me to conclude that she is of a lower order."

"What class does she belong to?"

"That is obvious: she is a prostitute."

His pronouncement was met with a sharp intake of breath among the onlookers. Another medical student raised his hand.

"Surely you knew that before observing her?"

"I assure you, I knew nothing except that she may have been a drowning victim."

"Then may I ask how you were able to ascertain her profession?"

"Nothing could be simpler," he said, holding up her hand and pointing to the nails, lacquered a fiery red. "No respectable woman would wear such a color in public. However, it is worn extensively by fallen women, especially in the houses of ill repute lining the Cowgate. I therefore deduce she is most likely one of those women."

Ian did not necessarily believe all of Bell's conclusions, but he had to admit it did make for an impressive bit of stage magic. Conan Doyle, however, hung on every word, gazing at Bell with admiration in his warm blue eyes.

"Shall we proceed?" he said, turning to Doyle, who plucked a scalpel from the tray of instruments and handed it to him.

The next hour or so was not a pleasant experience. Ian squirmed in his seat as the shining blades sliced into poor Margaret's flesh—even dead as she was, it was not an easy sight to witness. Dr. Bell punctuated his actions with commentary on everything from the state of her liver to the condition of her lungs, which were filled with a frothy pink fluid.

"It appears that the cause of death was in fact asphyxiation by drowning," he said. "That does not establish the *manner* of death, however—I'm afraid we must leave that to others to decide."

A frown crossed his face as he bent over the corpse. "Oh, dear. That is most unfortunate." He straightened up and addressed the assembly. "I regret to say that this poor woman was approximately three months pregnant."

Though Ian had already suspected this, there was something terrible in the blunt physical confirmation of it. He felt a heaviness in his chest that he knew would not lift until he had found poor Margaret's killer.

CHAPTER
THIRTY-FOUR

"So what now?" asked Donald as they stood in the corridor outside the lecture hall. Medical students poured like lava through the double doors. "Does this alter the course of your investigation?"

"It certainly gives me pause," said Ian.

"Perhaps she was murdered by the father of her child," Donald suggested.

"Or someone who believed they were the father."

"Or perhaps she wasn't murdered at all," came a voice from behind them.

Ian turned to see Dr. Bell, still in his white laboratory coat, speckled with blood.

"Hello, Dr. Bell," said Donald, his manner uncharacteristically deferential.

"Good morning, Hamilton," the great man replied. "Hello, Detective. I see you were disturbed by the autopsy." Ian registered the condescension, just subtle enough to be deniable. "You are perhaps new to them?"

"I had reason to suspect she was with child, but having proof— well, it's a sad thing."

"Yes, it's tragic—two lives are lost. But would her condition not be a possible motive for suicide?"

"When I met her, she struck me as neither depressed nor suicidal."

"You are hardly qualified to judge—"

"On the contrary; as my line of work brings me in contact with all varieties of human misery, I am eminently qualified to judge."

"So you believe—what?" Bell said with a smirk.

"I believe she was murdered."

"There was no indication of a struggle, no defensive wounds. Her nails, for example, were perfectly intact."

"Which is why I conclude she was poisoned first."

"Poisoned!" Bell snorted.

"There *was* water in her lungs," Donald pointed out.

"I believe she was sedated sometime before she went into the water," said Ian.

Bell crossed his arms and cocked his head to one side. "What evidence have you to suggest—"

"My suspicion is that she was killed by the same person who poisoned her client."

"Your *hunch*, you mean," said Bell.

"Call it what you like. But a toxicology report would tell us one way or another."

Donald glared at Ian and shook his head, indicating to back off, but Ian ignored him.

Bell frowned. "We have spent enough time on the death of a—"

"A fallen woman? Is that what you were going to say?" asked Ian.

"I was going to say suicide," Bell said evenly.

"If you really want to get to the bottom of this, you'll do a toxicology—"

"I am not accustomed to being told what to do by a policeman," Bell interrupted, pronouncing "policeman" as if it were synonymous with a species of cockroach. "And now if you'll excuse me, I am late for my morning rounds." With that, he turned and walked briskly away.

"Well," Donald remarked, watching him go, "I guess you told him, didn't you?"

"I didn't intend to put him off. I just—"

"He'll get over it. Or he won't, and my medical career is over."

"Surely he wouldn't—"

Donald laid a hand on his shoulder. "I was joking—relax, Brother. Dear me, you are in a bad way, aren't you?"

Ian was about to respond when the double doors swung open and Conan Doyle emerged, carrying the tray of instruments covered with a towel.

"Where's Dr. Bell?" he said.

"He said something about rounds," Donald remarked. "Though, by my watch, they aren't due to start for another hour."

"That's what he says when he wants to escape from people," said Doyle.

Donald gave Ian a meaningful look. "That makes sense."

"Did you say something to annoy him?" Doyle asked.

Donald shook his head. "I didn't, but—"

Doyle looked at Ian. "It was you, then?"

"Now see here," Ian said, fed up with the whole situation. "I just—"

Doyle burst out laughing. "Join the club! We've all gotten on the wrong side of him sooner or later—haven't we, Hamilton?"

Donald smiled. "I must admit, he can be rather touchy."

"I merely suggested that—"

"You could have asked him for the time of day, and if he was in one of his moods, he would take it as an insult," said Doyle.

"Excuse me a moment," Donald said, heading in the direction of the lavatory. "I'll be right back."

"By the way, I have something for that shoulder of yours," Doyle told Ian. "An old Jesuit priest showed me how to make it. Can you spare a minute?"

"Well, I—"

"Capital!" Doyle said. "Let me dispose of these instruments, and I'll be right back."

Standing alone in the corridor, inhaling the smell of antiseptic and floor polish, Ian felt strangely calm. Perhaps it was his aggregate exhaustion, but he felt himself slipping into a contemplative frame of mind.

He was roused from his peaceful state by his brother's hand jostling his elbow.

"Looks like you've made a friend as well as an enemy today," Donald remarked.

Ian saw Conan Doyle hurrying toward them, a silver tube in his hand.

"Here it is," Doyle said. "Just happened to have left it on Dr. Bell's desk. What exactly did you say to him, by the way? I've never seen his nose so out of joint."

"Can't we just let it go?" Ian said, feeling too exhausted to explain.

"Sorry, old man—of course. Put this on twice a day," Doyle said, handing him the ointment. "Really takes the sting out."

"What sting? What's it for?" asked Donald.

"His shoulder," said Doyle.

Donald frowned at Ian. "You never told me—"

"It's nothing," said Ian, slipping the tube of salve into his pocket.

"How can it be nothing when Doyle noticed it, for Christ's sake?"

"Thanks very much for that vote of confidence," said Doyle.

"Look," Ian told his brother, "you have your own—situation, and I didn't want to compound that with complaining about my—"

"Well, isn't that just too noble of you?" Donald said angrily. "Just like our dear sainted mum, eh? So I can be the 'problem child,' and you can suffer in silence and feel superior. Well, I'm just about fed up with that attitude, let me tell you!"

With that, he spun on his heel and marched away with as much speed as he could muster.

"Well," said Doyle, "this just isn't your day, is it?"

"Damn!" said Ian. "Donald was going to let me use a microscope, and now I've driven him off."

"I can show you one."

"Would it be terribly inconvenient?"

"Not at all," Doyle said, leading him to a room off a side corridor. On the frosted glass door was stenciled the word "Pathology." Inside, a few men in white coats were hunched over microscopes along the walls or working at the lab table in the center of the room. A couple glanced up when he and Doyle entered, but went straight back to their tasks.

Doyle showed Ian how to place the hair on a glass slide. "There you go," he said, sliding it under the lens. "What do you see?"

There was no denying that the hair was red—a rich auburn color, like autumn leaves.

"May I?" Doyle asked.

"Certainly."

"I want to study a cross section of the sample." Taking a sharp pair of medical scissors, Doyle carefully cut a small piece from the hair and placed it on the slide.

"Ah! Curly red hair," he said, studying it.

Ian frowned. "How do you know it's curly?"

"You see the oval-shaped follicles?"

"Yes," Ian said, a sour ball of dread forming in his stomach.

"Straight hair has round ones. This hair belongs to a curly-headed person."

"I am in your debt," Ian said, folding the hair back up inside his handkerchief.

"Pish tosh, old man. Have you eaten?"

"No, but I should be getting back to work."

"Nonsense—it's Sunday! The Sheep Heid Inn serves a decent ale. I'll buy the first round."

Ian sighed. He was too muddled to concentrate properly, and it was many hours since breakfast. "Perhaps the walk will do me good."

"That's the spirit!" Doyle said, rubbing his hands heartily. His enthusiasm was infectious, and his presence was reassuring.

"What about Dr. Bell?"

"He can get along for a few hours without me. Anyway, best to leave him alone when he's in one of his moods."

"Very well," Ian said. "'Lay on, Macduff.'"

Surprise crossed Doyle's frank, friendly face. "I say, isn't it supposed to be bad luck to quote that play?"

Ian shrugged. "It's difficult to imagine my luck getting much worse than it already is." But even as he said it, he realized the folly in his words.

CHAPTER
THIRTY-FIVE

The Sheep Heid Inn was tucked away in the village of Duddingston, nestled along the southeastern edge of Holyrood Park. It was a short walk from Arthur's Seat, the volcanic ridge dominating the park's landscape. If seated near the pub's front windows, one could watch the shadows cast by the rocky outcropping move as the sun made its daily journey across the sky.

The inn laid claim to being the oldest pub in Scotland, reputedly opening in 1360. The ancient structure cradled the past within its low ceilings, crooked walls, and uneven floorboards. Perhaps it was this sense of bygone times that appealed to the clientele—it certainly wasn't the gruff service or mostly unremarkable menu. But the Scots were a sentimental race, and looking back on the past was a national pastime.

Ian and Conan Doyle arrived just in time to scoop up the last two servings of lamb shank with roast potatoes and carrots. They finished the meal with a round of Glenlivet, by which time Ian was feeling considerably cheerier.

"This is quite an establishment," he said, gazing at the handsome curved bar with its brass footrails. The rumble of balls from the skittles lane down the hall punctuated their conversation like distant thunder.

"Have you never been here, then?"

"Once, long ago, with my father."

Doyle stared silently into his whisky glass.

"Is it true Mary, Queen of Scots played skittles here?" said Ian.

"That's what they say."

His companion's mood seemed to have suddenly darkened. Since Doyle had gone out of his way to be kind to him, Ian felt an obligation to cheer the man up.

"Fancy a game, then?"

"Oh, I don't know," Doyle replied, fingering his glass and heaving a sigh. "It's been a long week."

The silence between them was so thick Ian could hear snatches of conversation all around.

"Wonder wha's got intae wee Bobby?"

"Damned if I'd treat a son a mine like that, I kin tell you."

"There's aught but one way ta properly leaven bread, if y'ask me."

"Ach, ye don' shoe a dray same as ye'd shoe a racehorse, now, do ye?"

He turned to Doyle and cleared his throat. "Anything the matter?"

His companion gave a wry smile and shook himself, as a dog might shake water from its coat. "Sorry, old man, didn't mean to go all glum on you. How about that game of skittles, then?"

Swallowing his curiosity, Ian rose from his chair. "Right."

"I should warn you, I'm a keen cricket player."

"I expect you'll have the best of me, then, since my only sports are football and rugby. And a bit of wrestling."

"You don't golf?"

"Not really."

"We shall have to teach you, then."

The skittles court was located at the other end of a low, twisting corridor at the back of the pub, two lanes separated by a raised center trough with half a dozen wooden balls. A group of patrons was just finishing a game as Ian and Doyle carried their drinks to the alley, so they had the court to themselves.

"I did play skittles once or twice a long time ago," Ian said, "but I've forgotten how."

That was not entirely a lie, but it wasn't exactly the truth, either. In spite of his modesty, Conan Doyle was obviously a competitive sportsman. If Ian didn't pose any real competition, that might allow him to observe Doyle more closely. On the other hand, maybe Doyle was the kind who only respected other men of skill and accomplishment. Ian knew the type but wasn't sure if his companion was one of them.

"Now then, you take the ball like this," Doyle said, lifting one of the shiny wooden balls from its rack and holding it aloft in his powerful hands. "Then you sort of heave it, like so, between your legs." He bent over and demonstrated, sending the ball thundering down the polished wooden alley, where it knocked over half the pins before coming to rest against the brick backboard. "At least, that's how most people play. But some of us chaps prefer to play like this," he said, selecting another ball. Wrapping his strong fingers around it, he lifted it with one hand. Swinging it behind his body like a discus thrower, he hurled it at the remaining pins. The ball hit the alley hard, bouncing twice before slamming into the pins, scattering them every which way. Doyle smiled at Ian in an unsuccessful attempt to appear humble—he clearly enjoyed displaying his athletic prowess.

"Well done," Ian said.

"I was lucky," Doyle said, resetting the pins. "Go on, then, give it a go."

Ian grasped the ball in both hands—though a tall man, he was not as big-boned as Doyle. Swinging it to the side, he heaved it toward the pins as hard as he could. The ball spun and spiraled to the left, knocking down less than half the pins before scudding into the alley.

"Not bad for a first try," Doyle said, handing him a second ball. "Here, have another go."

His attempt to correct the left-sided spiral caused Ian's second ball to skid to the right, bringing down two more pins on the other side, leaving the middle three still standing.

"Well done," Doyle said. "You've got the makings of a first-rate skittles player."

Ian smiled. "Very kind of you to say so. As someone recently said to me, you should have been a politician."

Doyle threw back his head and gave a full-throated roar of laughter. Once again Ian was struck by the man's easygoing vitality and good humor.

As there were people waiting to play, they did one more ball each. Doyle nearly knocked down all the pins again, only leaving two standing, which he mowed down with a second ball. Ian did a bit better as well, clearing all the pins with his second ball.

"Let's have another round," Doyle said, sweeping up their glasses. "I'm buying."

"It's my turn," Ian protested, but Doyle shook him off.

"Nonsense; this is a treat for me. I'm rather keen on crime, you see. Wait—that came out wrong. What I meant is that it's not every day I get to drink with a member of the Edinburgh City Police, let alone a famous and celebrated detective."

"I'm afraid you've mistaken me for someone else."

Doyle signaled the barmaid as they slid into a seat in the corner booth. "My mother always said false modesty is as bad as bragging—and she was Irish, so she knew a little about bravado."

Ian took the seat across from him. "I'm neither famous nor cele—"

"Celibate? Is that what you were going to say?"

Ian smiled ruefully. "That I am, alas."

"Chin up, old man—no point in moping about."

"My aunt thinks I should pay more attention to women."

"And no doubt I should pay less," his companion replied, eyeing the comely barmaid as she brought them two snifters of scotch. Ian noticed she returned Doyle's smile. "Here's to the fairer sex," Doyle said, lifting his glass.

They clinked glasses, and Ian took a sip, letting the aromatic fire slide down his throat.

"Sounds like you really took on Dr. Bell today," said Doyle. "I must say, I was impressed—most chaps at the school are scared stiff of him."

"I'm not a medical student relying on him for a passing grade."

"What did you argue about, if you don't mind my asking?"

"He refused to do a toxicology screen on her blood."

"But why?"

"He concluded she drowned, and believes it was suicide. He doesn't welcome a second opinion from a *policeman*." Ian pronounced the word with disdain, imitating Bell.

"I'll test her blood for you."

"Aren't you afraid of incurring his wrath?"

Doyle shrugged. "I see no reason he needs to know."

Ian smiled. "You are more devious than I would have thought."

Doyle leaned forward, his broad face earnest. "Do you really believe that poor woman was murdered?"

"Does it not strike you as odd that her client is poisoned, then two days later she is found drowned?"

Doyle swirled the whisky in his glass, watching the golden liquid catch the firelight. "Wouldn't it be reasonable to assume that she poisoned him, then killed herself out of remorse?"

"Ah, but she didn't poison him."

"Are you certain?"

"There is no indication she had possession of strychnine at any time—nor any motive to commit the crime. By all accounts, he was kind and generous to her."

"Who, then? Did the same person who poisoned him also do away with her, and if so, why?"

"I think she was killed to prevent her from telling us what she knew."

"Which was—?"

"I don't know. Perhaps nothing. Maybe she was killed for the thrill of it."

"That's monstrous, Hamilton."

"I believe there exists a type of person the rest of us can neither perceive nor completely understand the way we understand the motives of ordinary criminals, say, pickpockets or thieves—or even your run-of-the-mill murderer."

"Surely there's nothing run of the mill about murder?"

"But the usual *reasons* people kill are quite mundane—jealousy, greed, and so on."

Doyle frowned. "I'm afraid I don't take your point."

"If such a person exists, then may not his or her motives lie outside what you or I might recognize as normal human behavior?"

"Such as?"

"What if the gain is not material—getting a rich relative out of the way or punishing a cheating husband—but rather, *the act of killing itself?*"

Doyle downed the last of his whisky. "That calls into question the whole of human nature, doesn't it? That such a creature could evolve within our species." He shuddered and pulled himself to his feet. "Sorry to be a soggy blanket, but I must get some studying done, and then I've got to help Dr. Bell prepare for tomorrow's lecture."

"Not at all," said Ian. "I appreciate you bringing me here."

"Must do it again sometime, eh?" Doyle said, affixing his hat at a jaunty angle. "Care to share a cab?"

"Why not?"

The two men left the pub together, a bit less steady on their feet than when they'd arrived, but in considerably better spirits. They stepped into the darkening streets, and the city closed around them like a fist.

CHAPTER
THIRTY-SIX

She sat at her window watching the gaslights flicker on all over Edinburgh. It was her favorite time of day, when the leeries came out to light the streetlamps, emerging from the shadows in their long coats and tall black hats, flitting from one lamp to the next, like bees pollinating the city with light. She craned her neck to see the leerie approach the lamp in front of her building. Long Jamie, they called him—tall and thin as the rod he carried to flare the wicks into brightness, a Prometheus bringing fire to comfort a lost and confused mankind. She watched as he raised his instrument skyward, held her breath as the light flared from pale blue to yellow.

Light from the flame illuminated his face, and she saw the disfigurement on the left side, where it was twisted and caved in. When she'd asked her neighbors what had happened to him, they said his father had done it, and the thought filled her with a fiery rage. Such power parents had over their children—and didn't she know it all too well, her father being the monster he was. She hadn't fully realized it at the time, of course—she was too young and confused—but later, that was the word she always thought of in connection with him: "monster."

And poor Long Jamie, with his mangled face, slinking around in the shadows, darkness hiding his shame from the gaze of a curious public. Fury roiled in her stomach, hot and bitter and implacable. It drove her, as it had on that night so many years ago.

It had been easy, actually—far easier than she'd expected. The idea had occurred to her when her mother sent her to fetch a tin from the pantry, and she saw the box at the back of the shelf. "Rat Poison," it said, and she remembered thinking if it worked on rats, why not a person? She dipped her finger into the white powder and put the tiniest amount on her tongue. It tasted sweet, with a little bitterness around the edges, but it wasn't unpleasant. It would be easy to add it to food without anyone noticing—oatmeal, for example, with plenty of sugar.

She had just turned twelve, and the thought took up residence in her brain, staying with her night and day. It was the last thing she thought before falling asleep, and her first thought upon waking each morning. She turned it over in her head, looking at it this way and that. Could it really work? Would she get away with it? And if not, would it matter all that much? She came to the conclusion it wouldn't be so bad to go to prison for life—after all, she was in prison now, even if she was the only one who knew it.

And so, one cold winter morning, she tiptoed into the pantry before anyone was awake, pulled the box down from the shelf, and made the oatmeal, just as she did every morning. Except that the bowl she served him was sprinkled with a liberal amount of the white powder, with plenty of sugar to conceal the bitter taste. She could hardly breathe as she set the bowl in front of him, her head spinning with fear and dread. What if he realized what she had done? But he didn't seem to notice, gobbling it down as he always did between gulps of strong coffee.

At first she was afraid she hadn't put enough in—he seemed all right, tossing his napkin on the table before pushing his chair away with a grunt. She held her breath as he suddenly stumbled and clutched his stomach with a groan, sweat pouring from his face. Her mother bent over him, clucking and cooing as she escorted him to bed, where he remained for the rest of the day and into the night. Her heart leapt as she heard his piteous moaning, followed by the sound of retching, as her worried mother scurried up and down the stairs with clean towels and warm basins of water. He lingered for days, attended by her mother as well as her aunt, his only sister.

By the time they fetched the doctor, it was too late, and when she visited him on the third night, lying next to his body, she could feel he was already beginning to go cold.

What surprised her was not the relief she felt—she had expected that—but she didn't anticipate the intense sexual pleasure, not only at the time but whenever she thought about it afterward. It was as if she had somehow managed to take back something that had been stolen from her. The shame she felt was still there, but now she had another, secret thrill, and she craved the feeling of power and mastery it gave her. For a while she experimented by poisoning the neighbor's cats, but it failed to give her the same satisfaction. Eventually she realized that only the real thing would do, and she resolved to become a nurse, and a punisher of wicked men.

She pulled the lace handkerchief from her pocket, her initials monogrammed on it in delicate gold thread. Unwrapping it carefully to reveal the string of black pearls inside, she held them up to the light, peering into their inky depths. Margaret was dead now, and would have no further need of the pearls—but she would make good use of them.

She sighed as she wrapped them up in the handkerchief again. Luckily for her, Margaret had forgotten to mention the handkerchief to the police—unlucky for Margaret, of course. It was easy enough to steal it back, but then Margaret said she had seen it, and if she told them about the monogram, it could ruin everything. Damn Geoffrey, stuffing it into his pocket as he left her to go see his whore—the man was a machine, insatiable and intractable. Margaret had said he was kind to her, but she had seen another side of him. Around men like Geoffrey Pritchett, no woman was truly safe.

So Margaret had to die, alas. She took no pleasure in it, cushioning the blow—she had learned from Kate that Big Margaret was especially fond of gin. She didn't dare do the deed at the brothel, since she was known there, so she'd tracked Margaret down to the river, where she'd offered to share her flask. After imbibing gin laced with a liberal amount of laudanum, poor Margaret was an easy target; she'd hardly struggled.

She gazed out the window as Long Jamie ambled down the street, his back to her, singing an air she recognized.

> Her voice is low and sweet,
>
> And she's a' the world to me,
>
> And for bonnie Annie Laurie
>
> I'd lay me doon and dee.

She never expected to be the world to anyone, and doubted anyone would ever write a song about her, but as for men laying themselves down to die—well, she thought with a smile, that was another thing entirely.

CHAPTER
THIRTY-SEVEN

"That was a splendid roast," Ian said, laying his napkin next to his empty plate. It was Sunday evening, and he was dining with Aunt Lillian as usual. He had come straight from the Sheep Heid to her flat after dropping Doyle off at his rooms near the university. In spite of having eaten at the pub some three hours earlier, he enjoyed his aunt's roast with good appetite.

"I'm glad to see you eating so heartily," Lillian replied. "No woman wants to marry a scarecrow."

Ian smiled. "So now I'm a scarecrow?"

"You're looking a wee bit better of late."

"Thanks to your repeated attempts to stuff me like a partridge."

"I've made chocolate cake for pudding," she said, clearing the dishes.

"Let me do that," he said, jumping up from his chair.

"Let's take our cake into the parlor," she suggested when he was done, settling herself in front of the fire in a way Ian knew meant business. She wasted no time getting to the point—donning her spectacles, she peered at him, her aged eyes keen as ever.

"Your brother tells me you've met someone."

"I meet quite a lot of people," he replied, if only to elicit the expected response.

His aunt did not disappoint—Lillian was nothing if not predictable. She rolled her eyes in the same overly dramatic way his mother used to. "I am referring to a young *lady*."

"Young she certainly is, though I doubt she merits the term 'lady.' I suspect she would be the first to agree with me."

Lillian wrinkled her nose. "Then what precisely *is* she, may I ask?"

"I suspect she's a suffragist, perhaps even an anarchist. As for what I know, she is a nurse."

"A noble occupation. What's her name?"

"Fiona Stuart."

"I can't say it rings a bell."

"But really, there is nothing romantic between us; I merely rescued her from some ruffians."

"Why, that is the very essence of romance!" Lillian cried.

Color flared on her papery cheeks, and her eyes sparkled behind the square spectacles. Caught in the glow of firelight, she looked half her age—and for a moment, Ian saw what Uncle Alfred must have seen so many years ago when courting his young bride-to-be.

"She was less than enthusiastic about my intervention," he said gloomily, hoping to temper her zeal.

"Shame on her! She should have swooned—or at least pretended to."

Ian smiled. "I'm afraid that kind of pretense is foreign to her nature."

"You must bring her to meet me," Lillian declared. "I shall make up my own mind about her."

"But I—"

"Until then, we'll speak no more of it."

"But, Auntie—"

"We'll speak nae mere!" Lillian repeated, and Ian saw there was no point in arguing. He knew from long experience when her Glaswegian accent emerged, it was time to retreat from the field.

"How's your brother getting on?" she said, changing the topic.

"Well enough, I suppose." He hoped to avoid mentioning their falling out earlier in the day.

"Staying away from the bottle, is he?"

"I believe so."

"Bring him along next week, if he's not too busy. Oh, goodness, look at the time," she said as the grandfather clock struck eight. "I must leave straightaway."

"Where are you going?" he asked, stacking the dishes on an enameled tray with a Japanese floral design, so fashionable these days.

"Madame Laroue was unable to hold her séance on Friday this week, so it is tonight instead."

Ian frowned as he carried the tray to the kitchen. "You don't really believe in all that nonsense?"

"Ach, what's it to ye?" Lillian called after him. Her accent thickened like pudding when she was irritated.

"I don't like to think of you throwing away money on that fraud," he said, coming back out to the hall, where she was busily preparing to go out.

"Do I tell you how to spend your money?" she said, pulling on her gloves.

"No, but—"

"Must ye natter on at me about this?"

"It's just that—"

Lillian threw her arms up. "I'm going to the séance, and there's an end to it! Now make yourself useful and fetch me my tartan scarf."

Ian shook his head but obeyed his aunt's command. The scarf was dutifully procured from the coatrack and wrapped snugly around her neck.

"Ach, ye needn't smother me," she said as Ian tucked it into her collar.

"There's a cold wind blowing in from the sea."

Lillian snorted. "It'll take more than a wee breeze to weaken my bones."

"I don't want to be blamed if you catch a chill."

She took his face in her strong, bony hands and kissed him on both cheeks. "When have I ere blamed ye for anythin'?"

Their eyes met, and the night of his parents' death flitted between them like a shadow, a thin, sad presence in the room. Ian pulled away from his aunt and straightened his shoulders, as if to cast off the reminder of what they had lost.

"Off you go, then," he said. "I'll tidy up."

"That's more like it. I'll make a proper man out of you yet."

Ian smiled. He knew Lillian's desperation for him to find a wife was the product of her own happy married life. Her attendance at the séances was mainly about contacting her beloved Alfred.

He finished washing the dishes and went into the parlor to check the fireplace screen. Though there were only glowing embers in the grate, his caution about fire was reflexive. After securing the metal screen, he was about to leave the room when an envelope protruding from the mahogany writing desk caught his eye. He walked over to push it back into place, but his toe caught on the Persian carpet, causing him to lose his balance. As he gripped the desk to steady himself, his hand brushed against the letter, and it fell to the ground.

He stooped to pick it up and recognized the handwriting immediately—it was his mother's. He felt a cold, hollow panic rise in his chest as he examined the envelope. It was unsealed, and read simply, *To Lillian*. Why, years after her death, was Lillian reading this letter from her sister? The question needled him as he reached out to return it to the desk. But his hand would not obey, and he stood motionless, his conscience warring with his curiosity.

He took a deep, ragged breath in an attempt to clear his head. To read the letter would be a betrayal of his aunt's trust, an invasion of her privacy. Perhaps worse, he would be keeping secrets from her, something he had never done. But what if she was keeping a secret from him? True, the letter was addressed to her—but his mother was dead now, and did that not mean her correspondence should be public to other family members?

He knew this justification was pathetic, but his curiosity was too great to resist. There was no rationalizing his actions as honorable—*virtue be damned,* he thought grimly as he slid the letter from the envelope. The blue ink looked so fresh upon the page, the writing so firm and resolute, he could scarcely believe the hand that writ it was now a pile of bones buried deep in Greyfriars Kirkyard.

Standing in the dimming firelight of his aunt's parlor, he read his mother's words.

> *Dearest Lillian, Sister and Friend (for so you have always been to me),*
>
> *If this letter finds its way to you, it means I am dead. I pray that is not for many years yet, but recent events have caused me to fear for my life in a way that makes me hasten to write this before it is too late.*

Ian's vision dimmed, and his legs turned to water as he read those lines. He clutched the arm of the chair nearest him and sank into it, barely aware of his surroundings.

> *There is so much I have not yet told even you, dearest sister—do not think ill of me if I have sought to protect the image of those who are undeserving. But if something happens, do not think it*

an accident but rather something much darker. If you have the stomach and the will, I beg you to consider pursuing the course of justice, if possible.

I dare not say more—indeed, I must hasten to put this in a safe place. I will endeavor to write a second letter soon, but I am pressed for time at the moment.

With deepest love and gratitude,

Emily

Ian let the letter fall from his hand and stared into the dying embers of the fire. His heart pounded with conflicting thoughts and emotions. The room no longer held any comfort—the long-familiar surroundings were drained of meaning, and his forehead burned with confusion. Who—or what—did his mother fear? Was it merely a coincidence, or did this letter predict the fire that killed his parents? If so, a very great crime had been committed, one that no one was able to prevent. The letter was undated, and there was no post office stamp, so presumably it had been delivered by hand.

A quote from *Hamlet* popped into his head.

One may smile, and smile, and be a villain.

What smiling villain was his mother protecting, and why? And why did he know nothing of this until now? Ian blamed everyone—the police, his mother and father, Lillian, Donald, but most of all, he blamed himself. He had an impulse to crumple the page and hurl it into the fire, but he folded it carefully and slid it back into the envelope. Replacing it on the desk, he pulled on his coat and slipped out into the night, locking the door behind him.

He arrived at his flat to find his brother asleep, snoring heavily. Ian longed to wake him, but he knew Donald had an early-morning lecture the next day. They had not seen each other since the incident outside the lecture hall, and Ian did not imagine a friendly reception if he roused Donald from a sound sleep at this hour. He tiptoed to the parlor and sat staring at the glowing embers of his own fire. He barely noticed when Bacchus slinked into the room and jumped onto his lap, purring. He stroked the cat absently, trying to make sense of what he had read. How could he broach the subject with Lillian without admitting that he had read a letter not intended for him? And why had she never mentioned it? What else was she keeping from him? Something was rotten in the city of Edinburgh, and he feared the source of decay was closer to home than he knew.

He was still in the chair, the cat on his lap, when the sun peeked through the front curtains. His brother saw him on the way to the kitchen to make breakfast, and thought perhaps to wake him, but decided against it.

CHAPTER
THIRTY-EIGHT

Ian arrived at the station house Monday morning to find the air thick with tension. Before he had hung up his cloak, Sergeant Dickerson crept over to him.

"DCI Crawford wants to see you, sir," he said nervously.

A couple of other policemen averted their eyes as Ian headed for Crawford's office. His knock upon the door was met with a growl.

"You wanted to see me, sir?"

Crawford regarded him as if he were an inferior species, perhaps a beetle or a snail.

"Detective Hamilton," Crawford said quietly, "you *are* aware that Dr. Bell often consults with us on investigations?"

"Yes, sir."

"And that he appears in court as an expert witness in criminal cases?" he continued in an ominously soft voice.

"Yes, I am."

"Then perhaps you can explain why you saw fit to antagonize him to the point where he sent me a curt message to that effect?"

"He rubbed me the wrong way."

Crawford's small blue eyes shot wide open with astonishment. "He *what*?"

"He was arrogant and dismissive."

"Good Lord, Hamilton, you can't be serious?"

"He refused to entertain the notion Margaret was murdered, preferring to assume she took her own life, simply because she was a fallen woman."

DCI Crawford looked as if he were about to burst at the seams like an overstuffed haggis. His flushed cheeks puffed, his eyes seemed about to pop out of their sockets, and his jaw hung open.

"You—are—the—most—bloody-minded," he said, wringing the words out one by one, "the—most—conceited—person—I have—ever—"

His tirade was interrupted by a knock on the door.

"What *is* it?" he bellowed.

"Sergeant Dickerson, sir."

"Don't just stand there—come in!"

The door opened a few inches, and the sergeant's face appeared in the crack.

"Yes?" said Crawford.

"There's, er, someone t'see Detective Hamilton."

"Tell them to wait."

"Yes, sir," Dickerson replied, closing the door quickly.

Ian turned back to DCI Crawford and was surprised to see the expression on his face had transformed. He looked positively grief-stricken. As soon as he saw Hamilton staring at him, he turned his back to gaze out the window.

"What is it, sir?" Ian asked.

"Never mind," Crawford replied gruffly. "Go attend to your visitor."

"Oh, sir," Ian said, hit by a sudden realization. "I just remembered. My brother was going to ask Dr. Bell about your wife. I am sorry. I didn't think—"

"That's your problem, Hamilton—you don't *think*. You just pursue what's in front of your nose, and if it's to do with a case, well and good, but God help us if other people's lives get in the way."

"I truly am sorry, sir."

"It makes you a good detective, I suppose, but not much of a man sometimes."

Ian's ears burned with shame. The chief was right—it *was* bloody-minded of him to react to Bell like that. Maybe the renowned doctor deserved it, but that was no excuse.

"I'll apologize to him, sir."

"Just leave it. Don't cause any more trouble than you have already."

"Yes, sir."

"Get along with you," said Crawford without turning around. "You've someone waiting out there."

"Thank you, sir," Ian said. Leaving the office, he felt a coward and a fool. When he emerged into the main room, there was no sign of Sergeant Dickerson. Fiona Stuart stood in the middle of the room, hand on one hip, lips curled in an expression somewhere between a smile and a challenge. She was smartly dressed in a pale-green riding habit with black trim, which set off her dark-red hair exquisitely.

"I have a message for you," she said, removing her tall black hat, which he noted was carefully brushed.

"Yes?"

"Arthur Doyle said to tell you there was a large amount of laudanum in Margaret's blood."

"Indeed?" Ian said coolly, trying to conceal his excitement. "Did he say anything else?"

"Only that if you care to discuss it more, he would be happy to meet with you."

"And how did you come by this knowledge?"

"I occasionally serve as Dr. Bell's scrub nurse. Arthur and I are well acquainted."

"It would seem there's no end to your abilities."

She examined the buttons on her riding jacket, then fixed him with a steady gaze. "Well? Are you going to offer me tea?"

He stared back at her. "I cannot help wondering if you manage to irritate everyone you meet?"

She frowned. "I merely asked for some tea."

He tried not to look at the dimple on her chin, which appeared whenever she frowned—or smiled. "Lacking evidence to the contrary, I must conclude your ability to exasperate people is universal."

She rolled her eyes—which were very round, and rimmed with dark-red lashes. "Why is it that women are expected to be meek and retiring, and never ask for anything?"

"I believe there is a way of asking for things without implying the person you are addressing is an idiot."

"I certainly did not mean to imply—"

"Never mind, Miss—"

"Stuart. I should think a police officer would have a better memory for names."

Ian turned away, permitting himself a little smile. He had not forgotten her name this time; he simply wished to annoy her. He was not in the habit of insulting young ladies, but she had it coming.

"So this is where you work?" she asked dubiously, surveying the room.

"That would be a fair assumption."

"What do you do beside catch criminals and rescue people who don't need rescuing?"

"Believe it or not, there is quite a lot of paperwork."

"It is the same in medical care," she replied with the first hint of sympathy he had heard. "If only we could devote all our time to care of our patients, we would be able to do so much more for them. Meetings are even worse—someone should outlaw committee meetings."

"My aunt says the same thing about her Amateur Photography Society."

"She is a photographer?"

"And an artist," he said, feeling an urge to brag.

"Your aunt sounds like an extraordinary woman."

"She is, though I wish she would stop going to those wretched séances." He instantly regretted his remark, as Fiona Stuart pounced on it, like a cat on a mouse.

"She attends séances? Whatever for?"

"She believes the medium is in contact with her departed husband. Such silliness is unworthy of her."

"It probably gives her life a sense of purpose."

"It is mere delusion."

"Delusion or not, who does it harm? Can you not understand how she feels?"

It was indeed hard to imagine the absence of such a person as Uncle Alfred—his large, shiny face and ruddy cheeks ablaze with goodwill and liberal amounts of gin. Such a solid physical presence, so keen a mind and energetic a personality—how was it possible for such a man to all at once be there no more? Ian did indeed understand how his aunt felt.

But he was not about to confess this to Fiona Stuart. "Superstition will be the ruin of mankind," he remarked darkly.

She burst into peals of laughter. "Will it, now? And what of our thirst for blood—our willingness to slaughter one another cheerfully as one might fry eggs for breakfast?"

"Many a war has been fought over religious differences."

"Oh, is it all religion you're calling superstition now?"

He took a deep breath before responding. "Yes."

She laughed again. "Aren't you a deep one, then?" He was about to protest that she was shallow for saying so, but she shook her copper curls, distracting him from everything but the way the sunlight glanced off the shiny surface of her hair. "Besides, religion is just an excuse."

"For what?"

"For our desire to slash and hack at one another. It's in our bones, I say, and any excuse will do. Religion, land, women—"

"Women?"

She pursed her lips and cocked her head to one side. "If we're to believe our Greek history, a whole war was fought over one lass. Do you really believe Helen of Troy was so much more comely than any other woman of that time?"

"No, but—"

"So there you have it—another excuse to fight a great bloody war."

"You seem to have an opinion on everything."

"Only things worth having an opinion on."

"You know," he said, "if everyone conversed like you, there would be no wars, because your opponents would be too exhausted."

For an instant her face darkened, then she burst into the strange chortle he found both irritating and compelling.

"Do you really find me so disagreeable, Detective Hamilton?"

"In my experience, women only ask a question like that if they are sure of their own attractiveness."

She reddened, but her voice was steady as her gaze. "You cannot deny you have been cold to me from the start. Is it too much to ask why?"

"Perhaps I am not accustomed to being pursued so aggressively by young women."

"Oh, you are much mistaken," she replied hotly. "I am not pursuing you—I am merely interested in your profession."

He noted with satisfaction that she was a hopeless liar.

She placed the hat back on her head, fastening it with a long hatpin. "I must be off—I'm expected at the clinic. You needn't see me out," she added breezily, as if expecting him to protest.

"Very well," he said, enjoying her surprised look.

"Good day, then."

He watched her go, as did most of the other policemen in the station. Fiona Stuart might be irritating, but even Ian had to admit she was a fine-looking woman. He could only imagine what Aunt Lillian would have to say about that.

No sooner had Miss Stuart left than Derek McNair sauntered into the room.

"Mornin', Guv," he said, tipping his hat in an exaggerated gesture.

"What do you want?" said Ian.

"Nothin', but I got somethin' you want."

"What's that?"

"Information."

"What sort of information?"

"The crime-solvin' type. What d'you think?" McNair said, eyeing the stack of breakfast pastries on the tea cart.

"Would you like a pastry?"

"If they're goin' to waste," he said offhandedly as Sergeant Dickerson approached his desk.

"Sergeant, would you please fetch Mr. McNair *one* pastry?"

Dickerson frowned. "Why do I have to—"

"Otherwise, he's liable to eat them all."

The sergeant sighed. "Yes, sir." As he shuffled toward the tea station, Ian thought he looked as if he could do with fewer pastries himself.

"Now then, what did you want to tell me?" he asked Derek.

"Kate says somethin' is missin' from Margaret's room."

"What is it?"

"Ye'd have t'ask her," he said, licking his lips as Dickerson handed him an almond tart.

"Is she there now?"

"She were when I left," he answered through a mouthful of tart, crumbs tumbling down his shirt.

Ian sprang up and grabbed his cloak from the rack. "Sergeant, you're with me."

"Right, sir," Dickerson said, following him.

"Oiy!" Derek called after them. "What about another pastry?"

"I'll buy you a whole box if this leads to an arrest," Ian called back. "Come along, Sergeant, there's no time to waste!"

CHAPTER
THIRTY-NINE

Sergeant Dickerson cursed under his breath as he followed Detective Hamilton along the damp, uneven cobblestones. Why couldn't the man ever take a bloody cab, for Christ's sake? At this pace, someone was liable to fall and break a leg, and with his luck, it would be him, making him look even more foolish in the detective's eyes. Sidestepping a pile of horse manure, he berated himself for not being fit, and cursed Hamilton for being so bloody fleet of foot, as they wove in between wagons of dry goods and carts piled high with cabbages and potatoes. Most of all, he hated himself for being so hungry for Hamilton's approval. Passing a blacksmith shop, Dickerson winced at the clank of a steel hammer upon the anvil, sparks shooting like thin red missiles into the air.

Kate threw open the door almost immediately in response to Ian's knock.

"I didn' expect ye so soon, but I'm glad, so I am." She wore a crimson frock that had seen better days. A sad red flower drooped in the midst of her cleavage, as if exhausted by the onslaught of flesh. Dickerson tried not to stare at it.

Hamilton closed the door behind them. "Derek McNair said you discovered—"

"Yes, yes—come wi'me, would ye?"

She took them upstairs, and as they passed a front bedroom, the sergeant heard the sound of a man grunting, interspersed with the occasional, "Oh, lovely, my dear, that's the way I like it—oh, yes!" He was struck by how similar the man's grunts were to the sounds made by a pig, and tried to shake the unpleasant image from his mind.

Kate appeared unaware of her customer's elucidations, talking rapidly as she opened the door to Margaret's room. "I was tidyin' up this mornin', puttin' her things in order, like, and everthin' seemed to be there except—"

The groans from the other bedroom increased in volume. Rolling her eyes, she poked her head out the door and called down the hall.

"Oiy—keep it down, will ye? Sorry 'bout that," she said, closing the bedroom door behind her. "What was I sayin'? Oh, yeah, Margaret's necklace. Can't find it anywhere."

"What sort of necklace?" asked Hamilton.

"It was beautiful—black pearls, they were, an' not the fake kind, but real ones."

"How did she come by it?"

"Some gentleman gave it to her years ago—I think he fancied her, but he moved down to London shortly afterward. She musta fancied him as well, or she would ha' sold it by now."

"Where did she keep it?"

Kate opened the middle drawer of the simple pine dresser. "In here, tucked away in the back."

"Did the other girls know about it?"

"What, you thought one o' them stole it?"

"It's a possibility."

Kate crossed her arms, pressing her bosom even higher, until she could have rested her chin on it. "They know if I catch any o' them stealing, 'specially from each other, there's hell t'pay."

"Maybe she were wearin' it when she were killed," Sergeant Dickerson suggested. "The killer coulda stole it or it might have ended up in't river."

"That's one possibility," Ian said. "Black pearls, you say?"

"Shiny as the inside of an oyster, they were."

"You have been most helpful," Hamilton said, leaving the room and striding back down the hall.

"Will ye let me know if ye find it, then?" Kate said, trundling after him, with Dickerson bringing up the rear.

"I will send McNair around as soon as we learn anything."

"He's a good boy," she said with a motherly sigh.

"That's hardly how I would describe him."

As they approached the front bedroom, a short, pudgy man crept into the hall, closing the door behind him before straightening his cravat and smoothing down what was left of his thinning hair. The sergeant noted with disgust that the man did indeed resemble a pig, with his pink skin, stubby fingers, and pug nose. When he spied Dickerson's uniform, alarm crossed his porcine face, but Kate shooed him away.

"Go on—get along wi' ye!"

With a sheepish smile, he scurried down the stairs. Sergeant Dickerson wrinkled his nose. The man smelled of carnality and stale sweat, and it depressed him to think of the girl behind that door taking in customers like him day after day—stinking sailors, filthy rail men, drunken dockworkers, and lewd lorry drivers. His sister would never have to worry about money, he vowed as he followed Hamilton and Kate down the steps.

"D'ye think it's significant, then?" she asked, opening the front door for them.

"I'll know more when I make a call to a certain gentleman," Ian replied.

Dickerson didn't know what he meant, but sometimes the answers to his queries left him even more in the dark. Hamilton did enjoy a bit of showmanship, he thought as they emerged back out into Edinburgh's teeming, dirty streets.

They didn't have far to go. Heading west along Canongate, Hamilton turned up St. Mary's Street, off of which was a narrow, grimy alley called Gullan's Close. Dickerson recognized it as the home of the city's most notorious "resetters," those who dealt in stolen goods. Some of them ran semi-reputable pawnshops, but they were always open to deals on the side, taking a hefty percentage of whatever they managed to procure for the stolen goods. Edinburgh being full of burglars, thieves, and pickpockets, they were rarely short of customers.

They descended half a flight of narrow stairs to a dingy basement entryway. A crooked, crudely painted sign dangled precariously from a single nail over the door: "J. R. McAllister, Pawnbroker." Ian pushed the door open, causing the bell overhead to tinkle, announcing their arrival. Dickerson squeezed in behind him—there was barely space for one in the tiny, crowded room, stuffed with everything from sleds and baby carriages to stacks of china and glassware. Everything was covered with a layer of dust and soot; the air inside was stale and close. Opposite the door was a counter, also covered with objects; behind it was a doorway leading to another room, covered by a tattered flowered curtain.

At first there was no response to the bell, and Dickerson wondered if the proprietor was there at all. But after a few moments he heard a shuffling, followed by a scraping sound, coming from a back room, as if someone was moving furniture.

"Jes a minute!" came a voice from the bowels of the shop. "Be right wi' ye." Another scraping noise, then the sound of a cat meowing. "Git along wi' ye!" That exhortation was followed by what sounded like crates tumbling to the ground. "Damned infernal creature," the proprietor muttered as he appeared in the doorway, pushing aside the shabby curtain.

Dickerson recognized him immediately—minus the sunburn and floppy hat, he was the exact image of Angus McAllister, the farmer Ian had spared from paying a fine for reckless driving earlier that week. A fire plug of a man, he had the same bulky shoulders and thick neck as his brother, the same small blue eyes. His skin was several shades paler, and a half-hearted beard sprouted in wispy clumps from his chin, but otherwise, the two men were identical. His face fell when he saw them.

"Good afternoon, Mr. McAllister," said Ian.

His face drew into an unconvincing grin. "Why, g'afternoon, gentlemen! Wha' kin I do fer ye?" His Glaswegian accent was as thick as his brother's, with the same guttural vowels.

"We're trying to locate a necklace."

"Wha' sort a necklace?"

"Black pearls."

The startled look of recognition that flashed across McAllister's face betrayed him. He glanced away and cleared his throat. "Can't say it sounds familiar."

Ian smiled and leaned an elbow on the counter, which made Dickerson wince—no telling what sort of vermin had scurried over that grubby surface. "Come along, Mr. McAllister—we know you've seen the necklace. Why don't you save us both time by telling us what you know?"

Crossing his arms across his broad chest, McAllister shook his head and smiled as innocently as was possible for a man of his appearance. "I wish I could help ye, but I don' know aught 'bout a pearl necklace."

Ian leaned closer to him. "I'll tell you what, Mr. McAllister. You tell me about the necklace, and I won't arrest your brother."

His broad face broke into a scowl. "Wha's me brother got tae do wae it?"

"Oh, didn't he tell you?"

"Tell me wha'?"

Ian related the run-in with Constable Turnbull, making it sound more serious than it was, adding something about a near collision with a mother wheeling a baby in a pram. Sergeant Dickerson stared wide-eyed listening to the detective's embellishments.

"He mentioned a sick child, so I took pity on him and let him go with a warning," Ian concluded. "Perhaps I made a mistake."

"Was it young Micky?" the resetter asked earnestly. "He's of delicate constitution, an' like tae come doon wi' catarrh."

His concern for his nephew made Dickerson feel sorry for the man, but Hamilton was unrelenting.

"He didn't say which son had taken ill—perhaps he was lying?"

McAllister was visibly sweating now, though the room was cool. "Look," he said, "I don' say I seen the necklace, but—"

"It's not the necklace I'm after. I want a description of the person you got it from."

McAllister's eyes narrowed. "*If* I had seen such a thing, it was a lady wha' brought it me."

"Can you describe her?"

"Young. Pretty. Educated, like. Tall, red hair, light eyes—maybe green, maybe blue. I can't say fer certain."

"What else can you tell me about her?"

"She wa' dressed as a nurse."

"If you think of anything else, here's my card," Ian said, pressing it into the man's grimy hand.

McAllister stared at the card, then back at Ian. "An' me brother? He's—"

"No harm will come to your brother unless he breaks the law again."

He smiled, displaying a row of blackened teeth. "Right, then."

"I suppose the necklace is in other hands now?" said Ian.

"If someone were tae show up wi' an item like you describe, it wouldn't stay here fer long."

"And how much would it be worth?"

"To the person wha' brought it? Ten pounds would be a fair price."

Ian raised an eyebrow. "That much?"

"If the resetter were honest, yeah."

"Thank you for your assistance," Ian said, picking his way through the narrow passage to the door. "Oh, one more thing," he said, his hand on the doorknob. "If such a person as you describe appears in your shop again, you will let me know, won't you?"

"A' course," he replied earnestly.

"Good day, then."

Sergeant Dickerson looked at Detective Hamilton, afraid to ask if they were thinking the same thing. James McAllister's description of the perpetrator sounded very much like Fiona Stuart.

CHAPTER FORTY

Donald was waiting for Ian when he arrived home that night. He stood in the doorway of the foyer as Ian removed his hat and cloak, leaning against the door frame. The aroma of pea soup and bacon hung in the air.

"See here, I'm not very good at these things," Donald said. "But . . . I'm sorry."

Ian didn't answer, smoothing out the wrinkles on his cloak before hanging it on the rack.

Donald flung his hands up in exasperation. "Oh, come along, I *said* I was sorry! What more do you want?"

"It's been a long day," Ian replied. He was exhausted and wanted nothing more than to crawl into bed and forget everything. *To sleep, perchance to dream . . .* He craved oblivion as one might crave shelter in a storm. His life had felt like a long, ugly storm lately—if only he could bury himself in a snowbank until spring . . .

His brother followed him into the parlor, where the cat was perched on his favorite chair in front of the fire. Removing Bacchus, Ian sank wearily into the chair. The cat flicked his tail peevishly before jumping up onto his lap. Too tired to object, Ian let him stay. Purring loudly,

Bacchus circled several times before settling down, pressing his big head into Ian's stomach.

"So you're still angry at me?" Donald said from the doorway.

"Let's just drop it, shall we?"

"What, then?"

"Nothing," Ian murmured, stroking the cat absently as he stared into the flames of the fire. The crackle and sputter of damp wood punctuated the still air; the only other sound was the steady ticking of the grandfather clock in the corner. Donald must have wound it up—Ian hated the sound of ticking clocks. He only kept it because Lillian had given it to him after Uncle Alfred died.

Donald crossed to stand in front of him on the Persian rug, another gift from Lillian. "And they say *I'm* the moody one. What is it?"

Ian gazed at him, trying to decide whether to tell him. Finally he said, "I found something at Lillian's."

"What did you find?"

"A letter."

Donald lowered himself into the chair opposite his brother. "Go on."

"It was from our mother."

"What's so unusual about that?"

"She seemed to think she was in danger of some kind."

Donald leaned forward, the glow of firelight catching the side of his face. Though considerably heavier than Ian, he had the same sharp, clean profile. "From whom?"

"She doesn't say. She asks Lillian to pursue justice if anything should happen to her."

His brother leaned back in his chair and pressed his fingers together. "'Curiouser and curiouser.'"

"Our mother wasn't given to paranoid fantasies, was she?"

"Not especially, though in the last year or so she seemed . . . preoccupied."

"How do you know? You were at medical school most of the time."

Donald gave him a withering look. "I notice things. So do you—it is our gift, and our curse. Does Lillian know you read the letter?"

"No."

"You have to tell her."

"That I read something addressed to her?"

Donald lit a cigarette. "She'll sense something is bothering you—you're not very good at hiding things, you know."

"Why didn't she tell me about it? How long has it been in her possession?"

"I couldn't say."

"Why is she hiding it from us?"

Donald inhaled deeply and released the smoke slowly, in a long, thin stream.

Ian frowned. "I wish you wouldn't—"

"Leave me my one remaining vice, Brother, or you shall certainly have a raving lunatic on your hands."

Ian leaned forward, and the cat murmured a protest before settling back on his lap. "You know something, don't you?"

"It's all in the past."

"If you had seen the letter, you wouldn't think so."

Donald rose and walked to the fireplace, hands behind his back. Ian recognized the posture as one he adopted when struggling with an unusually difficult problem. He rested one hand on the mantel and turned to face his brother.

"Do you know why our parents left the Highlands to move to Edinburgh?"

"Because there was more money to be made in—"

Donald shook his head. "That's just what they told us at the time."

"Why, then?"

"Our mother had taken a lover in Pitlochry."

Ian felt the air go out of his chest. "*What?* Why have you never told me this?"

"Because it didn't seem to matter anymore."

"'Frailty, thy name is woman,'" Ian muttered.

"Well, as long as you can spew out Shakespeare, everything is all right, I suppose," Donald said, flicking what remained of his cigarette into the fire.

"Give me a more appropriate response, and I'll be glad to oblige. What else are you and Lillian hiding from me?"

"I knew nothing of the letter, I swear. Where did you find it?"

"It was on the edge of her desk."

"That would indicate she had recently been reading it."

"But why would anyone read a letter written over seven years ago?"

"Why, indeed?" Donald said, fishing another cigarette out of a silver case. Catching Ian's look, he slid it back in with a sigh. "And would it have any relation to the fire that took both their lives?"

"The jealous lover returned from the Highlands to take his revenge, you mean?"

"Something like that, yes."

"So you never saw him?"

"Once, from a distance. Father and I had gone to town, and he spied a man across the street as we were coming out of a shop. I felt him go rigid, and I turned to see what he was looking at."

"How did you know it was—"

"I asked him what he was looking at, and he said, 'The man who is going to destroy our lives.' And then he pulled me back into the store. I didn't find out what he meant until years later, when Uncle Alfred told me why our parents had come to Edinburgh."

"So he told you and not me."

"You were younger, and also—"

"What?"

"Alfred and Lillian always tried to protect you from life's harsher truths. So did our parents, for that matter."

"But not you?"

Donald shrugged. "I was older, and perhaps they saw me as stronger, somehow." He looked at Ian sheepishly—or as close an approximation someone of his arrogance could manage. "Also, you never asked."

"And you did? Why?"

"I overheard Alfred and Lillian talking one night when they were looking after us. Our parents were out for the evening, and you were already asleep."

"You always did enjoy eavesdropping on people," Ian said, startled at how bitter he sounded.

"Interesting accusation from a detective."

"What did they say?"

"Nothing more than I've told you. She had a lover, gave him up, and they moved here to make a fresh start."

Ian gazed at the fire, wide awake now, trying to make sense of it all.

Donald lit another cigarette. "You certainly have given me plenty to think about."

"Think away," Ian said, rising abruptly from his chair.

Dislodged from his perch, Bacchus flicked his tail irritably, then walked stiff-legged toward the kitchen, no doubt hoping to entice Ian into feeding him.

"Turning in?" Donald said.

"Yes."

"Good night, then."

"Good night," Ian replied, heading for his bedroom.

His head was too muddled and full of confusing information to sort it out tonight. If he could coax himself into sleeping, he thought, he would face it all in the morning. But any fears he had about not being able to sleep were groundless—Morpheus pulled him almost immediately into a deep, dream-laden slumber. He found himself wandering an unfamiliar landscape, a rocky, barren heath with a tall, gloomy castle looming in the background, its gray stones silent as the grave. It was not like the Highlands of his childhood, yet somehow he knew it was. He also realized he was dreaming, in that strange state between wakefulness and sleep.

The ground was covered by a thin mist; he could not see his feet as he walked across the spongy soil, damp from a recent rain. The mist rose in thin gray fingers, clinging to his legs, wrapping wispy tendrils around his body. Looking down, he realized he was clad in medieval attire, a short tunic with leggings under long leather boots. A sword was strapped to his side.

As he approached a rocky outcropping, a thick swirl of mist gathered and spun, creating a whirlwind rising higher and higher into the air. As he watched in stunned amazement, the mist congealed into the translucent image of a man. The figure beckoned to him with a long, thin white finger, insubstantial as a flame.

Pulling his sword from its sheath, Ian brandished it in the air. Familiar words came from his mouth, as if by their own volition.

"'Where wilt thou lead me? Speak; I'll go no further.'"

He knew the lines were Shakespeare's and not his own, yet it felt entirely appropriate that he was speaking them. The apparition beckoned again, feathery tendrils of mist shooting into the air from its long, spidery appendages. Its hollow mouth opened in an attempt at speech, and when Ian heard the words, it was as though they came from his own head rather than the creature's mouth.

> *My hour is almost come,*
>
> *When I to sulphurous and tormenting flames*
>
> *Must render up myself.*

He realized with a shock the apparition was his father's ghost. He awoke, shivering, in his own bed, the cat curled at his side, a pale moon high in the sky. With the sound of his brother's rhythmic snoring in the next room, he lay awake for some time pondering the meaning of the dream. When sleep finally returned, the first cock had crowed, and an army of sleepy lamplighters ventured forth to extinguish their artificial flames as the sun peeked over the horizon at a dark and troubled land.

CHAPTER
FORTY-ONE

Vickie Caruthers sat in her shabby parlor, alarm stamped on her care-worn face. She was dressed in a plain gray frock, her belly even more distended than the last time Ian had seen her. The smell of boiled potatoes and pork sausage drifted in from the kitchen. It was a drab and lackluster Tuesday morning, and the sordid surroundings of Holy Land did nothing to ease Ian's depressed state of mind. Standing next to him, Sergeant Dickerson didn't look any more cheerful himself, fidgeting with his uniform buttons.

"You think he took somethin' a Tom's?" Vickie asked, frowning.

"He or she," said Ian. "We're not yet certain whether the killer is a man or a woman."

She shuddered. "Surely a woman wouldna—would she?" She gave Ian an imploring look, as if he held the key to human nature.

"I'm afraid so," he said gently. Mrs. Caruthers had an innocence that ignited his protective urges.

"So have y'noticed anythin' missing?" Dickerson asked.

"Such as what?"

"Anythin' valuable, fer example?"

She smiled sadly. "Tom didna' own anythin' valuable."

"A keepsake, then?" Ian suggested. "Something with sentimental value, perhaps?"

She frowned, concentrating. "Wait a minute—there was somethin'. Not really valuable, but unusual, y'know?"

"What was it?"

"A tiepin. Nothin' fancy, but I gave it t'him on our first anniversary."

"What did it look like?"

"It was a horse head, 'cause he used t'have a pony when he was a lad an' always liked horses." A sob welled up in her chest, but she swallowed it down, and her stoicism caused a lump to form in Ian's own throat.

"Can you describe it?"

"Nothin' special—made o' silver, wae a wee green jewel for the horse's eye; I'm sure it was only colored glass or some such thing."

"And it's missing?"

"I couldna find it when I looked th'other day but didn't gae it much thought. I'm sure ye can appreciate, I've other things on me mind."

"Of course," Ian said sympathetically, rising from his chair. "Thank you very much—you've been very helpful."

"D'ye think it'll help ketch Tom's killer, then?" she asked.

"It may very well," he replied, impulsively taking her hand. It was cold and dry, the palm rough and calloused. "We'll see ourselves out," he added as she began to struggle to her feet.

She sank back gratefully in the chair and nodded sadly. "I 'preciate all ye've done. Not many coppers what would care 'bout the likes o' Tom and me."

Rather than spring to the defense of the entire Edinburgh constabulary, Ian gave a little tip of his cap. She had a point, of course, but it was more complicated than that. No doubt the posh inhabitants of New Town received first-class treatment, but far more man-hours were spent on the drunken, dissolute, and disorderly denizens of places like Holy Land. It was a simple matter of numbers: most of Edinburgh's crimes were committed in Old Town, and the vast majority of criminals lived there. Like it or not, the average constable found himself banging on doors like hers more frequently than operating the burnished brass knockers of the polished Princes Street town houses with their matching masonry statues of lions.

"Oh, I meant t'tell ye," Vickie said, suddenly brightening. "The strangest thing happened—let's see, when was it?—yesterday, it was."

"What's that?" said Ian.

She opened the drawer of a small end table next to her—it was cheaply made but gaily painted in bright colors. "Tom found this table on the street, and painted it all nice for me," she said sadly as she closed the drawer. In her hand was a crumpled envelope. "I found this on the doormat jus' in the front hall," she said, handing it to Ian. "Someone musta slipped it under the door."

The envelope was unremarkable, the ordinary kind available at any stationery store. It was unmarked and unsealed, and inside were ten one-pound notes. He handed it to Sergeant Dickerson, who whistled softly. "That's the same—"

"*Yes*, Sergeant," Ian said sharply. Dickerson took the cue and was silent. "So you didn't see the person who left this?" he asked Mrs. Caruthers.

"I found it when I got up that mornin'," she said. "I'm an early riser, so it musta been left either late that night or before the sunrise. I'm usually awake by dawn. May I—may I keep it?"

"It was given to you, so it's yours," Ian said, handing it back to her.

"Thank you," she said meekly. "Who d'you think gave it t'me?"

"Maybe some kind soul heard 'bout your loss," Dickerson suggested.

"By why remain anonymous?" she asked.

"Some people wish to avoid publicity," said Ian.

"Well, if y'find out who left it, would ye let me know so I kin thank them?"

"I will," he lied. He already had a very good idea who was responsible, and had no intention of sharing that information with poor Vickie Caruthers, bereaved widow and mother-to-be.

He mumbled something about checking in on her later as he followed Sergeant Dickerson down the precarious flight of rickety stairs to the street. It occurred to Ian, not for the first time, that if Tom Caruthers had been another sort of man—the kind who didn't cheat on his wife, for example—he might still be alive. That sort of thinking was useless, of course, and it just made Ian angrier about his fellow man—what a pathetic lot of slobbish, unthinking idiots they all were. And that didn't exactly serve his job, which was to solve crimes, not sit in judgment of the entire human race.

His ruminations were interrupted by Sergeant Dickerson.

"Pardon, sir, but ten pounds were—"

"What Mr. McAllister claims to have paid for the necklace, if we are to believe him."

"So the killer pawns the necklace and gives the money to Mrs. Caruthers?"

"That is a reasonable conclusion."

"Why?"

"Perhaps out of some twisted notion of justice. Having robbed Vickie Caruthers of a husband, our killer decides to play God in a more benign way, as a way of atoning for her crimes."

"Her?"

"What?"

"You said 'her.'"

"So I did, Sergeant."

They stood in front of the dilapidated blocks of tenements comprising Happy Land and Holy Land, a blight on the city many called the Athens of the North. What paint once graced their wretched walls was peeling in patches; jagged shards of wood protruded from the stairs Ian and Dickerson had just descended. Even the surrounding cobblestones were unkempt, and the air smelled of soiled chamber pots and rotting cabbage. Somewhere deep inside, a baby cried inconsolably.

Ian shook himself, suddenly anxious to be far from the stink of so much misery.

"Where to now, sir?"

"Back to our friend in Gullan's Close," he said, turning his steps in that direction, the sergeant following after him like a faithful spaniel.

James McAllister was no gladder to see them than he had been the day before. Shuffling out of the back room, he sighed when he saw Ian and the sergeant standing at his cluttered front counter.

"Wha' is it now?" he said warily. "Somethin' else gone missin', then?"

"As a matter of fact, yes," Ian replied.

He described the tiepin, and McAllister dug his finger into his left ear as he listened. Ian glanced at Sergeant Dickerson, who looked horrified as McAllister wiped the tip of his finger on his shirt sleeve.

"Don't sound familiar," he said when Ian finished. "Who lost it, then?"

Ignoring the question, Ian leaned in closer. "The fact is, Mr. McAllister, we'd really appreciate any information you could dig up for us."

The resetter's eyes narrowed. "Ye want me ta check wi' me mates, is that it?"

"If you would be so kind."

"Wha's in it fer me?"

"Oh, now, Mr. McAllister, do I really need to spell it out? What's the usual sentence for resetters caught fencing stolen property these days?" he said, looking around the shop, letting his eyes wander over the objects stacked in piles in every corner of the room. When his gaze rested on a mahogany wall clock, McAllister visibly twitched. Ian turned to him calmly. "I'll wager that handsome clock has a story behind it, for example."

The pawnbroker glowered at him. "It'll take a coupla days tae hear from everyone."

"I shall leave you to it, then," Ian replied. "Oh, and might I assume that a necklace might be paid for in, say, ten one-pound notes?"

"That'd be a fair assumption, aye."

As they left the shop, a black cat darted in front of them before slinking back into the shadows and disappearing around the corner of a building. Sergeant Dickerson jumped backward involuntarily as the cat crossed his path. "Mother Mary o' God, saints preserve us," he muttered, wiping his brow.

"Steady on, Sergeant," Ian said, laying a hand on his arm. "It's just a superstition, you know."

"That's as may be, sir, but is there any harm in bein' careful, like?"

"No, I suppose not," Ian replied as they headed back toward the Canongate. Gullan's Close had a sour smell, like moldy laundry, and he couldn't wait to be clear of it.

"How did ye know Tom Caruthers' killer stole somethin' from 'im?"

"It was a hunch, based on the fact that Big Margaret was robbed, presumably around the time of her death."

"Further evidence it were the same person in both cases, y'think?"

"It seems increasingly likely."

"Y'know," Dickerson said, "I been thinkin' 'bout McAllister's description of the person who brought in t'necklace."

"Yes?" Ian said as they stopped to let a well-appointed carriage pass. It was drawn by a pair of gleaming black stallions, with two footmen dressed in crimson finery bringing up the rear. The horses trotted smartly along the Canongate, one of the succession of streets connecting Edinburgh Castle and Holyrood Palace. In Edinburgh, splendor and squalor lived cheek by jowl, sharing the same streets, the fetid air of Old Town detectable even amid the grandeur of the royal residences.

"Well," Dickerson continued, "it don' necessarily follow that the person wha' fenced the necklace were the killer."

"You mean he or she could have sent a confederate to the pawnshop?"

"Exactly. Maybe someone who weren't aware of the killin' at all, like."

"Excellent point, Sergeant. A poisoner like this one might take great pains to hide his or her identity."

And, he thought, that might mean the killer didn't so closely resemble Fiona Stuart.

CHAPTER
FORTY-TWO

"What do you say I come watch rehearsal tonight?" Ian suggested.

Back at the station house, the day shift was giving way to the evening shift as the sun slunk low over Castle Rock, hovering for a moment as if to do a final check on the city's inhabitants before sliding out of sight.

Dickerson looked at Ian apprehensively and shuffled his feet. "All right, then, sir—if y'ave the time, a' course."

"It is a sad state of affairs when one doesn't have time for the greatest play written in the English language."

"Yes, sir. Mind you, I'm not sayin' we do it justice, like."

"I don't want you to feel uncomfortable, or anything like that," Ian said, somewhat disingenuously. He knew very well his presence would make Dickerson nervous, but that couldn't be helped.

The sergeant gave a weak smile and donned his coat. "I'll be off, then, sir."

"See you in a bit," Ian called after him as Dickerson strode away in his peculiar wide-legged gait, his upper body lurching forward, as though it were in a hurry to get there before the rest of him. Dickerson walked like a man who had just wet himself, an observation Ian kept to himself, though he had on occasion heard the other officers snickering behind his back.

"There goes Wee Willie now," Constable Turnbull muttered under his breath as Dickerson passed, though whether it was a reference to Dickerson's gait, his stature, or something more personal, Ian didn't know. He glared at the constable, who winked and smiled at him without a hint of contrition. Turnbull was a master of ingratiating himself with his superiors while mocking anyone he saw as weaker. His air of bonhomie fooled some of the newer members of the force, but Ian had been onto him from the start. Consequently, of course, he loathed Ian.

Turnbull's response put Ian into a foul mood—he slammed the file folder onto his desk, causing everyone nearby to look at him, including Constable Turnbull.

"What are you staring at?" Ian snapped, and they all looked away, but he couldn't help noticing the sly smile on the corner of Turnbull's mouth.

Ian rebuked himself for giving the constable exactly what he wanted—this was not the first time the man had driven him into a temper. He took a deep breath and let it out slowly. Tucking the file folder under his arm, he threw his cloak over his shoulders and left the station house without looking back.

The Greyfriars Dramatic Society held its rehearsals in the main hall of the Masonic lodge on Blackfriars Street. The heavy stone plaque above the door, bordered by a brace of iron bells, informed anyone entering that it was lodge Number 8, and had been rebuilt in 1870, just ten years prior. Ian continued past the drafty foyer and down a long, narrow hall that opened out into the main meeting room. A few chairs were scattered around a raised stage with a red velvet curtain at the far end, and a dozen or so persons were deeply immersed in studying what looked to be scripts. Some moved their mouth as they read. There was no sign of Sergeant Dickerson.

Ian had no sooner entered the room than a thin, oddly dressed man with an elaborately waxed mustache rushed over to him. He wore a red silk kimono over black harem pants and slippers with gold tassels, like something out of *Arabian Nights*. As no one else in the room was in costume, Ian could only assume this was his regular dress.

"Look here," the man said. His speech was cultivated and rather affected—Ian couldn't quite place the accent. It unlike any he'd ever heard, a blend of a well-heeled Edinburgh accent and English upper-class speech, with a hint of a Southern American drawl. "You're Billy's friend, aren't you?"

Recalling that Sergeant Dickerson's first name was William, Ian nodded. "I've just come to watch—"

"I'm Clyde Vincent, the director. We need you," the man pleaded. "We've lost our ghost."

"I beg your pardon?"

"He just quit—walked right out of rehearsal! You know how actors are—high strung, mercurial."

It occurred to Ian that the description hardly fit Sergeant Dickerson, but he didn't argue. "I'm sorry to hear that," he said. "But I don't see what—"

"We open Friday—and you're just the right size for the costume!"

"But I'm not an actor—"

"You don't have many lines—a dozen or so at most. Please? You have a good strong voice."

"I'm afraid it's quite out of the question—"

The man clutched his arm with a grip Ian wouldn't have credited him with. "Please! I beg you—we open in three days! We only have four performances total."

"Can't you do without—"

"No! It's an important role, starts the whole plot in motion, you know. The most important thing is that you must say, 'Murder most foul!' Pushes everything into action, as it were."

"But I'm not really—" Ian began, and then he saw Fiona Stuart approaching them.

"What are you doing here?" she asked, frowning.

"I was about to ask you the same thing."

"May I introduce Fiona Stuart, our Ophelia," said Mr. Vincent.

"Miss Stuart and I are already acquainted," said Ian, thinking she was the least appropriate Ophelia he could imagine. Poor, passive Ophelia, whose only decisive action in the play was to take her own life—an entirely unsuitable role for Fiona Stuart.

"I see, Mr.—I'm sorry, I don't remember your name," said Mr. Vincent.

"Detective Ian Hamilton."

"Yes, of course—Billy has spoken of you often."

Ian couldn't quite manage to think of Sergeant Dickerson as "Billy."

Mr. Vincent turned to Miss Stuart. "I was trying to persuade Detective Hamilton to take over the role of King Hamlet's ghost. He's just the right size, you know, and has a good voice, don't you think?"

She gave Ian a withering look. "There's nothing wrong with his voice, but don't waste your breath. He's a thrawn puggy," she added, Scottish slang for "stubborn monkey."

Ian returned her glare, his hackles rising. Taking a deep breath, he turned to Mr. Vincent. "Very well," he said. "I'll do it."

Instead of gushing with gratitude, the director nodded brusquely, grasping Ian's elbow in his surprisingly strong fingers. "Come along, then—we've no time to waste!" he said as they ducked behind a flat with a florid oil painting of a castle. Ian imagined it was supposed to be Elsinore, but the resemblance to Edinburgh Castle could not be denied.

"Oh, don't be put off by my strange costume," Mr. Vincent said as he guided Ian backstage. "I had a little kerfuffle that resulted in a rather catastrophic coffee spill, so it was either go home and change or pluck something from the costume rack."

Ian couldn't imagine what he had to choose from that made him pick a costume suggesting he was about to board a magic carpet. He wondered if the spilled coffee had anything to do with the sudden departure of the actor playing Old Hamlet's ghost.

The backstage area was strewn with scripts, half-finished cups of tea, costume pieces, and used ashtrays. A few ratty-looking armchairs were scattered around. Ian's passion for order nearly led him to change his mind, but the memory of Fiona Stuart's smirk hardened his resolve. Standing in front of a bulletin board, drinking tea, was Sergeant Dickerson. He nearly dropped his mug when he saw Ian.

"Sir! Why—I mean, what—"

"Detective Hamilton is our new ghost!" Mr. Vincent proclaimed proudly. His announcement did not have the intended effect on the sergeant—he shot a panicked glance at Ian, who shrugged. The director seemed unaware of his consternation and rubbed his hands together with relish. "Let's gather the rest of the cast so we can introduce him properly."

The cast was a motley assortment, and included a banker, a florist, and two lawyers, amid representatives of all walks of Edinburgh society. Ian was pleased to see a familiar lithe figure with a halo of golden hair approaching.

"Good evening, Miss McNaughton."

"Hello again," she said with a sunny smile. "So you are to join our ragtag little company? We are lucky indeed."

"I look forward to learning from your example as an actress."

"Hardly!" she said with a laugh. "I'm more or less window dressing, I'm afraid. I play a lady-in-waiting at the court."

"Still," he said, "very attractive window dressing at that."

She gave another laugh and shook her blond curls, which occasioned a disdainful glare from Fiona Stuart.

From what Ian could see, the Greyfriars Dramatic Society appeared to be quite the fashionable organization. Jean Dalkeith, the lady playing

's mother, Gertrude, was a well-known philanthropist, and was
red to have dined with the queen herself. She was a spectrally thin
an in a scarlet frock; Ian estimated her age at anywhere between
ty and sixty, as her elaborate makeup probably made her look older
han she was. She appeared to be a grande dame of the Dramatic Society,
judging by the way she brandished her silk handkerchief.

"*Welc*ome to the *mag*ical world of theater," she said in a plummy
voice, peering at him through her pince-nez. "Have you ever acted
be*fore*, darling?"

"Once or twice, in school," Ian said, beginning to regret his hasty
decision. Fiona Stuart seemed to have a way of goading him into rash
behavior.

"Don't worry," she said. "I'll take you under my wing."

"Oh, she will at that," said Alan Jenkins, the handsome young office
clerk playing Hamlet. Though on the short side, he was blessed with
dark wavy hair and wide-set, gold-hued eyes, rosy cheeks, and prominent cheekbones. The only flaw was a rather thin, pinched mouth and
somewhat crooked teeth, which he attempted to hide by curling his
upper lip over them, the effect of which was that he was snarling. "And
you'd better watch out for her," he added. "She's quite rapacious, and
has a weakness for a pretty face."

"You're a naughty boy," Jean Dalkeith said, giving him a playful slap.

"Yes, Mother," he said, winking at Ian.

"You see what I have to put *up* with?" she said, rolling her eyes at Ian.

"Speaking of pretty faces," Alan said as Fiona Stuart walked by. His
hand snaked out toward her, but she swatted it away and glared at him. He
laughed lightly, as if it were of no consequence, but his upper lip twisted in
a snarl. He turned back to Ian. "I'm afraid I have yet to endear myself to
Ophelia, a situation I hope to remedy. She's thrawn and gallus, I'm afraid."

Jean Dalkeith frowned and fanned herself with an elaborate fan
made of peacock feathers. "*You're* the cheeky one, darling. Why don't
you leave the poor girl alone?"

"Ah, Mother, if only I could be as virtuous as you!" Alan said, seizing her hand and kissing it.

Jean clicked her tongue and assumed an expression of disapproval, but she was not a good enough actress to hide the blush creeping across her heavily powdered cheeks.

"Break's over, everyone," Mr. Vincent said, clapping his hands. "And now, if we could get started, please?"

The rehearsal went smoothly enough, and Ian didn't embarrass himself in his few scenes. A few people even complimented him, though Fiona Stuart was not one of them. He quite enjoyed skulking around the stage, and got chills when he heard the sound of thunder upon his entrance. It was so realistic he approached Mr. Vincent during the break to inquire about it.

"Ah, yes, it's quite a clever device," the director said, showing Ian a large wooden cylinder offstage. Raised up on four legs, it could be rotated manually by turning a crank on one side. "There's a cannonball inside," Vincent said, turning the handle. "The faster you rotate the drum, the louder the thunder."

"Fascinating," said Ian. "I really felt like a ghost when I heard it."

"It makes all the difference," Vincent agreed, "provided your stagehands stay sober," he added, casting a baleful glance at a couple of men in waistcoats and shirtsleeves, cigarettes dangling from their mouths.

"Don' worry," one of them said. "I'll make sure Robbie here don' miss 'is cue."

"You'd better."

The rehearsal refreshed Ian's spirit, taking his mind off the horrors of the past week. He felt a little bad for Dickerson but did his best to be kind to the little sergeant, even complimenting him on his interpretation of the Second Gravedigger—which, in fact, was quite credible. The sergeant made good use of his Lancashire accent, laying it on thick to great comic effect.

"Why did the actor playing the ghost quit so suddenly?" Ian asked him as they left rehearsal.

"I heard 'im tellin' Mr. Vincent he weren't puttin' up wi' anymore shenanigans from Mr. Jenkins," Dickerson said, buttoning his coat against the evening breeze.

"Such as what?"

"Well, sir, I'm not one t'judge, but Mr. Jenkins does favor the ladies, as it were."

"I noticed that."

"Apparently Mr. Davies—the fella playin' the ghost—caught Jenkins goin' after 'is wife. She were one a' the ladies-in-waitin', an' Mr. Jenkins took a fancy to her, y'see. Mr. Davies didn' like that one bit, so he tol' the director that it were either him or Jenkins. Mr. Vincent wouldn't fire his lead actor, so Davies left, and took 'is wife wi'im."

"I see."

"Mr. Vincent is all right—I know 'e felt bad fer Davies, but didn' feel it were possible t'find another actor who could play Hamlet on such short notice, like."

"Understandable, but unfortunate. Behavior like that should not be encouraged."

Dickerson sighed. "Well, this is where I turn off, sir. See ye tomorrow."

"Good night, Sergeant," Ian said, watching his retreating figure around the corner before continuing on his way. He was late again to meet Donald, and he quickened his stride as a full moon rose over Edinburgh Castle, casting shadows on its stark and rocky parapets. He wondered if any ghosts roamed its gloomy ramparts at night—surely there were more than enough murders in Edinburgh's dark history to produce an army of ghosts.

CHAPTER
FORTY-THREE

As soon as she came of age, she left home, cutting off all communication with her mother. Later, she heard the woman had taken to drink, wandering the streets clutching a bottle of whisky, singing Irish rebel songs. She was found one morning facedown in the chicken coop, surrounded by brooding hens and nest feathers. *A fitting end,* she thought, imagining her mother's body decomposing amid the smell of chicken feces and soiled straw.

She emigrated to Scotland, hoping to leave her past behind, but memories of her childhood trailed her like a sad, bedraggled dog. Looking for order and a sense of control, she worked as an office assistant until one winter a bout of pneumonia landed her in the infirmary. She awoke from a fever in her hospital bed to the soft rustle of crinoline and the scent of lavender water. Opening her cloudy, feverish eyes, she peered at an angelic figure in white hovering over her, gently bathing the sweat from her forehead. For the first time she could remember, she felt cared for.

And so, after her recovery, she became a nurse. She loved everything about the profession—the crisp white pinafore and the starched hat perched upon her head, proclaiming her calling to the world. She loved the accoutrements and tools of the trade—the basins and glass jars filled with swabs and puffy cotton balls, the shelves filled with rows of medicine bottles, all shapes and sizes and colors, with their exotic, beautifully printed labels. She loved the pungent tubes of ointments, and the sweet-smelling cedar closets filled with fresh linens and blankets.

Sitting in her kitchen now, she gazed at the familiar vial, with its neatly printed label. Licking her index finger, she delicately dipped it into the pile of white powder and raised it to her lips. She flicked the tip of her tongue over the powder, the sickly sweet taste bringing her back to her childhood and that first time she had tasted it so many years ago. What would it be like to swallow some, she wondered. Not enough to kill her, but perhaps enough to give her a taste of what her victims suffered. Replacing the lid, she slipped the vial into her pocket.

There was a knock on the door. She opened it to find the two men she had contacted about working for her.

"You're early," she said. "Come in, please."

It didn't take long to come to terms—they were in need of funds, and she was in need of manpower. She explained everything twice, just to make sure—she found them both a little thick, and didn't want anything to go wrong.

After they left, she sat down again at the kitchen table. Outside her window, the naked ground shivered as a gust of wind raked leaves and twigs across its barren surface.

She smiled and took another sip of tea. It had gone cold, like revenge.

CHAPTER
FORTY-FOUR

By the time Ian arrived at the White Hart to meet Donald, the dinner rush was over, and the innkeeper, a stocky fellow with brisk muttonchop whiskers, escorted Ian to a table near the window where his brother sat nursing a bottle of ginger beer.

"Too busy to turn up on time?" he said as Ian took his seat, which looked out onto the Grassmarket, the former site of Edinburgh's public hangings. Though the last one had taken place nearly a hundred years ago, the pub where condemned criminals had traditionally been offered their last drink still did a brisk trade. A few doors down from the White Hart, it was aptly named The Last Drop.

"I'm sorry," said Ian. "I do have a good excuse, but I apologize."

"I took the liberty of ordering," Donald said as the waiter delivered a roast pheasant on a pewter platter, surrounded by potatoes, carrots, and cabbage, with a garnish of dark-green winter cress. The aroma was heavenly.

The waiter set a bottle of Bordeaux on the table. "Don't worry—it's for you," his brother said in response to Ian's surprised look. "Allow me my vicarious pleasures." He tore a leg off the pheasant and took a bite. "Quite decent. Have some—you could use some meat on those bones."

"Have you been scheming with Aunt Lillian? She's forever attempting to fatten me up."

"Quite right, too."

Ian followed suit, tearing off the other leg, heaping his plate with a generous serving of vegetables. Tonight, he thought, he might just match his brother's robust appetite.

"Alas, you take after our mother," Donald said. "She ate like a bird. By the way, have you figured out what to do about the letter?"

"Not yet," Ian said, taking a large bite of roast pheasant and winter cress. It was as good as it smelled—deep, dark, gamey, the bitter cress a perfect complement to the rich, oily meat. "If I tell Lillian I read it, everything could go terribly wrong."

"But not mentioning it could be worse."

"Agreed."

"Damned if you do and damned if you don't," Donald said. He gulped down some ginger beer and wiped his mouth, greasy with fat. "Oh, speaking of hidden missives, I found this in your desk."

"What is it?" Ian said, peering at the folded piece of paper, yellowed at the edges.

"I think it's one of your poems. I wasn't snooping," Donald added quickly. "I was looking for some sealing wax, and it just fell from the drawer."

"Did it indeed?" Ian said, reading the first few lines.

October in the Highlands

Scotland is a land of ghosts

Pale riders galloping through fog

singing dreams of battles songs

and midnight massacres in the glen

On this windy night

Though I sit by a raging fire

I hear the cry of murdered clans

echo across the wind

"I wrote that when I was seventeen," Ian said, handing it back to him.

"I think it's rather good," said Donald, slipping it back into his pocket. "You certainly showed promise. Do you still—?"

"I scribble a little when I have time."

"Well, you shouldn't give it up. Who knows? You may be the next Robbie Burns."

"Hardly," Ian said, helping himself to more pheasant.

They ate in silence, listening to the clanking of glassware and the hubbub of conversation around them. Then, wiping his mouth again, Donald leaned back in his chair and sighed happily.

"That fig stuffing is brilliant. I must learn how to make that."

"I wouldn't object if you did."

"May I ask you something?"

"I suppose."

"Why did Dr. Bell get under your skin so much?"

"You ought to know—you have to work with him."

"I actually get on with him, believe it or not."

"I don't care for people who are stuck on themselves."

Donald gave a wicked little smile. "Like Fiona Stuart?"

Ian gulped down a substantial amount of wine. "Why bring her up?"

"You don't seem to care much for women."

"Why on earth would you say that?"

"You're not very comfortable around them."

"It doesn't necessarily follow that I don't like them."

"Perhaps you like them a little *too* much, then?"

"You don't seem very drawn to women yourself," Ian said, smearing a chunk of bread liberally with butter.

"Ah, but I *like* them. I just don't have any use for them."

Ian remembered the sharp, dismissive tone of Fiona Stuart's voice at the Greyfriars Society earlier. He smiled. "I'll have you know I'm in a production of *Hamlet* with Miss Stuart." He took a sip of wine and enjoyed the astonished look on his brother's face.

"How on earth did that happen?"

Ian told him the whole story, including his desire to spite Miss Stuart by accepting the director's offer.

Donald threw back his head and laughed. Several of the other patrons turned around—Donald's laugh was like the bellow of a bull. "That settles it. I do believe you're smitten, Brother," he said, ripping a chunk of bread from the loaf.

"Don't be absurd. Weren't you listening to what I was saying?"

"Oh, every word, I assure you. Old Hamlet's ghost, eh?" Donald said with a chuckle. "I should think that's a role well suited to you."

"How so?"

"You're always skulking about in that cape of yours. It's sort of wraithlike, you know."

"Tell you what," Ian said. "It's been a long day, and—"

"Very well, I know when to back off."

"Indeed? When did you acquire that ability?"

Donald grinned. "My lips are sealed."

Later, at home, Donald had a cigarette in front of the fire before retiring for the night.

"What did you mean you have no use for women?" Ian asked as his brother poked at the logs in the grate.

"Surely you must have guessed by now."

"Guessed what?"

"Good Lord, I should think it was obvious. You *are* a detective, if I'm not mistaken?"

"You mean—"

"Don't tell me you never suspected."

Ian stared at Donald. It was as if he had never truly seen his brother before.

"Close your mouth before you catch some flies," Donald remarked drily. "And before you say anything, I refuse to be ashamed of it."

"Good for you," Ian said finally.

"That's hardly the response I expected. I must say I am relieved."

"Is that why you—"

"Why I drink?"

"Why *do* you drink?"

Donald gave a little snort. "Why do you breathe?"

"To live, of course."

"I drink to live—or to die. I drink to forget, I drink to remember. I drink because it is who I am."

"Poetic but rather evasive, don't you think?"

His brother flicked a cigarette ash into the fire. "It's as much of a mystery to me as it is to you."

"Isn't that a bit convenient?"

Donald's face went pink. "If only I could be like *you*, with your oh-so-enviable control and self-restraint!"

Ian felt his own face flush. "I didn't mean—"

"That's the problem with you, Brother—you often don't *mean*, and yet you say it anyway."

"I'm sorry. I'm afraid I have much to learn about you."

His brother's face softened. "Never mind."

"You're not drinking now—that's the main thing, right?"

"Yes," Donald replied, though he looked unconvinced, and the old sadness had crept into his voice.

"Right," Ian said with forced cheerfulness. "I'm going to draw a bath."

Before either of them could utter another damaging remark, Ian turned and went into the bathroom. Bent over the hot water as it splashed into the tub, the steam rising to fog the windows, filling the air with a filmy mist, he wondered if there was something missing in him. Perhaps he lacked the ability to truly love another person. He had believed his parents' love for each other was selfless and all-consuming, but now that image was crumbling before his eyes. He stirred the water and watched the whirlpools form around his hand, enveloped by the swirl of liquid.

He loved Aunt Lillian, to be sure, as he had loved his parents, and his affection for Donald, though complicated, was real enough. But why did he not long for a woman in his life? He seemed to possess a cold, hard center that precluded the warmth of another person's presence. Something deep within him resisted intimacy. He lived for justice; its pursuit was the only thing that could ease the gnawing ache that he had lived with ever since his parents' deaths.

He went back into the parlor to ask his brother if he wanted a bath, and found him asleep on the sofa. Donald's face had the softness of a baby's in repose, his cheeks ruddy in the glow of the fireplace. Ian covered him with an afghan and crept out of the room.

CHAPTER
FORTY-FIVE

The November sun was yawning its way into a pale dawn early the next morning when Jedidiah Corbin stood up from his desk in the *Scotsman's* editorial department. He glanced at the massive wall clock hovering over the untidy, spacious room like a stern schoolmaster. The owners of the desks scattered around the room answered to the movement of its stark black hands, ticking inexorably from deadline to deadline. They felt its rhythm in every word they scribbled, in every sentence they typed on the few precious typewriters lined along the far wall. But the room was quiet now, the morning issue having been put to bed several hours ago.

Jedidiah stretched and stifled a yawn. Apart from one or two rumpled, sleepy-eyed copy editors hunched over their writing tables, readying texts for the afternoon printing, he was alone, surrounded by empty desks, stale cups of coffee, used ashtrays, and the smell of worry sweat. It was a worrisome business, being a newsman.

Jed Corbin was proud to call himself a journalist; his awareness of the perils and pitfalls of the profession only spurred his passion for it. He loved everything about it—the heart-stopping pace, the thrill of the hunt, the mad dash to break a story, score a scoop, file an exclusive. He even loved the chaotic newsroom with its stink of tobacco, stale air, and cheap whisky. The very smell of it made his loins buzz with excitement.

He walked stiffly toward the exit, printing presses grinding and whirring in the basement below; the boards beneath his feet vibrated with the sound. In underground rooms, men in smudged leather aprons and green visors had spent the night laying out sheet after sheet of Linotype; now they tended to machines spitting out reams of broadsheets. Within the hour, stacks of newsprint would be piled onto lorries lined up at the back of the building, to be driven far and wide, to Edinburgh's boundaries and beyond. Soon newsboys, their faces grimy with printers' ink, would be crying the headlines from every corner of the city. Jedidiah pictured it all with satisfaction—he was never happier than at the moment a new issue hit the streets. It was theater, primal and exciting, and he was at the center of it, by God.

An acknowledged up-and-coming star at the *Scotsman*, Corbin basked in the glow of his fame and notoriety. Both were the result of his tenacity, ruthlessness, and cunning, his disregard of the laws governing normal human interaction. Traditional niceties and delicatesse meant nothing to him—if he had to bring an aged widow to tears to get his story, no matter. If it was necessary to break into a house, lie to a policeman, or pursue a known criminal through a dark alley, that was part of the job, as far as he was concerned. He had a reputation for having professional integrity, but he would sacrifice even that in the interest of a good story. In the end, nothing else mattered.

But this morning he had an assignation. He stood for a moment outside the building, constructed especially for the newspaper, its logo emblazoned in gold over the fourth floor, with its carved stone balcony. Built in the Scots baronial style, the building blended in with its fellows, with its restrained gray stone and tall windows; the steeply graded roof included a staircase of bricks in the Dutch manner.

The *Scotsman*'s current editor in chief, Charles Alfred Cooper, was now a man of great wealth, but he had risen through the ranks, beginning his career as a lowly reporter for the *Hull Advertiser*. Cooper gave his more talented reporters free rein, and Corbin was only too eager to take advantage of it. Once or twice he had been called out for his behavior—there was the time he posed as an English lord in order to gain admission to a party at Balmoral Castle, which nearly got him sacked. Though his actions were officially condemned, they were secretly (and not so secretly) admired among his colleagues. Of course, Jedidiah Corbin also drew his share of envy, which he purported to dismiss, but the truth was it worried him—the news business was full of ambitious backbiters.

None of this was on his mind as he walked along Cockburn Street, turning south onto Jackson's Close. The air was still, the city not yet awake as the early-morning light bloomed a delicate oystershell pink in the eastern sky. A few hansom cabs lingered in front of the Tron Kirk, steam rising from the horses' backs as their owners removed their wool blankets in preparation for the day's labor. Crossing the High Street, Corbin continued on toward Stevenlaw's Close. He could have taken a more widely traveled route, such as South Bridge, but did not wish to be spotted by anyone who knew him. If this meeting was as big a scoop as he hoped, it could make his already-promising career.

He passed a line of street vendors pushing heavy wooden carts toward the Grassmarket, where hungry buyers and sellers would soon gather for the midweek market. The wheels of their carts rumbled over the uneven cobblestones, and he watched as they labored, backs bent, up the incline toward the western end of town, the castle glowering down on them all. Looking at the vendors, struggling with their cumbersome burdens, he felt a chill of gratitude that he wasn't one of them. Theirs was a rugged life, and a few hard winters could wear a man out.

He fingered the crumpled note in his pocket, the handwriting so coyly feminine, the letters curling on the page like wanton strands of hair. He wondered if she was pretty, and whether this meeting offered him something more than just information. He glanced at the address as he turned onto Hastie's Close. The crumbling bricks and rotting timbers of the buildings lining the narrow alley were not reassuring—this was Old Town at its most desolate. He shivered as a blast of cold air rushed at him from a basement window; overhead, frozen-looking laundry hung forlornly over the street, tattered gray bedsheets flapping half-heartedly in an anemic breeze.

Finding the building, he knocked on the door, which, to his surprise, was half-open. Getting no response, he knocked again, then called out. He was met with silence. Looking both ways to make sure he had not been followed, Corbin took a deep breath, pushed the door, and stepped inside.

CHAPTER FORTY-SIX

Ian arrived at the police station early Wednesday morning to find DCI Crawford already there. Ian barely had his cape off when Crawford came barreling out of his office, heading straight for Ian's desk. Ian instinctively tensed up, but to his surprise, the chief inspector seized him warmly by the hand, shaking it vigorously.

"Thank you, Hamilton!"

"For what, sir?"

"For putting me in touch with Dr. Bell. He's going to have a look at my wife later today."

"I'm very glad to hear it, sir," Ian replied, feeling sheepish—in the heat of the investigation, he had quite forgotten Crawford's personal woes.

"Quite a coup, the great Dr. Bell," Crawford continued, stroking his whiskers. "I won't forget this, Hamilton."

"Think nothing of it, sir."

"Please thank your brother for me."

"I will, sir."

"I met that young friend of yours—Conan Doyle, is it?"

"Yes, sir—he's Dr. Bell's assistant."

"Stout fellow. With that build of his, he'd make a bloody good policeman."

"Quite right, sir."

"How's the investigation going?"

Ian filled him in on the details of the case, and though he listened politely enough, Crawford looked distracted—clearly his mind was on his wife's illness. Ian found the chief inspector's devotion to her touching and wondered if he would ever feel that way about a woman.

"Good work, Hamilton," Crawford said as policemen began filing in for the day shift. "Never mind all the bosh and bunkum—you'll get there."

"Oh, one more thing, sir."

"Yes?" Crawford said as Sergeant Dickerson came in, shaking snow from his shoes.

"I'm in a play," said Ian.

Crawford's prodigious eyebrows shot up, and his mouth dropped open. "A *play*, is it? What sort of play?"

"*Hamlet*. I'm playing his father's ghost."

"And a right proper ghost you are, sir, if you don' mind me sayin' so," Dickerson added, taking off his coat.

"What exactly *is* a proper ghost?" said Crawford.

Dickerson swallowed hard. "I m-mean DI Hamilton is a good actor, sir."

"Well, then, I shall have to come see you both perform," Crawford said, rubbing his hands together. "Carry on." And with that, he turned and charged back toward his office.

"He's in a jolly mood today, sir," Dickerson remarked.

"Dr. Bell is going to have a look at his wife."

"How'd you manage that?"

"It seems my brother arranged it."

"Your friend Mr. Doyle is quite close to Dr. Bell, isn't he?"

"He is Bell's assistant," Ian said. Something in the sergeant's voice and manner made Ian suspect Dickerson was jealous of his relationship with Doyle. "What do you say to a trip to Dr. Jex-Blake's clinic on Grove Street?"

Dickerson's face brightened. "Shall I call us a cab?"

"I thought we'd walk. It's a fine day."

"It's snowin', sir."

"A brisk walk is good for the circulation."

Dickerson's shoulders sagged. "Yes, sir."

"Come along, Sergeant," Ian said, throwing on his cape. "We can't let a few snowflakes deter us."

"Right you are, sir," Dickerson answered dutifully, trudging after him.

Ian knew the sergeant didn't share his passion for treading the streets of the city, but he believed a policeman should be physically as well as mentally fit. Ian couldn't force Dickerson to like it, but at least he could make the sergeant get a little exercise.

Snow swirled around them as they swung onto Johnston Terrace where it intersected with the High Street. The air was sharp, the sky increasingly opaque as they crossed King's Stables Road in the shadow of Edinburgh Castle. They continued southwest onto Spittal Street, the castle behind them now. Even when not in sight, its presence was felt—majestic and moody, it watched over the city day and night.

"Why are we goin' to the clinic, sir?" Dickerson said, huffing to keep up with Ian's long strides. The snow was coming down in earnest now, gathering on the ground, obscuring the cobblestones beneath their feet.

"Dr. Jex-Blake has been a valuable source, and I thought she might have some information on one or more of our victims."

Sophia Jex-Blake's clinic occupied the first floor of a four-story stone building. The place was immaculate—the polished floors gleamed, and a fresh coat of white paint brightened the somewhat cramped foyer. A multicolored crocheted rug added a touch of cheer, and an ornately carved coatrack gave a sense of elegance in an otherwise utilitarian setting.

A shy young nurse in a snowy-white apron and crisp starched cap escorted them to a small waiting room just off the main hall, where half a dozen women of various ages sat in the rows of chairs along two walls. Young or old, they all had the weary, stoop-shouldered look of those worn down by hardship. The near wall was occupied by a tea station, complete with tins of tea, mugs, and a pitcher of cream; a receptionist sat at a small desk along the far wall.

"If ye'd just wait here, Dr. Jex-Blake will be out shortly," the nurse said in a lilting accent suggesting the rolling hills of Ireland.

"Thank you, Miss—" Ian said, removing his hat.

"Mary's my given name, sir." She was pale and elfin, with wispy blond hair and light-blue eyes with delicate pink lids. She reminded Ian of a rabbit he'd had as a child.

"Thank you, Mary," he said, sitting next to a thin, elderly woman with yellowed, papery skin.

The young nurse disappeared behind a folding screen behind the receptionist's desk, and Ian heard a door being opened and closed. A few moments later, Dr. Jex-Blake emerged, resplendent in a long white apron over a navy-blue frock, her smooth, dark hair pulled back in a tidy bun as usual. Upon seeing Ian and Dickerson, her dour expression dissolved into a smile.

"Detective Hamilton, what a pleasant surprise. Please, come through," she said, leading them into a small office on the other side of the door behind the screen. It was simply furnished, with a plain oak desk, a hooked rug, and a glass cabinet full of medical supplies. On the walls were handsomely framed prints of birds Ian recognized as the work of the American naturalist and painter John James Audubon.

Seated in a chair next to the desk, to Ian's surprise, was Arthur Conan Doyle. Seeing the detective, he rose immediately and shook Ian's hand heartily.

"I say, Hamilton, this is an unexpected pleasure! What brings you here?"

Doyle's cheerful manner and ruddy cheeks brightened Ian's mood instantly. The same could not be said of Sergeant Dickerson, who bit his lip and cast a baleful glare at the young medical student.

"We were hoping to interview Dr. Jex-Blake and her staff," said Ian.

"Capital idea," Doyle said.

"An' what are you doin' here, sir, if ye don' mind me askin'?" Sergeant Dickerson asked. His voice was polite, but his narrowed eyes made it plain he did not like the man.

"Mr. Doyle is kind enough to volunteer his time at our clinic," Dr. Jex-Blake said, "for which we are immeasurably grateful."

"I'm afraid it's not much," Doyle said modestly. "Only a couple of hours a week—but medical school does really seem to occupy most of my time."

"Whom did you wish to interview?" Jex-Blake asked.

As if on cue, there was a knock at the door. The doctor opened it to admit Abby McNaughton, looking fetching in a blue nurse's uniform and white apron. Surprise crossed her attractive face when she saw the detectives, but it was quickly replaced by a smile.

"Oh, hello," she said.

"Nurse McNaughton, this is Detective Inspector Hamilton and—" Dr. Jex-Blake began, but Nurse McNaughton cut her off.

"Oh, we're old friends by now. We're all in a play together."

Dr. Jex-Blake frowned. "Why did you not tell me?"

"It never came up."

Ian noticed Nurse McNaughton offered no apology, and he was impressed that she seemed more than capable of standing up to the intimidating Jex-Blake.

"Never mind," her employer replied. "You're here now, so please answer any questions DI Hamilton has for you."

"Actually, I was wondering if any of you had occasion to see signs of poisoning prior to the fatal incident," Ian said. "Perhaps when Mr. Caruthers accompanied his wife to the clinic?"

"I did."

They all turned to see Fiona Stuart in the doorway, hands folded in front of her, crisp and fresh in her white apron and cap. She must have slipped in through the open doorway. Ian was struck once again by the firmness of her chin and the frankness of her green eyes.

"What are you doing here?" Ian said.

"Surely that is obvious. I work here."

"Nurse Stuart comes in twice a week," said Dr. Jex-Blake.

Ian frowned. "So you saw signs of poisoning prior to Mr. Caruthers' death?" he asked Nurse Stuart. "Why did you not tell me this earlier?"

"Because you never asked. I was waiting to be questioned, but apparently your aversion to me led you to postpone it."

"What signs did you see?" Ian asked, feeling sweat gather at his collar. The room was too full now, and his aversion to cramped spaces was beginning to make him feel dizzy and weak.

"I did not remark upon it at the time, but in retrospect, I think it was symptoms of arsenic."

"What did you see?" Doyle said eagerly, evidently unable to contain his curiosity.

"Darkening of the skin, as well as lesions and bumps on his hands," Fiona replied.

"Come to think of it, I noticed that as well," said Abby.

"At the time, I put it down to his being a railway worker," Fiona went on. "But now it's clear it was far more sinister."

"How long before his death did you observe these symptoms?" asked Ian.

"About two weeks, I'd say."

"And you?" he asked Abby.

"That's about right, yes."

"That would indicate it had been going on for some time," remarked Dr. Jex-Blake.

"Which makes it more likely he was poisoned by someone close to him," said Ian. "Someone he saw on a regular basis."

"Well done!" Doyle said. "Dr. Bell himself would be impressed."

Ian was amused by the medical student's enthusiasm, but Sergeant Dickerson glowered at him. "Sir," he said to Ian, "don't you think we should be conducting interviews without outside . . . interference, like?"

"Quite right," Doyle said. "My apologies—working with Dr. Bell has engendered a certain keenness for this sort of thing. I assume you have eliminated the wife as a suspect?" he asked Ian.

"Not entirely," Ian replied, "but I fail to see her motive. With a child on the way, she's lost her only breadwinner."

"Well, I'll leave you to it—I've patients to attend to anyway," Doyle said.

"Before you go, I wanted to ask if any supplies are missing from the infirmary pharmacy."

"Such as arsenic?"

"Yes, but also strychnine and laudanum."

"I haven't heard of anything," Doyle replied. "But I can ask around."

"I would be most grateful, thank you."

Doyle slipped out the door, and Ian felt the air in the room collapse a little in his absence.

Sergeant Dickerson, however, breathed a sigh of relief and turned to Nurse Stuart. "Now then, miss, you were sayin'?"

"I've already described everything I noticed. I failed to notice striations on his fingernails, but then, Mr. Caruthers wasn't our patient—his wife was."

"Presumably she still is?" said Ian.

"We've not seen her for a while, actually," said Dr. Jex-Blake. "I was about to send someone to her rooms to check on her."

"I'll go," said Nurse McNaughton, a smile on her heart-shaped face.

"Very well," Dr. Jex-Blake agreed. "See to the patients you have first, and then you may go check on her."

Abby McNaughton gave a little curtsy, and Ian thought how what might seem obsequious from someone else was becoming on her. It pleased him even more when he saw Fiona Stuart glowering at him from the other side of the room.

"Before you ask, Detective, we've not had any supplies missing either," said Dr. Jex-Blake. "Though those substances are easy enough to procure—too easy, if you ask me."

"Would you like me to do a thorough inventory?" Abby asked.

"Good idea," said her employer, and Ian saw Fiona Stuart's face redden as she abruptly turned and left the room.

"What got into 'er, I wonder?" Dickerson mused.

"Some people are just moody," Abby replied sweetly.

"Yes," Ian agreed. "Moody and ill-tempered."

CHAPTER
FORTY-SEVEN

By the time Ian and Dickerson left the clinic, there was just time for a hasty meal before rehearsal. As Jean Dalkeith had an evening commitment, Mr. Vincent had called an afternoon run-through with the entire cast.

When Ian stepped onto the stage for his first speaking scene, he was surprised to find his legs shaking. It was odd that he was more comfortable pursuing dangerous criminals than reciting a few lines of dialogue in an amateur theater production. In the previous rehearsal, there had not been time to be nervous, but now as he stood stage left, he wiped sweat from his brow. He enjoyed his earlier entrances, where he had no lines and had only to stand looking mysterious and forbidding, but as he opened his mouth to deliver his first line, he felt faint. Drawing a deep breath, he spoke:

Mark me.

His voice shook a little, but he realized it added an otherworldly aura. Alan Jenkins, as Hamlet, looked startled as he delivered his line.

I will.

Rather than fight the tremor in his voice, Ian let it inform the next line.

My hour is almost come,
When I to sulphurous and tormenting flames
Must render up myself.

He felt a surge of pleasure, a tingling that rose from his toes to his forehead, suddenly overwhelmed by the thrill of speaking lines from what he believed was the greatest play ever written in the English language. He felt the loss of his own father, imagining what it would be like to speak to his ghost. Tears sprang to his eyes, clouding his vision, as he played the rest of the scene with his "son." Whatever sort of man Alan Jenkins was, he was a gifted actor, listening carefully to Ian's lines before giving passionate and believable emotional responses. Caught up in the drama, Ian's self-consciousness disappeared as he forgot himself, really believing he was Old Hamlet's ghost come to beg his son to avenge his murder.

When the scene was finished, the rest of the cast applauded, and Ian felt a euphoria that neither wine nor career victories could produce.

"Well done, sir!" Sergeant Dickerson said as the cast broke for tea after the first act. "How'd ye make yer voice shake like that?"

Ian smiled. "I'm afraid I can't take credit—it was quite involuntary."

"You're a natural, sir, if y'don' mind my sayin' so."

"You're very kind, Sergeant."

"You were better than I thought you would be," said a woman's voice.

Ian looked up to see Fiona Stuart, dressed in a long white gown that hugged her figure most becomingly, her hair loose around her shoulders. A simple gold belt dangled from her slim waist.

"I shall consider that a compliment, coming from you."

"Consider it whatever you like," she said. "You make a good ghost, at any rate."

"Thank you," he said, but she was already walking away, her red curls bouncing.

"She's quite attractive, innit, sir?" Dickerson said, watching her. "Pity she's so prickly an' all."

"Ah, well," Ian said. "One can't have everything in this life, Sergeant." He looked up to see Clyde Vincent approaching. Dressed in striped gray trousers, a maroon waistcoat, and a black frock coat, the director looked quite normal, not nearly as exotic as the first time Ian had met him. There was something theatrical in the way he moved his hands, and his lean face was unusually expressive.

"I say, that was excellent!" he told Ian. "I got chills, I honestly did. Well done!"

"Thank you," said Ian, relieved he had not embarrassed himself. He had even managed to memorize his lines, though Mr. Vincent had told him it wasn't necessary.

Rehearsal continued smoothly, everyone pulling together, as opening night was only two days away. When it was time for the scene with the two gravediggers, Ian sat in the back so as not to make Dickerson nervous. The two actors entered carrying shovels as they prepared to bury Ophelia. The actor playing the First Gravedigger was an accountant named Kenneth Lloyd, a jolly, rotund fellow well known to local audiences for his portrayal of Falstaff in the previous production. He was a great favorite among the other cast members, garnering laughs for most of his lines.

Ian was pleased to see Sergeant Dickerson holding his own, his Lancashire accent thickening as he bantered with Lloyd in one of Shakespeare's typical "low comedy" clown scenes, full of puns, jokes, and double entendres. The first line was Lloyd's, as he questioned Ophelia's burial in a churchyard, when she had reputedly committed suicide.

Is she to be buried in Christian burial when she willfully seeks her own salvation?

Dickerson mimed industrious digging, as if he just wanted to get the job over with.

I tell thee she is. Therefore make her grave straight. The crowner hath sat on her and finds it Christian burial.

Lloyd settled himself on a mound of "dirt" (a burlap sack full of cloth) and unwrapped a sandwich as he watched Dickerson dig, his indolence getting a laugh from the assembled cast.

How can that be, unless she drowned herself in her own defense?

The line itself got a laugh as well.

Dickerson interrupted his digging to pluck an invisible worm from his shovel, which occasioned another burst of laughter from the audience. Hands on his hips, he delivered the next line as if he had had just about enough foolishness.

Why, 'tis found so.

The rest of the scene continued merrily, the comic relief providing a counterpoint and commentary on the more serious action of the play, with its themes of betrayal, vengeance, and death. Amusing as the scene was, Ian couldn't help thinking of Big Margaret.

Watching the scene between Hamlet and his mother, Gertrude, Ian thought about his own mother's letter. Were his parents murdered, and, like Hamlet, would he be called upon to avenge their deaths? If so, would he suffer the same tragic fate as Hamlet, or, as a policeman, would he be able to bring their killer to justice? He did not believe in the afterlife, but he found himself wishing that he could have a conversation with his departed parents' spirits.

After rehearsal, he headed to the greenroom to speak with the costumer, and as he passed through the wings, he saw Alan Jenkins cornering one of the younger members of the cast, a girl who looked to be barely in her teens, who played a lady-in-waiting in the court. She was backed up against the rear wall backstage, next to a pile of scenery flats and coiled rope.

"What does a fellow have to do for a kiss around here?" Jenkins was saying, looming over her, one arm leaning on the brick wall above her, preventing her escape.

As Ian approached, her eyes darted frantically to his, her expression pleading. Without interrupting his stride, he sauntered over to Jenkins and clamped his hand firmly upon his shoulder. Taken by surprise, the actor gave a start and looked at Ian apprehensively.

Tightening his grip on the man's shoulder, Ian said, "I just wanted to say what a fine Hamlet you make."

"Oh, ta v-very m-much," Jenkins stuttered, turning to face Ian. As he did, the actor removed his hand from its position, so that the girl was able to slip away. Darting past both men, she cast a grateful glance at Ian before disappearing into the wings. Jenkins' eyes followed her ever so briefly, and he turned back to Ian with an unconvincing chuckle. "Just giving a bit of acting advice there," he said. "Young Carrie wants to be an actress, you know."

Beads of sweat trickled down the actor's forehead as his legs twitched with the desire to flee, but the detective held his gaze. "I was wondering what it's like to be so . . . talented," Ian said languidly, enjoying the man's frustration.

"Oh, I'm not all that gifted," Jenkins said. "Just a big fish in a small pond, don't you know."

"Well, you have your fans," Ian said, giving him another pat on the shoulder—though not so hard as the first one, it was firm enough to deliver the message that he had better watch his step.

Jenkins swallowed hard and gave a sickly smile. "Well, I'd better be on my way."

"Yes, you had better," Ian agreed, removing his hand. He watched as the actor scampered away, nearly tripping over the red velvet curtain as he stumbled out to the auditorium.

When he arrived in the greenroom, Carrie was putting on her coat. Seeing him, she rushed over to him and clasped his hand in hers. It was tiny, like the hand of a child.

"Thank you so much, sir," she said, tears springing to the corners of her big brown eyes.

"Not at all," he said. "Please inform me if you have any more trouble with Mr. Jenkins."

"Oh, sir, I wouldn't want to—"

"If you have *any* more trouble," he repeated, "I shall expect you to let me know."

"Oh, thank you, sir," she said, her voice faint.

"Promise?"

"I promise."

She hurried from the room as if she were being pursued. Ian watched her go, then turned to the costumer, Mrs. McCafferty. She was a plump, middle-aged woman with a kind face and a harried manner, and always seemed to be in a hurry. She was busy tidying up the costume rack, hanging up discarded items and organizing the rack. Each actor had their own hanger, their name written in capital letters on a piece of paper fastened to the hanger with safety pins.

"Hello, dearie," she said. "What can I do for you?"

"I wondered if I should try on my costume?"

She looked him up and down. "Not unless you want to, dearie. You're pretty much the same size as our last ghost. We can do all that tomorrow at dress rehearsal. Oh, fiddlesticks!" she said, turning back to the rack. "Where has that thing gone?"

"What's that?" said Ian.

"That blasted red wig," she said, clicking her tongue. "It's missing."

"Do you need it for this production?"

"No, but it was expensive, and we can't afford to keep buying props and costumes."

Sergeant Dickerson entered the greenroom with a mug of tea.

"I thought you had gone home, Sergeant," Ian said.

"I stayed t'give the stagehands a bit o'help, sir. Many hands make light work, me mum always used to say."

"Quite right," Ian said. "Good man."

The door to the greenroom was thrown open, and Derek McNair burst into the room.

"Good heavens!" Mrs. McCafferty said upon seeing the disreputable-looking ragamuffin.

"Master McNair," Ian said. "How did you find me?"

"You *know* this personage?" said the costumer.

"Ye'd better come with me," the boy said, panting heavily.

"What on earth—?" said Ian.

"I'll explain on the way," said Derek. "There's naught time t'waste—a life is at stake!"

Ian didn't need any further convincing. "Come along, Sergeant," he said, throwing on his cloak.

The three of them hurried from the room, leaving a very puzzled Mrs. McCafferty standing in the middle of the greenroom, holding a hanger in each hand.

"Goodness me," she said, shaking her head. "What next?"

CHAPTER
FORTY-EIGHT

He did not know how long he had been there, or when he had lost consciousness. To the man on the bed, time blended into a blurry swirl of dreamlike images. He stirred, trying to pull himself from oblivion's embrace, but it was a struggle, and he kept sinking back into the arms of Morpheus. The drug had loosened the bonds of reality, so he hardly knew what was real and what was a product of opium-laced hallucinations.

He had been dreaming he was being pursued by scores of demons in red flannel pajamas wielding medical syringes. He could not see their faces, but when they ran it sounded like rats scuttling. He awoke to realize that though the demons were the product of his fevered mind, the rats were real. When he thrashed in the bed, they disappeared into the corners of the room, but he feared they were growing bolder, and he shivered at the thought of their cold little feet scampering across his body.

In moments of semiconsciousness, he realized he had been given laudanum, having had it once before during a tooth extraction. He knew the drug's effects and vaguely remembered feeling the needle in his shoulder just after he'd entered the tenement house—collapsing to the floor, his knees hitting the ground as he cursed himself for being lured into such an obvious trap. He cursed his own arrogance and ambition, his rash and headstrong nature. A more temperate man might have alerted the police, but he was too proud, greedy for all the glory—he alone would crack the case and bring a murderer to justice.

Throwing aside the threadbare wool blanket covering him, he saw that he was still in the same clothes he had worn to this ill-advised meeting, minus his shoes. He hoped they were in the room somewhere. He had the feeling that he must flee, that it was now or never. Groaning, he put a hand to his throbbing head, struggling to sit up. He felt no hunger, but his throat burned with thirst, so dry he could barely swallow.

What did they want with him? Even worse, what were they planning to do with him? He had no way of knowing if the person who had drugged and abducted him was the same party responsible for the rash of poisonings plaguing the city.

Raising his head slightly, he could see the iron bedpost at his feet—to his addled mind, it seemed like prison bars. He didn't know if it was morning or evening, or how many days had passed. An anemic bit of sunlight pushed through the single window over his bed, its pallid gray light stretching across the tiny room, as if it, too, longed to escape these wretched surroundings. He was aware of the odor of mildew and rotting wood; the cobblestones beneath his window reeked from years of steaming chamber pots emptied day and night on unsuspecting streets. There was another smell he couldn't place—a sickly sweet aroma mingled with the stench of human waste.

Swinging his legs over the side of the bed, he stepped onto the uneven floorboards in his stockinged feet. He took a few unsteady steps, but the room began to swim, and he retched. But his stomach was empty, so nothing came up. Grasping his head with both hands, he staggered back to the bed and fell onto the dusty mattress as blackness closed over him.

He awoke again to the feel of soft hair on his face and a soothing female voice in his ears. At first he thought he had been rescued, and tried to sit up, only to find his hands and feet were tied to the bedposts. Opening his eyes, he squinted into the darkness but saw only the outline of a feminine form hovering above him. He tried to speak, but a cloth was shoved into his mouth. Confused, he struggled to free himself as he felt the buttons of his shirt being undone. Hungry hands explored his body, with feverish, frantic passion, touching him in private places, all the while the soft voice murmuring in his ear. When he writhed and struggled harder to free himself, he felt the needle in his arm, and the blackness returned once again.

CHAPTER
FORTY-NINE

"What d'ye mean ye didn't get my note?" Derek said as they rushed out to the street. "I left it at the station early this mornin' sayin' it were urgent. A matter o'life an' death, so help me, Guv."

"Who did you leave it with?" said Ian.

"He were a thin, unpleasant fella wi' a face full a' pockmarks."

"That'll be Constable Turnbull, sir," Dickerson said as a cab rattled by, its wheels skittering on the wet cobblestones. The snow had continued to fall, and now several inches lay on the ground. "I knew 'e were a lout, but you should 'ave his badge fer this."

"I just might," Ian murmured as yet another cab splashed by without stopping, the snow in the gutters already turning to slush beneath its wheels.

"At this rate, sir, we'd be better off walkin'," Dickerson remarked glumly.

"Hang on a minute," said Derek, focusing on something across the street, though with the flakes falling thicker and harder, it was difficult to see what he was looking at. "Oiy!" he cried, scampering across the street, narrowly avoiding being run down by a coach pulled by a pair of black geldings.

"Watch where you're going!" the driver shouted, flicking his whip at the boy, who ducked so the tip of the lash missed its mark.

"What on earth's 'e up to now?" asked Dickerson, shielding his eyes from the cascading flakes.

"We'll find out soon enough," Ian said, stepping onto the street with more caution. Crossing to the other side, they found the boy holding the bridle of an enormous chestnut gelding attached to a milk cart.

"Let me 'andle this," Derek said.

"Very well," Ian agreed, intrigued.

"This is Timothy," the boy said, stroking the horse's neck.

The animal gazed at them with large, mild eyes, plumes of steam pouring from its nostrils in the cold air. Timothy appeared completely unconcerned by either the weather or the presence of strangers—indeed, he looked half asleep.

"And this is Cob," he added, as a tall man with ruddy cheeks and shaggy gray hair emerged from the other side of the milk cart.

Ian recognized him as a familiar figure around town, though he'd never known his name until now. On fine days the man wore a white jacket, but today he had donned a dark-green sou'wester and matching oilskin cap.

"Cob," Derek said, "this is Detective Inspector Hamilton and his sergeant."

"How 'do?" Cob said pleasantly, slinging an empty milk can onto the cart.

"Y'see, Cob," Derek said, "these policemen need yer cart."

"How's that?" the milkman said, arranging the empty cans, their metal sides clanking against each other. He didn't seem particularly bothered by the suggestion, as if it were a common, everyday request.

"You're done w' your route, aren't ye?"

"Pretty much, yeah," Cob replied, wiping the snow from Timothy's head while feeding him a handful of oats. The big horse chewed slowly, his eyelids half closed.

"They're catchin' a murderer, see? An' they can' find a cab, so—"

"I'll give it t'you fer half a guinea," said Cob.

"Half a crown," Ian said, fishing coins from his pocket.

"Done," Cob said, taking them. "Ye'll find me in yonder pub when ye've finished," he said, pointing to a corner establishment across the street called the Mole. Over the entrance was a large sign depicting an anthropomorphic version of the creature, wearing a top hat and round spectacles, carrying a white-tipped cane. "I live upstairs, so if ye get in late, leave ol' Tim in the barn 'round back, eh? There's more oats there in't back of th' cart." Handing Ian the reins, the milkman strolled off in the direction of the pub.

Sergeant Dickerson shifted his feet and chewed on his lip. "You, uh, been around horses much, then?"

"I grew up on't farm in Devon," Derek said. "An' Timothy and I are old friends. I kin drive."

Dickerson gave Ian a panicked glance, but the detective handed the boy the reins. "I assume you wouldn't lie about something like that."

"Course not," Derek said, hopping up onto the cart.

"Come along, Sergeant," Ian said. "Master McNair here is in a hurry to take us somewhere."

"I'll explain on the way," the boy said as Dickerson reluctantly climbed aboard the cart. With the milk cans filling the back, there was just enough room for the three of them—with Ian sitting next to Derek, Dickerson was forced to sit behind them, legs crossed, looking cramped and uncomfortable.

Derek turned the horse expertly, lifted the whip, and gave a little flick. Timothy broke into a brisk trot, and off they went into the swarm of flying snowflakes.

CHAPTER FIFTY

Derek McNair was as good as his word, driving the milk cart with ease and skill. Turning south on Grove, he took it to the end, then headed northeast on Fountainbridge. Timothy's hooves struck the cobblestones in a steady rhythm, muffled by the gathering snow. In spite of the slick streets, the gelding trotted confidently, steam rising from his broad back. Nearly blinded by the thickly flying flakes, Ian pulled his cap lower over his eyes, grateful the horse knew these streets so well.

"So what is the life-or-death situation you pulled us out to investigate?" he asked Derek.

"It were that newsman—the one wha' ye don' like."

"Jedidiah Corbin?"

"That's 'im."

"What about him?"

"He's missin'."

"How do you know?"

"Never ye mind."

Ian peered at him, but the boy stared straight ahead as Fountainbridge jogged onto West Port. He turned around to see how Dickerson was faring. The sergeant clung on to the side of the cart with one hand, the other clamping down on his hat to keep it from bouncing off his head.

"You all right, Sergeant?"

"F-f-fine, s-sir," he said, shivering.

"Chin up—it won't be long now," he said, taking pity on the poor fellow.

"N-n-no, sir," Dickerson replied manfully.

Ian turned back to Derek McNair. "Very well, so he's missing. Where are you taking us?"

"To th' *Scotsman*, sir. I were thinkin' there might be some evidence there as t'where he might 'ave gone."

"Good thinking," Ian said as they swerved to avoid a street vendor. They were approaching the Grassmarket now, where a smattering of customers lingered at the midweek market. Everyone looked sodden and miserable, except for the gaggle of children having a snowball fight, squealing gleefully as they pummeled one another with wet missiles. "You might want to avoid this route," Ian said, "since it's market day."

"Right-o," said Derek, swinging north onto King's Stables Road, to the south of the castle. High overhead, its outline blurred by what had now become a proper blizzard, the castle looked dreamlike and oddly serene.

By the time they turned onto Johnston Terrace, Ian, too, was shivering, and he clutched his cloak closer to his body. He glanced at Derek, but the boy seemed oblivious to the cold—eyes narrowed, he focused on the road ahead. Luckily, the weather had driven more sensible people inside, so even the High Street was nearly empty by the time they turned onto the Royal Mile where it met Johnston Terrace. It wasn't far to the *Scotsman* offices on Cockburn Street, and they were able to shelter both cart and horse beneath a portico to the side of the building. Finding a dry blanket in the covered back of the cart, they draped it over Timothy, attaching his feed bucket to his harness. Shoving his massive head into the bucket, he began munching on his oats, flicking his tail and snorting softly.

"That means he's happy," Derek said in response to Dickerson's look. "Aren't ye, old Tim?" he added, patting the horse's muscular back. Timothy gave a little shake of his head and resumed eating.

Brushing the snow from their outerwear, the three were met in the foyer by a freckle-faced young clerk with a thatch of coarse sandy hair. Clad in a short jacket and matching breeches, he carried a pen in one hand and a sheaf of paper in the other.

"Hallo," he said in a scratchy, high-pitched voice. "I'm Felix. You the detectives what were sent 'round to find our missing fella?"

"I am a detective, yes," Ian said. "But what—"

"Come along, now—he's waitin' for ya."

"Who is?" asked Ian as they followed Felix through a room of such bustle and activity as Ian had seldom seen. In all his years working at the City of Edinburgh police station just down the street, he had never been inside the offices of the city's most popular newspaper, even though he had passed it hundreds of times. There was a wary distrust between members of the news and law-keeping professions. Their goals were not always aligned, and many policemen felt newsmen fed off them rather than helped them. But now, in the newsroom, Ian couldn't help looking around with fascination.

Men in shirtsleeves hunched over desks, scribbling. Occasionally they would hold up a few pages, calling, "Copy boy!" at which point a young lad would appear, snatch the pages, and carry them into an office at the far end of the room. Some of the men looked as though they hadn't slept in a while—a few were disheveled with a day's beard growth—but most were so engrossed in their work they barely seemed to notice the three strangers in their midst.

Except that one of them wasn't such a stranger. Several men looked up from their desks and hailed Derek with a wave or a friendly smile.

One or two even called him by name as the three visitors followed the bushy-haired Felix through the room.

Ian looked down at Derek. "You're popular around here."

"Too bad I ain't so popular with you lot," the boy replied, wiping his nose with the back of his sleeve.

"If this pans out, that could change," Ian remarked as Felix stopped them in front of the office at the far end of the room. The name stenciled on the frosted glass read, "Charles Alfred Cooper, Editor."

"Here we are," Felix said, brushing a lock of sandy hair off his freckled forehead. "I'll just let him know you're here." He raised his hand to knock, but a voice boomed from within.

"Come in, come in!"

Felix opened the door to admit them to an elegantly appointed office with leather wainscoting and tall French windows overlooking Cockburn Street. A plush green Oriental carpet covered most of the floor; a handsome oak desk commandeered the far end of the room, behind which was a floor-to-ceiling glass cabinet full of reference books and encyclopedias.

Behind the desk was seated a bulldog of a man, his stocky body clad in the most expensive threads a Princes Street clothier could offer. Ian could practically smell the aroma of money emanating from the expensive cigar smoldering in the ashtray, and from the flashing gold signet ring on the man's finger.

But his frank, open affect put Ian at ease. Charles Alfred Cooper might be a man of means, but as he came around the side of his desk, there was no mistaking the worry on his short, pug-nosed face.

"Thank you, Felix, that will be all," he said, dismissing their guide, who backed out of the room, closing the door behind him.

Their host turned to the two policemen. "Thank you for coming," he said earnestly in a deep, rounded voice that seemed odd coming from such a stubby body. "I appreciate you venturing out in this wretched weather."

Cooper gestured to a leather couch opposite his desk. When Sergeant Dickerson hesitated, the editor said, "Do sit, please," at which the two policemen sat on either end while Derek remained standing.

"Uh, sir," he began. "I were wonderin'—"

Cooper raised a meaty hand to cut him off. Smiling, he gestured to the door. "Tell the tea lad to give you all the biscuits you can eat. Take a few home with you as well, eh?"

"Thank *you*, sir!" Derek said, scurrying out of the room.

"Ask if there's a cheese-and-jam sandwich for you," Cooper called after him.

Returning to the chair behind his desk, the editor ran a hand through his rather luxuriant black hair and studied his visitors for a moment. "So," he said, "no doubt you're wondering what's so damn important."

"Well, I've been given to understand it concerns Mr. Corbin," Ian began, but the editor leapt from his chair.

"Jed's missing—no one's heard a peep from him since he was seen leaving the office early yesterday morning," he said, pacing back and forth in front of his desk. "And it's not like him to miss a day of work, especially with this poisoner on the loose. Jed's been pursuing the story relentlessly."

"Is it possible he's sick?" Dickerson asked.

Mr. Cooper snorted. "Jed Corbin doesn't *get* sick. And if he did, he'd show up all the same. I've never seen anyone so dedicated to his work. The man is damned ambitious."

"Perhaps he's been out following a lead?" Ian suggested.

Cooper dismissed him with a wave of his hand. "He reports in at least once a day. Felix went 'round to his digs first thing today—his landlady said he didn't come in last night."

"Is it possible—" Dickerson started.

"I'm telling you, something's wrong, man! He was dead set on the trail of this—this criminal, and then—whoosh! He vanishes, just like that."

"You've convinced me, Mr. Cooper," Ian said, rising from the couch. "May I see his desk, please?"

"Of course—certainly! Right this way," he said, leading them from the office into a secluded corner of the main room, beneath the eaves. "He likes it here. More private, you know. Says it helps him concentrate."

In contrast to Cooper's meticulously tidy office, the desk was a masterpiece of chaos. Papers sprouted from every surface like spring mushrooms—in piles and stacks, or single sheets jutting out from one of the many tomes on its overcrowded surface. Appointment books, dictionaries, encyclopedias, birth records, social registries—a small library of reference material was heaped upon its overburdened surface.

"Not the most orderly of fellows, I'm afraid," Cooper said, frowning as they contemplated the disarray before them.

"It'd be quite a feat sortin' out a clue to 'is whereabouts from this lot," Sergeant Dickerson said, scratching his head.

"Let's not panic," Ian said. "Let every man be master of his time."

"Weren't sayin' naught 'bout panic," Dickerson muttered. "I were jus' sayin'—"

"Hang on a minute," Ian said, spying a single cleared-out hollow in the mountain of miscellaneous objects. A discarded lead pencil lay next to a loose-leaf binder, the top page haphazardly torn off so that only a jagged remnant remained. "Someone was in a hurry when they tore this off."

Dickerson frowned, but Cooper's face registered hope. "I see what you're driving at. Do you think—"

"No doubt he took the hastily scribbled paper with him. Hopefully he used this," Ian said, seizing the discarded pencil next to the notebook. "And, given that he is a man of great energy and force, let us hope his penmanship displays the same qualities."

Using the blunt edge of the pencil, Ian carefully shaded in the apparently blank top page of the binder. As he did, the imprint of what had been written on the torn-off page appeared before their eyes.

27 Hastie's Close

"It's an address—I know the place!" Dickerson cried.

"Very clever indeed," Cooper remarked, rubbing his hands together. "Do you think that's where he went?"

"I think it likely enough," Ian replied. "Come, Sergeant, we haven't a moment to lose! We will keep you informed as best we can," he called over his shoulder to Cooper as he strode away.

Before the editor could utter a word of thanks, the two men were on their way out of the building and into the cruel, dark night.

CHAPTER FIFTY-ONE

Timothy had finished his bucket of oats by the time they returned and was standing with his left rear leg slightly lifted, resting on the tip of his broad hoof. His eyes were closed, and Ian could hear gentle snoring emanating from the muscular body. He gently touched the horse's neck and the big chestnut flicked his ears and opened his eyes, turning to Ian as if to say, "What, you again?"

"Fancy another journey by milk cart?" Ian asked Dickerson, who, he noticed, avoided going anywhere near Timothy. "Sergeant, are you afraid of horses?" he asked, detaching the feed bucket and storing it in the back of the cart.

"Course not!" Dickerson snorted.

Ian smiled as he climbed onto the cart and took up the reins. "There's no need to be ashamed of it. We all have our foibles, as it were. Might I remind you of my own aversion to—"

"I jes don' like 'em, is all," Dickerson said, climbing onto the cart.

"I see," Ian said, flicking the reins.

Timothy obeyed, if a bit sullenly, and off they went.

"What about t'lad?" asked Dickerson and they jostled along the nearly deserted streets. The vast majority of citizens had taken the weather as a cue to remain indoors, except the poor souls who had no choice.

"He'll find his way home," Ian replied. "Or they'll let him stay the night. I saw some cots in a back room."

The snow had finally abated but lay deep all around them as they launched out into the night. The sky remained starless, but the leeries had done their job even in the dreadful weather, and scores of lanterns twinkled all around them as Ian turned onto Old Fleshmarket Close.

"Hastie's Close is just off the Cowgate, isn't it?" Ian asked Dickerson, who huddled next to him on the driver's seat.

"Yes, sir."

"How is it you know this place?"

"Me sister has a school chum on Hastie's Close. Lives next door, at Number Twenty-Five."

"Not a very nice street."

"Her folks haven't much money."

"How is your sister, by the way?" Ian asked as they clattered past a pair of leeries trudging toward the High Street, long coats flapping at their knees, carrying their ladders and lamp-lighting sticks.

"Well enough, sir, thanks for askin'. She's a good girl, is my Pauline," he said with a sigh. "Wants t'be a nurse someday."

"Good for her," Ian said as they reached Cowgate. It was only a short jog to Hastie's Close, and Ian pulled the cart up in front of the entrance. "I was going to ask you to return Mr. Cob his cart while I went inside, but we'll sort that out later."

"I'd best stay with you," Dickerson said, peering into the dark alley, lit by only a single streetlamp. "It may be dangerous."

"I shouldn't wonder if you're right," Ian said, turning into the close. The buildings teetered and listed toward one another like tired old men, their crumbling exteriors exhausted with the weight of years. Their interiors brimmed with misery, mishap, and mayhem, the lot of the poor in Scotland's wealthiest city.

Even Timothy seemed ill at ease, snorting and tossing his head as they advanced deeper into the darkness. The sound of a baby crying came from inside one dilapidated tenement, while in another, a dog barked nervously.

"There it is, sir," Sergeant Dickerson whispered, pointing to a forlorn two-story building, as if he were afraid to awaken evil spirits dwelling in its ramshackle interior.

Ian secured Timothy to a lamppost, and the two men crept toward the front door. Ian raised his hand to knock, but as he did, he heard a faint groan from within, then the sound of scuffling, following by what sounded like a body dropping to the floor.

"Stand back!" he commanded Dickerson and then hurtled his body full force at the door.

The old wood shuddered and splintered, the ancient iron clasp giving way beneath the force of the blow. Ian felt pain slicing through his back—in the excitement of the moment, he had forgotten about his injured shoulder. The shock nearly brought him to his knees, but he staggered and regained his balance. The pale glow of the streetlamp showed the front room to be empty, save for a small table near the door and a pile of rags in the near corner, next to an empty fireplace. Ian fished around in the drawer for matches—finding a box, he fashioned a hasty torch with a couple of rags and handed it to Dickerson.

"This will do until we find something better."

Lighting the torch, the two of them peered around the deserted room. Spying a closed door on the far side, Ian beckoned the sergeant to follow him. There was an eerie quiet following the commotion of their entrance, but Ian had the feeling someone was on the other side of that door. Just as he was about to open it, they heard the sound of someone running at the back of the building, then a door opening and slamming.

"Around back—quickly!" Ian shouted. "Someone is trying to escape—try to cut them off!"

The sergeant dashed out the way they had come, while Ian tried the door handle, finding it locked. As he prepared to lunge at it, he heard another groan from the other side of the door, and a faint voice said, "Help . . . please help me." Gritting his teeth, Ian launched his body at the door, nearly blacking out from the pain as his shoulder received another blow. But the door gave way, and he stumbled into a tiny room with a single window on one side. A bed had been pushed against the wall opposite, and lying upon it, looking more dead than alive, was Jedidiah Corbin.

He looked wretched. His hair was matted, his clothing torn, and there was a terrible gray cast to his skin, visible even in the dim light. His shirt was spotted with what looked like bloodstains, and he wore no shoes. Ian quickly knelt by his side and felt for a pulse. Corbin's head was sunk upon his chest, but he raised it to give a weak smile.

"Just my luck. Should have known it would be . . . you . . . to the rescue."

And then he lost consciousness.

CHAPTER
FIFTY-TWO

Though Ian was taller than Corbin by half a foot, and heavier by several stone, lifting the dead weight of his inert body was no mean feat. There was no question of Ian slinging him over his shoulders—the detective's back was already aflame with pain—so he carried the reporter in his arms, as one might a child, out to where Timothy stood patiently waiting. Laying the reporter carefully in the back of the wagon, propped up against empty milk cans, he went to see what had become of Sergeant Dickerson.

But before he had taken more than a few steps, the sergeant emerged from the narrow gap between Number 27 and its neighboring building, wiping soot from his brow.

"Sorry, sir—whoever were in't house managed t'get away. Prob'ly jumped fence at back of property. Wi' the nest of alleys back there, no tellin' where they are."

"We'll worry about them later," Ian said, climbing onto the cart. "We must get Mr. Corbin to a doctor."

"Where to, sir?" Dickerson asked, heaving himself up to the seat.

"The Royal Infirmary," Ian said, giving the reins a flick. Timothy responded immediately—if he was tired, he showed no sign of it, trotting smartly back up the alley. "What an excellent horse," Ian said, turning west onto Cowgate. "I'll give him a double portion of oats while we're in the infirmary."

"Wha' about Mr. Cob, sir? Won't he be wonderin' wha' happened to his cart?"

"I imagine by now Mr. Cob is sound asleep in the back room of the Mole."

"Sir?"

"Half a guinea buys quite a lot of ale."

They spoke very little the rest of the way to the infirmary, but when they arrived, Ian was glad to see Conan Doyle conversing with several other medical students near the main entrance. When he saw Ian and Dickerson carrying Corbin between them, Doyle immediately went into action, directing a couple of orderlies to place the unconscious man on a gurney.

"How long has he been out?" Doyle asked, checking Corbin's pulse.

"About half an hour. He was in bad shape when I found him."

Lifting Corbin's eyelids, Doyle peered at his eyes. "That's not good."

"What?" asked Dickerson.

"The pupils are constricted. Let's get him to a treatment room straightaway."

They hurried through the halls, Doyle leading the way—the building bustled with nurses, doctors, and patients.

Scurrying to keep up with them, Sergeant Dickerson touched Ian's sleeve.

"Uh, sir? I hope you don' mind my askin', but it's late, like, an' my sister is home by herself—"

"By all means, go to her," Ian said. "You should have said something earlier."

"Thank you, sir."

"I'll see you tomorrow. And, Sergeant—"

"Yes, sir?"

"Good work tonight."

"Yes, sir—thank you, sir," he said. As Dickerson walked away, Ian thought there was a bit of a bounce in his step.

As Ian and Doyle rounded a corner with the gurney, a familiar figure approached them.

"Doyle! What have you got there?"

"Detective Hamilton just brought him in, Dr. Bell."

Acknowledging Ian with a brief nod, Dr. Bell leaned over the gurney to examine Corbin, who still hadn't regained consciousness. He looked at Corbin's eyes, felt his pulse, and put his ear to the reporter's chest. After a few moments, he straightened up, ran a hand over his bushy hair.

"This man is suffering from a laudanum overdose."

"Treatment, sir?" asked Doyle.

"Administer emetics and keep an eye on his respiratory response. His breathing is ominously shallow."

"Yes, sir," Doyle said, instructing the orderly to wheel Corbin into a treatment room.

When Doyle was gone, Bell turned to Ian. "He's lucky you found him. Another hour and he'd be dead. Where *did* you find him?"

Ian told him.

Dr. Bell listened carefully, arms crossed. "Who do you think did this to him?"

"The same person who is responsible for the deaths of Tom Caruthers, Geoffrey Pritchett, and probably Margaret Callahan."

"You know, young Arthur is quite keen on crime solving," Bell said. "He'll deny it if you ask him, but with his energy and love of action I sometimes think he's more suited to law enforcement than medicine. Don't tell him I said so."

"I won't."

Doyle reappeared, walking briskly toward them. "He's asking for you," he told Ian.

"He's awake, then?" Bell asked.

"Yes. Apart from being very thirsty, he claims to feel much better."

"Well done, Doyle," Bell said. His obvious affection for the young student made Ian like him more than he had initially.

"Follow me," Doyle told Ian. "The room is just down the hall."

Corbin was still lying on the gurney when they arrived, but when he saw Ian, he sat up. His gaze was clearer, though his cheeks were sunken and his eyes rimmed with red.

"Any chance of something for this pounding headache?" he asked Doyle.

"Best thing is to keep up your fluid intake," he answered, handing Corbin a cup of water.

Corbin drank it down greedily, then turned to Ian. "I am in your debt. I don't know what would have happened if you didn't chance to find me."

"It wasn't chance, Mr. Corbin."

"What, then?"

"Your colleagues were concerned about you. When we were alerted something was amiss, went to your offices—"

"But I told no one where I was going."

"We found an imprint of the address on the top page of the notebook you had written it on."

"Capital!" Corbin exclaimed, slapping his knee. "First-rate detective work!"

Ian shrugged. "Elementary. It was fortunate your penmanship was so forceful."

"Are you up to answering some questions?" asked Doyle.

Corbin nodded. "Anything that will bring us closer to capturing this fiend."

Ian looked at Doyle, but he showed no intention of leaving. After debating it with himself for a moment, he decided to let the man stay. It was, strictly speaking, unorthodox, but the young medical student had been so helpful, and appeared so keenly interested—and besides, Ian liked him. He suspected most everyone liked Conan Doyle. He was uncommonly affable and sweet-natured, yet entirely manly—the kind of stalwart fellow Ian would want beside him in a crisis.

He turned to Corbin, who was holding a damp towel at the back of his neck.

"This is much better, thanks," Corbin told Doyle. "Now then," he said to Ian. "How can I help you catch this monster?"

CHAPTER
FIFTY-THREE

It would not do.

She sat at her kitchen table, surrounded by her beloved objects—the fine linen tea towel with the picture of a rooster, his feathers red as blood; the Chinese tea set, delicate bone china so thin it was nearly transparent; the heavy lead crystal vase that sparkled in the afternoon sun. Each had a story and was precious to her because each represented a small piece of her past. She was all too aware of the impermanence of life—her horrific early years had tattooed it onto her soul, and her work as a nurse ground it in like the heel of a boot.

But objects lasted longer than people, and people were unreliable. Objects were solid, durable, and forgiving—they didn't come in the night and do terrible things to you, or turn their back on you because the truth was just too unbearable to face.

No, this would not do. Her plans, her carefully constructed scenarios, were in danger of being derailed—first by that horrid little reporter, and now by this busybody detective. A secret smile crept across her face as she thought of what she had done to the reporter—too bad he got away before she was finished with him. She had used laudanum before—it was easier to control the dose, and she was able to have some fun without having to worry about a sudden attack of vomiting.

But now she saw all her plans turning to mush like the snow in the fickle Scottish weather. One day the ground was covered in white, and the next it had melted, leaving the ugly browns and grays of an Edinburgh winter. Her hand tightened around the vial she held, the lid gleaming silver in the gaslight.

No, she thought, this really would not do. Throwing on her hat and cloak, she crept out into the night.

CHAPTER FIFTY-FOUR

By the time Corbin had finished recounting his ordeal, the chimes of midnight had rung, and most of the city had gone to bed. Doyle encouraged the reporter to stay the night at the infirmary, but he insisted on going home.

When Ian suggested Doyle might accompany him in returning the milk cart, his friend agreed enthusiastically. Timothy was fast asleep, his empty feed bucket dangling from his harness, but seemed glad to see them when he woke, tossing his head and neighing softly.

"He likes you," Doyle remarked.

"He associates me with a full stomach," Ian answered, climbing onto the cart.

They set off through the sleeping city, the air crisp and clear. The storm had blown over, and a shy sliver of moon hung high in the sky above. They soon arrived at the Mole, Timothy's strides lengthening the closer he got to home. At the pub, the barkeep told them Cob had gone up to bed, so Ian unfastened the horse and put him away in his stall, making sure he had plenty of water and clean hay.

He stood for a moment next to the horse, his hand on his flank, listening to the soft crunching sound as he munched on another bucket of oats. The aroma of sweet hay and horse sweat propelled him back to the days of his youth in the Highlands, riding a long-maned pony across the windswept hills of his ancestors, hunting for wild mushrooms along the streams and creeks snaking through the valleys. Ian seldom allowed himself to dwell on those times for fear emotion would overtake him. Shaking himself free of the memory, he stepped out to greet his companion.

If Doyle sensed Ian's emotional state, he had the good sense not to mention it. "The first round is on me," he said, pulling open the door to the pub.

Ian had never been so glad to be greeted by the hubbub and raucous good cheer of a Scottish pub. After a long night spent riding through dark alleys and icy streets, the warmth and bonhomie enveloped him like a fog, and he sank gratefully into its embrace. For just a little while he could forget that the city depended upon him to catch a ruthless killer stalking her inhabitants.

"Here we are," Doyle said, balancing two brimming pints and a couple of meat pies with chips as he walked carefully to their table next to the roaring fire. "We were lucky to get these," he said, putting down the food. "The kitchen is closing—some fellow ordered them but was so inebriated he forgot. He left before it came out, so it's ours for the taking."

"You are a magician, Dr. Doyle," said Ian, the smell of the food making him light-headed.

"I'm not a doctor yet," Doyle replied, plucking a chip from the plate. "Please, help yourself."

"What do I owe you?"

"Not a farthing," Doyle said. "You deserve it, after all your chasing around." He set a bottle of Glenlivet on the table. "I took the liberty of procuring this from the landlord. I thought the weather called for it—protect us from the elements, you know."

"I am in your debt," Ian said as Doyle poured them each a shot of whisky.

"I am rather in yours, for providing me with a most engaging evening. I'm afraid adventure runs in my blood, and you've given me a taste of it."

If food had ever tasted better, Ian could not remember it. Golden, crispy crust, hearty chunks of lamb and vegetable, chips as thick as his fingers. He didn't so much chew as inhale the food, and when he finished, he sat back in his chair, stupefied.

"That's better," Doyle remarked. "You must have been famished. You've had quite a night."

Ian wiped his mouth with a napkin. "I'll admit I've had few like it."

Doyle leaned forward, his eyes shining. "I want to hear all about it."

"Well," Ian said. "Maybe some—"

"I understand," Doyle added quickly. "It's an ongoing police investigation."

"I wish everyone were more like you. You wouldn't believe the people who fancy themselves amateur detectives."

Doyle smiled. "Maybe I'm one of those people."

"But you've the good sense to appreciate the difference between armchair sleuthing and actual detective work."

"Please don't tell me anything you feel would compromise your case," he said, pouring them each another dram of scotch.

Perhaps lulled by the warmth of the fire, a full stomach, and strong drink, buoyed by Doyle's interest, Ian launched into the story of the poisonings that began with the demise of Tom Caruthers and ended with the kidnapping of Jed Corbin, who had revealed some of the disturbing events he'd suffered during his ordeal.

"Why him, do you think?" asked Doyle.

"Presumably because he was on the killer's trail. At least we know now there's a woman involved, one way or another."

"But can we be sure of that? He admitted he might have been hallucinating."

"I intend to return tomorrow in the daylight. I want to comb the scene for physical clues. She may have left something behind."

"Do you think she really did—those things he claimed?"

Ian took a substantial swig of whisky. "Yes, I do."

Doyle shuddered. "I cannot conceive of the fairer sex behaving in such a depraved manner."

"Perhaps I have a more jaundiced view of human nature. And poison is a woman's weapon of choice more often than you might imagine."

"It makes sense, I suppose, since women lack the physical strength of men. Do you think it's significant that she used different types of poison in each of the three cases?"

"I take it to mean she's a risk-taker, and very confident. I wonder . . ."

"What?" Doyle said, his voice tight with excitement.

"I wonder if this is not her first foray into killing."

"You mean—"

"Would it be possible to look for suspicious poisonings in the infirmary's medical records?"

"If one had the time, I suppose it would."

"Oh, never mind," Ian said. "You are far too busy with your studies."

"But now you have intrigued me, and I want to help."

"No—it's far too much to ask."

"Pish tosh," said Doyle. "I feel very much involved already. By Jove, I'll do it!"

"Are you sure?"

Doyle leaned forward, his eyes shining. "I've never been surer of anything in my life."

"Good man," Ian said, finishing his drink.

"This calls for another round," Doyle said, pouring them each a glass.

Ian sipped his thoughtfully. "It's a game to her, I think. It reminds me of a painting I'm fond of in the National Gallery."

"Which one?"

"An Old Woman Cooking Eggs."

"Oh, yes, the Velázquez. I know it well."

"I've often thought how the people in that painting exist more as background to the objects, which are the artist's true subjects."

"I think I know what you mean. But how does that relate to—"

"Maybe I'm just being fanciful, but I feel this killer treats other people as objects."

"A chilling thought," Doyle said. Finishing his whisky, he poured them both another. "I nearly poisoned myself once, you know."

"You did?"

"I was experimenting on myself with gelsemium. But the effects got to be so unpleasant, I was forced to discontinue."

"Good Lord. Don't you think that was a bit foolhardy?"

"No more than rushing unarmed into a dark alley. Devotion to one's vocation can lead to all sorts of risky behavior."

"Speaking of which, how is my brother getting along? I hope you don't mind my asking."

Doyle took a long swallow from his glass. "Not at all. Donald has the keenest intellect I have ever encountered."

"It is his emotional state that concerns me."

"He's holding his own in that regard—better than some of the other lads, I'd say."

"I'm very glad to hear it."

"I think Dr. Bell is quite taken with him."

"Well, then, say no more," Ian remarked with some sarcasm.

"Why don't you like Dr. Bell?"

"He seems a bit stuck on himself."

"With good reason. I tell you, Hamilton, his diagnostic genius is like nothing I've ever seen. If he can teach it, it will revolutionize medicine."

"Some gifts are hard to pass on to others."

"Speaking of which, your brother tells me you're quite the poet."

"I used to fancy myself a writer. Now I'm a policeman."

"Why can't you be both? Look at James McLevy—I've read his memoirs. They're very good, don't you think?"

"Yes—and Carmichael's as well."

"The Glaswegian detective?"

"Yes. I'm not sure I see myself in that mold."

Doyle poured them both another drink. "I've done a bit of writing myself, you know. Not that I fancy myself any great shakes, but it's a nice change of pace."

"I should like to read it sometime."

"That's very kind of you. My point is that you shouldn't give up your writing just because you're a policeman."

"I write mostly for myself."

"Tell you what, Hamilton: I'll show you some of my scribblings if you show me yours."

Ian smiled. "All right. But now," he said, yawning, "I think it's time to call it a night. Thank you very much for the sustenance."

"The pleasure was mine. I appreciate not having to talk about seizures and sutures for just a few hours."

By the time they parted, last call had come and gone, and the city was in a deep slumber. Ian nearly fell asleep on the cab ride home. Bacchus met him at the door, and the last thing he remembered after falling gratefully into bed was the cat's cold, thin breath on his face.

CHAPTER
FIFTY-FIVE

Charles Odhran Buchanan yawned from his perch atop the milk cart as his horse, Timothy, trotted up Victoria Street early Thursday morning. He barely had to touch the reins—the big chestnut knew the route as well as he did. Being a horse, Tim was a creature of habit and enjoyed routine, knowing just where to stop for each delivery. Known to everyone as "Cob," Charles O. Buchanan was born and bred in Edinburgh and had barely strayed beyond its borders his whole life. The son of a laborer, he had watched his father worn away by toil and cheap gin at a young age, and vowed he would not suffer the same fate.

He managed to keep half of that vow. When Robbie Cavanaugh, longtime milkman of Edinburgh's East End, decided he needed an apprentice, Cob jumped at the chance and never looked back. He loved the early-morning rambles through the sleepy city, the sweet smell of the horse barn, the waves of his customers as he showed up with each day's bounty. Solitary by nature, Cob had just enough interaction with his fellow man to stave off loneliness, but not so much as to irritate him. Any leftover need for companionship was filled in evenings of drinking at one of Edinburgh's many public houses.

He remembered his father trudging wearily home from the Leith docks, his face bruised from fights with the hard men who worked the ships coming in from the Firth of Forth, his skin roughened by the cold winds blowing in from the North Sea. Cob's customers were always glad to see him, and some days his work was over by midafternoon. He even enjoyed the sound of the milk bottles clanking softly in the cart behind him as Timothy clopped up and down Edinburgh's ancient cobblestone streets.

Holding the reins in his right hand, Cob rubbed his throbbing temples with his other, groaning as the cart bounced over a pothole. He had not done well keeping the second part of his vow. His father's love of the bottle had been passed onto him—try as he might, Cob couldn't resist a night of drinking, especially if someone else was paying. Last night he had really tied one on. He'd bought rounds for everyone at the Mole, buoyed by the generosity of that police detective, who had also stuffed Timothy with so many oats the big gelding actually looked fatter today, if a bit sleepy from his late night. The fellow had even left a few additional shillings for feed, so Cob decided to treat the horse to carrots and fall apples from the fruit and vegetable sellers along the Grassmarket.

There wasn't room for the horse and cart on narrow Victoria Terrace, so Cob left Tim napping next to a lamppost while he lugged a rack of bottles up the steep staircase. He didn't mind—his customers on "the Terrace" always tipped generously at Christmas. As he dropped off the last bottle, he caught some movement out of the corner of his eye. Turning to look, Cob thought he saw a flash of black disappearing into the far alley, but it could have been a trick of the light. It was early enough that not many folks were awake yet.

He didn't give it a second thought as he carried the empty milk rack back down the stairs, where he was greeted by Tim's low, welcoming whinny. It looked to be a fine day, he thought as he swung the rack onto the back of the cart and climbed up onto the driver's seat. If he was quick about it, he might just make first call at the Mole.

CHAPTER
FIFTY-SIX

Ian awoke Thursday morning to the sound of retching coming from Donald's room. Instantly alert, he sprang from bed and, without throwing on his robe, banged on his brother's door. The cat, roused from a deep sleep, followed him stiff-legged.

"Come in," Donald said, his voice weak.

Ian threw open the door to find his brother sitting on the side of the bed, a basin in his hands.

"What happened?"

"Can't understand it. One moment I was fine, and the next—" He broke off, shaken by spasms of vomiting.

"What did you eat?"

"Nothing—I just made some coffee."

"With cream?" Donald liked his morning coffee very light—half cream, half coffee.

"The usual amount. The milkman had just arrived, so I skimmed off the cream, and left some for the cat—" He was interrupted again by a violent bout of retching.

Ian bounded from the room and raced to the kitchen, where Bacchus was sniffing at a bowl of cream next to the icebox. Snatching it up, Ian threw the contents in the sink. The cat flicked his tail irritably and protested by shoving his head into Ian's ankles.

Ian returned to his brother's room to find Donald perched on the edge of the bed, pale and exhausted.

"We're going to hospital. Now," Ian said.

"But—"

"Now," Ian repeated.

Too weak to object, his brother complied meekly. Before they left, Ian grabbed the open bottle of milk, fastened the lid securely in place, and tucked it into a canvas satchel.

"Why are you bringing that?" said Donald.

"I am fairly certain you've been poisoned."

"By the milkman?"

"By someone who tampered with this bottle. And I mean to have proof, so we're going to get it tested. But first we need to get you treated."

Twenty minutes later, they were seated in the Royal Infirmary waiting room. The door to the treatment room was flung open, and Conan Doyle came flying through it. Apart from a slight redness around his eyes, he seemed to have survived the excesses of the previous night rather well. He approached the brothers, concern in his blue eyes.

"What happened?"

Ian told of the sudden onset of symptoms and gave him the milk bottle from his satchel.

"Good thinking!" Doyle said. "I'll get it tested straightaway. How are you feeling?" he asked Donald.

"Better. The cramps have abated."

"We're going to admit you for observation."

"I don't think that's necessary."

"I'm afraid I must insist."

Donald shrugged—he looked frightened and cowed, and Ian couldn't blame him. After escorting his brother to a bed in the semi-private wing of the hospital, Ian joined Conan Doyle in the pathology laboratory.

"I am beginning with the Reinsch test," Doyle said. "If it is not conclusive, we can proceed to the Marsh test. I added hydrochloric acid to a sample of the suspect milk, which I then boiled," he said, pointing to a beaker of white liquid on the lab table. "Now all that remains is to insert a copper strip and heat it."

Ian observed the process with interest, his fascination with the process temporarily overcoming the growing knowledge that he and his brother were very likely in danger. Placing the copper strip over the open flame of a Bunsen burner, Doyle held a piece of clear glass above the strip. Ian watched as a dark silver deposit appeared on the glass.

"The results indicate the presence of a heavy metal," Doyle said. "The Marsh test will confirm if it is arsenic, but there can be no doubt the milk was indeed poisoned. But who did this, and why?"

"I feel certain it's the same person or persons responsible for the crimes I am currently investigating."

"You must be getting closer to finding them out, which is probably why they took such a drastic step."

"Precisely what I was thinking," Ian said. "And now, I must be on my way."

"Please be careful," Doyle said, following him out of the office and down the hall. "You are clearly dealing with a driven and desperate character."

"On that we agree," Ian said. "Thank you for all you've done, and if my brother—"

"He is in good hands," said Doyle. "Fortunately, he seems not to have ingested too much of the poison, and should make a full recovery. Oh, that reminds me—I did a bit of digging into the infirmary records, and I found one poisoning that was ruled a suicide, but I'm not entirely convinced."

"Oh?"

"A few months ago, a schoolmaster at Leith Walk Primary School by the name of Richard Brown was admitted to the infirmary suffering from arsenic poisoning. He had recently been fired, so it was assumed he had tried to kill himself."

Ian leaned forward, hanging on every word. "Go on."

"But here's the strange part. Upon being admitted, he rallied, but then, mysteriously, he took a turn for the worse and died."

"What does that suggest to you?"

"That your theory that this perpetrator may be a medical professional may be correct."

"If that is the case, none of your patients is safe."

"Just so."

"Can you think of anyone you might suspect of this heinous behavior?"

"No one. And I hasten to add that it is just a theory."

"My brother—"

"I will personally supervise his care. Please don't trouble yourself."

"How can I thank you for all you've done?" Ian said.

"By catching this murderous fiend."

"I will not rest until I do. What was the name of that schoolteacher?"

"Richard Brown."

Wrapping his cloak around his body, he left the infirmary, hailing a cab to take him to the station house.

It was early yet when he arrived, and apart from a sleepy desk sergeant, only Constables Bowers and Turnbull were there. Bowers greeted him with a shy smile, his pale-blue eyes beneath blond eyebrows wide with good humor. When Constable Turnbull saw Ian, however, he attempted to slink away into a little side office the officers used as a break room. Ian followed him, determined to have it out.

"Good morning, Constable," Ian said, catching up to him in the hall.

Half turning to face him, Turnbull looked cornered, a sickly smile on his sallow face, his hairpiece slightly askew, like a lopsided muskrat.

"I understand you received a message for me," Ian remarked.

Turnbull frowned. "Did I?" he said unconvincingly.

Ian put his face close to the constable's, so near he could make out each pockmark on his heavily rutted skin.

"If you were upset by my intervention in your dealings with Angus McAllister, you should have taken it up with me, rather than attempting to sabotage an investigation behind my back."

"Are you talking about that scruffy little ragamuffin?" Turnbull said, the corner of his mouth lifted in a sneer. "I wouldn't trust anything he said. I'm surprised you would."

"Thanks to your petty meddling, Turnbull, a man almost died. If you ever attempt to thwart an investigation again, I will not only see to it that you are fired from the force, but I will have you thrown in jail."

Trembling with rage, Ian turned on his heel, leaving the constable cowering in the corner of the hall. He emerged into the main room feeling lighter for having his say but aware that he might have made an enemy for life. The trouble was, he had no idea how dangerous that enemy might prove to be.

CHAPTER
FIFTY-SEVEN

Eleanor Atkinson was just sitting down to elevenses in her second-floor flat on Royal Terrace when the doorbell rang. She wasn't expecting anyone, and was a little annoyed at the timing—the first-flush Darjeeling had steeped for five minutes; if she let it sit much longer, it would turn bitter.

Peering through the peephole, she saw a well-dressed young lady in a smart green traveling suit with a matching handbag. She looked eminently respectable. Intrigued, Eleanor opened the door.

"Good morning," the young woman said. "My name is Harriet Sloan. Forgive me for bothering you, but I was hoping I might ask you a few questions about Thomas Caruthers."

"Oh, yes—you sent me the note about meeting at the funeral! I looked for you, but—"

"My apologies. Something came up."

"I'm not entirely clear what your relationship was to Tom," Eleanor said.

"I was his personal nurse, and I'm helping the police with their investigation of his death."

"Surely they don't think I'm involved?"

"Oh, it's nothing like that—at least, I don't think so. May I come in?"

"Yes, of course," Eleanor said, admitting her visitor into the foyer.

"What a very nice place you have," the young woman said politely.

"It belonged to my parents, and I inherited it after their death," she said, leading her guest through to the parlor.

"What a comfort it is to know that some parents can be counted on," Harriet replied, removing her hat to reveal a mass of red hair.

"Will you join me for some tea?" she asked, pondering her visitor's odd remark.

"What a lovely notion, thank you," Harriet said, lowering herself onto the pink chintz settee as though she were a frequent and welcome visitor.

Eleanor sensed something strange beneath the veneer of politesse, but being a well-brought-up girl, she would never consider saying or doing anything that might be construed as rude or inhospitable.

"Milk and sugar?" she said, pouring them each a cup of tea.

"Both, please," Harriet replied, helping herself to lemon cake.

After serving her guest, Eleanor raised a cup of the golden liquid to her mouth. "Now then," she said. "How can I help you?"

CHAPTER
FIFTY-EIGHT

James McAllister looked surprised to see Ian and Sergeant Dickerson enter his cluttered pawnshop later that morning. Picking their way through the bric-a-brac, the two policemen stood next to a gaily painted wooden carousel horse, still on its metal pole. Its lips were drawn back in a lurid grin, teeth bared in an expression of fury or defiance, or perhaps fear—it was hard to tell. Ian ran his hand over the red-and-yellow saddle, the paint chipped in several places.

"I trust you have had a chance to confer with your colleagues regarding a certain tiepin," he said as a nervous smile replaced McAllister's initial expression of alarm.

"I did indeed," said he, "an' none a 'em seen anythin'."

"I wonder," Ian mused. "Can we believe you?"

"Wha' cause ha'e I t'lie to ye?"

"I can think of three or four."

"I swear it, on me dear old mum's grave."

"Your mother is alive and well," Ian replied. "I saw her Wednesday last at the market with your brother."

"Ach, it's jus' an expression," McAllister said. His eyes darted around the shop, falling on Sergeant Dickerson, whose hand rested on an elaborately carved figurine of a mermaid, evidently from the prow of a ship. "See 'ere," McAllister said, "I'll gae ye that mermaid for free—she's worth two guineas at least."

"What are you so afraid of, Mr. McAllister?" said Ian.

"I ain' afraid a naught."

"Then why are you carrying a revolver?"

The pawnbroker's eyes widened. "What are ye, some kind o' magician?"

"There is a bulge in your right jacket pocket, and whatever you have in there is obviously preying on your mind, since you continuously slide your right hand inside the pocket to check on it. As you evidenced no such behavior the first two times we saw you, it is either something of great value, or—the more likely explanation—a firearm."

"Mary, Mother of God, y'are a magician!"

"What terrifies you so that you carry a loaded pistol in your own store?"

Dickerson cleared his throat. "Sir?"

"Yes, Sergeant?" said Ian.

"Maybe this is the reason," Dickerson said, pointing to the front-door lock, which had clearly been tampered with. The wood on the door was chipped and splintered, as if someone had been trying to pry the lock off.

"Well spotted, Sergeant! Someone has tried to break into your shop," Ian said to the pawnbroker.

"Aye, but only took th'one thing."

"Let me guess: a tiepin in the shape of a horse."

McAllister's shoulders sagged in defeat. "Ach, it weren't worth *that* much. Why break in only t'steal that?"

"That is indeed the question. How did you come upon it in the first place?"

"A great hulkin' fellow wi' yellow hair brought it."

"Did you happen to catch his name?"

"Aye, I think his companion called 'im Gordy."

"Isn't that the fella y'said ye fought in t'pub?" Dickerson asked Ian.

Ian nodded. "It would seem he's turned up again, like a bad penny. You said he had a companion," he said to McAllister. "Can you describe that person?"

"Aye. Little runt, he was, wi' a crooked nose."

"Thank you, Mr. McAllister," Ian said. "Had you told me the truth from the beginning, you might not have suffered the burglary."

McAllister took the pistol from his pocket and waved it around. "If they so much as show their ugly mugs 'round 'ere, I'll unload this on 'em, I swear."

"That would be unwise. I shouldn't like to add murder to your list of crimes," Ian said.

The pawnbroker frowned and scratched his head.

"In any case, I shouldn't worry about another break-in. They seem to have found what they came for. Good day, Mr. McAllister."

They left the shopkeeper muttering to himself, and stepped into the street.

"Well, well," said Ian as he and the sergeant stood outside the building, a cold wind whipping in from the Firth of Forth. "The plot thickens."

"D'you think those fellas also poisoned Tom Caruthers and th'others?" Dickerson asked as they turned their steps west along the Cowgate.

"It seems apparent they are connected somehow, though in what way escapes me." Ian stood aside to let a tired-looking mother wheeling a baby carriage pass by on the narrow sidewalk. Another small child trudged at her side, bundled up against the cold.

"Why would they steal a worthless tiepin?" asked Dickerson.

"Maybe there was something incriminating about it . . . or maybe the killer wanted it as a sort of keepsake."

"Wha' for?"

"As a reminder, a memento of the crime."

Dickerson shivered. "That's cold, that is."

"Actually, I think it's quite human."

"Where to now, sir?"

"Leith Walk Primary School," said Ian. Flinging his hand into the air, he shouted, "Taxi!"

After he interviewed the headmaster, James McIntyre, it was clear to Ian the man was hell-bent on revealing as little as possible about the reason Richard Brown had been fired after five years at the school. After delivering some mumbo jumbo about "disappointing job performance," he made it clear he had nothing more to say.

"Regrettable business," he said as he ushered the policemen out of his book-lined office. "He wasn't a bad chap. Been on the staff nearly since the school's inception. A real pity, his suicide."

"Was it? A suicide?" Ian asked.

McIntyre frowned. "What else would it be?"

"That's what I mean to find out," Ian said. "Good day."

As they made their way down the long hallway toward the exit, a door to one of the classrooms opened slightly, and a man's face peered out.

"Pssst! Detective," he whispered.

Ian stopped walking. "Yes?"

"May I have a word?"

"Certainly, Mr.—"

"Simpson. Henry Simpson," he replied, opening the door all the way. "In here, if you please."

Mr. Simpson looked both ways down the hall before closing and locking the door behind them. It was evidently a geography classroom, judging by the maps pinned to the walls and the large mounted globe of the world in the front of the room.

"Please don't think me terribly nosy, but I happened to overhear your conversation with the headmaster."

"And?"

Simpson adjusted his thick black glasses. He was a slight man, his suit hanging so loosely it appeared several sizes too large, as if a child had wandered into the adult section of a clothing store. His brown eyes were large and myopic beneath the heavy lenses; he licked his thick lips nervously as he beckoned the policemen farther into the room.

"It won't do to let the headmaster know I've spoken to you," he said.

"I see no reason he should know," Ian replied.

"Very well." He licked his lips again and tugged at his shirt collar, though it was already loose on his scrawny neck. "Richard Brown was . . . how can I say it? The fact is, Detective, he was a pervert."

"And by that you mean—?"

Simpson wiped sweat from his upper lip, though the room was quite cool. "He preyed on the children. Girls, mostly—young as eight or nine, some of them. That's why he was let go. The school won't admit it publically, but it's no secret among the faculty."

"Do you believe Richard Brown committed suicide?"

Simpson bit his lip. "That's the devilish thing, you see—I don't, really."

"Why not?"

"He didn't strike me as the type. When he was fired, he hardly seemed surprised. Took it all in stride, you know. He certainly wasn't repentant. He wore the same smirk he'd always had."

"Thank you, Mr. Simpson, you've been extremely helpful," said Ian.

"You won't let on that I told you, will you?"

"You have my word."

Simpson opened the door a crack and peered up and down the hall. "Go ahead—the coast is clear."

"Thank you again," said Ian as he and Dickerson quickly left the building.

"D'ye think Brown was murdered, sir?" the sergeant asked as they strode up Leith Walk in search of a cab.

"If so, it would fit in with what I now believe to be the killer's motive."

"An' wha's that, sir?"

"Vengeance, Sergeant. I believe she sees herself as an avenging angel, bringing her own form of justice to those she sees as deserving of her wrath."

"It's a twisted kind o' justice, sir."

"She is a twisted individual, though what made her so I cannot say. 'Vengeance is in my heart, death in my hand, blood and revenge are hammering in my head.'"

"That's not from *Hamlet*, sir."

"No, it's *Titus Andronicus*."

It didn't take long to find a cab. After a short ride to the station house, they were mounting the steps to the building when a voice called out behind them.

"Detective Hamilton!"

They looked up to see a man running full tilt toward them. As he got closer, Ian saw it was Jed Corbin.

"Good heavens," he said. "What is so urgent?"

"It's Eleanor Atkinson," Corbin said, panting.

"Tom Caruthers' mistress?" said Ian.

"The same. I saw you talking to her at the funeral and—well, the fact is, she's disappeared."

"What do you mean, disappeared?"

"I went 'round to her place to ask a few questions about Caruthers, and her landlady said she'd left a note that she'd gone to Devon," he said, wiping sweat from his forehead.

"That hardly strikes me as—"

"But the landlady said it was all quite strange because she wasn't aware of her having any connections to Devon."

Ian frowned. "Still—"

"And the landlady said the note wasn't in her handwriting! I asked if she was certain, and she said she'd swear to it."

Ian exchanged a look with Sergeant Dickerson. "I have to admit, that does sound odd. Thank you for bringing it to our attention."

"You saved my life. I am forever in your debt."

"I should like to think you also want to prevent harm coming to an innocent young lady."

"Of course," the reporter replied, coloring.

"Well done, Mr. Corbin."

"I have the address if you care to go 'round to her place."

"Actually, we were about to revisit Hastie's Close. Whoever has her may very well have taken her there. I don't suppose you'd like to accompany us."

The reporter hesitated. "Well, I—"

"I can understand if you'd rather not, but it could be most helpful."

"Very well. If it helps you capture this demon."

"I assure you, we are looking for someone very much in human form," Ian said, though it seemed to him these days that the line between person and demon was a thin one indeed.

CHAPTER
FIFTY-NINE

The corridors of Hastie's Close were as dank and dusty as ever, and Sergeant Dickerson gave a hacking cough to clear his lungs as the three men alighted from their cab and made their way down the narrow maze of streets. Now that the weather had decided to take mercy on Edinburgh's residents, cabs were plentiful—the more you needed the bloody things, the harder they were to obtain, Dickerson mused as he trotted after DI Hamilton and Jed Corbin.

"Well, here we are," Hamilton said as they stood in front of Number 27.

The door stood ajar, a single slip of dingy sunlight coming through the lone window of the front room. Dust particles danced in the shaft of light, a strangely mesmerizing sight.

"Did you find out who owns it?" Corbin asked.

"The same landlord who owns Number Twenty-Five," said the detective. "But this one has been unoccupied for several weeks after the previous tenants were evicted. He seemed surprised to hear someone had broken in. Are you up to going in?"

"Certainly," said the reporter, but Dickerson thought his voice shook a little, and he looked unsteady as he stepped over the sill.

"What do you remember?" Hamilton asked as they stood in the barren foyer, with its rough-hewn plank floor. A few abandoned cobwebs dangled over their heads.

"Not much. I took a few steps in, then called out to see if anyone was here." Corbin turned to his right, pointing to the empty wall. "There was a curtain here."

"We saw no curtain there when we arrived."

"I remember wondering what was behind it. I heard a loud noise in the back of the room, called out in alarm, and that's when I felt the needle go into my shoulder."

"Presumably the perpetrator was hidden behind the curtain."

"Yes," Corbin said. "I'm fairly certain that's what happened."

"What else do you remember?" Ian asked as they walked through the empty front room to the back room where Corbin had been held.

"The smell," he said with a shudder. "Every time I started to come to, there was this terrible sickly sweet odor."

"Any idea what it might have been?"

"Possibly perfume, but it was awful, like decaying flowers. I suppose my reaction could have been a result of the drugs in my system."

"Do you smell it now?"

"No," Corbin said, sniffing the air. "It seems to have disappeared."

"What does it mean, d'you think, sir?" asked Dickerson.

Hamilton shook his head. "It could be a clue to the woman's identity, but it might be coincidental." He pointed to a single bed on the far side of the room. "Were you tied up the entire time?"

"No. Sometimes I woke to find myself unbound, but I was too drugged and confused to muster the energy necessary to escape."

"Were you aware of anyone apart from the woman you encountered?"

Dickerson saw the reporter's clenched jaw, remembering his description of the perverted and degrading things she'd done to him. The sergeant didn't care to think of women as capable of such disgusting behavior, even though years as a policeman had taught him otherwise.

"I could have dreamed it, but I thought I heard a man's voice at some point—maybe even two."

"Anything you remember about them?"

"One had a stutter."

"A stutter, eh?"

"Do you know who that might be?"

"I have an idea, yes. Did you get a glimpse of them at all?"

"I'm afraid not. I wish I could be more helpful, truly, I do," he said, and Dickerson thought he saw tears at the corners of the reporter's eyes.

"Never mind," Hamilton said gently. "You have been through an ordeal none of us would envy."

He proceeded to examine every corner of the room. Lifting the moth-eaten blanket, he shook it carefully over the bed, then bent over to examine the dusty mattress.

"Ah!" he said, plucking something from it.

"What is it, sir?" Dickerson asked.

"This," Hamilton said, showing him what looked to be a curly red hair. "Of course, it could have been here all along," he added. Folding it carefully in a handkerchief, he tucked it away in his coat pocket.

Dickerson was immediately put in mind of Fair Kate, whose effect on him still stunned the sergeant. She was motherly and matronly, alluring and attractive—she roused so many conflicting feelings that his breath quickened just thinking about her. And her masses of curly red hair—was it real or dyed? He could not tell; it seemed to go with her white skin and pale eyes, but William Dickerson had not enough experience to judge. In spite of having a sister and a beautiful girlfriend, he was still in many ways an innocent when it came to feminine wiles.

He deeply hoped Fair Kate was not guilty—he could not imagine her poisoning anyone, let alone poor, gentle Big Margaret. Still, he was learning the hard way that all too often things most fervently hoped for were the ones most readily denied.

"Look at this," Hamilton said. On his hands and knees, he was peering under the bed. Reaching his long arm underneath it, he drew out an object and held it up to the light. Dickerson was surprised to see a human skull, the empty eye sockets set over the grinning mouth.

"What on earth—?" Corbin said, staring at it.

"It would seem whoever kidnapped you has a morbid sense of humor."

Dickerson scratched his head. "But why, sir? Why a skull?"

"This reinforces my theory that, on some level, this is a game to our killer. 'Alas, poor Yorick.'"

"Do ye—do y'think they know 'bout us bein' in the play, then, sir?"

"I wouldn't be surprised. I do think they left this to taunt us," said Hamilton. "And now," he told Corbin, "if you would point me the way to Eleanor Atkinson's abode, I should like to question her landlady for myself."

"Certainly," the reporter said, following them out of the building.

Sergeant Dickerson breathed more easily once they had pulled the rickety door closed behind them. To his relief, DI Hamilton called a cab to take them to Royal Terrace—he didn't fancy a walk on what was becoming an increasingly cold, nasty day.

After parting from Corbin, the two men found themselves in the back of a hansom cab as it rattled across town, the sky darkening as day slipped into dusk. Leaning back in the cushioned seat, DI Hamilton gazed out the window as light sleet began to fall.

"It does occur to me that these murders mirror much of the action in Hamlet. Had you remarked upon that, Sergeant?"

"No, sir," Dickerson replied. He liked it when the detective rhapsodized philosophical, but also feared being left behind Hamilton's rapidly advancing train of thought.

"Big Margaret dies like Ophelia, drowned beneath a willow with leaves in her hair, then Jed Corbin is stabbed from behind a curtain like Polonius—not to mention the poisonings, of course, which are both an overriding theme and the climax of the play. And now the skull."

"You've a good point, sir, though I'm not sure where it leads."

"Perhaps nowhere. One thing is certain: this killer is more determined than our hesitant prince to wreak vengeance." The detective sat lost in thought the rest of the ride, staring out the window as Old Town gave way to the elegant Royal Terrace.

The interview with Miss Atkinson's landlady yielded nothing of interest, other than a confirmation that the note did not match the handwriting she was familiar with; she was quite insistent on that point. As to enemies her tenant might have, she could not think of any, further stating that Miss Atkinson had few visitors and kept largely to herself.

When DI Hamilton offered to drop Dickerson off at home, the sergeant readily agreed; the sleet had not abated, and it looked to be a miserable night. Dickerson had just enough time for a quick supper with his younger sister before dress rehearsal for the play. He relished any extra time he might be able to spend with Pauline. He hadn't seen much of her since this case started, and had virtually no time to see his beloved Caroline. He hoped she would come see him in *Hamlet*, he thought as he trudged up the front stoop to his flat.

Across the street, a pair of eyes watched as he opened the front door and went inside. Their gaze turned to the street, following the cab as it rolled away and disappeared into the night.

CHAPTER SIXTY

Lillian had invited Ian over for a quick supper before dress rehearsal of *Hamlet* that evening. He had not spoken with her since his discovery of the letter, and as he sat in the back of the cab on the way to her house, anger seeped into his soul like acid. And what, really, was he angry at? At people for not being perfect? As if he himself were a paragon of virtue—he knew that was absurd, yet each time someone disappointed him, part of him shriveled and died. He didn't expect much of humanity in general, but when it came to individuals, hope, it seemed, sprang eternal. Every new person he met had a chance to *not* disappoint him, yet they invariably did.

In that sense, Fiona Stuart was refreshing, because her flaws were so immediately apparent. Most people tried to show themselves better than they actually were, whereas Fiona seemed to do just the opposite. Getting to know someone like her could be a series of pleasant surprises instead of a long litany of disappointments.

He gazed out the window at the jagged shards of freezing rain. Was his reaction to disappointment a personality flaw, a rift in his character like the jagged fault lines running down the steep sides of Castle Rock? In the winter, they filled with layers of ice, gleaming, white and cold. His own heart felt frozen; he wondered if it would ever thaw out completely, or if the tiny ice crystals were embedded forever deep inside him.

And now Lillian had disappointed him, freezing him out of something so important. That he held her in such high esteem only made it worse. He was furious but afraid to confront her. He wished he could forget he ever saw the damn thing, yet he could not leave it. Donald was right: she would notice something was off if he tried to continue as if he had never seen the letter.

When Ian arrived, Lillian was in the kitchen preparing dinner. He took her offer of a glass of whisky, and after she refused his offer of help, he sat in front of the fire, sipping his drink, trying to decide how to approach the matter. Finally, he went back into the kitchen, where she was chopping vegetables. Two fat loin lamb chops sat on the counter, and he could smell potatoes and turnips boiling on the stove. Leaning against the door frame, he watched her quick, capable hands chopping carrots and cabbage.

"Did you know my brother is a homosexual?" Ian said suddenly, wanting to shock her, shake her up, maybe even hurt her.

To his surprise, she went right on chopping the vegetables as if he hadn't spoken.

"Did you hear me?" he said louder.

"Oh, aye," she replied calmly, stirring the pot. "I heard ye."

He noted with satisfaction her vowels were thickening—a sure sign she was agitated, even though she was trying to hide it.

"Well?" he said. "Did you know?"

"Are ye really just discovering this now, Ian?" she said, the steam swirling around her face, droplets catching on the frizzy fringes of her hair.

"Why? How long have you known?" he said, astonished.

"It was evident to me when he was very young."

"Why have you never mentioned it to me?"

"I didn't see the necessity of it," she said, scooping the chopped vegetables into the boiling water.

"Did my parents know?"

"Your mother and I spoke of it once, years ago," she said, wiping her hands on a dish towel. "She saw signs of it when he was just a wee bairn."

"And my father?"

Lillian frowned. "I don't think he ever quite accepted it in a son of his."

"And the letter?" he blurted out. "Why did you keep that from me?"

Her expression was opaque, but her mouth twitched. "What letter?"

"The one from my mother I found in your desk."

Lillian took a deep breath, staring into the pot. "What cause did you have to be snooping among my things?"

"It was protruding from the side of the desk, and I chanced to see it."

"So you took it upon yourself to read something not addressed to you."

He had no defense against her remark. He stood, hands at his sides, swallowed in miserable silence. This was the only quarrel he could remember having with his aunt since the age of ten, when he'd poured salt into her sugar bowl as a Hallowe'en prank.

She folded her arms over her thin chest, and for a moment, she looked like a tired old woman. He longed to wrap her in his arms and beg forgiveness, but his pride and anger were deeper than his shame, keeping his spine rigid.

"So you read it," she said quietly.

Her reaction was surprising. He had half expected her to rail at him, but her voice was calm.

"Why did you not tell me?" he said.

"What good could possibly come of it?"

"It is a potential clue in apprehending a murderer!"

"Revenge is a dark alley no man should tread, Ian."

"I'm speaking of justice, not revenge. My mother feared something—what was it?"

She sighed heavily, and he sensed all the disappointments of a long life in that extended exhale. "Can ye not let the dead rest in peace?"

He stared at her. "What peace can there be for those who met so cruel a fate?"

"Ian," she said, "some things are better left unexamined." There was an odd tone to her voice he had never heard before, a wary resignation, as if she were repeating a conclusion she didn't believe in herself yet felt compelled to stick with.

He stared at her, studying her face. It was the same face he had loved all these years, the face of his mother's own sister, with the same keen eyes and firm mouth, but there was a defeat in her eyes that shocked him to the core. She wasn't daring him to defy her—she was telling him it was no use to try.

"So you know, but you won't tell me?" he said finally.

"Not exactly, no."

"What, then?"

"Ach, Ian, must ye be so stubborn?" she said. "There are places it is not wise tae tread. I couldn't bear to lose ye. More I cannae say."

There was no mistaking the fear in her voice. Ian took a step backward. "All right, Auntie," he said softly. "I will leave this—for now, at least."

Dinner was a strained affair. Though on any other occasion he would have found the food delicious, Ian barely tasted it. Making an excuse to leave early, he fled his aunt's house for the cold embrace of a November night.

Wrestling with his conflicting thoughts and emotions, Ian went home on foot. The sleet had stopped, but the air was biting; the icy cobblestones glistened beneath flickering gaslights. The city had become a magical fairyland, as dangerous as it was beautiful. One misstep and disaster could follow.

As he walked, he tried, as he had so many times before, to remember the last thing he'd said to his mother. The time before the fire blurred into an indistinct series of days, full of vague images, but he could not conjure up any words exchanged between them.

There was always a last time, he knew, in the brief, mortal lives of human beings. A last meal, a last morning coffee, a last conversation with loved ones. Ian yearned for something to hold on to—the memory of a moment, an embrace, a kind word with his mother before the conflagration took her.

Turning onto Chambers Street, Ian sank deeper into contemplation. Some people fell gratefully into death's embrace, relieved to have an end to their suffering. He wondered which camp he would fall into—would he fight till the last or welcome death like an old friend, glad for the release from life's slings and arrows? Like Hamlet, would he lean into the darkness, yearning for that undiscovered country from which no traveler returns? More than he cared to admit, he understood Hamlet's dark imaginings, his fascination with suicide as a means of taking fate into one's own hands.

Ian was so deep in thought that he failed to notice the two figures trailing him at a distance as he turned onto George IV Bridge. When they caught up with him as it passed over the Cowgate, it was too late, and they were upon him.

CHAPTER
SIXTY-ONE

Donald Hamilton was about to turn in for the night when he heard a sound at the front door, like the scratching of an animal. Imagining Bacchus had somehow got out, he turned up the gas in the parlor to find the cat sitting on an armchair in front of the fireplace. Thinking the sound must be another bout of sleet, he went to close the front curtains against the draft. As he walked past the front door, he heard it again. Wary but curious, he unlocked the door and opened it a crack.

Crumpled in a heap on the front stoop, bloody and bruised, was his younger brother, Ian.

"Good Lord," Donald muttered. Leaning over, he scooped his brother up in his arms and carried him inside.

"What have you gotten yourself into now?" he said as he examined his brother's injuries, which included numerous head contusions and abrasions.

"Our old friend Gordy and his little pal," Ian murmured. "The idiots from the White Hart. Two-to-one odds they were paid to attack me."

"You're lucky they didn't kill you," Donald said, peeling off Ian's shirt to reveal bruises on his torso. "Why didn't they, do you suppose?"

"Even a cold-blooded killer knows there's a great difference between a dead policeman and a live one."

"You mean the lads on the force wouldn't rest until your death was avenged?" he said, examining Ian's injuries.

"Something like that."

"Though from what you've told me, you're none too popular."

"True enough. How bad is it?"

"I haven't found any broken bones, if that's what you're asking."

"I'm sorry, Donald."

"And so you should be. Keeping me up when I should be asleep. Shame on you," he said, getting up to fetch the carbolic acid. "This may sting a bit," he said, returning with the bottle and clean gauze. "But it's necessary to keep infection at bay."

"Bloody hell!" Ian yelled as Donald applied the antiseptic.

"I wouldn't have to do this if you weren't so damn reckless," Donald said through clenched teeth. "Hold still."

Perched on the armchair opposite, Bacchus watched calmly through half-open eyes.

"What are you looking at?" Ian said to the cat, who yawned and began grooming himself.

"He's just thinking what a bloody fool you are," Donald said, applying antiseptic to a gash on Ian's forehead. "You need a few stitches, but this should hold you until you get to hospital."

"No time for that," Ian said. "Can't you just sew me up here?"

"I'm a first-year student."

"And smarter than most of the faculty teaching you."

"That doesn't mean I can suture a wound."

"Give it a try, would you?"

Donald sighed heavily. "You do try one's patience, O Brother Mine."

"That makes two of us," Ian muttered. "Oh, damn."

"What?"

"I've missed dress rehearsal. The director will have my hide."

"What's left of it," Donald muttered. "Now hold still."

Donald did not sleep well that night, waking from time to time to the sound of his brother moaning in the next room. He had done his best to stitch up the wounds, using ample amounts of antiseptic, and he could only hope he had done a good enough job. Most of the cuts weren't too deep, but there was one over Ian's eye that worried him. He was tired of arguing with his brother about every little thing and resolved not to fight about whether or not he went to hospital.

Finally drifting off to sleep, he awoke to brilliant sunshine pouring through the French windows in his bedroom. Throwing off the covers, he went into his brother's room, but the bed was empty, and there was no sign of Ian anywhere. Cursing under his breath, Donald fed the cat, grabbed a cold slice of beef and a chunk of bread, and left the flat.

CHAPTER
SIXTY-TWO

She waited impatiently for the knock at her door, and when it finally came, launched herself from her seat in the parlor, nearly tripping over the hooked rug in the foyer in her haste to answer it.

"Well?" she said as she let the two men into her flat. "Did everything go as planned?"

"Aye," said Gordy, taking off that bowler he always wore to reveal his spiky hair, so light blond it was nearly white. "We gae 'im a right good pummelin'."

"R-r-right g-good," said his companion, the little man with the crooked nose. She always had trouble remembering his name. Something common, like John or James. Roger, maybe? No matter—after tonight, she wouldn't need to remember. She made a point of only retaining useful knowledge, not crowding her brain with stray tidbits.

"I'm glad to hear it," she said. "That will make up for your foolishness with the tiepin."

"Sorry fer misunderstandin' there," Gordy said. "But I got it back fer ye."

"So you did," she said. "Let me pay you for your efforts. But first, how about a cup of tea? It's a cold night."

"That's awright," said Gordy, fidgeting with his hat. "We don' need—"

"I have some very good cake."

The little one gave Gordy a pleading look. "C-cake?"

"Really," Gordy said, frowning. "We'd best be gettin' on."

"Nonsense. I insist." She looked back and forth from one to the other, then burst into laughter. "You don't think—"

"No, a' course not," Gordy said unconvincingly.

"Well, that's ridiculous. Besides, I'm going to have it with you. Come along, now," she said, leading them into the kitchen.

The little one followed her eagerly, but Gordy went slowly, dragging his feet like a man on the way to the gallows. Outside, an owl hooted from the branches of a sycamore as it prepared to pounce on an unsuspecting mouse.

CHAPTER
SIXTY-THREE

"Don't waste your breath," DCI Crawford said when Donald Hamilton charged into the station house like an enraged bull, demanding to see Ian. "He won't listen to anyone."

"He'd bloody well better listen to his brother," Donald replied, looking around. "Where is he?"

The chief inspector's face reddened, and he gave a strange little chortle. "He's in the back room."

The other policemen in the main room watched as Donald strode to the rear of the station house. As he approached, he heard loud voices coming from a closed room. One was his brother's; the other belonged to a woman.

"What, then?" said the woman. "Do you think they should be ashamed of what they do?"

"That's not what I was saying—" Ian protested.

"Which is a fine bit of hypocrisy, as it is you men who demand their services and keep them as a permanent underclass."

"*I* do no such thing, Miss Stuart!"

So it was that bluestocking nurse—served Ian right, Donald thought, taking her on in a debate. She was a firebrand, that one—he liked her. He just wished his brother would admit that he did, too.

"I wasn't speaking of you in particular, but men in general," she said.

"I am not a 'man in general,' and I should think someone of your intelligence would not make such an elementary mistake in reasoning."

"I just meant—"

Donald knocked on the door, but they ignored it.

"When one goes about tarring everyone with the same brush, there is likely to be a considerable margin of error," declared Ian.

Donald knocked again, louder this time.

"What do you know about margin of error? Are you a scientist?"

"Certainly not."

He pounded on the door. Still no answer.

"Because that is a concept one learns in medical training," said Miss Stuart.

"It is also applicable to police work, believe it or not," Ian replied.

Grasping the doorknob, Donald abruptly threw open the door. The two of them stared at him as if he were an apparition, though it was Ian who resembled a ghost. Pale and wan, with a bloody bandage wrapped around his forehead, he looked like a war casualty.

"Donald!" he said. "What are you doing here?"

"He's probably come to rescue you from your suicidal impulses," Miss Stuart said. Though her voice was tart, there was no mistaking the concern in her eyes.

"Good morning, Miss Stuart," Donald said. "How nice to see you again."

"Miss Stuart was enlightening me on the nature of social injustice," said Ian.

"I was trying to knock some sense into his head," she said.

"I've already tried that," Donald said. "You see how much good that's done."

Miss Stuart gave her head a disapproving shake. "He won't go to hospital. Why can't you be sensible, like your brother?" she asked Ian.

Sergeant Dickerson appeared in the doorway.

"Sir?" he said tentatively.

"Yes, Sergeant?" Ian said, turning to face him.

"Wha' in God's name?" Dickerson cried. "Y' look terrible, sir."

"What did you want to tell me?"

"I'm th'one wi' sommit to tell ya," came a voice from behind the sergeant.

Donald recognized the voice as belonging to the ragamuffin Ian had befriended. Even though he was wearing an overcoat several sizes too large, with a newsboy cap thrust haphazardly on his head of shaggy brown hair, intelligence shone from the boy's sharp brown eyes.

"What is it?" Ian asked him.

"Mr. Doyle would like t'see ya at the infirmary, as soon as it's convenient," said the lad.

"It's convenient now," Ian replied. "Thank you for your instruction," he said to Miss Stuart, throwing on his cloak. "And now, if you'll excuse me—"

"I cannot imagine what Conan Doyle sees in you," she said. "At least ask him to have a look at your injuries while you're there."

"Come along, Sergeant," said Ian.

"Don' worry, sir—I'll see to it," Dickerson told the others as he trotted after him. The urchin tipped his hat and winked at Miss Stuart before scampering after them.

When they were gone, Miss Stuart turned to Donald. "Your brother is entirely too stubborn for his own good."

Donald sighed. "My dear, you have no idea."

CHAPTER
SIXTY-FOUR

"Good Lord," Conan Doyle said when he saw Ian. "What on earth happened to you?"

"I had the misfortune to run into two gentlemen who mistook me for a punching bag."

They were seated in Doyle's tiny office in the Royal Infirmary. Suddenly aware he hadn't eaten that morning, Ian had sent Dickerson off to fetch some food from a street vendor, instructing him to buy Derek as much as he could eat, as well as some extra to take with him.

Conan Doyle leaned back in his chair and stroked his waxed mustache. "Were you attacked to put you off the investigation?"

"I think it's a fair assumption."

"Did anyone examine your injuries?"

"My brother."

"At least let me change your bandages," Doyle said. "The one on your head is coming undone."

"Very well," Ian agreed, not wanting to let on how much pain he was actually in. "What did you want to see me about?"

"The Marsh test was conclusive—the milk was laced with arsenic."

"Thank you for doing that," said Ian. "I looked into the school-teacher, Mr. Brown."

"And?"

"His colleague didn't believe he killed himself. And he shared an important trait with the other victims."

"Which is—?"

"The habitual mistreatment of women. In this case, it was even more egregious—he preyed on young girls."

Doyle's face darkened. "It is difficult to regret the death of such a monster."

"I feel the clues point more and more to a member of the medical profession."

"Someone on staff at the infirmary, you mean?"

"Who else had access to him while he was here?"

"The records do not mention any visitors," Doyle said, removing the bloody bandage from Ian's head.

"I procured another hair from the location where Mr. Corbin was held prisoner," Ian said.

"Do you happen to have it on you?"

"As a matter of fact, I do," Ian said, carefully extracting his handkerchief from his pocket.

"May I see it?" Doyle said, wrapping a clean bandage around Ian's head.

"Certainly," he replied, handing Doyle the hair. "What are you looking for?"

"It's just a hunch," his friend said, laying it on a microscope slide and slipping it beneath the lens. "This is quite instructive," Doyle said, peering into the microscope.

"What is?"

"See for yourself," Doyle answered, stepping aside. "Observe how evenly the end of the strand is cut, how blunt it is. There is no jagged edge, no tearing."

"And what might that signify?"

"I examined several different female human hairs and found a much more jagged structure in every one of them."

"From what sources were these hairs?"

Doyle smiled. "I was able to persuade several nurses to volunteer a sample in the interests of science. I compared that with samples from two different wigs I purchased."

"And what is your conclusion?"

"It is by no means a certainty, but I would venture to suggest that this hair is from a red wig."

"So the killer is using a disguise."

"Which would make it more difficult to ascertain her identity."

"Indeed, it would, unless—thank you for your assistance," he said, abruptly rising from his chair and throwing on his cloak. "Excuse me, but I have an urgent call to make."

"Mind you don't rush around too much," Doyle said. "I don't like the look of that head wound."

"Thank you for your concern," Ian replied. "I shall do my best to keep you posted."

And with that, he left the office and strode swiftly from the building. He had completely forgotten about Dickerson's errand, when suddenly he saw the sergeant approaching, two greasy bags clutched in his hands.

"Sorry it took a while, sir," he said. "The one fella had—"

"Never mind," Ian said, hailing a cab. "We can eat on the way," he said as they climbed in.

"On th'way to where, sir?"

"Holy Land."

"Why are we goin' there, sir?"

"I have a few questions to pose to Fair Kate."

Twenty minutes and two meat pies later, they arrived at Holy Land.

"No, luv, none o' my girls have a red wig that I'm aware," Kate said in response to his question as they sat in her cozy kitchen, which smelled of fried kippers. It was then Ian remembered it was Friday—as a Catholic, Kate would be eating fish. "Would ye like me t'ask them, then?"

"I would appreciate it," said Ian.

Sergeant Dickerson fidgeted with the brass buttons on his uniform while Kate went from room to room to speak with her "girls." He looked nervous, as if he wanted to say something. Several times he looked as if he was about to, then stopped.

"Well, out with it," Ian said finally. "I won't bite you."

Dickerson took a deep breath. "Will we make it in time t'do *Hamlet* tonight, sir?"

"I hope so, Sergeant. Was Mr. Vincent very angry at me last night?"

"A bit, sir."

"We'll just have to make sure that we get there early tonight. The show must go on, eh, Sergeant?"

"You sure you're all right, sir?"

"Everyone keeps telling me I look half dead anyway, so maybe that will enhance my performance as the ghost."

"Yes, sir."

Fair Kate returned to the kitchen with the news that no one in her employ confessed to having a red wig.

"Wish I could be more helpful, luv. Anythin' else I can do for ye?" she asked, running a crimson-polished nail over her plump lips.

Sergeant Dickerson blushed and looked away.

"Thank you," Ian said. "We must be on our way."

The rest of the day offered no breakthrough in the case, and before long, it was time to go to the theater for the evening performance. Ian was glad to take his mind off work for a few hours, and suspected Dickerson felt the same. A thin sliver of moon hung in a starlit sky as they made their way to the Greyfriars Dramatic Society, the city unnaturally quiet, holding its breath in anticipation of an approaching storm.

CHAPTER
SIXTY-FIVE

Ian stood in the wings, listening to thunder shaking the rafters of the theater as lightning flashed and rippled across the stage. The effect was so real there were gasps from the audience. Ian was half persuaded himself, though he was aware of the stagecraft that produced the thunder—the lightning was created by rapid flickering of overhead limelights.

He drew a deep breath, inhaling the aroma of greasepaint and gaslighting, orange peels and perfume. Edinburgh theater was a sensual experience in every way, spectacle and social venue, with intermissions often lasting half an hour or more, as audience members gossiped while gulping down ginger beer or mulled wine, slurping ale and oysters.

Ian's first entrance was coming up, and as most of his role consisted of merely standing about while other characters spoke, his mind was free to ponder the difficult questions raised by the case. Meanwhile, he let Shakespeare's words roll over him, the poetry of the language smoothing the rougher parts of his soul.

Hearing his cue approaching, he prepared to enter, as the actor playing Bernardo spoke of the ghost's appearance the previous evening.

Last night of all,
When yond same star that's westward from the pole
Had made his course to illume that part of heaven
Where now it burns, Marcellus and myself,
The bell then beating one—

Ian stepped out onto the stage and was gratified to hear more gasps from the audience. Dressed entirely in white, his face powdered, his eyes highlighted with dark greasepaint, he was indeed a spectral sight. To heighten the impact of his entrance, a stagehand flapped bedsheets over a block of dry ice offstage, creating a thin white mist floating across the stage.

The director had instructed him to remain upstage in order to heighten the otherworldly effect, and from where he stood, Ian could see the entire audience. The room was packed, with one row of spectators standing along the back wall. Sitting in the third row, looking utterly enraptured, was DCI Crawford. Directly behind him was Aunt Lillian, and to her left sat, of all people, Derek McNair, chewing on a licorice stick. Donald sat to his aunt's other side, arms crossed over his generous middle. Ian felt a pang of guilt at having confronted Lillian about the letter, but also anger that she had kept secrets from him for so long. He felt the rift in their relationship, and knew she felt it, too.

Hearing his cue to exit, Ian took a few steps toward the wings as the actor playing Horatio intoned his lines:

Stay! speak, speak! I charge thee, speak!

Doing his best to "glide," as the director had instructed him, Ian exited the stage, glad to be out of the glare of the stage lights. Gaslights were hot enough, but the limelights were worse, and even the backstage area was hot. Wiping sweat from his powdered brow, he adjusted the bandage over his forehead. Fortunately, his wound dressings fit in with his ghostly apparel; he had been costumed in overlapping strands of white cotton, meant to look like the ragged wrapping of a dead body, as if he had just dragged himself from a moldering grave.

Ian's big speech came in Act I, Scene V, when the ghost tells Hamlet he is the spirit of his murdered father. The audience was silent as a held breath when Ian intoned the famous lines:

Murder most foul, as in the best it is;
But this most foul, strange and unnatural.

Ian felt chills slither over his body—were his parents, too, victims of "murder most foul"? And if so, why did his aunt never want to speak of it? What did she know? And was he, like Hamlet, a congealed stew of procrastination, not taking action until it was too late?

He delivered the speech describing his own murder with a passion he had not known existed in him, and saw corresponding emotion on the face of Alan Jenkins. By the time Ian reached the end of his monologue, Alan appeared on the verge of tears.

Adieu, adieu! Hamlet, remember me.

Waving his raggedly clad arms, thunder booming through the room, Ian glided through the ground mist to exit as lightning crackled across the painted sky. The audience gave a cheer and broke into spontaneous applause, and several stagehands clapped him on the back as he made his way to the greenroom. Suddenly exhausted, he sat heavily on an upholstered armchair next to the costume rack.

Eyes half-closed, he gazed idly at the rows of gowns and frocks, doublets and jackets, boots and slippers, hats and—wigs. His languorous mood abruptly vanished. There on the rack was the red wig that had been missing two days earlier. Forgetting his fatigue, he sprang from the chair to find the costumer. He located her making tea in one of the dressing rooms.

"You look dreadful," she said. "Well done."

"Where did you find the red wig?" he asked.

"It just reappeared by itself."

"You didn't see who put it back?"

"No. It was there when I arrived this evening. Why?"

"Thank you," Ian said.

"You look like you could use a cup of tea, dearie," she said, but he was already halfway out of the room.

Not wanting to tip his hand, Ian queried the actors during the intermissions, and then moved on to the stagehands. No one claimed to know anything about a red wig, and several people looked at him askance. He didn't mention it to Dickerson, not wanting to distract him from his own performance—the sergeant seemed nervous enough at the prospect of performing in front of a full house.

Watching Fiona Stuart play the doomed Ophelia, Ian had to admit she was good, delivering her lines with such conviction and clarity that he found it easy to believe her as the lovesick mistress of a disturbed prince feigning madness.

At the opening of Act V, Ian stood in the wings watching the grave-digger scene. Dickerson acquitted himself well, and the audience was laughing heartily as Hamlet and Horatio entered.

As was the custom, the Greyfriars production was abridged, and the final duel scene followed not long after. Nearly all the other cast members were onstage, leaving Ian and Fiona alone in the greenroom. She wandered over to the coatrack and fished something out of her coat. As she did, Ian's eye was caught by the flash of a brooch on a jacket. He walked over for a closer look. The jacket was forest green, and the jewel was a silver horse's head, the animal's eye represented by a small emerald. Vickie Caruthers had said it was only colored glass, but it looked like a real gem to his untrained eye.

"Whose jacket is this?" he asked Fiona.

"Oh, that's Abby's."

"Are you quite certain?"

"Yes. Why?"

"So is this her bag?" he asked, holding up a green velvet purse with black-and-gold trim on the same hanger as the jacket.

"Yes. What are you up to?" she asked as he removed the bag and opened it. "That's private property!"

"I am investigating a murder," he muttered through clenched teeth.

"You don't think Abby—" She stopped, mouth open, staring at him as he rifled through the purse.

Inside he found a number of red hairs that matched the wig perfectly, as well as a small vial of white powder.

"What's going on?" said Fiona.

Without replying, he dashed from the greenroom. As he approached the wings, he heard the actor playing Osric deliver his line:

A hit, a very palpable hit.

Ian charged past the mystified stagehands, leaping onto the stage just as Queen Gertrude was lifting a poisoned cup of wine to her lips. Crossing to her in three long strides, Ian dashed the cup from her hands. A cry of alarm went up from audience, and for a moment, everyone onstage froze in astonishment.

Abigail McNaughton, however, sprang into action. In a flash, she seized the dueling sword from Laertes, striking it across a wooden column to remove the safety tip, and brandished it at the assembled company. "Not one step closer!" she hissed, her face a mask of rage.

As the other actors shrank back, Ian grabbed Hamlet's sword. He did not remove the safety tip, however—perhaps something within him rebelled at the idea of harming a woman. Turning to the rest of the cast, he commanded, "Get back!" They obeyed, eyeing the pointed steel blade Miss McNaughton wielded.

By now the audience was in chaos. Realizing only dimly what was happening onstage, they shouted and catcalled, railing at Ian for taking arms against a woman.

"What're ye doin', man?"

"She's just a wee lassie—gae out wi' ye!"

Out of the corner of his eye, Ian could see DCI Crawford trying to squeeze out of the middle row. But people were in clumps now, some even fighting among themselves, in the Scottish tradition, where any disruption was a good excuse for a fight.

It was only an instant of inattention on Ian's part, but that was all Abigail McNaughton needed. She lunged at him, but he parried her attack, and the sword clattered from her hands. As it did, it grazed her face, leaving a red slash across her cheek. Grabbing her face, she gazed with horror at the blood dripping onto her palms.

"You fool!" she cried. "You have killed me! I am undone!"

Ian took a step toward her, but before he could reach her, she crumpled to the floor. Everyone onstage gasped, and several people rushed to her aid. Conan Doyle dashed down the aisle, vaulting onto the stage, and knelt next to the fallen woman as the chaos in the room crescendoed.

As the actor playing Claudius reached down to pick up her sword, Ian shouted, "DO NOT touch that sword!"

The assembled company ceased their chatter and looked at Ian, their eyes wide, as he knelt and carefully picked up the sword by its handle. Even the audience had gone quiet, a breathless hush descending over the room.

By then Sergeant Dickerson had rushed onto the stage, his ruddy face flushed.

"Y'all right, sir?" he panted.

"Quite all right," Ian said, holding the discarded sword carefully by the handle. "How is she?" he asked Conan Doyle, who held his fingers to Abby McNaughton's neck, feeling for a pulse.

He looked up at Ian and shook his head. Everyone in the room knew what the gesture meant. Ian looked down at the dead woman, surprised at the grief he felt at the sight of her pale face. He began to stand up from his kneeling position, but suddenly his legs wouldn't hold him. The edges of his vision darkened and blurred, and he sank back to the stage as oblivion overtook him.

"Wake up, sir! Wake up!"

As Ian slid back into consciousness, he became aware of someone slapping him. Opening his eyes, he saw Sergeant Dickerson's panic-stricken face.

"Please . . . stop . . . doing . . . that," he said.

To his relief, the slapping ceased. He tried to sit up, but several pairs of hands prevented him. Still very groggy, he turned his head to see his aunt Lillian and, hovering behind her, DCI Crawford.

"What—where is—" he began, but he was having trouble making his mouth obey his brain.

"Who?"

"Conan Doyle," he said.

"Right here," said the medical student, bending over him.

"Is everyone . . . all right?"

"Everyone except Miss McNaughton."

"Her sword . . . poisoned?"

"I would imagine so. Something very fast acting—curare, perhaps. Well done, Hamilton."

"Yes, well done," said another voice. It was Aunt Lillian.

He reached a hand toward her. "Please forgive me."

"Ach, there's naught to forgive," she said, but the corners of her eyes glistened.

Ian smiled, and then he fell into a long, dark tunnel.

CHAPTER
SIXTY-SIX

A few days later, Ian sat in DCI Crawford's office, looking out the window at the soft rain falling upon the city. Like its people, winter in Edinburgh was unpredictable. Tomorrow might be balmy as a Mediterranean summer, or fierce as a North Sea gale; there was no telling. But that was one of the things he liked about living in the Athens of the North—not that he would ever feel as much at home here as he did in the Highlands. Still, he thought, gazing in the direction of the Scottish National Gallery, the city offered certain embellishments Highland life did not. Maybe he would pay a visit to the Dutch Masters wing on Friday evening.

DCI Crawford lumbered into the room, closing the door behind him. "The lab results are in," he said, tossing a report on the desk before sitting heavily in his chair. "Doyle was right—the sword had been dipped in curare. She must have intended for Hamlet to die from the poison in the duel."

"Just like in the play."

"And the entire audience would have seen it," Crawford added with a shudder. "Thank goodness you figured it out in time."

"And the wine onstage?"

"It was clean. Apparently, Alan Jenkins was her only target." He sighed. "Her victims weren't exactly admirable—all cads, by the look of it. Oh, speaking of which, those two ruffians who attacked you—"

"Gordon Kinsey and his mate? What about them?"

"Looks like they were her final victims. They turned up in the alley outside her flat."

"Poisoned?"

"It appears so."

"Rosencrantz and Guildenstern," Ian murmured.

"What?"

"The unlucky pair King Claudius pays to kill Hamlet. He's far cleverer than they are and betrays them so they end up dying instead. They're murdered offstage."

Crawford stroked his whiskers. "'To all that fortune, death, and danger dare, even for an eggshell.'"

"Well done, sir—that's from Act Four, I believe?"

"I've been reading it in my spare time. Can't have you the only one around here spewing quotes, Hamilton."

Ian smiled. "How is Eleanor Atkinson?"

"She'll be all right. Dunno why exactly Abigail McNaughton kept her alive, but she was lucky to survive. We found her locked in the back room of McNaughton's flat. Don't know what she was planning to do with her."

"Perhaps it's best we don't know."

Crawford shook his massive head. "How do people become twisted like that?"

"It's a mystery we may never solve, sir."

There was a knock on the door.

"Yes?" said Crawford.

Sergeant Dickerson poked his head in. "Pardon, sir, but you've a visitor."

"Who is it?" the chief inspector asked.

"Dr. Jex-Blake."

Crawford groaned.

"Shall I send her in?"

"Yes, I suppose."

"Good evening, Detective Chief Inspector," Dr. Sophia Jex-Blake said, planting herself in front of his desk. Smartly dressed in a gray wool suit, she was the picture of competence and control.

"Good evening, Dr. Jex-Blake. What can I do for you?" Crawford said.

"I just wanted to thank you."

"For what?"

"First of all, for taking the matter seriously, and of course for solving the case."

"You've Hamilton to thank for that."

"I know. But I wanted to thank you both anyway. I know you were initially resistant, but—"

"*Resistant?*" Crawford said, his small eyes narrowing. "Why, I—"

"You're quite welcome," Ian told her. "Thank you for bringing it to our attention in the first place."

"It was my duty," she said, "nothing more."

"Thank you anyway."

"Well, I must return to the clinic. I just wanted to thank you in person. Oh, and you made a very good ghost," she said to Ian.

"I didn't realize you were in the audience."

"I arrived late and was forced to stand in the back. Mind you don't overdo it," she told him. "You've been through quite a lot, and you need time to recover. Oh, I almost forgot—Miss Stuart sends her regards."

"Please thank her for me," Ian said.

"I shall. Goodbye, Detective Chief Inspector."

"Goodbye," Crawford muttered. "'Resistant?'" he said when she had gone. "What on earth does she mean?"

"You were a bit . . . reluctant at first, sir."

"Bosh and bunkum!" Crawford sputtered. "Why, I—"

"If you'll excuse me," said Ian, "I am expected at home." Standing up, he made his way stiffly to the door.

"You really should take some time off, Hamilton. You're not exactly shipshape."

"I'll think about it, sir."

"Give my regards to your brother."

"I will. And your wife, sir? Has Dr. Bell seen her yet?"

"He's seeing us later this week."

"Good luck, sir."

"Thank you, Hamilton. Good night."

"Good night, sir."

Sergeant Dickerson was still at his desk when Ian emerged into the main room.

"Isn't it high time you went home?" Ian asked him.

"I'm jus' goin', sir," he said, putting on his coat. "Oh, and sir?"

"Yes?" Ian said, fetching his cloak from the rack.

"This arrived for you while you were in wi' DCI Crawford," he said, handing Ian a telegram.

Ian opened it and read it.

JOIN ME FOR DINNER TOMORROW? SHEEP HEID INN. GHOSTS HAVE TO EAT, TOO. I'M BUYING.—CONAN DOYLE.

Ian smiled and slid the note into his pocket.

"Who's it from, sir, if ye don' mind my askin'?"

"A friend, Sergeant."

Dickerson frowned, looking down at his shoes. "Mr. Doyle, innit, sir?"

"Sergeant?"

"Yes, sir?"

"You are invaluable. No one could ever replace what you have been, and done, over these past months."

Dickerson looked away. "Yes, sir," he said, his voice thick. "Thank you, sir."

"Have a good evening, Sergeant," Ian said, opening the door leading to the stairwell.

"You, too, sir."

Outside, the rain had lifted, so Ian decided to walk. Donald was making roast pheasant tonight, and Lillian would be there. He was surprised at how much he looked forward to seeing them both, but first he needed some time to be alone with his thoughts. As he passed St. Giles', he heard a familiar voice behind him.

"Ye weren't half bad, y'know."

"I assume you refer to my truncated thespian efforts," Ian replied without turning around.

"I mean th'play," said Derek, catching up to him. "Ye made a good ghost."

"I can't tell you how gratified I am by your critical appreciation."

"Goin' home, then?"

"Your deductive powers continue to amaze me," Ian said, rounding the corner onto George IV Bridge.

"Yer aunt's there already."

Ian stared at him, then laughed. "I was about to ask you how you know, but I'm not sure I want the answer."

"Speakin' of yer aunt . . ."

"Yes, you may come for dinner," said Ian. "But no, you may not have any beer."

"But—"

"Or wine, or mead, or anything alcoholic."

"If it weren't fer me, ye would never ha' solved—"

"You are too young to be drinking spirits."

"I'm sixteen."

"We have been through this before."

"Fifteen, then."

Ian laughed. "Come along," he said, quickening his steps, "before it starts to rain again."

Later, lying on his bed after dinner, Derek snoring loudly on the couch, Donald sitting by the fire studying, Ian experienced a sense of peace that had eluded him these many long weeks. He was glad of the people in the other rooms, and of their presence in his life, but he was just as glad for his work.

Work was the antidote—to faithless friends, determined killers, and a society more bent upon revenge than justice. It was something that could be *done*, whereas all one could do with life's slings and arrows was to bear them, bravely or not. Without work, Ian knew he might very well agonize about things he could not change. When it all became too much, he would throw himself into his work as if his life depended upon it. And for all he knew, perhaps it did. Stronger men than he had collapsed beneath life's unpredictable sorrows. He could not look to others for his salvation; other people were unreliable, changeable. He could only count upon his own resources, his own courage, his own need for truth. But for now he was glad for the presence of other people in nearby rooms.

He gazed at the windowpane covered in droplets, listening to the rain falling all over Edinburgh—a pure, cleansing rain. It cascaded down from the heavens, slipping softly through tree leaves, pattering on rooftops, washing the city clean of sin and soil and human folly. He listened for the sound between the raindrops, the stillness that lives inside, that carries no grudge, and has neither hope nor despair. Truth was not the answer, he knew, and would not save him. But there, lying on his bed surrounded by the hiss of rain, he felt the presence of grace. Not God, not even goodness or wisdom, but simply grace. Unlooked for, unexpected, it might not answer all his questions, but tonight, for now, it would do. He stretched and breathed in the good, clean smell of rain.

Yes, he thought, it would do.

ACKNOWLEDGMENTS

Thanks as always to my wonderful agent, Paige Wheeler, for her continued support, advice, and wisdom. Deepest gratitude to the fabulous Jessica Tribble and Anna Rosenwong for their superb editorial acumen and good cheer, and to Laura Barrett for her eagle eye.

Heartfelt thanks to Alan Macquarie, scholar, musician, and historian, for vetting the manuscript from a uniquely Scottish perspective, and for being such a wonderful host in Glasgow. Thanks to my friend Anthony Moore for his research assistance, and for prowling the streets of Edinburgh with me. Deepest thanks to Liza Dawson for being the best friend ever (and an awesome agent), to Hawthornden Castle for an amazing month during my fellowship there, and to Byrdcliffe Colony in Woodstock, where I enjoyed many happy years of residency, as well as the magical Lacawac Sanctuary and the Animal Care Sanctuary in East Smithfield, Pennsylvania, and to Steph Spector of Gotham Writers for making my residency there possible.

Thanks to my friend and colleague Marvin Kaye for his continued support, and for all the wonderful dinners at Keens Steakhouse, where we toasted Scotland over a single malt. Thanks to my virtual assistant and techno-sensei, Frank Goad, for all his work and expertise. Thanks, too, to my good friend Ahmad Ali, whose support and good energy have always lifted my spirits. Special thanks to Robert "Beaubear" Murphy and the folks at the Long Eddy Hotel, Sullivan County's best-kept secret. Deepest thanks to my mother, Margaret Simmons, for all those bedtime stories, for reading to us and doing all the character voices so brilliantly, and for teaching me the transformational power of a good story.

ABOUT THE AUTHOR

Photo © 2017 Patricia Rubinelli

Carole Lawrence is an award-winning novelist, poet, composer, and playwright. Her previous novels include *Edinburgh Twilight*, the first Detective Inspector Ian Hamilton novel. She is also the author of six novellas and dozens of short stories, articles, and poems—many of which appear in translation internationally. She is a two-time Pushcart Poetry Prize nominee and winner of the Euphoria Poetry Prize, the Eve of St. Agnes Poetry Award, the Maxim Mazumdar playwriting prize, the *Jerry Jazz Musician* award for short fiction, and the Chronogram Literary Fiction Award. Her plays and musicals have been produced in several countries as well as on NPR; her physics play *Strings*, nominated for an Innovative Theatre Award, was recently produced at the Kennedy Center. A Hawthornden Fellow, she is on the faculty of NYU and Gotham Writers, as well as the Cape Cod and San Miguel Writers' Conferences. She enjoys outdoor sports such as hiking, biking, and horseback riding, and you can often find her cooking and hunting for wild mushrooms.